Vivi il Momento

MARY BELLE

Bird Books

Vivi il Momento | Mary Belle

ISBN: 979-8-9885228-0-5

eBook ISBN: 979-8-9885228-1-2

www.marybellebooks.com | info@marybellebooks.com

Edited by Elizabeth Lyons | www.elizabethlyons.com

Cover design by Debbie O'Byrne | www.jetlaunch.net

❀ Created with Vellum

*For my husband; of all the love stories ever written,
us fighting for our happy ending will forever be my favorite one.*

Vivi il Momento

"Il vostro compito non è cercare l'amore, ma, semplicemente, cercare e trovare dentro di voi tutte le barriere che avete costruito contro di esso."

"Your task is not to seek love, but simply to seek and find all the barriers within yourself that you have built against it."

——Rumi

CHAPTER 1
Mia

I was driving eighty-two miles per hour west on Highway 80 with the windows down to get the smell of cigarette smoke out of my hair. Twenty-four years old—attempting to spend another weekend with my "boyfriend" who was really anything but an actual boyfriend—and Reina's classic "Find Another Woman" blaring through the speakers of my black Mustang GT.

I had a flair for the dramatics when scorned.

Two hours prior I was hoisting my boobs so they'd delicately protrude from my sequin halter top, which was far too small to fit one of them, let alone two, while staring back at myself in the bathroom mirror of yet another night club in Northern New Jersey. Sweat dripped down the side of my face causing my once perfectly flat-ironed hair to tendril at the nape of my neck. I had just finished my second vodka soda with lime, giving me a light buzz for some added liquid courage, and had an overnight bag filled with lingerie in my trunk to show my not-so-boyfriend-boyfriend how goddamn lucky he was to (not really) be dating me.

I smelled of Christian Dior's "Hypnotic Poison" perfume (about seven sprays too many of it), secondhand smoke and sweat, and tasted like strawberry lip gloss with a vodka overlay. And, I was absolutely ready to make some horrible decisions since, somewhere along the line, a majority of us young women convinced ourselves the more we tried to tell or show them our worth, the more desirable men would find us. Wrong we were, but still, I marched out of the bathroom to grab "my" man and attempt to drive back to the wildly romantic $75 per night motel room we'd reserved on a whim.

"I want to go back to the motel," I said matter-of-factly. He was talking to his friends, but grabbed my hand, rubbed his lips alongside my neck and whispered back, "We'll leave in a little bit, baby."

"No, I want to leave now." My gray eyes had turned green, which meant I was either tipsy, tired, or both. I happened to be both at that point, and seeing her name on his phone hadn't helped any.

"Why are you in a rush? We've barely been here an hour and we waited longer than that to get in."

"Why is she texting you?" I asked, half with my classic *"lie to me and I'll punch you in the face"* look, the other half hurt, already knowing the answer.

"She was just saying hi." He rolled his eyes and shook his head, aggravated with my line of questioning rather than concerned by it.

I felt my blood pressure rising, and while I knew better not to make a scene in public, this had happened way too many times before. "On a Saturday night at 1 am? The only thing she wants to say 'hi' to is your dick."

"Don't start this shit again, Mia."

"Start what? You slept with her when I was away at school and you refuse to admit it. Are you still? And don't lie to me." There was about five percent of me who assumed he wouldn't lie to me when I told him not to lie to me because isn't that what liars do? They lie. Even when they say they aren't lying. It's exhausting.

"I'm not doing this here," he replied, staying true to his avoidant nature.

I kept forging forward because that's what *I* stayed true to. "Doing what? Confirming what I already know?"

"Please stop. I wanted to have fun tonight."

What a dickhead.

"Yea, well, I want to be with someone who's not banging someone else," I retorted, hurt but mostly on a mission to verbally assault him.

His shoulders slumped before looking down at the floor. My face flushed again, knowing what he was going to say. My stomach gurgled, from both the vodka sodas and the stress I voluntarily put myself through while convincing myself that the men I fell for wanted to be in a relationship —even after they declared, "I'm not looking for a relationship."

I was smart, kind, funny, pretty enough, and a good time to be around. I generally had my shit together. And, as I would hear over and over again through the years, "You are such marriage material, Mia Luciano!"

Problem was, most men ranging in age from eighteen to twenty-nine didn't want to get married. They wanted to reserve $75 per night motel rooms, give me what I mistook to be mind-blowing sex, and then have absolutely zero further attachment to me after they had finished. They took advantage of me—because I let them.

Why buy a whole cow when you can get the milk for free? I should have put that on a graphic tee and worn it to the clubs instead of a push-up top. I constantly threw myself at unavailable men who didn't deserve me and continued to wonder why I wasn't finding actual *boyfriend* material. To be fair, it wasn't just me. It was also a large majority of women I knew.

"I'm sorry," he said, his big, brown, bloodshot eyes staring back at me.

"I hate you. I really fucking hate you," I responded, more calmly than I actually felt, and then pushed myself away from him and headed towards the door. We had taken two cars that night, which was great for my dramatic exit but not great for my blood alcohol levels and the need to operate a motor vehicle. I bulldozed my way through the crowd, passed a bunch of couples making out and at least one pair fighting with each other, and finally made it to the front door.

A cold burst of air covered me and the sixty percent of skin showing, and I finally felt like I could breathe.

"Mia! Do not even think of getting in that car," he yelled after me as I marched through the parking lot. I popped my trunk open, opened the zipper of my overnight bag, grabbed the lingerie I had packed, and threw it in his face.

"Here. She can wear this for you later instead!" For a level-headed girl, a couple drinks mixed with some heartache made for quite the dramatic scene. He stood there looking mildly defeated, and for one brief moment I contemplated staying with him. *Again.* But, it wasn't the first time it had happened. It was the third. And, it was going to be the last.

I turned the ignition, the CD player began playing "No One's Gonna Change You," and I sped off.

It was the perfect exit—*if you were the star of a daytime soap opera.*

In the midst of my heartache, with mascara running

down my cheeks, I briefly cringed at the thought of my parents ever witnessing any part of this scenario.

I wasn't drunk by any means, but I did what any sane, rational woman would do while waiting to sober up a bit and mend a freshly broken heart. I pulled into the McDonald's drive-thru.

"Double cheeseburger, no pickles. Four-piece nuggets with sweet and sour sauce. Large fry. And, a small Diet Coke, please."

"Is that all?"

...*and some of my dignity back, if that's available.* "Yes, thank you."

I pulled into the nearest spot under a bright light, turned my car off, took my keys out of the ignition, and made sure my car was locked no less than three times. Lessons from my parents were deeply ingrained in me, with an emphasis on personal safety and potential security breaches, along with a few more specific ones.

From Mom: *"Someone always has it worse than you. Feel sorry for yourself for a short while, then dust yourself off, pick yourself up, and keep it moving."*

And from Dad: *"Assume everyone is an asshole, and be pleasantly surprised when they're not."*

He always got his point across in the fewest words possible.

I was lucky to call them mine. Sure, growing up they were strict, but I was the baby of the family. As birth order would have it, they softened significantly by the time it came to parenting me. I was allowed to do more, got away with more, and experienced more than my siblings as a result, but I also always had a good case for why I should be able to. More often than not, they couldn't say no to my post-dinner explanations or occasional PowerPoint presentations espousing the pros of allowing me to do certain things.

They instilled a huge love of family. I was the teenager who went to dinner at Nana and Poppy's house while many others my age were at pool parties, sneaking beers behind the shed. Every once in a while, I felt like I was missing out. But, I had plenty of friends, was sociable, involved with lots of school activities, and I enjoyed all that high school and then college had to offer.

After graduating, I vowed to focus on my career so I could start saving money and move out on my own. Even though I was employed, I hadn't yet nailed down the art of saving money, nor did I quite have the nerve to move out. It didn't stop me from daydreaming though. I couldn't wait to decorate my own place, buy my own groceries, and eventually, fall in love and be with someone who would sit and watch me cook dinner for him while I was dressed in an oversized, off-the-shoulder sweater, big hoop earrings, and barefoot on the kitchen floor with a glass of wine.

What can I say? I had extremely specific aspirations for someone who now found herself at 2 am in a McDonald's parking lot, drowning in chicken nugget crumbs and fry salt with a few small dots of sweet and sour sauce staining my beloved sequin halter after yelling—Jerry Springer style —at a man who barely appreciated me before returning home to my bedroom at my parents' house.

A tear rolled down my face.

Get yourself together, Mia.

Emotional eating had been my thing since I came out of the womb. I grew up accumulating the best and worst of memories, all of which revolved around food. Someone was born? Fry some eggplant, assemble a giant tray of parmesan, and celebrate their arrival. Someone died? Book a restaurant reservation, order your favorite family style appetizers, entrees, and desserts, and celebrate their memory. Coworker got a promotion at work? Hit the sports bar on the way home for some nachos, mozzarella sticks, and boneless wings while simultaneously toasting them and feeling sorry for yourself that they'd no longer work in your department. Commuter traffic on a Friday night? Order a pizza and drink three glasses of wine in sweet silence immediately upon arriving home.

I sat in my car, music still playing at high decibels in auxiliary mode, finishing the last of the bottom-of-the-bag fries, realizing I needed to make a change.

I was uncomfortable in the worst way. I'd given a man all the tools to make me feel devalued by allowing him to be dishonest not once, not twice, but three times.

I made a public spectacle of it, shouting in a parking lot and throwing a brand-new Victoria's Secret lace-up teddy at him—one that now laid on the damp ground. By this time, it had probably been run over a few times, was stained, and had some holes in it—a lot like my heart and my ego.

What an asshole I was.

Nearly an hour later, I started my car and prayed to my angels above to get me home safe. The cool breeze blowing through the car windows helped to air out my hair from questionable decisions and moderate regret while also keeping me awake.

Around three in the morning, I turned onto our quiet street, lowered the volume, and pulled into the driveway. I opened and closed my car door as quietly as possible before sticking the key in the front door and turning it to find my dad slowly walking down the stairs, squinting at me.

"You're just getting home now?"

"Yea. I stopped to eat."

"I can smell that." I sensed a little judgment from him.

"I'm going to bed."

"You do that. Your brother and sister will be here later. We want to talk to you all."

"About what?" My interest was fully piqued.

"Go to sleep," he instructed me.

I was too tired to ask any questions but alert enough to know something wasn't quite right. I climbed the steps, washed my face, brushed my teeth, changed into my vintage gray Matchbox 20 t-shirt with a pair of fresh undies, and climbed into bed.

My ears rang from the loud music, my head hurt from crying, and my phone screen lit up displaying a text message from him.

Asshole: I'm sorry

Asshole: Call me tomorrow

I narrowed my eyes, and my lip curled up in disgust.

Mia: I'm home

Mia: Not like you care

Asshole: You know I will always care about you

"Not like I care abo…" I deleted it. It was the same cycle I always put myself through. I'd be sad enough to make him feel worse, and he'd always do or say something to waltz his way back into my heart, or more accurately, my pants.

I blocked his number and deleted the message thread, and with a right-before-bed moment of mental clarity, I promised myself a few things.

Goal 1: "Never cry in public over a man ever again."
Goal 2: "Let my value speak for itself, without ever having to convince someone of it."
Goal 3: "Find growth in the uncomfortable."

My stomach turned, and I wasn't sure if it was the McDonald's or the stress. Perhaps both—but I was too tired to figure it out. I closed my eyes, hoping I'd wake up and not remember the details of the night. As it turned out, I wouldn't be focused on any of it when I woke up, but not for the reasons I had hoped.

CHAPTER 2
Gennaro

My eyes opened and I blinked a few times to bring everything into focus. I was definitely in my own room because it felt like the dead of winter even though it was, in fact, spring time. The rolling hills of the Italian countryside had a way of heating you up from the inside out while bouncing sunbeams off your shoulders midday, quickly turning into the arctic overnight thanks to a lack of insulation inside the villa walls.

I grew up here and was an integral part of our family's holiday villa business since I was old enough to help my parents run it. I had dedicated the first part of my life to this place—and because of it—I knew what to expect from the local weather patterns, among many other things.

Always prepared, I had extra blankets at the foot of my wrought iron bed-frame and a pellet stove nearby. It was a fun game I'd play with myself, refusing to touch the dial of the stove unless it was actually fall or winter. In fact, I often liked to test the limits of my mind and body. If someone told me I couldn't do something, it became a personal goal to get it done. If I did something well the first time, I'd vow to do it better the next. When I made dumb decisions, I was harder on myself than anyone else ever could be.

So, when I woke up with my head pounding and remembered I had consumed four Peronis and two Grappa shots too many the night before, I was livid. I had way too much manual labor to get done. The thought of cleaning a chicken coop, power washing the pool landing, trimming the hedges, and moving furniture from one villa to the next before new guests arrived, turned my stomach and made my head throb even more. As if that weren't bad enough, I rolled over from my right side onto my back only to realize another person was in bed with me.

"Gezu Cristo!" I whispered in a huff.

She didn't budge, her long blonde hair draped over the side of my other pillow, with the air around her smelling like stale beer and floral perfume. Wearing her own clothes and buried underneath every extra blanket I had available, the Italian countryside chill appeared to have taken hold of her.

Then, as was always the case the morning after a few too many drinks, I started to piece together the important parts of the night before.

My best friend, Vincenzo Massaro, had recently graduated from the local police academy, and like old times, we hit the Osteria down the road to celebrate. We grew up together, have similar interests, and are both stoic in nature. Where he tenses up at the thought of speaking to most people, I have the ability to socialize with most people, in any type of crowd, *so long as I want to.*

Rounding out our threesome, on the complete opposite side of the spectrum, is Salvatore Rosa. The youngest of five, Sal has an uncanny way of making his way through life unbothered. Nothing's a big deal, no huge consequences for any mistakes or wrong turns, and he's blissfully unbothered by anyone's expectations of him. He leaned on his siblings as he got older and always felt the comfort of a strong network of people around him.

Vin and myself though, the oldest children in our families, have responsibilities—a lot of them. With fathers who are relentless with their parenting styles and expectations that would crush most people, we leaned on *each other* an incredible amount throughout our younger years. He was my rock, and I trusted him more than my own brothers, of which I have two, Giovanni and Giuseppe Beletta.

Giovanni is two years younger, and he flew the coop faster than you could say *"Scusi!"* when he was nineteen years old. He studied law at the University of Florence, is gleefully single with no kids, and visits home only once in a while—usually when he's had his temporary fill of practicing law and the city life that surrounds it. As middle children usually do, he marches to the beat of his own drum, observes from afar, and keeps to himself most of the time.

Giuseppe, our youngest brother, still lives at home with absolutely zero insight as to what he wants the rest of his life to look like. My father gave up a long time ago trying to "make a man" out of him. He doesn't do much of anything useful, but is wildly happy with himself while not doing it. Papa tends not to care as much, so long as he stays out of jail. I could never understand why his expectations of me were so much higher while he let Giuseppe skate, but even years later, nothing has particularly changed.

My angel of a mother, Giovanna Beletta often found herself in the middle of our arguments growing up while also trying to calm down our father, Rocco (Papa). In all honesty, Papa would have benefitted from a few Peronis himself to let loose and relax a bit. While I understand the importance of running the family's business, an exquisite, sprawling property where we host both local and international guests alike, what's the point if you don't allow yourself some time to enjoy the fruits of your labor here and there?

Because of it, I've always been turned off by the business itself. Rather than focus on the beauty of the property and all that was built by my parents and our family before them, I grew resentful over the years and, in truth, wanted to move away years ago.

I wasn't exactly afforded the luxury to do so, however, given our family history.

Instead, I tried to enjoy local hot spots like the Osteria and the benefits of knowing everyone within a 1 km radius, benefits that, last night, came out as far too many on-the-house Peronis in celebration of Vincenzo's graduation.

I noticed blonde hair from across the restaurant about an hour after I settled in at the bar with the guys. While I'm not necessarily into blondes, and I'm usually not in the habit of going home with strangers, watching my best friend start the next chapter of his life while I was still living at home was making me particularly miserable. Since blonde hair isn't typically a local thing, my interest piqued. Like any rational, self-soothing person would do, I looked to cure my discomfort with the temporary warmth of someone I'd likely never see again.

I kept shooting glances across the room, partially to uncover her levels of interest but also to make sure a rogue husband or boyfriend wasn't lingering. I could only see an older couple and a younger guy, likely a brother, at her table for four. A nice Italian vacation for the American family, it appeared. I shook my heads the larger and smaller one—and told myself to relax. I couldn't go around bedding visiting guests, especially when I didn't know if they were staying at our property.

After my third beer, I walked down the hall to the restroom, taking in the local artwork that hung on the walls with a significant layer of dust covering their frames. The Osteria was a local staple of nearly thirty years. It had opened right after I was born and was an "old faithful" source of comfort, especially during the times I wanted to live anywhere but here. I often tried to understand if I disliked growing up here because of my father's dictator-like rule or because I wanted to get out and see what else the world had to offer. Likely, it was a bit of both. I stared at myself in the mirror while washing my hands and vowed to come up with a plan for my life by summer's end.

I opened the bathroom door and found myself face to face with long, blonde hair that smelled like flowers and mint. It wasn't my first choice for a female scent, but at least I knew personal hygiene was high on her list. She spun around, looking a lot younger than she had from across the restaurant. She was twenty years old, at most.

"Do you speak English?" she asked.

I internally rolled my eyes. I don't know why this question always bothers me from Americans, but it does.

"Yes." I suddenly didn't have the energy or desire to communicate in my normal engaging tone.

"I saw you looking at me, and I wanted to say hi." Her direct, blunt, and very boring opening line instantly negated any remaining physical attraction to her.

"Hello." I continued walking back up the hallway to the bar. Part of me felt bad for being rude, but the majority of me had no interest in whatever this was turning out to be. It wasn't exciting, it wasn't fun, and I had too much to do the next day.

I decided to self-soothe a bit longer with nothing more than another Peroni.

Once back at the bar, I felt her standing behind me but

didn't turn around. Vincenzo looked at me with a raised eyebrow, and before I could shrug my shoulders, Sal approached from the right. "Gennaro! Man, I've missed you! Give me a hug."

He came in for the squeeze, knocking my phone out of my hand onto the floor, and subsequently, the beer straight down the back of blondie. She screeched, far more dramatically than necessary, and jumped into my arms. I stood motionless, looking up at the ceiling in defeat.

"Oh man. I'm sorry," Sal winced with regret. Impossible to stay mad at, because he didn't have a bad bone in his body, I shook my head and smiled at him. I was more aggravated than anything that my shirt was now cold and wet, my personal space was being impeded on, and she was still lingering.

"We usually don't let him out without a babysitter, but she was booked tonight." She laughed a little too hard, and I immediately regretted saying anything, sensing she took it as more interest than I actually had.

"Do you mind if I hang out with you for a while? I told my family I was going to stay and hang with Gianna, and they left to head back." Gianna was the daughter of the Osteria owner, eighteen years old, sweet, and incredibly immature. She was like the little sister I never had and also never wanted.

"Grappa for everyone to celebrate!" the usually silent Vincenzo yelled across the bar. Either he was trying to distract me, had a few too many Peronis himself, or maybe both. In either case, it worked. He ordered eight shots, when only six of us were there—himself, two of his academy partners, his brother, Sal, and myself. Then, without hesitation, he handed one of the extras to the American girl and the other to me. "To new friendships!"

I wanted to punch him in his face, but I sucked that shot down faster than I could muster a witty response.

"Your friends are a lot of fun," she said. "We should hang out more before I leave."

"When are you leaving?"

"Sunday." It was Thursday, I'd be busy tomorrow with manual labor, and Friday through Sunday would be working regularly for arriving guests, which meant surveying the property as an underpaid, hidden security guard since my father trusted no one else to do it. I not-so-kindly responded, "Listen, I have too much to do tomorrow to entertain any of this, and on top of that you're way too young. I hope you have a great rest of your trip."

She blankly stared at me, not knowing what to do with what I had said, which furthered my disinterest in her.

The beers had made me significantly dizzy, the shots had sealed the deal, everyone was getting louder, and my shirt was still soaking wet. Once I got into a bad mood, it was hard to get me out of it, which meant it was time to head home. I said goodbye to everyone and offered a congratulatory hug and a whisper of "*Fanculo*" to Vincenzo before heading out since it was just our thing. And then, I walked a quarter mile down the road back home.

The property was dark and silent, as it usually was anywhere after ten in the evening. I fumbled with my keys to open the door to my villa and immediately took my shirt off to rinse and air dry it a bit. If my mother smelled it the next morning, she'd think I was far drunker than I actually was—although I definitely did have too much to drink— and I'd get a fifteen-minute lecture on leaving my younger days behind me. She wanted the best for me, always, and while I appreciated her soft way of delivering her messages, I wasn't in the mood to hear it.

When I turned off the sink water to wring out the shirt, I heard a knock at the door. It wasn't the first time Sal stumbled down the road to stay with me because he couldn't make it the extra quarter mile up to his house, and I was sure it wouldn't be the last.

I swung open the door with an open mouth to jokingly tell him there was no vacancy, only to be met with that same head of long blonde hair.

My eyes widened and my heart skipped a beat. I wasn't sure if it was pure shock or the twenty percent pique in interest given the balls she had to actually follow me. Three seconds later, when I came to, I grabbed her arm and pulled her inside, because the last thing I needed was for one of my parents, or a guest, to see my twenty-eight-year-old self with a tourist as young as she was.

"You dropped your phone at the bar, and Sal suggested I bring it to you," she blinked, waiting for my reaction.

I would kill him tomorrow.

"I appreciate that, but you really need to leave."

"It's kind of scary out there. The road is really dark." She gave me her best puppy dog eyes, but I wasn't budging.

"Yea, that's why it's frowned upon to walk on it by yourself, especially when you're not from here." I sounded aggravated and was too tired to care.

"Sal drove me to the end of your driveway," she said with a shrug.

Could you kill someone twice? Because I'd do that tomorrow, too.

"Ok, so is he waiting for you?" My impatience was on full display.

"No, he said I could stay here and you'd drive me back early in the morning." I blinked twice, completely stunned, and started laughing.

"Listen. I don't mean to be rude, but these are guys I

grew up with, and I'm sure they're messing with me. If you want to stay on the couch over there, I will bring you back in the morning. Nothing else is happening, and no one can know you're here. My parents run this property, and there are other guests staying here overnight."

"Uhm, ok." She had to be the most boring woman I'd ever encountered.

I gave her a bunch of blankets, a pillow, and some water, and shut off the light after she laid down on the couch. She was asleep in minutes, and I followed suit. Arm behind my head while lying on my back, looking up at the ceiling, I shook my head and vowed to figure out my life (again) by summer's end.

When I woke up, a few rays of sunshine were peeking through the blinds I hadn't completely shut, which was good since it was already seven in the morning. Problem was, those rays of sunshine felt like they were burning a hole through my skull. My head was pounding, my mouth was dry, and I felt terrible.

When I rolled over and was stunned, yet again, by the blonde hair that would just, not, quit, I truly began contemplating my life's choices. I wasn't attracted to or interested in this girl, *I didn't even know her name*, and she ended up in my bed? What the hell was I doing?

I nudged her. "You need to wake up, because I need to drop you off back at your place. Let's go."

She grunted at me.

"I'm not kidding. Get up, put your shoes on. We need to go before people start walking around."

"You know, Sal is a lot nicer than you are," she mumbled.

"Then you should have gone home with him last night. How did you end up in my bed, by the way?" I was hoping for a good answer since I didn't remember anything after I put her on the couch.

"I woke up around three and was freezing. I asked you for some pants and a long-sleeved shirt, but you refused to wake up so, I climbed into the bed hoping for some body heat instead." She was resourceful, I'd give her that much.

"So we didn't…" I flinched, waiting for her answer.

"No. We didn't. Your personality makes you a lot less attractive."

I smirked. It wasn't the first time I heard that. "Well you're very astute for a teenager."

"I'm twenty," she said with an eye roll.

"Same shit," I retorted as I peered out the window, making sure no one was up and walking around yet. "I'm going to go get my car and pull it up to the top of the circle drive. Meet me there."

I walked along the gravel, down the hill, and around the corner to our garages, where vines had taken over the cement walls but boasted a collection of bright pink roses, hydrangeas, and white lilies. Even though I have every reason to want to be far, far away from this place, I can't deny that when my world would fall apart in various ways, it always reminded me how beautiful life could be if you paid attention to the good parts.

She was standing in the middle of the driveway when I drove up. Following directions wasn't her strong suit, it would appear, and I ushered for her to get in the car quickly. We drove in silence down the road to her villa, and for once in my life, the Gods had smiled down on me. She hopped out of the car without saying a word, and I was free to leave.

For one brief moment, I felt a wave of relief, which quickly vanished when I pulled back up the gravel driveway with my still pounding head, a slight wave of nausea, and my father standing there waiting for me. He never looked particularly happy, so his present demeanor wasn't out of the ordinary. I wasn't supposed to start work until eight and it was barely seven thirty. Maybe he saw me leave with her and thought I'd been romancing tourists on property.

I parked the car and walked up the drive to meet him. "Mama is waiting in the kitchen. We have some bad news."

"What is it?" I asked with a raised eyebrow

"Giuseppe was arrested last night."

CHAPTER 3

Mia

I woke up feeling like I ate sandpaper in my sleep, which is the quintessential sign of "You probably made bad decisions last night, and you're about to feel like absolute shit." Room darkening shades have a way of making you think it's three in the morning but since I came back home at that time and there was an ever-so-subtle blinding ray of sunshine pounding on my forehead through the side of said shades, it surely wasn't.

I hadn't drunk too much the night before, but between the emotional wreckage, the late-night McDonald's run, and the lack of sleep, I was feeling the effects. I blinked a few times, rolled over to grab whatever water was available, chugged it, and peeked at my phone. At a quarter to noon, I rolled my eyes in self-disgust having wasted half the day away but let out a sigh of relief for no missed calls, no missed texts, and a great appreciation for the "block this caller" feature. Bonus points for deleting the entire message thread before I fell asleep so I couldn't obsess over any of it when I woke up with a "Let's pretend this never happened" approach.

The front door opened downstairs, heavy footsteps barreled into a heavier man hug, and I knew my brother had arrived. I headed towards the bathroom for a scalding hot shower to wash away some of the remaining cigarette smoke, sweat, and lingering embarrassment. When I turned off the water, I heard the door open again and the faintest newborn cry. My sister had arrived, too, with her husband and our family's first grandchild. A few swipes of mascara with a freshly blown out hairdo and I almost felt like a complete human again. *"Gang's all here,"* I thought.

Let's get this over with.

In the grand scheme of weird or annoying families, mine isn't one. We're a tight knit crew who generally love spending time together with an occasional roast or zinger thrown in. I poured myself a giant cup of room-temperature coffee after saying hello to everyone and joined them at the table.

"Late night?" my mom asked.

"A tad," I responded.

"Why are your eyes puffy? Were you crying?" she asked with a fifty-fifty split of concern and judgment.

"I'm preparing to live alone with a lot of cats the rest of my life, but other than that, it was fine," I responded with an attempt at humor since my face could never really tell a lie.

"You don't even like cats," she said matter-of-factly.

"Depressing isn't it?" I didn't like where this was heading, but also felt I deserved it, because she always knew what was good (and not good) for me. A few months prior, I had shown up to night-club-disaster-lingerie-in-the-parking-lot-guy's place with a bag filled with Christmas gifts and got an incredulous, "Why do you do this when I don't even celebrate the holiday?"

"Uhm, you're welcome?" It was another attempt at

making a non-relationship into one, and I ended up coming home crying from that, too.

As my mom, she was tired of seeing me get hurt, especially by people who didn't deserve me. As my built-in best friend, she was running out of patience with me in general.

"When you stop looking, you're going to find exactly what it is you've been searching for," she reminded me.

I stared off into space, knowing she was right but tired of hearing it because, to be honest, I didn't even know what the hell I *was* looking for. I just felt exhausted.

I was exhausted from shitty men, from living at home in order to financially survive the demanding but low-paying event planning career path I was on, and from life in general. I started daydreaming about my own place like I always had, thinking it was going to solve all my problems.

"Your mom and I are moving," my dad interrupted my daydream long enough to create the immediate realization that apparently, it now *was* time for me to move out.

We all blankly stared at them. We grew up in this house, we celebrated so many things in this house, my sister had even started raising her own kid in and out of this house, and we couldn't exactly picture what life would be like without it. Not necessarily that I was planning to stay forever, because obviously I was looking forward to being on my own, but I was not quite ready to not be able to come and go as I pleased.

"I object," I retorted, straight faced.

"You can object all you want, but it's too much to maintain and it's time to downsize," he replied.

"Overruled," I tried again. He was powerless against my baby of the family charm, or so I liked to believe.

"Ah…nice try." I looked back and forth from my sister to my brother and back again.

My brother shrugged his shoulders, unphased. "Whatever you guys need, Pop. How can we help?" Men. Often level-headed with the big stuff, but catch them on a day when something small derails them and they'll go full psych patient on anyone within reach. I'll never understand it.

My sister, the ever-so-quiet one, sat there with tears in her eyes. Granted, we were acting like they had two weeks left to live, but *hello*, the memories, all of them. Our hearts were breaking.

"Where are you moving?" she asked.

"A few hours south. We need it a little bit warmer, and we found a spot in a nice community where some of our friends are," he explained.

"So, you're turning into country club people?" my sarcasm was acting up with a side of not pleased.

"If that's what you want to call it, sure. This really shouldn't be too big of a deal. All we want is to get rid of a lot of *stuff*, simplify our lives, and go to Italy next year to celebrate our fiftieth anniversary—to which you are all invited." He had a way with both words and timing. Hit us with some surprise info and then soften us into a pile of gelato with some Italian pipe dreams.

"Ok, forgive me for not jumping on the 'Buongiorno' bandwagon as my childhood memories are being flushed down the shitter, but when is this all happening?" I was twenty-four and testing my limits, still mildly afraid of one of those classic Italian-American backhanded love taps from my mom or look of disapproval from my dad.

"Moving in a month once closing is finalized, and Italy sometime next May," he said as my brain computed what the next few months would look like.

"I'm getting kicked out of here in a month, and I'm

supposed to feel better about that with a trip to Italy next year?"

There it was, just a step too far.

"You're twenty-four years old. If we were going to 'kick you out' we would have done that years ago. And you mispronounced *thank you.*"

Oh, he was good.

My sister kicked me under the table, and when I looked at her, she gave me the "Let's review this later" look. Fine. My mind was in overdrive. I was a rational person but an emotional one. I was super attached to anything I loved. I had totaled my first car after a rogue deer threw itself in front of me one night and I swerved up and over a snowy ice-filled embankment to avoid it. The car got towed away, and every time I passed the mechanic whose parking lot it was wasting away in, I started crying. Real, human tears—over a car.

So, to think about what would happen when I left behind my childhood house, the one in which I previously adorned my bedroom walls with *NSync, Backstreet Boys, and Vin Diesel posters, choreographed dances in the base-ment, competed in summer Olympics in the pool outside, stole my sister's clothes straight out of her closet, and sat on the kitchen counter when having heart to hearts with my mom, simply gutted me.

"Mia, come help me with the baby," my sister urged me. We pretended to go change a poop-filled diaper but mostly exchanged some WTFs.

"We knew this was coming," she said.

"Yeah, but not this soon," I retorted. I was still feeling irrationally upset given all our parents had sacrificed for us over the years. "Where are we going to have the holidays? Where are you going to have all of your parties?"

"We'll figure it out," she responded. "They're not the

only people to ever move. You've been wanting to move out anyway and Daddy's right; it's time to get out on your own."

I felt moderately judged, but also knew she wasn't wrong. Part of me always rationalized staying home longer to help them when they needed it. Mostly though, I was stuck working a job that paid a minimal salary while expecting maximum output. My finances were hurting, which always seemed to keep me from leaping forward. I wasn't sure which direction I wanted my life to take as far as a career path was concerned, but I was certain that working all these hours as a reliable perfectionist thereby making someone else's company a lot of money—with zero benefits for myself—was not for me.

Cheated on? *Check.*

No solid career? *Check.*

Kicked out of childhood home? *Check.*

With a mental white flag waving, my brother, well known for his less than stellar delivery skills, walked into the room as I was about to cry, giving me *the* face and a loud, "You've got to be shitting me."

"About what?" I gave him *the* face right back.

"It's time to grow up, Mia. You've got the world by the balls. Go find an apartment, do whatever it is you want to do, whenever you want to do it, and live," he said.

I stared at him blankly.

"This is exactly what you need. You're Miss Independent until it comes to leaving this place, and life is passing you by. How many people in their mid-twenties want to date someone who's still living at home? None that I know." His words ripped through me, but again, I knew he was right. Everything he said was true. I *was* Miss Independent. I wanted to do things the way I wanted to do them. I wanted to do what I wanted when I wanted.

As I thought hard about why I had such a hard time with the idea of leaving, I remembered I was a creature of habit and planned more than I sometimes should. I tried to control situations rather than live presently. When I lost that control, it innately bothered me.

Whenever I felt this pang of pressure in my chest, I'd default to needing my honest-even-if-it-kills-ya best friend. I walked outside and called my best girl since kindergarten. "Wait, wait, slow down," Allie said. "They're both ok? Your parents? Neither of them is sick?"

"No, why would you think that?" I asked.

"Oh, I don't know, because you're acting like a friggin' lunatic."

Friends, the sisters we choose.

"You know how I am with life changes. It's too much, too soon," I said.

"I get it, I'm the one who still lives in the same place since birth because I don't like driving over bridges, but come on Mia," she replied.

"Jesus Christ, you and my brother. Come on what?" I started mildly fuming.

"You're more capable of things than you allow yourself to be. You're fun, smart, talented, and you just need to spread those wings and fly a little. I really think this is going to be great for them, and even better for you. It's time."

Allie was another one who had a way with words. And the best part—she meant every one of them.

I started crying again. "They want us all to go to Italy with them for their anniversary next year," I told her.

"That sounds horrible, too," she responded and I felt her eyes roll through the phone. "I'm here for you like I always will be. But seriously, get it together."

I was known for getting in my feels for short outbursts

at a time, hating the way it felt, then quickly snapping out of it and concocting a plan, much like I had after gracing the McDonald's drive-through the night before.

"You're right, like you always are, thank you."

"Anytime," she said before she hung up, off to wrangle one of her two beautiful kids yelling in the background.

I walked back inside to find everyone sitting at the kitchen table. My brother yelled, "Yo, Drama Llama, want to come finish this conversation with the adults?" I envisioned kicking him straight in the nuts and felt moderate relief.

"You ok?" my mom asked.

"Yeah."

"Ok, good." My dad continued, "We're splitting some of the proceeds from the house sale among the three of you now rather than waiting until we're…"

"Dead? Are you about to say dead?" I was clearly on edge and everyone side-eyed me.

"Relax," he put up a stiff hand and continued. "That'll happen eventually, no sense in pretending it won't. The point is, this money can help you in your own homes, if you have to find a new one." He looked directly at me with a raised eyebrow.

Well, he certainly had that planned out, didn't he? Oftentimes, I felt like I didn't deserve to grow up in the manner I did, and this was one of those times. Here I was, crying all over myself because they were selling a house too large for them to maintain while still thinking of ways to give back to us, like they always did.

I hugged them tight and thanked them, poured myself a glass of wine, curled up on the couch with a notebook, and closed my eyes. What was the actual reason that I was so upset? I was self-aware enough to do some quick soul searching, fully knowing something just didn't feel *right*.

Things didn't feel whole, for me, for my life, for where I was, or for where I was destined to go. I was in one of those awkward, transitional stages of life, and it felt uncomfortable.

I needed more, I wanted more, and the mere thought of traveling to Italy made my heart skip a beat. Maybe all of this was happening to force me into my next chapter? If I leaned into the changes rather than fight them, perhaps I'd figure out what it was I was meant to be doing, where I was meant to be, and who I was meant to be with.

First up was finding a new place, which, as much as I resisted it, really did excite me to think about. I also had to do some soul searching. Was an event planning career really what I wanted? Was it going to push me towards where I envisioned myself ending up at forty years old? Fifty years old? Did I even have an idea of what that vision looked like?

I didn't have the answers to any of these questions, but I opened my notebook and made a short Italian bucket list to distract myself instead.

Mia's Italian Bucket List

- *Experience villa life in Tuscany*
- *Gondola ride in Venice*
- *Unlimited guilt-free pizza, pasta, gelato, and wine*

Seemed relatively basic upon review, and I immediately decided it needed a little spice.

Extra Credit

- *Have incredible sex with an Italian hottie—no strings (or expectations) attached*

Perfect. It went against every fiber of my being to even

think I was capable of being romanced by someone without planning our wedding the following morning, but I promised myself I'd at least try not to be *opposed* to it.

The new plan moving forward was to plan (a little) less, do (a little) more, and enjoy my life to the absolute fullest which included looking forward to a future trip to Italy.

But first, it was time to find a new place to live.

CHAPTER 4
Gennaro

"Did you have to mangle his face?" I asked Giuseppe as we walked out of the police station.

"He's lucky I didn't kill him," he responded, without an ounce of remorse. "He was talking shit about Papa, our property, our business, everything."

"Oh, *our* business. As in, the one you want nothing to do with and don't ever help with? Classic." I don't know why I'm continually surprised at his lack of maturity or ownership of anything in general. "Let's actually try to understand what the actual issue is here. You're pissed. At what? I still have no idea after years of trying to figure you out. You found an opportunity to take it out on someone who, yes, probably deserved it, but come on. You're better than this. I'm tired of bailing you out."

"Vin bailed me out, actually," he smirked, referring to my best friend, the ink not even dry on his academy graduation certificate.

"Thanks for noticing," Vin chimed in, "but your brother's right. You've got to move past all this little kid shit. That's the first and last time I'm helping you out."

Growing up in Italy where we own hundreds of acres felt at times like we were being raised on undiscovered land at the turn of the twentieth century. Cowboys and Indians? No, more like everyone's great grandparents making property deals, arranging marriages, or joining each other in business ventures to secure as much as they possibly could.

I know I sound extraordinarily ungrateful for all we have, but it's been a huge burden my entire life. There was never any question as to what I wanted to do when I grew up, just an assumption, or more accurately, an expectation, that I'd continue maintaining the entire property to host guests, both locally and internationally sourced.

It's a spectacular place with rolling hills, mountain views for miles, buildings constructed by our ancestors alongside exquisite stonework, and an in-ground pool with an infinity edge overlooking the vineyards. A barn filled with animals paired with an expertly tended to garden, provides fresh produce, dairy, and meats that we use daily in our cooking. It has everything you'd expect from a traditional Italian property.

It's a place people dream of visiting, staying at, and living in, and as someone who grew up here, I feel constant resentment towards it. I don't see the beauty in it anymore —I see the hardships. The sheer manpower it takes to upkeep it all, the constant needs to be met from visitors who pay to stay there, and the years required to ensure our land stays ours alongside some of our closest neighbors.

All of those years produced great friends and local allies, same as they produced scum who would never be satisfied seeing us thrive. As we grew up and barely made it through school, we encountered more of those families than we cared to admit. People who wouldn't ever do anything to better their own situation, but instead used all of their energy trying to tear down someone else's accomplishments. What they saw was a successful, lucrative business that shined light on the beauty of the Italian countryside to all of the "wrong people."

We're viewed as sell-outs for hosting international guests at premium pricing, rather than for doing what we actually do, which is share our culture and ways of life with people who have genuine interest in learning about us. The back breaking, round-the-clock working hours to maintain the integrity of the property and the Italian way of life in general? They merely glaze over that before running their mouths.

So, it came as no surprise that I started shutting it all out over the course of the last few years, desperately trying to figure out possible next steps for myself. Giovanni escaped to Florence with his law aspirations to legitimize his leaving, and Giuseppe repeatedly acted out in sheer denial of pretty much everything.

I'm the oldest sibling, trying to hold it all together, but the resentment of it all has left me reeling. Picking up my little brother from a police station after working sixteen hours sent me over the edge. As friendships would have it, I unloaded all my frustrations on Vincenzo after we dropped Giuseppe off at home.

"I don't want to do this anymore. Any of it. The property, the countryside, the same old shit day in and day out. I never asked for any of this, and I never wanted any of it," I rambled from the Osteria parking lot. "I know I sound ungrateful, but I'm closer to thirty than I am to twenty, and I don't have one thing that makes me excited to wake up in the morning."

"I get it," he responded. "I felt the same, which is why I went to the academy. I wanted the salary security and the ability to get out and do something different. I think my parents were blinded with pride that I'd be a cop, so they never busted my balls too much for leaving the farm."

"Man, we always dreamed of going to the academy together when we were younger. I'm happy for you, I really am. I just don't know what I can do," I said. At this point, I was annoying myself with uncertainty and what felt like a whole lot of complaining. It's not my natural style. I'm more of a do-it-and-shut-up-about-it kind of guy, but that strategy has seemed to hit maximum capacity.

"What's stopping you from doing it?" he asked, simply.

"You know my parents would absolutely lose it if I wasn't here," I said.

"No, they wouldn't. It feels that way now, but if you leave, they'll figure out a plan B because they'll have to. You really think they're going to disown you for choosing another path? They didn't disown Giovanni for moving to Florence, and they have yet to disown Giuseppe, although maybe they will after this last one." We laughed.

Vin was my brother by choice and my sounding board. A hard ass by day and night, he protected me like I was his little brother. Very few people ever saw his softer side. A hidden heart of gold, he's like a lion protecting his cubs when it comes to anyone he really loves. I'm lucky to have him because I'm not able to talk to my brothers in the same way.

Our relationship spans back to grade school. We were the athletic kids, smart enough, well liked, but slightly unapproachable at times. Not by choice, he was just always a big guy with a face that screamed, "Please don't talk to me," and I had limited patience with, well, mostly everyone. For whatever reason, women loved that sort of thing —the whole "hard to get" notion—but in my case, I didn't do it on purpose, and the more it attracted people, the more annoyed it made me.

So here we are, two "by choice" brothers, trying to navigate life's journey together. We want to make our families proud but still do something we actually feel good about.

"Let's go get a beer," Vin suggested.

"I'll meet you there in a few. I have to grab some wine from Taglia's for dinner tomorrow."

He shot me a look, and I immediately put my hand up and shook my head back and forth once. "It's the closest market, and I'm not driving back into town tomorrow," I explained.

"Whatever you want to tell yourself. See you in a bit," he said.

I walked next door to Taglia's Family Market and breathed deeply before turning the knob and walking inside. The smell of freshly baked bread smacked me in the face, temporarily distracting me. My carbohydrate coma ended abruptly when I saw her fire-engine-red hair behind the counter. She looked as happy to see me, as I was her, which was to say…not at all.

"Francesca," I mumbled while avoiding eye contact.

"What do you need?" she asked somewhat aggressively.

In hindsight, I should have thrown back a few beers with Vincenzo *before* walking over here, but at least now I'd have fully earned them before indulging.

"I need some wine for dinner tomorrow," I said abruptly.

"Who are you trying to seduce now?" she glared at me with the same lack of trust she had since we were teenagers, and my eyes instinctively rolled in the back of my head.

"Ti odio!" I hadn't been there a full minute and she was already screaming that she hated me. Vin always predicted things, and he knew better than for me to walk in there.

"Listen, I don't like coming in here any more than you want me coming in here, but it's the only market for miles. I need three bottles of wine for my *family* dinner tomorrow. I don't need to seduce anyone, I don't have time for all that bullshit." She had an incredible way of getting me fired up in all the wrong ways.

"Yeah, you never have time for anything, do you?" If I engaged any more, she wouldn't stop. I grabbed the three closest bottles of red wine, threw some money on the counter, shook my head, waved my hand over my shoulder, and walked out.

"Arrivederci," I said calmly. I wasn't about to get worked up again, especially over her. We had never seen eye to eye and we never would, no matter how much our families wished it to be different.

I put the wine in my car and walked into the Osteria to see Vin talking to a group of guys, all of whom looked like cops. "Gennaro! Let me introduce you."

"Give me a minute, I need a drink first," I said, visibly agitated.

"She did it again, didn't she?" He slid over and started interrogating me.

"I don't even blame her, I'm just tired of it, all of it." I was truly exhausted. Insane expectations from my family had finally reached their boiling point, and I knew I needed a change. Francesca still holding on to disappointment and heartache from ten years ago was the final straw.

"Well, I have good news." Vincenzo turned me around and introduced me to a Deputy Chief he met during his academy. "This is my best friend, Gennaro. He's wanted to be a part of the force since he was little and probably the only guy I'd personally vouch for."

"We have a test coming up for new recruits, but the openings are in Rome. Are you interested in moving?" he asked, wasting no time with his recruitment.

"To be honest, I haven't thought about it in that much detail. I always…"

"Well think about it quickly, you'd have to register by Monday," he interrupted.

It was Friday night. Saturday I had to work, then have dinner with my family. And Sunday, I was planning to do absolutely nothing for my first day off in months. This all felt like unnecessary pressure and seemed to be escalating quickly, which isn't how I typically deal with stuff. Then again, the ways in which I've been dealing with life lately— slow, methodical, predictable—isn't really doing me any favors either. Maybe I need to make a rash decision for once.

In the middle of my personal brainstorm, my phone dinged with a text from my father. "Thanks for getting Giuseppe home, we'll talk about this tomorrow."

How Giuseppe getting arrested turned into a personal problem of mine, I had no idea. I put my phone back in my pocket without responding, wanting to be left alone, but the more I thought about it, the more furious I got. I didn't want to spend another second talking about either of my brothers, my parents' expectations, the villa work schedule, any of it. I'd finally had enough.

I shook the Deputy Chief's hand, thanked him for the information, and let both him and Vincenzo know I was going to get things in order over the weekend and register for the academy on Monday. Vin's face showed both pure shock and excitement. I could tell he was happy at the thought, but not necessarily convinced I'd go through with it.

The next day, I'd tell my family, and Vin would see exactly how serious I was about needing and wanting a change after all.

"Absolutely not!" Papa bellowed while Mama sat with her face in her hands, holding back tears as though my wanting to become a police officer was the same as enlisting in the military and heading off to an actual war.

Giovanni chimed in, "What's the big deal? He'll only be a couple of hours away and can come back some weekends."

We weren't that close as far as brothers were concerned, but he was very rational, very straightforward, and very matter of fact. Those qualities were the exact reason he'd been able to pick up and move to Florence as easily as he did, and for once, I appreciated them.

"I'm getting too old to maintain this on my own, and I don't trust strangers to run things. Who will help me?" Papa asked.

I started to wonder to myself how this was *my* problem and *my* responsibility, much like Giuseppe's arrest seemingly was, but before I could muster a rebuttal, someone else responded. "I will." We all turned our heads to the patio door to find Giuseppe standing there. "I'll take over Gennaro's responsibilities, and I'll do whatever else you need me to do."

No one said anything for what felt like minutes but was actually seconds until Mama got up, as moms do, and hugged him. Giovanni was smirking with raised eyebrows, holding back laughter. My father's eyes darted to and from each of us while I poured myself another glass of wine.

"Listen, I'm sorry about last night, but I'll save everyone the long lectures about me needing to grow up. I know I do. I'll do it here. And Gennaro, you can go to Rome, or wherever you want to go without worrying. I've got this." Giuseppe sounded a whole lot more confident in his plan than I did, but for once, I actually felt moderately relieved.

"Are you going to be ok with this?" I asked Papa.

"Do I have a choice?" he retorted.

"You have as much choice as I ever did getting started with it all, I guess. I'm not a kid anymore, and I need to see what else is out there." I started shaking my head, the way I always did whenever I dared to explain that my dreams didn't necessarily revolve around my father's. "Maybe I'll hate it, maybe I'll turn right around when I get there, but I at least need to try. And I need you to support that."

"Rocco, this is a good plan. I know you don't like change, but it's a good plan, a good opportunity for Gennaro, and a good chance for Giuseppe to get more involved," Mom softly said.

We all held our breath, waiting for his final response, but he sat at the head of the table in his arm chair holding his glass of wine and staring off into space. I love him as sons love their fathers, but in that moment, I realized he'd never truly be happy with any outcome.

If I was finally going to live my life for me, the time to make a change was now.

"I'm registering for the academy on Monday, and it starts in a month. I'll come back on weekends when I can to help out with things." I felt myself exhale and finished, "Giuseppe, thanks for stepping up."

He stood there, proud of himself with a big grin. He

was in for a rude awakening, but it wasn't anything he couldn't handle. In fact, he'd probably handle it better than I would, since he wasn't ever bothered by much. Where I was overly observant, slightly temperamental, and always needing to be in control, he'd actually end up being exactly what my father would appreciate: a gritty worker without much opposition. The guests would end up loving him and his crazy personality, too.

I felt better. Lighter, optimistic, and like I was carrying a little less weight on my shoulders than I was a few minutes prior. Sure, a police academy would have its own demands, but I'd be able to navigate those on my own terms, not under constant observation of my father. I'd get out of town for a while, and head into a bigger city filled with more people, more excitement, more of everything.

I grabbed my glass of wine, walked to the courtyard, and laid down on the outdoor couch, looking up at the stars, breathing a few more sighs of relief. I thought about daily life in Rome, but mostly, what I'd be leaving behind.

I had a solid family life, but it was laced with extremely traditional gender roles. Papa did everything outside of the house and Mama did everything inside of it. I was never particularly convinced they had a deep, true love for one another, and as a result, I never saw them demonstrate much affection. They worked *well* together, but it wasn't the type of relationship that anyone would necessarily write a romance novel about.

It had left me jaded as far as love and relationships were concerned.

Many of my younger years were spent having limited interactions with girls and women, because heaven forbid anyone or anything tarnish our family's reputation. I got used to sneaking around, not because I wanted to, but because I didn't really have a choice. With that came the label of being a *bad boy*, which was actually the farthest thing from the truth. I figured I'd have a hard time convincing an entire town otherwise though, so I kept to myself, which many people took to mean I was a rude asshole.

I was ready to get out of here, ready to be an individual and not just another member of the Beletta family. A chapter was closing, and the next one was an open book of blank paper waiting to be written upon. I wasn't sure exactly what was ahead of me, but I was certain the path would lead me to greater things. There was no backup plan, and there was no other option. I was going to prove to myself, and to Papa, that there *was* life outside of this place.

What I wasn't aware of was how much one decision and one city would change my life and my heart.

Forever.

CHAPTER 5
Mia

I straightened the brightly colored abstract wall art complete with gold flecks of paint that hung over my cream-colored couch. The rest of my apartment was a combination of gray and ivory neutrals, which generally put me at ease. At the urging of Allie, who came to help me decorate, and thanks to this newer and somewhat improved version of myself, I quickly realized the importance of brightening up my life with a pop of bold color, living a touch outside the lines I was used to.

An hour and a half north of my parents' new home, I had settled in nicely right along a part rural, part suburban border in northern New Jersey. It was close enough to New York City, not that I particularly liked venturing *into* New York City, yet far enough away to actually live peacefully.

The apartment complex I found was relatively new, bustling with people in their twenties and thirties. I started meeting my neighbors once winter was over and we all began venturing outdoors a bit more, and had even made a connection at the gym with someone who needed bartending shifts filled at his local restaurant. Working random night and weekend shifts when I wasn't traveling for my regular job helped me to pocket extra money.

I unintentionally blocked outside distractions, and the after effects of fully focusing on myself were more than evident.

If I wasn't working, I was exercising or visiting my family. I was finally getting used to feeling like a mature adult, which was probably why seeing my family a couple times per month simultaneously filled my heart and reminded me how much I loved having my own space to come back to.

I felt the best I ever had, with only a mild nagging feeling that something wasn't quite *right*.

As I was reflecting on what it could be one night while mixing a drink at the bar, a deep voice behind me distracted my inner dialogue.

"If you were a cartoon character, there'd be smoke coming out of your ears right now." I spun around to find a confident smile and blazing blue eyes burning a hole right through me. My lady parts reacted accordingly.

"Is that so?" I smiled back as I slyly assessed his muscular build and the tattoos peeking out of his crewneck t-shirt while pretending to remain cool. The way the sleeves of his tee hugged the curve of his biceps told me he didn't miss a workout often, and the extreme eye contact he continued to make confirmed he didn't suffer from any self-esteem issues.

"You looked deep in thought, that's all," he followed up his original ice breaker, watching me intently as I moved back and forth serving other people around him.

"I'm always thinking about something," I honestly responded. "What can I get you?"

"What's your favorite drink to make?" He was equal parts inviting, charming, and mysterious, asking me something I hadn't been asked before in my short career as a bartender.

My eyes kept pulling towards his neck tattoo, leaving me curious as to how far they stretched down the length of his body. When I snapped out of the temporary stupor I was in, I responded, "Whichever drink will make you enjoy your night the most."

"I don't need a drink to enjoy myself here. I just need to look at you." He didn't take his eyes off of me while he said it, and for a split second my conscious self—paired with the involuntary twitching between my legs—knew he was too good to be true. There were plenty of men who came in and hit on me as well as every other woman behind the bar, but I'd politely declined them all. I rationalized though, that I'd give in just this one time to see where it would lead me, and shared my number with him when he asked for it at the end of the night.

I was a woman who was beginning to *plan* a little less and *do* a little more. What, exactly, I was *doing* hadn't been ironed out yet, but I was *rolling* with it like Tina Turner.

He followed up with some texts over the next two weeks, communicating with me consistently between seven in the morning and seven at night, never later in the evening, and never on the weekend. My Spidey sense had been partially activated due to the fact that no one I worked with knew anything about him. In addition to that, he had asked to take me out on a *Thursday*—but I was trying to give him, and my hormones, the benefit of the doubt.

There seemed to be a fine line between being close-minded and a complete idiot who ignored warning signs, but I was trying to simply enjoy things, let go of expectations, and keep on rolling.

Proud Mia keeps on burning…

Sing it, Tina!

Now, having changed purses from the large, daily handbag that occasionally doubled as a suitcase to a small, date night clutch, I looked up to study my reflection in the full-length mirror perched in the corner of my living room. Having to adjust to an unseasonably cold April night, I chose a classic black, form-fitting, long-sleeved bodysuit that I tucked into dark jeans and finished with a pair of black, slouchy, knee-high boots. Satisfied, I nodded at myself, put on a final layer of lip gloss, and checked my phone after hearing it ding from my clutch.

> Date: Hey, I'm really sorry but I can't make it tonight

I squinted at the phone and assessed the twinge I felt in my gut. While I was trying to figure out if I was pissed off that he canceled, annoyed with myself for not listening to my inner Spidey, or frustrated that I wasted time shaving my legs, putting makeup on, and blow drying my hair, some more messages rolled through.

> Date: He's lying to you

> Date: He's also an asshole

> Date: This is his girlfriend

> Date: Trust me, I'm doing you a favor

Lord, have mercy.

I started to type back but shook my head and blocked the number instead. My gut instinct turned out to be right, as it always was. As quickly as the text messages came through, I was undressed with a washed face, hair piled on top of my head, jammies on, and a bowl of ice cream, catching up with the DVR.

I felt myself starting to doze off on the couch some-where around ten and abruptly woke to that punched-in-the-gut feeling of dread that I had to go to *regular* work the next day. Thankfully, it was Friday, the last day of the work week, but it was still an unnerving feeling.

As life would have it, even as I figured out certain portions of life—living on my own, situating my finances, and not allowing letdowns from men to derail me—another part of life began to feel uncertain.

I was gleefully happy living on my own, but unhappy and uneasy in my career.

While I loved the frequent travel associated within the event planning industry, I could feel, somewhere deep within my bones, that I was beginning to resent it. It had a different appeal back when I'd just graduated college and moved back home. Getting used to living with parents again after four years of autonomy was a difficult thing to do. So being able to travel, legitimately, while someone else paid for it, was the perfect win/win scenario where I could get out of the house, respectfully, and also save money.

But once I had the freedom of an entire apartment, coming and going as I pleased, the thought of traveling for work rather than pleasure didn't have much of an appeal anymore. Three years of planning events for corporate executives or pharmaceutical sales reps had proven to be plenty. Problem was, my coworkers—and even the owner of the company—had become like family, which made it extremely difficult to leave. I didn't want to disappoint anyone; but most importantly, I couldn't even envision which industry I might move towards next.

I shook my head, shut off the television, double checked the locks on all my doors and windows, and headed towards my bedroom.

After climbing into bed, I set my morning alarm, and

pressed shuffle on my spa music playlist. Obviously, this was an attempt at drowning out the noises of any potential murderers lurking beyond my apartment walls.

Still slightly dramatic even though I had evolved into a full-fledged responsible grown-up.

Eight hours later, my body began to waken—with eyes still closed—as my brain finished processing the most vivid of dreams. Bright blue skies had opened up to an expansive vineyard. I sat in a chair next to someone with my feet perched on the edge of a stone wall, and a glass of red wine in my hand. As my head turned to bring this person's face into view, my eyes finally blinked open to instead reveal my ceiling fan rotating on its lowest speed.

I laid there motionless for a few minutes, willing myself to fall back asleep so I could relive the scene, but to no avail. Instead, I begrudgingly showered, dressed myself, packed a lunch, and headed to work.

"Happy Friday!" One of my least favorite coworkers bellowed from her cubicle. I found it impossible to muster words back to her. Why was it always the annoying coworkers who felt the need to be the friendliest first thing in the morning? I bypassed her desk and my own, walking straight into the corner office of our lead planner and my best work friend, Nancy.

Still wearing sunglasses as I slumped over in her visitor's chair, she assessed me with her fingers still typing away at her keyboard. "I can't tell if your date went well and you're running low on energy from a night of wild sex, or if your eyes are swollen and puffy under those glasses you're wearing, in which case, I'd love to know what happened so I can try to remind myself why I thought being married was the answer to a happy life."

She was a tough cookie, honest as all hell—even when

you didn't want her to be—and she rarely, if ever, minced words.

"The date didn't happen," I began, "Apparently he's with someone. His girlfriend texted me through his phone. I blocked his number, and then I went to bed."

She pursed her lips together and nodded her head while raising her eyebrows as if to say, "Whelp, I did *not* have that on my Mia's-Dating-Life bingo card."

"I'm not particularly surprised," I continued, "I felt something in my gut that wasn't right. Not too broken up about it though. Actually, I felt worse having to come here this morning than I did as this was unfolding last night."

"Well that says a lot about your career choice," she said, the corners of her lips curling upwards.

"Thanks for the reminder, asshole," I said, lovingly, as we often talked to each other.

Her phone rang. "Yes, sure, I'll send her in." She looked at me with an ever-so-slightly concerned look on her face. "Rob wants you in his office. Didn't say why."

I shrugged, assuming I spent too much on incidentals during my last trip. When I sat down in the office next door, though, his lack of initial eye contact was unsettling. Whatever he was about to tell me involved much more than airport snacks and an occasional happy hour cocktail.

"Mia, I…" He stopped to rub his temples and scratch the back of his neck, visibly uncomfortable. "We are hurting here as more and more of our clients turn to internal employees to plan their conferences, and…" he exhaled deeply and finally looked at me. "I can't keep you on full time."

My eyes went wide, and I could feel the tight squeeze in my throat that usually occurred right before I'd start crying about something. Thankfully, he called Nancy in to help us along since my mouth wasn't capable of forming words.

"We value all you've done for us, which is why I want to try to offer you a part-time position, but it'll be less than half your current salary and you'd serve as more of an on-site assistant," he explained.

Nancy interjected, "You're saying she'd be traveling more than she is now with less pay?"

I was glad she said it, and when he nodded to confirm, I felt the final sucker punch.

"Unfortunately, you're the last one in and had to be the first choice to go." He was a kind soul, and I somewhat agreed with his logic, but he and everyone in the office knew I had recently moved out on my own. Here I was, not *quitting* because I considered us family even though I didn't like the job itself, and in an instant my life was flipped upside down—the same courtesy not being offered to me.

He continued on, saying he'd pay me my full salary for the next month regardless of which option I chose, but if I decided to leave, I'd only be required to stay on for the next two weeks to tie up loose ends and hand off my remaining events and projects. I nodded through it all.

"You don't have to make up your mind right now," he began, but I put up a hand. This was the life change I needed, and I felt it in my gut, the same way I knew Ol' Blue Eyes at the bar was a bad news bear.

"I'll give you two more weeks, and then I'll be done. I don't want the part-time option, but thanks for the offer," I responded confidently before walking out.

Back in Nancy's office, she chimed in, "Mia, it doesn't feel like it right now, but this," her voice trailed off as she looked out the window and then she continued, "is a blessing."

"Are you high?" Words finally formed, but not in the manner I hoped they would. "How the hell is this a blessing? I'm completely fucked." The confidence I had a minute ago in my boss's office had already vanished.

"No, you're not." She swung her chair around to face me again. "You saved up some money these last few months, right? And you have the money your parents left you?"

"Yea…" I had no idea where she was going with this, but I could hear the passion in her voice.

"Go to Italy." She leaned closer towards me, over the top of my desk, drilling a hole through my soul, or so it felt. "Call your parent's friend who lives there, what's her name?"

"Pesca," I answered.

"Yes, her. See if they have any last-minute cancellations, which I'm sure they do, and get your ass on a plane and go." She was a lady on a mission to help me keep forging forward.

The Mia who colored *in* the lines was reeling while the Mia who was trying to add pops of bold, abstract color— thinking a little less and doing a little more—was fully picking up what Nancy was putting down.

My face transformed from a deflated sad sack to wide-eyed excitement.

"You're a genius, you know that?" I smiled big.

"Stop it," she flapped her hand at me and smiled. "Ok fine, keep going."

"It feels like this might be happening on purpose. I had a weird dream this morning that I was somewhere overlooking a vineyard, and didn't know who I was with," I told her.

She shook her head from side to side, "I don't believe all that astrological witch shit, but I see an opening for you with this. Take the paycheck for the two weeks you don't have to work, use it as a down payment for the trip, and use your saved miles to buy your airfare before your last day of work. Go! Experience a couple of weeks in Italy and worry about what's *next* when you come back."

It clicked.

She was right.

This was my opening. My parents had invited us all to Italy with them next year, but my newfound desire to tap into my spontaneous side said there was no reason I couldn't go before then, too.

I went back to my desk and turned on my computer. While I waited for it to boot up, I texted Pesca, one of my parents' best friends.

> Mia: Paging my favorite pretend parent

> Pesca: Returning page to my favorite pretend daughter

> Mia: Just lost my job

> Pesca: Shite

> Mia: Rather than be dramatic about it, I want to finally book my trip to come see you

> Pesca: Say less

> Pesca: When are you thinking?

> Mia: As soon as possible

> Mia: I have two weeks left here and then I'm done

> Pesca: Let me figure something out

Two hours later, I had grabbed lunch from the cafe downstairs and was eating it at my desk, avoiding any and all conversations that were occurring in the employee lunch room. When my phone dinged and I saw her name, I felt excitement course through my veins.

> Pesca: There's an opening during the last week of May and first week of June

> Pesca: Does that work?

It was only one month away, but I quickly buried any hesitation.

> Mia: The dates do, yes

> Mia: But how much is it?

> Pesca: Don't worry about that

> Pesca: It's taken care of

> Mia: Nope, I can't do that

> Pesca: You can and you will

She was a feisty little thing.

> Pesca: I'll send an email with more details

> Pesca: Take care of your flight, I'll take care of the rest

> Mia: ...

> Pesca: Just say thank you

> Mia: Grazie!

> Pesca: Atta girl

I called my parents on the way home to fill them in and was pleasantly surprised that they were also...pleasantly surprised. I was losing a job, but I was gaining independence with every decision I was making.

Apartment. Check.

Trip to Italy. Check.

Eventual new job. Check-ish.

I pushed back the fears and welcomed this new chapter with open arms.

Plan a little less and do a little more.

Next up...Italia.

Andiamo!

CHAPTER 6
Gennaro

"Beletta, Gennaro." I stood up as they called my name during the graduation ceremony from the Accademia di Polizia di Roma.

"Bianci, Marco." My soon-to-be partner stood beside me and nudged my shoulder with his. It was a grueling couple of months both physically and mentally, but we made it through.

Marco was born and raised in Rome, and I was utterly grateful that he was the first person I met at the academy. He was instantly friendly, warm, and fun to be around, which was a whole lot different than I was used to back home. I had planned to stay at a local, relatively affordable hotel while trying to find a place to live, but he kindly offered for me to stay with him for as long as it took to sign a lease agreement. We went from complete strangers to roommates in less than twenty-four hours, and it worked out, thankfully.

About a month after the academy started, his some-what crazy but seemingly lovable uncle, Giustino, had told him of an available apartment for rent in his building. It was right down the street from where we'd be stationed, so I checked it out the same day and signed the paperwork the morning after.

It was definitely a man's apartment, with the bare minimum of decor, furniture, and appliances, but it was all I needed or wanted. Newly renovated, it had dark, walnut-stained wood floors throughout, a deep charcoal blue color on the walls, with medium gray and cream-colored furniture and rug accents. With sweeping views of the city, it was close enough to the action but far enough away for some peace and quiet, plus there was an amazing rooftop restaurant and bar down the street, perfect for a date night spot, should I ever decide I had the energy or desire to get into all that.

It was my simplistic modern getaway a few hours from the traditional Italian home I grew up in, and it worked perfectly for me. My head felt clear here. There were fewer distractions, I had more time to myself, and more time to think, which had a way of occasionally being a bad thing. Every once in a while, I felt like something was missing, but I couldn't quite put my finger on it. I was thankful for Marco, though, who reminded me frequently to get out and enjoy as much of it as I could.

Having been in the apartment for a month and Rome for two, we were finally graduating. I was proud of myself and excited for what was to come. The utter lack of support from my own family, albeit disappointing, was not surprising.

Giuseppe and Mama had texted with congratulatory words, but I didn't hear a single word from my father. On top of that, the only one able or willing to come to the ceremony was Giovanni. He was a busy guy working at a prestigious law firm in Florence, but made the time to drive up and support me, which I took note of. I found him relatively quickly after the ceremony, and any residual disappointment due to the rest of my family's inadequacies quickly turned itself around.

"Congratulations, brother," he hugged me tightly, shook Marco's hand and congratulated him as well. He then got right down to business. "Where are we eating?"

Marco chimed right in with details surrounding the party his entire family was throwing for him and had added me to as a guest star. It was absolutely unnecessary, very much appreciated, and very much reminded me of why I left home when I did.

As Marco's graduation party wrapped up, Giovanni decided he was going to stay with me overnight, which meant he planned to hit up a few more bars and clubs before we returned home. The three of us hopped into an Uber and headed towards one of Marco's favorite spots, which he promised would be busy enough for Gio but mellow enough for me. What I mostly looked forward to, though, was watching them duke it out for the reigning Ladies' Man title. Who would take it home—Marco, the friendly guy-next-door, or Giovanni, the charming city slicker?

We piled into a corner lounge area, complete with a leather couch and small cocktail table thanks to Marco knowing the owner. I was elated that the buzz of the graduation ceremony was behind us, our new career was ahead of us, and the world could stop spinning for a few hours in the meantime.

As quickly as they sat down, both Marco and Giovanni stood right back up to scope the place out. When the server came back with all three of our drinks, she asked, "Your friends bail on you?"

I smiled and responded, "Oh no, they're just on a

mission," and nodded my head to the corner of the main bar where they had found two women to talk to.

"And you didn't want to be part of that mission?" She was obviously curious as to why I had stayed back, then asked, "Married?"

"Just not interested in complicating my life," I honestly answered.

"Definitely married," she winked.

"Whatever you want to believe," I held my hand out to shake hers. "I'm Gennaro."

"Alessia," she shook my hand firmly without taking her eyes off of me and then walked away.

She was absolutely gorgeous, and still, I had no interest in playing the rest of the game.

"Gezuuu, who was that?" Giovanni asked, staring at every inch of her as she walked away.

"Our server," I replied before resting the ankle of my right leg atop the knee of my left, sinking a little further into the leather couch I was seated in.

"And?" Marco looked at me like I was nuts.

"And, I'm not interested," I smiled faintly, and shrugged my shoulders.

"Did someone rip his heart out when he was younger or something?" Marco asked Gio, desperately searching for a reason as to why I was unaffected by mostly all of the women we came in contact with.

I took after Papa, standing at six feet two inches tall with dark brown hair and caramel brown eyes. My brothers ragged on me that I got all the good physical genes but the bad temper, to which I always responded, "Don't give me a reason to activate the temper, and you won't have to witness it."

Most of my life I felt misunderstood, like I was some hard ass who was always in a bad mood, but truthfully, I simply didn't like dealing with bullshit. I didn't like fake people, awkward interactions, or anyone telling me what to do. I generally preferred to be left alone but had a small circle of good friends plus my immediate family, and that was more than enough for me.

If I loved you or even liked you, you'd know it.

"He didn't tell you?" Gio looked to Marco and then to me, but I quickly shook my head at him in an effort to keep his mouth shut.

"Tell me what?" Marco's interest was piqued.

"He's gay," Gio didn't miss a beat from my non-verbal cues, which wasn't surprising, given he was the lawyer of the family.

"That explains it then." We all whipped our heads around. Like a tigress on the hunt, our server had returned, completely undetected, and was smiling from ear to ear.

"No more drinks then?" she asked as Marco and Giovanni ogled her, refusing to take her eyes off of me.

I held up my still full drink to signal I was good. She pursed her lips, shook her head, smiled ever so slightly, and headed towards another private table.

"If you tell me you don't find *her* attractive, I may actually start believing that you *are* gay," Gio blurted.

Marco chimed in, "I think I agree with him," and they both stared at me.

"I can find women attractive and still not have any interest in getting to know them," I retorted.

"Getting to know them and bedding them are two very different things," Gio said. He was insatiable.

"I have no interest in bedding just anyone, you already know that," I reminded him.

"Yeah, yeah, yeah," he rolled his eyes.

A couple hours later, they were both sufficiently

liquored up, had finally stopped breaking my chops, and were more interested in finding late night food than determining my sexual preference.

We headed to the nearest pizza joint for late night pies and Peronis. As I watched them chat up yet another group of women, I sat by myself, realizing that even though I had made a large-scale change starting a new career and moving from the country to the city, I still had more soul searching to do.

Was I ever going to fix the scars of the past, the ones I didn't like to talk about, with anyone, so that I could allow myself to experience a normal, healthy relationship?

Did I even want to?

My Nonno had told me years ago before he passed, *"Tutti hanno almeno un vero amore,"* which translates to "Everyone has at least one *true* love." He always emphasized *true* as if to say, all love is not equal love.

True love would feel different, look different, and be different than anything I had ever experienced before.

"Devi essere impavido per trovarlo," he would constantly remind me, and it stuck with me.

I had to be fearless to find it, if I wanted it.

I didn't know how he knew that, he never quite elaborated, but he was a man I trusted. He raised Mama, who is a romantic at heart, and because of that I believed him.

Fearlessness brought me to this new city and gave me a new career. Perhaps the thing that was missing from my life would find me here, too.

CHAPTER 7
Mia

"Benvenuti a Roma. La temperature ora è di 21 gradi con us massimo di 28 gradi. I cieli sono per lo più soleggiati e il fine settimana sarà lo stesso. Buon soggiorno. Ciao!"

"Welcome to Rome. The temperature is currently 70 degrees with a high of 82. Skies are mostly sunny and the weekend will be the same. Enjoy your stay. Ciao!"

My eyes blinked open a few seconds before my brain computed we had finally landed. I lifted the window shade and was met with the blazing sun bouncing off the tarmac. It looked like any other airport runway I had ever seen and I was thoroughly exhausted, but my mouth immediately shaped into a smile.

Nine hours soaring through the air had brought me here, and it felt surreal. I spent the first few hours of the flight a bit wired. My innate need to plan everything had me trying to predict what it would be like, who I would meet, what I would experience, and even how I would feel while I was here for two whole weeks.

I didn't do it on purpose, it just happened naturally. The pros and cons of being a "planner" by nature was a double-edged sword that had my brain constantly churning, even though I was no longer a "planner" by trade. In any case, right before I finally dozed off to sleep, I promised myself I would do my best to live in the moment, or *vivi il momento*, as Google translate had taught me.

It would be my Italian vacation motto.

As we deplaned, I received a message from Pesca.

> Pesca: I see you landed. I'm here waiting for you outside of baggage.

> Mia: See you soon!

I replied with an exclamation point to hide the red-eye flight side effects I was feeling. It felt like I had a hangover, completely foggy and run down. I didn't operate well on limited sleep, ever, but I was finally here, and I was, without a doubt, going to take advantage of every single moment.

I grabbed whichever fancy Italian coffee I could find as I walked through the airport towards baggage claim. So far, I hadn't been blown away by anything feeling particularly "Italian" besides a whole lot of signage and some overhead announcements, none of which I could read or understand.

I spotted her slim frame and curly black hair almost immediately, although it was now peppered with some grays. I hadn't seen her in years, but a beautiful, confident smile remained. She was a small package, but a fierce one. Wildly intelligent and extremely cultured, Pesca was a Parsi with origins in Persia, having grown up in England. She was well traveled throughout the States and, obviously, Italy. She was as interesting as she sounded, too, with a *fabulous* British accent.

"How was your trip, Darling?" she asked as we walked over to the carousel.

"It wasn't bad. I think I need three days of consecutive sleep, though." As someone who requires a decent amount of rest, add in a red-eye flight, the European time change, and the days of anxiety prior to leaving, and I felt like partial death.

"Well, you're going to want to stay up as long as you possibly can before going to bed so you can get back on a regular schedule. How about we head to Siena, get some fresh air, grab some food, and check in to the villa after that?" She was my unofficial tour guide, and I felt extremely comfortable doing whatever she told me to do. In fact, it was nice to not be the decision maker for once.

"You're in charge," I responded. Her smile told me she was as comfortable being my tour guide as I was letting her be.

We were a travel match made in heaven.

My eyes almost immediately began to roll into the back of my head as we drove away from the airport towards Siena, which was located in Tuscany. The warm morning sun was beaming through the windows of her small sedan, fatigue had fully settled in, and I felt totally comfortable.

She must have seen me starting to doze off as she carried on with conversation, asking how my parents were doing. "They settled into their new place, and I think they're already a little jealous that they aren't here with me."

"I don't blame them," she responded. "They're always telling me how this is their favorite place on Earth."

My mom and dad first traveled with Pesca and her

then-husband, Michael. Dad and Michael worked together and became great friends, which meant that Michael and Pesca were an extended part of our family. Soul crushingly, he passed away a few years back, which was devastating to all of us. It was no secret that I loved my parents, but I loved their friends just as much. When we lost one of them, it felt like we had lost a family member.

Pesca vowed that she'd continue visiting the villa where they had always stayed in his honor, and I think my parents did, too. It was, after all, the reason they were so intent on my brother, sister, and me coming here. Over the years, I had kept in touch with her, and she became an unofficial distant relative, one whom I deeply admired, respected, and looked up to.

We chatted back and forth for the little over two hours it took to arrive in Siena, and while I was underwhelmed by the Rome airport, the ride through Tuscany was anything but. The contrast between the plush, rolling green hills, the bright blue sky, and the white fluffy clouds was like an actual painting. Sun beams would break through the cloud cover every few minutes, and somehow, I felt like I was closer to heaven because of it. If the drive to Siena satisfied my visual expectations of Italy, Siena itself was about to satisfy the aromatic ones I didn't even know existed.

It was somewhere around noon local time when Pesca parked outside of the Piazza del Campo and I, thankfully, got a second wind. Unsure if it was from pure excitement, the aroma of freshly brewed espresso from every angle, or a little of both, I stepped out of the car with the sun shining on my face, ready to immerse myself into Italian culture.

I immediately noticed the beautiful yet slightly dangerous cobblestone walkways and mentally noted that half the shoes I had packed would land me in an Italian emergency room if I attempted to wear them here. There was the hustle and bustle of locals mixed in with the laid-back nature of tourists, and you could absolutely tell the difference between each. Pesca looked the part until she surprised people with that British accent of hers, which was one of my favorite things about her. You never knew what you were going to get, but you could trust her with anything.

She led us past the crowd through quiet, narrow back streets toward the piazza with understated ease. The sun was now hidden behind centuries-old buildings, and as I looked up to inspect them, I found myself struggling to catch my breath. A few hours earlier, I was groggy and suddenly, I felt an instant buzz from my surroundings alone. I didn't know exactly where I was or where I was going, but I knew it was where I was meant to be at this precise moment.

We dipped into quite literally a hole in the wall to grab a small bite to eat, or so I thought. Pesca asked what I was in the mood for, and I responded with "Whatever you think I'd like, so long as it's not seafood."

She rattled off a bunch of Italian words to the shop owner, we sat down at a small corner table for two, and within minutes I had my first glass of homemade Italian wine sitting in front of me. Like most "Americanized" Italian things, I was initially disappointed that the glass was so small—that is, until I tasted it. Stronger, more flavorful, so robust you could immediately tell this little glass of homemade crushed grapes would knock you on your ass a whole lot sooner than the stuff at home. It tasted absolutely delicious, too.

Next, a platter overflowing with thinly sliced meats and rough-cut cheeses alongside a hot, crusty loaf of fresh bread and a small bottle of extra virgin olive oil. My mouth instantly began salivating. It reminded me of home, whether it was lunch time with my grandparents or antipasto on a Sunday afternoon before "dinner" at three o'clock, but it was so much better.

I vowed at that moment to slow down and truly savor every part of this trip—every sight, every smell, every taste, every sound. Everything I touched I would try to etch into my memory forever. From this meal, I would remember how delicious the simplest of food from the most inconspicuous of places could be.

Pesca suggested we burn off some of our lunch before indulging in any coffee or dessert, so we kept walking along the cobblestone paths closer to the piazza. I was in constant awe of the architecture. No matter which corner you rounded or street you walked down, you could feel the history of every single building etching its way into your soul. I had truly never felt anything like it.

As we walked closer towards the piazza itself, the pathways and streets became wider, a bit more commercial, lined with bakeries, gelato, markets, clothing, and a whole lot more people bustling about. Out of nowhere, I inhaled one of the most incredible scents I had ever smelled. Having just eaten, it wasn't a fresh pizza or a hot crispy sfogliatelle that I was overdosing on. Rather, it was a distinct, fresh burst of…*something*. I couldn't quite figure it out until I rounded a corner and saw a storefront that boasted floor-to-ceiling windows with the most beautiful turquoise hue shining through.

I looked up and read the sign. "Acqua dell'Elba." Pesca, watching me, smiled and ushered me through its doors. "Buongiorno," a tiny, middle-aged woman with long brown hair and a beautiful face with little-to-no makeup greeted me.

"What is that incredible smell?" I asked, assuming, as Americans do, that she spoke English.

Every inch of the space was clean, neutrally decorated, but adorned with that beautiful shade of blue. I felt like I was at the beach, but was in the middle of one of Europe's greatest medieval squares. That's the power of scent; it can immediately transport you anywhere. She grinned back at me, and waved for me to walk towards the counter.

She introduced me to the scents, the story behind them (of three founders who went sailing, determined to bottle a perfume that encapsulated the aromas they discovered along the way), and the entire line of available products to choose from. Turned out the scent I loved most was the Eau de Parfum Classica for Men, but she explained it could be considered a unisex fragrance.

"It's a masculine perfume with fresh, marine notes ranging from mandarin, lemon, and rosemary, to marine algae, finished with woodsy Mediterranean musk and shrubs," which was likely my favorite part. If there were ever a scent that screamed "Italian man of your dreams with his arms wrapped around you while you sailed the ocean," it was this one. I was dying to have it but had bought a new perfume for myself before I left. I didn't want to start spending money so soon, given the newly unemployed situation, but I rationalized that I'd come back in a few days to get it if I was still thinking about it, which I already knew I would be.

I thanked her profusely, told her I would be back for sure, and Pesca and I headed next door to Nannini's, a *pasticceria* (or bakery), famous for its Ricciarelli cookies. We sat at yet another small corner table, with a small plate to share, and a single espresso for each of us. It was by far the best cookie I had ever tasted—absolutely delicious, mouthwatering, chewy, and bursting with almond flavor. I closed my eyes, savoring the flavor in every bite.

My senses were on overload in the best way possible. From the salty, savory flavors of lunch paired with crisp, cool wine to the refreshing yet soothing smells from Acqua dell'Elba to the present sweet and bitter aromas from fresh brewed espresso and almond cookies, I was only a few hours into my Italian journey and already felt core life memories being unlocked.

We stopped at a small store to grab a few groceries before heading back to the car. "There's a nice family market down the road from the villa, but we can go there during the week. Let's get you unpacked and settled."

A half-hour trip back down south was packed with more incredible views. I couldn't get over how everything almost seemed fake, too beautiful to be real. People actually lived here. Some in quaint, small homes; others on hundreds of acres of land. The history ran deep, and somehow you could feel the ancestry, familial lines, heritage, and traditions combined into this immense sense of pride amongst neighboring properties.

We pulled into an understated yet long gravel driveway that was surrounded by tall shrubs and a lot of trees. I couldn't see too far ahead and couldn't yet make out the buildings on the right side of us, but to the left were rolling hills lined with crops.

After slowly cruising down a small hill and parking, I grabbed my enormous suitcase and we walked back up to a row of stucco covered buildings, all overgrown with green vines. Pesca led me to my villa. "They had a last-minute cancellation. You'll have this whole place to yourself."

She opened a solid wood door with large window panes into a small sitting room complete with a couch, cozy fireplace, and coffee table. Off to the right was a bedroom—my bedroom—that had its own private bathroom and a window to the front yard, which boasted a gravel walkway, a variety of sitting tables and chairs, and the most beautiful assortment of red and pink roses alongside bright green bushes. I could hear the birds chirping and saw the sun starting to set in the distance.

The kitchen was just past the sitting area. It was spacious with dark brown cabinets and a center island. The brown, wooden kitchen table was surrounded by four chairs, and to the right-hand side was a larger dining room table with eight chairs, in case I made seven new friends during my two-week stay. Behind the kitchen, were two more bedrooms and a full bathroom. While it could easily accommodate at least six grown adults, I was elated to have it all to myself.

"How are you feeling?" she asked, breaking me out of my trance.

"I can't believe I'm here," I responded. I realized I hadn't even let my parents know I landed, which was a huge security breach according to the family rules. I looked at my phone and saw three missed messages from my dad asking for confirmation that I had arrived.

> Dad: I saw that you landed. Get in touch with Pesca yet?

> Dad: Let me know when you're on the road.

> Dad: You have your phone in your hand every minute of the day and you pick today to decide not to answer me. Unbelievable.

> Mia: 10-4, the package has landed. Sorry for the delay, I've been busy falling in love with The Motherland.

I responded with some humor to lighten him up.

> Dad: OK

> Dad: Now put your phone away and enjoy it all. Wish I was there.

> Mia: Yessir

I wished he was, too, because I knew how happy this place made him.

Pesca suggested I unpack and take a shower and told me she'd bring over some food. I did exactly that, with hot water pouring over me until there was no more left. That filthy feeling after traveling for nearly twenty-four hours swirled down the drain, and while I initially felt refreshed and invigorated, as soon as I changed into some lounge clothes, exhaustion consumed me. I walked into the kitchen to a small plate of creamy mozzarella, bright red tomatoes, freshly torn basil leaves, a few slices of warm bread, and olive oil alongside a short note:

> *"Eat and rest up. We're heading to Rome in the morning."*

I couldn't have asked for a more perfect traveling partner and I did exactly as instructed.

I ate, slept (for twelve hours straight), and woke up wrapped up in four different blankets with a cold nose. The bedroom itself felt frigid, but I could see a bright, warm sun teasing me through the curtains.

I had a smile on my face and excitement in my bones. Italy had already begun to leave an everlasting imprint on my soul, and a quick trip to Rome was about to change my life forever.

CHAPTER 8
Gennaro

"Excuse me, do you know which direction the Trevi Fountain is?" I internally rolled my eyes but gave walking directions with a half-ass smile on my face to help yet another lost soul find their way. I don't know what I expected from a foot post in one of the most heavily visited tourist spots in the world, but I thought I'd be doing a little more than standing around, barking out Google Maps results on a daily basis.

Besides a few store robberies, some nightly altercations when the bars and clubs closed, and managing the homeless population, I mostly watched people. People of all nationalities, languages, genders, and ages, some friendly, some not, and most so immersed in touring that they barely lifted their eyes from their phone, map, or brochure.

It always amazed me, the amount of people constantly on their phones. Most of them were taking photos and video to remember their time here, sure, but was footage from every rolling second of action necessary? Life seemed to be passing everyone by while their heads were buried.

"You want to grab some drinks at Savoy tonight?"

Marco snapped me out of my thoughts right as I felt myself getting unnecessarily aggravated at complete strangers.

"Absolutely. I'm going to get in a quick workout first and then shower."

"Ok, pretty boy." They had called me that since my first day on the job, and I found it only mildly irritating. If having high grooming standards with a kick-ass beard, showering twice a day, and always smelling good made me pretty, then I guess I was guilty. I was used to double showers when I worked the property at home, one in the morning to wake up and one afterwards when I was absolutely filthy. The same went for working here with dark uniforms, blazing sun, and walking up and down city streets for hours on end, and I, for one, liked everything to smell good—all of the time.

As I walked back to the precinct to change, I saw a car alongside the street a block ahead of me with its trunk open, a huge suitcase on the sidewalk, and a female lunging across the back seat to grab something. I tried not to, but whenever I saw someone who blatantly overpacked, I always assumed they were from the States.

As she put both feet back on the ground and climbed out of the car, I immediately noticed long, dark brown, *almost* black, hair that fell below her shoulders. As if she was in slow motion, she grabbed her hair with her right hand and pulled it over her right shoulder, exposing large hoop earrings and a gold nameplate necklace, another telltale American sign, but it hit me *right* in my dick.

She had on a white spaghetti strap bodysuit, tucked into dark, high-waisted jeans, a dark brown belt with a gold clasp, and tan, strappy sandals that made her already long legs appear even longer. When I reached the side of the car and was standing a mere few feet away from her, I noticed she didn't have on a lot of makeup. Some mascara and lip gloss paired with sparkly cheek stuff—whatever that's called—with nails and toenails painted white.

A weakness of mine.

She took off her sunglasses, rested them on top of her head, and stared back at me with big, light eyes and a beautiful smile to match.

There weren't many times in my life that I found myself speechless, but this was one of them. I kept walking, my mind in a bit of a fog, because besides my legs continuing to put one foot in front of the other, the rest of me was frozen. Did I even smile back?

I clearly needed some time to myself, but I wanted to get my workout in first. I headed straight towards the small gym on the top floor. It had basic equipment, which was all I needed for a little bit of cardio, some push-ups, pull-ups, and sit-ups. I was old enough to still require some workouts to prevent weight gain but young enough that only a few exercises for a half hour kept me in solid shape.

I thought back to the girl from the street earlier. The corner of my lips curved into a smile and finished with a head shake. I didn't often find myself immediately attracted to someone like that, but I absolutely had a type. If brunettes who didn't realize how gorgeous they were could be considered a *type*, it was definitely mine.

"What are you smiling about?" I whipped my head around to find my neighbor and Marco's uncle, Giustino, leaning against the doorway with a wet towel around his neck. He was pushing seventy years old, sharp as a tack, slightly crazy, and one of the few people I looked forward to bumping into. "It's a girl, isn't it?"

"A beautiful woman actually," I smiled.

"Isn't it always. What's her name?"

"Hell if I know. I walked past her on the street before," I told him.

"And?" He was hilariously relentless and I knew he wouldn't let up until I gave him some juice.

"Unfortunately, that's the beginning and the end. When I got to the door here, I turned around and she was already inside the hotel."

"So you know where she's staying? You could figure out the rest if you really wanted to." His logic was so flawed yet so simple.

"I'm a cop, not a stalker, if you recall. And I'd like to stay that way." He shrugged, clearly disappointed in me, and walked away.

I laughed again and then thought about her again, finishing my workout and heading back downstairs to my apartment. A girl I'd never see again had gotten me more worked up than I wanted to admit, and I had to take care of it before I left the house.

I put on some slow Italian pop music, yet another thing everyone got on my case about, poured some Dol Gin over ice with a splash of blackberry seltzer and a torn basil leaf, and turned the shower on. The water was just shy of boiling as it poured down my head, neck, shoulders, and back. I turned around, both hands on the wall below the shower head, hunched over, rounding out my back to stretch it out. I could hear my phone dinging but was focused more on the sound of the water and *her face*.

My hand made it downtown, requiring only a few strokes before I exploded. It had clearly been a while since I'd had a release of any kind, and I blamed the quick finish on that rather than the picture burned into my brain of her long dark hair, bare shoulders, light eyes, and big smile that radiated through her entire body. As the hot water slowly began to run out, I stood there, frozen in place, wishing I had done something more, had said something more. I even wished I had taken a picture the way I always judged everyone else for doing. I finally snapped out of my trance when my phone started ringing.

I wrapped a towel around my waist, took another sip of my drink, and answered, "Ciao, Marco."

"I'll be over to you in a half hour, and we can head there together, cool?" He was easy to make plans with, and I was happy for the distraction. "Sounds good, see you then."

I sprayed cologne all over me and put on a dark pair of jeans, a black v-neck t-shirt, and black leather boots. My beard and hair both required a variety of products and about fifteen minutes of styling time, but I still finished with ten minutes to spare. I took a look in the mirror and felt the best I had in a while. I threw back the rest of my drink, blew out the candle burning on the kitchen island, locked the sliding door to the outdoor balcony off the living room, and went downstairs to meet Marco.

"Ciao, Gennaro! Did you eat?" His question reminded me that I hadn't eaten a single bite of anything since lunch. We grabbed something quick on the way, talked about work briefly, and then vowed it would be the last work-related commentary we'd have for the rest of the night. I could tell he was on the prowl, while I was just looking forward to a few more drinks, some music, and a little liveliness before heading back to countryside solitude and the always unpredictable family time in the morning.

It was sometime around ten o'clock when we walked in and grabbed two seats at the square-shaped bar, right alongside the dance floor. There was a small stage set up for the DJ and a few small tables and chairs across the dance floor in a back corner, all of which were occupied. We ordered a round of drinks, and before I could take my first sip, Marco had already started talking to someone. I shook my head with a smile. He was *beyond* predictable. As for me, I sat back and enjoyed my drink and the music for the next half hour or so, completely unbothered and finally able to relax.

I excused myself to use the restroom, but Marco barely heard me, still talking intently and getting closer with their physical touch as the minutes passed on. When I returned, they were headed toward the dance floor. Marco was an absolutely terrible dancer, but he knew how to have fun, and the woman he was with was having equally as much fun. I motioned for the bartender to come over. She acknowledged me, and as she turned around to grab a bottle off the back wall, the person she was serving came into view.

Long dark brown hair, an off-the-shoulder, plum-colored shirt tucked into a tight black skirt, and the same oversized gold hoop earrings I saw earlier on the street.

She was here.

I attempted to swallow the brick that had risen into my throat, and I couldn't take my eyes off of her.

"What can I get you!?" the bartender yelled. I have no idea how many times she asked me before I finally heard her, but she quickly ran out of patience. "Sorry, another gin and seltzer, please."

When I looked back, girl-from-the-street was gone. My stomach formed knots, but after quickly canvassing the room, I found her again. She was tucked away across the dance floor in one of the leather chairs alongside the tables, by herself, drinking what looked like an Aperol Spritz or something similar. Was she waiting for someone? A date? A friend? I had no idea, but I couldn't stop staring.

I contemplated going over to talk to her but didn't really know what to say. "Hey, I ran into you on the street earlier and jacked off in the shower thinking about you afterwards?"

Jesus Christ, I'm an embarrassment to myself.

But, she was here for the second time in one day, and I wasn't a man who believed in coincidences, especially when I was usually unaffected by other women. I spent some time watching her watch others and was most intrigued that she didn't seem to be on her phone that much. She was really taking in her surroundings—the music, the dancing, the people—all of it. I assumed if she was meeting someone they would have shown up by now. I felt a little relief, but it was short lived. In the next instant she was standing up, adjusting her clothes, grabbing her small purse, looking like she was ready to leave.

Maybe it was my third gin, or wanting to give Giustino a more interesting report tomorrow morning, but I quickly stood up and started walking, hoping to intercept her before she got to the door. The place was packed as she reached the middle of the dance floor where mostly everyone was dancing. I wasn't a confrontational person by nature, but if there were ever a time to throw some elbows, it was now.

Time seemed to stop, and everything around me slowed down as I came within a few inches of her. She accidentally dropped her purse right in front of me, and while I wanted to grab it for her, I found my hand on the small of her back supporting her as she stood up instead. She stumbled a little bit, squinted her eyes trying to figure out who was touching her, and then turned towards me.

With a slight smile on her face, I caught her taking a quick, deep breath. With one of my hands still on her back, the other pushing strands of her hair away from her face and over her bare shoulder, she reacted to my touch instantly. Her skin was covered in goosebumps, and while she initially seemed a bit shy, there was something brewing deep within her.

I could absolutely feel it.

"Vuoi ballare?" I asked for likely the first time ever in my life, although it was more of a polite demand than a question.

"I'm sorry, I only speak English," her American accent confirmed my large suitcase theory, and I smiled.

"Dance with me," I repeated, *"please."*

CHAPTER 9
Mia

"Why the hell did I wear these shoes here tonight?" I asked myself while sipping the last of my third Pirlo, a better version of an Aperol Spritz that tasted like delicious, refreshing, morning regret. There were three other pairs of shoes scattered across the floor of my hotel room, but I had convinced myself that if there were ever a time and a place to wear four-inch heels with straps that tied around the ankle, made of "real" Italian leather, it was while one was in Italy.

Pesca had urged me to wear comfortable footwear before I left the hotel room that we checked into earlier in the day, but did I listen?

Nope.

It was somewhere around eleven, and while I had finally adjusted to Italian time, it was still way past my mid-twenties bedtime. After the hotel concierge told us this *discoteca* was the place to be on a Friday night, I decided to check it out for myself. Pesca and I were sharing a hotel room and had eaten dinner together earlier after we arrived. She invited me to meet up with an old friend of hers, but I wanted her to enjoy her own time and, selfishly, wanted to do a little exploring by myself. The next day we'd be touring the Colosseum together, and while I was a sociable person most of the time, other times I liked to be alone.

It also seemed to be a rite of passage as one aged to successfully go to a restaurant or bar solo. There was a freeing element associated with it combined with an increase in self-confidence to know you could go anywhere and be comfortable in your own company. So, since I had traveled across half the world by myself, I figured going out to a bar with no one other than me, myself, and I would be the icing on the Italian cake.

I had spent the previous hour people-watching while nestled comfortably in a soft leather chair across from the dance floor in a makeshift lounge area before I briefly flashed back to the uniformed hottie that I had smiled at outside of our hotel. I didn't know what kind of academy these guys graduated from, but there must have been a full curriculum surrounding the need to be perfectly groomed with just the right amount of snug in the fit of their uniform sleeves. I thought I noticed him smile back at me but figured he felt bad for the American who couldn't speak a lick of Italian, had overpacked, and could barely maneuver her suitcase out of the Uber.

I had finally gotten up to my room, sweating in places one shouldn't sweat from, and peeked out of my room window to the sidewalk to see if he was still there. Gone. Probably for the best, since I have a weakness for dark hair, dark eyes, beards, muscles, and men in uniform.

Dio mio.

"*My God*" indeed.

When I came to, I got up to order one more drink at the bar. I had paid for each one separately since open bar tabs lead to bad decisions. Then, I immediately returned to my leather chair before anyone else could discover how comfortable it was. It was a great feeling to explore on my own and people-watch while enjoying new scenery without any expectations.

I sipped the last of my drink and decided I had enough. My feet were starting to hurt, my eyelids were getting heavy, and if I was going to enjoy visiting The Colosseum in the morning, I would have to be asleep by midnight. Those were the rules my body abided by as I crept closer to twenty-five.

Quarter-life crisis was a thing for sure.

After peeling myself out of my beloved leather chair, I pulled down my tight, black, high-waisted pencil skirt, adjusted my "girls" nestled comfortably underneath an off-the-shoulder, plum-colored top, ensured both oversized gold hoop earrings were securely in place, and began my walk to the exit.

I caught a glimpse of my full outfit, complete with the four-inch ankle strap shoes from hell in a full-length mirror and muttered, "*This* is why we wear the shoes." Smiling to myself and shaking my head that I had gotten dressed up to sit by myself all night, I pushed through the crowd of dancers towards the exit.

The bass thumped, the overhead lights changed colors and tempo to match the music playing, and a sea of sweat and diluted alcohol filled the air. As a couple gyrated directly into my personal space, I stumbled a bit, and accidentally dropped my wristlet onto the dance floor.

Three Pirlos made my trip from the ground back to my fully upright five foot, eight inches (plus four-inch heels) a whole lot harder than it should have been. The room spun a bit as I waited for my vision to readjust, and I inhaled him before I even caught a glimpse of him. Every part of my body reacted to the scent surrounding me, and my inner thighs twitched as I felt his hand on the small of my back. I spun around to see who was touching me and was just shy of eye level to bold but comforting brown eyes, a perfectly groomed beard, and the same smile that had watched me step out of my Uber.

Before I knew it, he pulled me in close, one hand on the small of my back, the other pushing a few strands of hair from my face, and whispered in my ear, *"Vuoi ballare?"*

I managed to tell him that I only spoke English, so he translated for me. "Dance with me, please," he all but begged, with eye contact that made Blue Eyes back home at the bar look like an absolute rookie. I thought about it for just shy of a nanosecond before locking eyes with him, feeling an immediate protective connection, wrapping my arms around his neck, and allowing him to pull me in even closer.

The tip of his nose trailed the length of my neck as he breathed me in. Lightly stroking the side of my arms, over my shoulders, and down my spine, he settled his thick hands on the smallest part of my waist.

Dancing slowly with the music bellowing around us, he finally broke the silence between us, "You smell incredible." With his forehead connected to mine, he briefly closed his eyes before opening them again, staring at my lips like he wanted to feast on them.

"Can we grab a drink somewhere quieter?" he asked after about ten minutes on the dance floor, as we pretended the world around us didn't exist.

"Where?" I asked, intrigued but cautious, eying him up and down trying to understand why I wasn't more skeptical of his intentions.

"There's a rooftop restaurant right down the street, close to where you're staying. You can head home after whenever you want." He winced, likely embarrassed that he made mention of where I was staying like a stage-five clinger.

"I'll give you one chance to explain how you know where I'm staying before I call the *polizia*." My eyes glimmered with equal parts sarcasm and skepticism.

"Well, first, I *am* the *polizia*. And second, it's hard to forget the sight of someone who looks the way you do when she gets out of an Uber in a foreign country." He was smiling, and I was still at a loss for how safe I felt with him. "I saw you on the street earlier when I was heading home after work. And…" He hesitated briefly but continued when he saw the corners of my mouth curl up into a smirk. "I haven't stopped thinking about you since."

I bit my lip, quickly shook my head, and looked up towards the ceiling. As I lowered my head back down and exhaled, trying to figure out what the hell I was about to do, we locked eyes. My inner critic was fighting with her own damn self at this point.

> *Inner Critic: Girlllll, what are you doing*
> *Mia: Living in the moment, bitch!*
> *Inner Critic: Okay yes, but this is a stranger in a*
>   *foreign country…*
> *Inner Critic: And you're thinking of leaving a bar*
>   *with him*
> *Mia: Vivi il momentoooo!*
> *Inner Critic: How many drinks have you had?*
> *Mia: Mind ya business!*
> *Inner Critic: I'm going to have to ask you to*
>   *calm down*
> *Mia: Stop being a buzz kill; he's beyond hot*
> *Inner Critic: He totally is, but…*
> *Mia: But nothing; this is why we came here*

Inner Critic: To get murdered on the streets of
     Rome?
Mia: No, to have incredible sex with a hot Italian!
Mia: Please refer to Mia's Italian Bucket List,
     Extra Credit section
Inner Critic: You need to calm down
Mia: Refer to the list, lady
Inner Critic: FINE, you're annoying me
Mia: Yea, well, you're annoying me more

She had a small point, I guess, but I could clear that up quickly.

"How do I know you're not completely full of shit?" I asked without so much as a flinch.

"My mother would haunt me in the afterlife if I ever disrespected or mistreated a woman." Call me crazy, but I believed him.

Take that, Inner Critic.

Pleased with his response and my willingness to live for the now, my smile grew wider. I quickly texted Pesca, grabbed his hand, and nodded towards the door.

I am American, hear me roar. Now, let's do this thing, whatever that thing is going to be.

We were both a little tipsy, not drunk by any means, as he led us towards the exit. I could feel his hand tighten around mine as we weaved through the dense crowd of people, an unspoken bond of trust between two strangers. The cool air when we finally made it to the street was exhilarating and calming at the same time.

He stopped walking and turned around, looking directly at me, which I felt in the deepest parts of my soul. Moonlight and streetlight combined to light his face up clearly. His eyes were soft and bold at the same time. It was obvious he was thinking of kissing me and I instinctively licked my lips at the thought but he changed his mind and kept walking.

Under normal circumstances, I would have had my personal safety at the forefront of my brain and wouldn't be leaving a club in Europe with a complete stranger all by myself. Whether it was his cologne that I still couldn't quite pinpoint, his unwavering but not at all creepy eye contact, the innate feeling that he was a protector by nature, or the fact that he mentioned his mother's disapproval if he acted out, there I was, walking hand in hand with someone I'd just met, who also knew exactly where I was staying.

Cringe topped with a little bit of "take me now."

I briefly flashed back to my days of throwing lingerie in my ex's face in the middle of a parking lot and thought to myself, *"Look at me now! Still an idiot."* My dad would be less than thrilled. But, because I was spending my last hours before potentially being murdered in Italy, and not a dusty parking lot in New Jersey, maybe he'd forgive me.

I remembered how my body reacted when I saw him on the street earlier, having flown up to my hotel room to try and catch another glimpse of him from my window. He was already out of sight, but the memory of him in uniform was etched into my brain. Now, having seen him twice in one day and a lover of romance, I was trying to understand if this was all coincidental or the universe's way of testing me.

"How much have you learned, young grasshopper? Will you relax and let things be without needing an answer and a plan for every goddamn thing?"

- The Universe, probably.

In the middle of my thoughts, he stopped walking yet again, let go of my hand, turned to face me, and slid both arms around me, gripping my lower back. He couldn't have been more than a few inches from my face, looking down at me, smelling like cologne and a little bit of spearmint, when he said, "I don't even know your name."

"It's Mia," I managed to loudly whisper. I still felt myself catching my breath when his eyes met mine.

"Mia…" he repeated it like he was trying to figure out if he liked it or not and then told me his: "Gennaro." He had a slight smile, shook his head, then grabbed my hand again while he held a door open for me. We had made it to the hotel and squeezed ourselves into a packed elevator as the doors were closing. He stood behind me with one arm wrapped around the front of me, and I could feel his steady breath right above the back of my neck.

A man standing to my left inched closer as he prepared to get off at his floor, and Gennaro instinctively tightened his grip on me. In a matter of minutes, I had gone from worrying about him potentially murdering me to imagining him murdering someone who tried to hurt me. Was I concerned that this was all happening very quickly?

Slightly. Was I turned on by it? *Abso-fuckin-lutely.*

The elevator reached the top floor and the doors opened, revealing a stone walkway surrounded by deep, dark greenery. It was lit up beautifully with rows upon rows of warm white string lights. We followed the walkway through the front doors of the restaurant, past the hostess, to whom he nodded his head. I was probably the thirty-seventh woman he had taken here, but I didn't care in the least. I'd sacrifice myself to the Italian Gods for whatever was about to happen, so she could add me to the long list if she wanted.

The front half of the restaurant was more of an

indoor space with a roof covering, while the back half boasted outdoor tables with a pergola covering, more greenery, and even more white lights. The far-right-hand corner, where we were heading, was a completely uncovered lounge area. He man-hugged the guy running security by the tables, and we were ushered towards the last one available. It was a small table top—only about two feet high—with a small leather bench-seat that could perfectly fit two people.

I went to sit down, but he tugged on my hand and led me towards the balcony instead. The security guy looked me up and down, and while I wasn't sure if it was a good or bad look, I felt safe in the arms of this extremely hot still-stranger. Finally, I snapped out of it. "I…I need to know more about you. Or actually, something more than just your name," I stammered.

I turned around to face him, my back to the balcony, and saw him giving me the same smirk from earlier. "What do you want to know?"

"Oh, I don't know. What do you do for a living? How often do you kidnap women from bars and bring them here? How many sprays of that cologne did you put on before you left the house?" I didn't know where my somewhat hilarious shortness was coming from, but I assumed it was partially due to my lack of orgasms in the last few months paired with currently raging hormones and a dollop of nervous energy.

His smirk grew into a full-blown smile. "Do you want me to answer those in order?"

And take my clothes off, please.

"Yes," I said with as much confidence as I could muster.

"As I said earlier, I'm a cop here in Rome. Can it really be considered kidnapping if the person willingly goes with you? And…that's classified information." I loved a solid, confident, witty response. *God dammit.*

I obviously remembered I first saw him in uniform but wanted to confirm *what kind* of uniformed man he was. I did indeed leave the club willingly with him to walk the streets of Rome and end up here, on an incredibly romantic rooftop terrace. And Jesus Christ, that cologne was doing things to my innards.

I stared up at him, blinking slowly and soaking him all in. He was equal parts beautiful and rugged, confident without arrogance, and while I had joked about how many women he'd perhaps brought here before me, he really didn't give off player vibes. He did, however, seem like a man who knew exactly what he wanted and how he wanted it—with a kindness in his eyes and a softness in his touch. His entire demeanor set off a five-alarm fire inside me while calming me at the same time. I was intrigued by him; I was curious about him; I absolutely wanted him, and *somehow*, I fully trusted him.

He trailed his hands up and over my shoulders to my neck and then my chin, tracing his thumb over my bottom lip. At the exact moment my eyes started closing, thinking he was about to kiss me, he leaned in and whispered in my ear, "Turn around, Mia."

He ushered me to the edge of the terrace, placed each of his hands on either side of the balcony railing, pushed the front of his body closer to the back of mine, and hunched down a bit so that his chin was right above my left shoulder, with us both looking in the same exact direction. "This is the best view in the city," he said.

And, it was a hell of a view. You could see city lights and streets for miles, an outline of the Colosseum in the distance, pedestrians walking, and building after building of historical architecture. For a second or two I breathed it in, still somewhat in disbelief that I was there. But without missing a beat, I slowly turned around to face him, and with his hands still firmly placed on the railing surrounding me, I slid mine up his chest to the base of his neck. I surveyed his lips and instinctively licked my bottom one before looking into his eyes and telling him, "This is the only view I need tonight."

I left my face hovering right in front of his for a few seconds, and then, as I continued to be a grasshopper the Universe would be proud of, I slid both arms around his neck, closed my eyes, and placed my lips on his. I didn't have to do much work from there as he pushed off the railing, stood straight up, wrapped both arms tightly around my lower back, and pulled me in closer, eliminating any open space that was left between us, melting into me.

He kissed me back, ever so slightly tugging at my bottom lip with a soft bite, and then sliding his tongue inside to meet mine. Finishing by softly brushing his lips over mine, he pulled away for a second to catch his breath. Our eyes slowly opened, staring so intently at one another in the heat of a single moment, that our surroundings now paled in comparison.

"Only one, by the way," he whispered as he backed up a bit.

"One what?" I had no idea what he was talking about.

"You asked how many women I've kidnapped and brought here. You're the only one," he clarified.

"Someone once told me you can't kidnap the willing," I smiled.

"How long are you in Rome for?" he quickly snapped me back to reality.

"I leave tomorrow afternoon actually." I watched him calculate something in his head, looking side to side, lightly gripping his chin.

"Stay with me tonight," he said. There was no question mark, because it wasn't a question. It was a polite, somewhat forceful suggestion.

My phone dinged, and I looked down to see Pesca responding to my text from earlier letting her know I'd be home a little late.

Pesca: Have fun!

I thought about my response for only a brief second before firing it off.

Mia: I met a great group of girls

Mia: Heading to their apartment right up the street from our hotel now.

I *hated* lying, but I also hated being judged by someone I respected, and I couldn't possibly admit to the ferociously hot one-night-stand I was considering.

Pesca: Be careful

When I looked back up at Gennaro, he was softly staring at me, and the corners of his mouth had curved into yet another smile. He tilted my chin up, kissed me softly, looked into my eyes, and repeated himself. "Stay with me tonight, *please*."

"Promise you're not a kidnapper?" I ridiculously asked.

"Promise."

"...or a murderer?"

"Promise."

"Ok, let's go."

Twist my arm why don't you.

I returned my phone to my purse. He firmly grabbed

my hand and led me back through the restaurant towards the elevator. I quickly glanced over at our would-have-been table and saw that it was already occupied. Mr. Security must have been watching the entire exchange and knew without a doubt we weren't making it back there to sit down.

I, on the other hand, was entirely certain that my ability to live presently without feeling the need to overanalyze or force expectations was about to be tested to the max.

As if this man didn't smell good enough on his own, his apartment was the final aromatic straw. It was immaculately clean and minimally decorated, but somehow still cozy.

He lit a candle on the coffee table that began to flicker like my insides before opening the double doors from his living room onto the terrace. A light breeze blowing through kept circulating the scent of the candle and his cologne. I wasn't drunk on anything but my own senses, which was good, because when he handed me a gin and seltzer I drank the entire thing almost immediately.

Getting tipsy to provide some temporary comfort was typical of *old* Mia—confident, saying all the right things in the heat of the moment, and then innately worrying once the overthinking kicked in. She had a tendency to fall for anyone she got physical with, because, well, she wouldn't get physical with anyone she didn't feel an actual connection with. Being good looking was fine and all, but she wanted more, which is why she hadn't *ever* gotten involved with one-night flings before.

Parts of Old Mia were still buried within me. It's

impossible to abandon the core of what makes you *you*, after all, but post-job loss, new home, traveling alone Mia was different.

I was trusting my instincts, all of which were telling me that I was about to have the night of my life. The hard part was figuring out if I'd be able to accept the possibility of it never happening again.

Would I begrudgingly return home to the States completely jaded, knowing I'd never find another man or have another encounter even remotely close to this one?

Or could I just enjoy what was quite literally standing right in front of me and push the worries and doubt aside?

He must have smelled my brain cells burning, because before I knew it, he was within inches of me, catching me off guard with a "*Vivi il momento*, Mia."

I instantly felt everything come full circle. I had spent a large portion of my life overthinking, planning, and letting mild anxiety consume my life. The last half of a year had matured me as a person and helped me find my inner strength as a woman.

An opportunity—or more accurately, an experience—had presented itself to me.

What was I going to do about it?

I quickly texted Pesca the address, threw my phone on the couch, finished the last few melted sips of my drink, and exhaled for what felt like a solid five seconds. He dimmed the lights and turned on some Italian music. It was equal parts slow and fast, and entirely sexy. Just like he was.

Him. I was going to do him.

I had successfully turned my brain off to quite literally everything else in the world and was focused solely on this beautiful man standing in front of me. He moved closer, wrapping his arms around my lower waist, and surprised me by dancing with me slowly. After a few minutes swaying to the beat of the music and breathing each other in, he sat on the couch, situating me right in between his legs.

I was still standing, with my hands on his shoulders and my hair dangling in front of his face. Looking up at me, he glided his hands underneath my skirt, over the front and sides of my thighs, before working his way towards the back, firmly squeezing each available square inch of my ass. I squirmed, not because it hurt but because every part of my body was already reacting to his touch.

He grabbed one of my hands and moved it from where it was resting on his shoulder towards his mouth and kissed it. I traced my thumb along his lip this time. Then, he began to slowly lick and suck it while looking at me, as I let out an audible groan.

That's all he needed to hear before he stood up, inched my skirt higher, and picked me up by gripping the sides of my waist. He walked us a few feet over to the kitchen island and set me down. Then, he grabbed a glass as I wrongfully assumed he was about to make another round of drinks. Instead, he filled it completely with ice, held it in one hand, slid me off the counter and steadied me on my feet with the other, grabbed my hand, and led me to his room.

The music playing from the living room was piped through to the bedroom, which was another clincher, not like I needed anything else to seal the deal at this point. He put the glass of ice on an end table and spun me around so I was facing the bed and he was standing behind me. Pushing my hair to one side, it fell forward and exposed both my shoulders. He grabbed a cube and traced a line slowly from behind my ear, down the back of my neck, over my shoulder blade, and then around the front of me to right above my chest. He held it there and let it melt before pulling down the top of my bodysuit.

Thanks to whatever youth I had left, my full C cups still had some perk in them, and the bodysuit's shelf bra had successfully served as their sole support. As he pulled it down, his fingers lightly grazed each of my nipples. It didn't matter how much ice he introduced my skin to from that point on; I was radiating straight fire.

I helped by unzipping the back of my skirt, but before I could take it off fully, he spun me around. "I want to watch, if you'll let me." So, I did what any girl who was living boldly and confidently would do and pushed him slowly into the armchair that was alongside the wall behind him. I turned the bedside lamp *on*, something that previous Mia would *never* have considered.

I slowly pulled my skirt down my thighs, turned around with my back facing him, and let it slide down the rest of me until it hit the floor. I stepped out of it, with my ass and the thong portion of my bodysuit in full view before turning back around and straddling him in the chair. Since he had already pulled down the top of my bodysuit, my tits were on full display, inches from his face, which made him inhale deeply again.

Before I knew it, he had snapped open the bottom of my bodysuit like an Italian magician, and his fingers met my very warm, very wet lower lips. He lightly rubbed the top of me with his thumb while sliding the next two fingers inside me, expertly. Where most men needed GPS, a magnifying glass, and a cheat code to find the right spot, he had located it effortlessly. I began gyrating and breathing rhythmically for the next few minutes, fully knowing and feeling that he had found *the* spot. I refused to slow down once I felt the rush.

With red flushed cheeks, I grabbed the sides of his face,

pulled his mouth off of my collarbone where he was licking me, and all but suction-cupped myself to him as I climbed to the quickest finish of my lifetime. My head fell into the crook of his neck where I briefly rested afterwards. I was drunk on his smell, his touch, his everything, and now I needed him inside of me.

Clearly a mind reader, he stood up, gently laid me flat on his bed, grabbed a condom from the side table, and crawled on top of me with both of his palms on either side of my head. With my legs now wrapped around his waist, my body begged for him to enter me. Brushing his mouth over mine, I felt his strong hand trail up and over my chest towards the base of my neck. His eyes peered into mine, watching my expression as he gently held me down, and firmly pushed inside of me.

While sex itself, when done properly, was amazing, I couldn't deny the fact that his body, his stature, his scent, him in general was what was turning me feral. He had reached parts of me I didn't know existed.

I simply couldn't get enough.

A short while later, he slowly pulled out, lowered himself to kiss me again, and whispered, "Get on your knees, Mia." Flashbacks of assholes I had given myself to in years past crossed my mind, but he was anything but. Everything he said was laced with both passion *and* respect. It was the first-time sex actually *made* me feel sexy, because I felt both wanted and protected at the same time.

I had already turned over on all fours when I felt him come behind me. With one hand slowly gliding up my lower back to my shoulder and the other on my hip, he slowly but firmly entered me again, and again, and again. My lower back arched, my head and hair fell backward, and I exposed my neck hoping he'd take the bait.

Of course, he did.

I could feel him release at the exact time his lips and tongue made their way to where my neck met my shoulders. My entire body felt like there was electricity running through it, as a result.

We both deflated into the bed, him still resting on top of me, my legs in a figure four. As he began playing with my hair, I felt myself consumed by pure exhaustion. I tried to stay awake, but he pulled a blanket over us both, whispering, *"Vai a dormire."* Him kissing my shoulder was the last thing I remembered before I did just that. I slept what was the best night's sleep of my entire life, comfortably, peacefully, and satisfyingly, next to the most gorgeous man I had ever met and knew barely anything about.

CHAPTER 10
Gennaro

Sun beams were fiercely shining through my bedroom curtains, which meant it was somewhere around seven in the morning. I was still in a spooning position with my chest towards her back, but with a few inches between us to prevent the heat radiating from our skin from turning into sweat. Normally by now, if someone had stayed over (which hadn't happened in quite some time), I'd be three feet away on the other side of the bed, planning my departure, and figuring out a way to get them out of my apartment. I wasn't often a one-night-stand guy, but when it *did* happen, I tried my best to let them know up front that I had somewhere to be in the morning. Color me prepared.

I didn't mention any of that last night. In fact, I don't think I've ever spoken fewer words in a shorter amount of time before deciding that I absolutely had to have someone. I rolled over on my back, my right arm resting behind my head, still naked from hours earlier, looking at the ceiling and trying to remember every detail. It wasn't because I over-drank and couldn't remember it, I certainly hadn't. In fact, I hadn't slept this well or felt this great waking up in a while. I just didn't want to forget a single thing.

From seeing her on the street earlier in the day to thinking about her in the shower to having her take my breath away in the club to the rooftop and back here, everything flowed easily. Maybe we skipped out on some personal life details to get to know each other more, but we *felt* plenty. I was comfortable with her, and I could absolutely tell she was comfortable with me, especially after confirming that I wasn't a murderer.

I found myself hesitating to look at her while she was lying next to me, still sleeping, not because I didn't want to bask in the sight of every inch of her, but because I didn't want to think of what my bed would look or feel like when she was gone.

I couldn't help myself, though.

I rolled back over to my left side to see and breathe in every inch of her. Her long hair was still wavy with the slightest bit of frizz, immediately reminding me of her breath near my ear, her lips grazing over my neck, her cheeks flushing as her body tightened right before she finished on top of me in the arm chair.

God damn.

The bed sheet was pulled up to her natural waist and had settled in the narrowest indent of her frame. It also highlighted her curvy bottom half. She was thick in all the right places, an hourglass figure, but most important of all, she was confident in her own skin. I knew this from watching how she carried herself, how she slowly removed each piece of clothing last night, never taking her eyes off of me while she did it. She was ravenous, I could tell, but she was tasteful about it.

She was independent, she was observant, she was cautious, she was just…with it. Her discreet humor was a bonus. And her physical attributes were turning me on again as I looked her up and down.

I felt myself getting hard, and while I wanted to move in closer and slip inside of her again, this was real life, not the movies. Morning breath was present, and so were a variety of heavily used body parts from the night before, all of which needed a little refreshing.

I quietly got up so I wouldn't wake her, put loose-fitting sleep pants on, shut the bedroom door behind me, turned on the espresso machine and the same music playlist from the night before on the lowest volume, and opened the doors to the balcony. It was a clear day with bright blue skies and a slightly cool breeze blowing through, which meant that by lunch time it would easily reach twenty-seven degrees Celsius.

After heading towards the bathroom, brushing my teeth, and turning the shower on, I spun around to find her standing there in one of my white v-neck t-shirts. My entire body reacted to the sight of her, but most notably, I felt myself smiling from ear to ear, which I realized hadn't happened in quite some time.

"I'm going to need some mouthwash or some tooth-paste immediately," she broke the silence with an embar-rassed smirk. If I needed another sign that she was my soulmate, it had arrived.

I opened the small closet door next to her to grab a new toothbrush, and I felt her eyes following my every move. "I didn't notice the tattoo on your back last night," she said. "What does it say?"

"Impavido," I said as I closed the closet door and slowly turned around to face her. "It means *fearless*."

"Of course, it does," she smiled with the slightest eye roll and bit her lip, taking the toothbrush out of my hands, and turning away from me towards the sink to brush her teeth.

"Why do I feel like you're making fun of me?" I asked, now standing with both hands resting on the bathroom counter on either side of her, staring at each other through the mirror reflection.

"Oh, I'm definitely not making fun of anything that makes me want to get back in bed with you," she looked up at me, her gray eyes had turned a light shade of green, and my pants were a little tighter than they had been a few seconds prior.

"How about we try out the shower since it's closer?" I suggested.

I lifted the bottom of the shirt she was wearing and slowly pulled it up and over her torso, ensuring my finger-tips grazed her skin while I did it. I felt goosebumps form before I slid the rest of it over her head and dropped it on the floor next to me.

The shower water had filled the bathroom with steam, fogged the mirror over, and surrounded us in a thick, hot cloud. We stood there staring at each other for what felt like forever but was actually only a few seconds. Then, she slowly pushed me towards the opposite wall, grasped both sides of my waistband, came in close, and whispered, "It's my turn to take your breath away."

My head fell backwards and I deeply exhaled with a muffled moan. I was used to being the one in charge, but maybe that was because I hadn't yet found someone who knew what I wanted, and when I wanted it. She started kissing my neck and slowly traced her lips down to my chest. Her hands followed forcing my senses into complete overdrive. I felt the soft touch of her fingers paired with the sharp scratch of her nails, and it sent blood rushing through me. In slow motion, she lowered herself to the ground, pulling my pants with her.

I made the mistake of looking down at the same exact time she grabbed the back of my knees and gazed back up at me. With a slight smirk, she slowly stood back up and led me to the shower. It was a large one with a rainfall shower head and a wooden teak bench on the opposite side. I thought back to when I toured the property before signing the lease and wondered what the hell I would need a shower this size for. I now had the answer.

She sat me down on the bench after lathering up a cloth, kneeled down to situate herself in between my legs, and began slowly washing me. From my face to my beard, down my neck and shoulders, over my chest to my stomach, and finally to my thighs and shins.

Mia motioned for me to stand up, and as I was rinsing off the front of my body, she finished washing the back of me. I had turned around to face her again when she softly pushed me towards the wall behind me. The shower head was positioned far enough away where we were no longer underneath the stream of it.

Before I knew it, she kneeled in between my legs. My skin shivered, partially because I was in the open air without hot water to keep me warm, but mostly because she started tracing the outline of her lips along the side of my exceptionally hard dick.

She teased me for a few seconds, licking and nibbling before taking all of me in her mouth.

I saw stars.

I quickly remembered that if I wanted to finish with her back in bed, I had to prevent myself from prematurely doing so here.

"Mia, I want you back in the bedroom," I said, somehow managing to form words again.

"Uhm, I'm soaking wet," she smiled.

Game on.

"I'm sure you are. Let's go take care of that." I turned the water off, we quickly pat dry with some towels, and as she was about to crawl onto the bed, I grabbed her hand to quickly turn her towards me instead.

Both naked with damp skin, dripping wet hair, and a cool breeze blowing through the window, I pulled her face towards mine to kiss her deeply and inched as close as our bodies would allow. Heat radiated off of her skin as I grabbed the bottom of each ass cheek and lifted her up to my waist. Instinctively, she wrapped both legs around me, and I lowered us on the bed as one unit, using my knee on the edge of the bed to guide us.

I slid myself inside of her slowly at first before wrapping my arms underneath and then up and around her shoulders. When I had my intended grip on her, my mouth met her neck, and I plunged deeper inside of her. She moaned—loudly and repeatedly—as her nails settled in the skin of my upper back.

My windows were open, which I absolutely did not give a shit about.

Giustino would be proud.

On the verge of finishing—again—she nudged me to roll over. I did as requested, never letting go of her shoulders while still inside of her. Now on my back, I enjoyed a front row seat to the most beautiful performance I had ever witnessed—her long hair, dripping shower water all over my stomach, her palms pressing into my chest, and her tits a few inches away from my face. She was determined to finish and had invited me to watch the show.

It didn't take her long as she expertly rode me, never breaking stride, until the skin of her neck began to glisten, and muffled moans turned into the shriek of a satisfied finish. I felt her twitch and then tense around me before completely releasing when she fell off of me to one side. I was in awe of what I had watched her accomplish in such a short amount of time before she rolled back over onto all fours and took me in her mouth to finish me, too.

We laid there, motionless.

If Rome were on fire, I wouldn't have noticed it over the heat that was still permeating from us. Her feet were by my head, her head by my shins, and I was holding her left hand with mine as we both stared at the ceiling.

I couldn't tell you what she was thinking, but I knew I wasn't ready for her to leave.

"I'm starving," she broke the silence, and I smiled.

A woman who always knew what she wanted. I absolutely loved it.

"Let me make us something. Anything you don't eat?" I asked.

"Seafood."

"Ok good, that wasn't on the menu," I responded with a smile.

I put on a clean pair of black sweatpants, handed her another pair with a kind-of-small-on-me t-shirt, and closed the door behind me so she could get dressed in privacy, as though we hadn't spent the last eight hours mostly naked. In the kitchen, I turned the music up a little, brewed two double espressos, and quickly scrambled some eggs. Then, I plated them with some fresh berries I found in the fridge and warmed up the last *cornetto* from a box Giustino had brought me earlier in the week.

We sat at the island eating and sipping our coffee. I asked her a bunch of questions about herself—where she was from, what she did for a living, and even a little bit about her family since she had mentioned earlier that she was staying with a family friend.

We hadn't talked about me much, which I was fine with. I didn't want to get into the family dynamics, the villa, any of it. Really, all I wanted to do was to stay with her the rest of the day, but at the exact moment I thought that, her phone started ringing.

She had a short conversation with her friend and ended it by agreeing to meet her downstairs.

"You're leaving now?" I asked, not at all trying to hide my disappointment.

"She's meeting me downstairs in twenty minutes. We're heading to see the Colosseum today before we leave tonight," she told me before asking, "Would you want to come with us?"

I felt the corners of my mouth twitch, happy she thought to ask, but I then came crashing down to reality. I was already late getting back to the countryside. "I'd love to, I'm a great Colosseum tour guide. Been there five times since I moved here, but I have to leave for work soon."

I didn't know why I kept avoiding telling her that I was going home to work on the property, rather than a police shift. Likely it had to do with not wanting to waste time talking about stuff that aggravated me. I put the breakfast dishes in the dishwasher, and when I turned back around, she had quietly moved to the terrace.

The weather was perfect, a slight breeze blowing through as I walked up behind her and put both of my arms on either side of the railing, exactly like I had the night before on the rooftop. I kissed the corner of her neck, rested my chin on her shoulder, breathed her in deep, and exhaled slowly. I had never spent so little time with someone who made as big of an impact as she did. It wasn't just the sex—even though that was incredible. It was everything combined.

Her quiet confidence, her accent, the way she spoke,

and the way she knew exactly what she wanted made her even more attractive to me. But I could also tell she had a big heart. Her face lit up when she talked about her family, and upon thinking about it further, she was the only woman I had ever slept with who was more concerned about me finishing than herself.

She must have felt my brain cells burning, because she slowly turned around, brought her hands to either side of my face, and stared deeply at me before taking a deep breath, closing her eyes, and putting her lips on mine. Slowly she kissed all around my mouth before nibbling my bottom lip, which I had now determined to be her signature move. Our tongues slowly twirled around each other before we finished with one more lip nibble, her head falling to my chest, my arms around her, standing together, completely silent.

Her phone dinged again. "She's downstairs, I need to go." Grabbing her clothes from the bedroom, trying to figure out what to do with the items of mine that she was still wearing, I quickly helped her solve the problem.

"Keep them," I tried to calm her mind. "I don't need them."

She smiled again, nodded, and said, "I don't know how often, if ever, you're in the States, but I'd love to keep in touch. I mean, if you want to." It was the first time she'd shown even an ounce of doubt.

"I *absolutely* do," responding with zero hesitation.

We exchanged numbers and found each other on Instagram.

"Guess this is what the kids do these days?" I smiled, trying to lighten the moment a little.

"Kids *and* two grown-ass adults who had a lot of great sex," she responded with a wink.

My dick moved again, but I restrained myself as I

walked her to the door. I was about to head down with her like the gentleman I am, but she stopped me. "Ehh, I sort of told her I was staying with a group of girls I met last night."

I laughed. Didn't matter how old we got, our parents were our parents, even when they were our parents' friends. "I get it, no problem."

I pulled her in close again, pushed the hair away from her eyes that had somehow turned a gray-green, and kissed her like I'd never see her again.

She must have felt it, because she had a hard time letting go of me. At the elevator, she pushed the down button, and looked back. I hadn't moved, leaning on the doorframe watching her every move. She ran back to me, kissed me one last time, and turned back around when the elevator doors opened. I felt a pain in my stomach as I watched the doors close with her behind them, but didn't have time to focus on it because I heard my phone ringing inside.

"What happened last night?" Marco sounded like he was walking home, but from where I didn't know.

"What *didn't* happen last night. Want to meet for coffee in fifteen?" I suggested.

"You bet your ass I do," and he hung up. I went into my bedroom to pack a small backpack to bring home with me for the weekend and felt like I got punched in the gut. The disheveled bed reminded me that she had been in it not too long ago, the sheets were still a little damp, and I could see some of her dark hair strands there, too. I wasn't ready to make it and decided to leave it like that until I got back.

I hadn't stopped thinking about her since the minute she left and wanted to send a message, but had bargained with myself to wait until later in the afternoon. It would be the bright spot in an otherwise stressful weekend. On top of that, she had ditched her friend overnight for me, and I didn't want to intrude on their time together.

My phone dinged while I was locking up the balcony doors. I grabbed it off the counter and headed towards the elevator. I expected it to be Marco, but it wasn't.

> Mia: I'm sure I'm supposed to wait a few hours to build up the suspense but...I miss you already

My stomach twisted in the best way possible.

> Gennaro: I missed you before you even left

I was smiling when I walked off the elevator and bumped into Giustino. "You're smiling again," he noticed. "Who is it this time?"

"Same one," I responded.

He laughed out loud and waved a finger back and forth in the air, *"Sei finito."*

It was just getting started, actually.

The best, and worst, was yet to come.

CHAPTER 11
Mia

I opened the double doors from his apartment building to meet Pesca on the street below. If eyes could burn a hole straight through a person, I'd have been a melted pile of flesh on the floor.

She had been out walking this morning, stopping at his building on the way back with the assumption we'd head straight to the Colosseum from there. Since I hadn't gotten into my outfit change details (or the reason behind them) on the phone earlier, it came as a small surprise to her that I wasn't actually ready to head over there yet.

I greeted her with damp, frizzy hair piled on top of my head, wearing black men's joggers, his white v-neck t-shirt that I'd knotted right above my belly button, and the strappy black four-inch heels from the night before.

To be fair, this was actually a pretty modern outfit choice, except we were planning to walk the streets of Rome for half the day. If I wanted to preserve the health of my feet for the duration of our trip, and I did, I'd have to change into sneakers.

"I was expecting you to look worse for wear if we're being honest," she said with her trademark dry humor.

"Thank you, I think?"

"Oh, you're quite welcome," her half-smile let me know she was partially on to me. "Do you need breakfast? Change of shoes? Advil? A confessional?"

My lips formed a straight line, trying their best not to morph into a smile, but to no avail.

"We ate breakfast a little bit ago, definitely need shoes, no Advil necessary, and pass." When I looked at her again, her smirk had turned into a full-blown smile.

"Dare I ask who 'we' refers to?" No wonder she's best friends with my parents. I'm incapable of lying to her as well. "Because I wrongfully assumed you'd have packed some clothes for today to bring to the girlfriends-you-just-met-at-a-night-club sleepover you had last night."

We walked into our hotel lobby and headed straight for the elevator.

"Is this a judgment-free zone?" I asked, already knowing the answer as the doors slid open.

"Always is, Mia."

The doors shut in front of us to take us to our floor. "Well, the pants and shirt belong to a very hot Roman *polizia*," I closed my eyes and inhaled.

"Since you didn't call needing to be bailed out, I assume this *polizia* didn't apprehend you?"

"Not in the traditional sense." I looked at her through the reflection of the elevator mirror and we both let out a belly laugh. "I'd say the Rome portion of this trip might be hard to top."

"I can only imagine," she responded as the elevator doors opened to our floor.

"Maybe we should pack our things now and leave the bags with the valet so we can get on the road quicker? We need to be back to the villa by around three." She was always on it.

We only planned to stay in Rome for the one night since Saturday nights were *"famiglia dinners"* at the villa. They incorporated a few basic cooking lessons for anyone who wanted to participate before all the guests were invited to enjoy the meal together.

"Sounds perfect to me," I assured her.

We had a few hours to head to the Colosseum before driving back to Tuscany. I quickly packed all of the clothes and shoes that were lying on the floor from last night's fashion-show-rejects, into my entirely-too-large-for-one-night suitcase. Before I zipped it up I grabbed the outfit that *had* made the cut, now rolled into a ball, and breathed it in deeply.

It smelled exactly like him, and it instantly clicked where I had smelled his cologne before.

Acqua dell'Elba Classico—from Siena. He was wearing the scent I had fallen in love with behind the turquoise shop windows.

I felt a pang in my stomach and a twitch in my thighs, and I could swear my brain computed an entire slideshow of last night's flashbacks within seconds.

"You ok?" Pesca must have seen me staring off into the distance.

"Depends on what you mean by ok," I smiled, "but yes, I'm fine."

"Listen, I don't ask a lot of questions. I don't like to pry, and I don't like being nosy. But I'm always here for you if you want to talk about anything."

"I know you are, thank you. It was a great night, he's an incredible person, and I'll probably never see him again." I sounded like a sad sack, but it was all hitting me at once.

"How do you know that?" she was trying to keep me upbeat, but really, how would I ever see him again? We'd probably text back and forth for a few weeks or months before we remembered how far we live away from each other and resolve ourselves to *"What the hell is the point of this?"*

"I don't, I guess. I just promised myself I'd come here without any expectations. I don't necessarily want a guy to get in the way of my enjoyment of anything," I said, mostly as a reiteration to myself.

"Seems like you enjoyed yourself plenty last night, darling," she said matter-of-factly, without judgment.

"The only part I didn't enjoy was saying goodbye to him."

"He showed up *because* you weren't looking. Happens all the time. Now you've got to try to push it towards the back. Doesn't mean you forget about it; just means you don't let it consume you. Whatever is meant to be, will be. I sound like a self-help novel, but it's true."

I playfully saluted her, "Yes, ma'am."

"Now come on, we've got a Colosseum to tour."

We had hopped on a tour bus weaving in and out of city streets when, out of nowhere, we turned a corner to be met with the giant structure towering over us. I don't know what I expected, but it surely wasn't to see this enormous piece of history so close to everyday civilized life. We deboarded and walked past a few officers, which immediately made me think of him, but I snapped back to reality, following Pesca on foot to get in the proper line. She was a quick little thing, and I didn't want to miss learning about the epic piece of history staring me in the face. I also had to pay attention so I wouldn't get taken out by a distracted tourist, of which there were thousands.

If anyone wants to feel how small we all truly are, to feel the insignificance of most of our life challenges, I urge them to stand in the middle of the Colosseum. It was simultaneously noisy but quiet. Impressive but also heart breaking. Historical but almost felt fictitious. We took our time walking around, taking it all in, and I appreciated the wholesome comfort it brought me. Nothing quite like brushing up on ancient history to make me temporarily forget the soft porn star I was emulating a few hours prior.

Like he was still reading my thoughts, my phone dinged and his name was staring at me from my lock screen. My cheeks completely flushed and I threw my head back, looking at the sky before closing my eyes and letting out a long exhale.

All I wanted to do was open his message, but the need to remain present was crucially important to me. I put my phone away and felt myself regaining a slight sense of control. I didn't do it in a game-playing manner; I didn't feel that I needed to one-up him in any way. It was just something I needed to do for my own sanity.

Inner Critic: You go, girl
Mia: Thanks, Bitch

"Do you want to have lunch before we head back to the villa?" Pesca asked, and since my stomach rumbled at the sound of it, I quickly said yes.

Much like Siena, the best food came from hole-in-the-wall restaurants. It was somewhere around noon, late enough for a glass of red wine because I was on vacation after all, and I decided on pizza, because why wouldn't I?

I savored every bite of it, realizing I was hungrier than

I thought I was. Maybe it was my brain recirculating memories causing a spike in adrenaline, or perhaps it was the cardiovascular exercise from the morning, but either way I was starving. It was also a great distraction from the unread text message sitting in my phone that I desperately wanted to look at. I told myself to wait until we got in the car to head back to the villa and focus on the culture surrounding me instead.

I told Pesca a little bit more about the previous night, leaving out *specific* details, and then we discussed the rest of the two weeks that I'd be there. I knew I wanted to take a gondola ride in Venice, and I planned to overdose on pizza, pasta, gelato, and wine, in no particular order. Other than that, and maybe a day or two relaxing by the villa pool, I had no requirements. She suggested we hit Florence and Venice for some overnight stays, and plan for a Tuscan day trip or two.

I was itching to finally read his message as we paid our check, hopped in an Uber to grab our things from the hotel, got in her car, and started the two-hour trip to the villa.

Gennaro: Vivi il momento, Mia

That's all it said, but it was plenty. It was our theme from the previous night, after all, and we'd most certainly done exactly that, having experienced more than a few unforgettable moments already.

I pressed my phone to my chest and felt Pesca look at me quickly before turning her eyes back to the road.

"He reached out to you?" she asked with a smile.

"Yes. I think he actually thinks I'm heading back to the States tonight. I'm realizing I never told him we were going back to Tuscany."

"Well, it's not that far of a ride. I'm sure there's time to see him again if you really want." My partner in crime seemed rather supportive of a man I met just one day ago.

I sat there thinking in silence. On one hand, last night was about the most romantic one I've ever had. I met someone I was wildly attracted to, trusted, was comfortable with, and enjoyed every second with, effortlessly.

On the other hand, I wasn't moving to Italy anytime soon, and I doubted he was about to leave a law enforcement career to follow me to the States, so what exactly was the end game here?

Live in the moment and enjoy as much as I could? Or stop torturing myself with what would likely never be? On top of that, I was sitting there thinking of *relationship* stuff when I had no reason to think he wasn't solely thinking of when we were going to have sex again.

Inner Critic: Classic chick move
Mia: Eat glass

I unlocked my phone screen and effortlessly crafted a reply to him.

> Mia: I'd like to relive every single moment of last night (and this morning)

He instantly texted back.

> Gennaro: I've been reliving it in my mind all day long

> Gennaro: How was the rest of the day?

I felt the infamous inner thigh twitch again and flashed back to sitting on his lap in the armchair, receiving the quickest manually stimulated orgasm of my entire life. I was already dying to smell him again, see him again, and touch him again, but I also couldn't spend the entire trip ignoring Pesca, running around together like we were dating, when the goal of the trip was to do so much more. I was acting a bit lovestruck and needed to snap out of it.

For the first time in my life, I left someone on "read."

It felt terrible.

I reiterated to Pesca that I was there to sightsee and take in all the history and culture. That while I wanted to explore all things, hot Italian men included, I didn't want it to fully consume me. Not that she was judging—she wasn't—but my verbal affirmation served as confirmation for me.

"I understand, I truly do. But I also know that I found the love of my life when I should have been paying attention to other things. You're smart and observant, and I find it hard to believe you'd let anyone waste your time, especially while you're here. Just some food for thought."

"You're killing me," I shook my head with a smile.

"Shouldn't have worn the strappy shoes," she smiled back. "They do it every time."

We made it back to Tuscany a bit before three in the afternoon. It already felt like home even though I had only spent one night there, which consisted mostly of sleeping and unpacking, and I was excited to meet the owners, learn how to cook some new dishes, and explore more of the property.

"Why don't you go rest a bit? I'm going to help Gigi set up. Come on down to the kitchen around four or five. We don't eat until later on."

I nodded, gave her a hug, opened the door to my place, and walked straight into the shower. If I had laid down, I wouldn't have gotten up again until the morning. Hot water streamed down the back of my body, and I could still smell the remains of my perfume and his cologne. It made me both excited and a little nauseous. I thought back to the few times he grabbed my hair, secured in a low ponytail, gently tugging my head back and kissing from the base of my neck up to my chin and lips. There was not one thing that man did to my body that I didn't like.

I sat on the bed with a towel wrapped around me, and one around my head, and finally picked up my phone. I answered a few family messages, letting everyone know I was alive and that I had crossed the Colosseum off the to-see list.

Then, I opened his message. I felt two things: emotional, because I did actually miss him, and sexual, because I was clearly still thinking about the previous night.

On one hand, an emotionally charged message might have him jumping off the Colosseum walls, whereas a sexual one might convey the wrong sentiment entirely. Yes, the sex was more than great, but I tried to be honest with myself—a five-thousand-miles-away sexual partner was less than convenient.

There I went again. Worrying about two weeks from now, not *living in the goddamn moment.*

What did I want *right now?*

Him. Badly.

What was I scared of?

Everything.

A lightbulb turned on in my brain, and rather than text him, I dialed Allie.

"Oh my GOD. You called. How is it going?!" she screamed into the phone.

"It's going. I've got to get ready for dinner, but long

story short, I met a guy at a nightclub in Rome. He's a cop with tattoos, he's gorgeous, he smells great, I went back to his apartment last night, and we had sex. A lot of it. And he's waiting for me to respond to a text message."

Silent pause.

"Why aren't you saying anything?" I asked.

"I'm trying to figure out if you're not happy about this for some reason?"

"I came here trying not to get wrapped up in any sort of man issues, remember?"

"Right, but I didn't hear anything that was an issue," she said matter-of-factly. "If he was going to kill you, he'd have done that by now. If he's an asshole, you won't ever have to see him again. If you fall in love with each other, I'll be your maid of honor and we can go to Rome for the Bachelor/Bachelorette reprise."

I could tell she was smiling and also meant every word.

"Is anything ever a big deal to you?" I asked with pretend attitude.

"Yeah, important shit. I wished for someone to kidnap me the other day so I'd have a few hours of peace and quiet, and here you are getting laid by someone who sounds like everything you've ever dreamed of, yet you're overthinking everything," she continued. "Ever hear of the phrase 'When in Rome?'"

"Well, I'm in Tuscany now so…"

"Ok, Jake from State Farm. Just text him back. If he's worth your time, he'll come see you there, too. If he doesn't make the effort, chalk it up to Italian men being exactly like Long Island men, and become a lesbian."

There was a reason why she was my go-to for honest, not-at-all-subtle advice.

I thanked her, hung up, and opened his text again.

~~Mia: My friend told me to tell you to come visit me in Tuscany or I'm going to become a lesbian~~

That wouldn't work.

~~Mia: I think you think I left to go home to the States because I was too chicken shit to tell you that I wasn't.~~

Neither would that.

What did I actually feel? *That I wanted to see him again.*

> Mia: Today would be better if it ended with the same view I had last night.

Sent.

I put my phone down, styled my hair in a low, slicked-back bun, dusted on some cheek highlighter, mascara, and lip gloss, and added my signature gold hoops, since I was now convinced they were good luck. Then, I decided on an ivory colored outfit, pairing an off-the-shoulder lace top with a high-waisted, loose, flowing skirt with gold sandals. I kind of looked like J. Lo, but the Italian-American version, and I felt pretty great. Lastly, I finished with approximately fourteen sprays of perfume.

After a quick mirror glance, my phone dinged.

> Gennaro: Are you referring to the rooftop city views or the views from the balcony terrace?

> Mia: I'm referring to the bedroom and shower views.

> Gennaro: Gesù Cristo

I loved how quick he was. Once I started, I could continue bantering like that for hours. It was a skill set best showcased with the right counterpart, and I already knew he was it.

I took a quick picture of myself and sent it to him.

> Mia: I forgot to tell you I wasn't actually leaving to go back to the States today.

He hearted the picture.

> Gennaro: Where are you then?

> Mia: Tuscany

> Gennaro: ...

I saw three bubbles pop up, then disappear, then pop up, then disappear again.

Five minutes later, he hadn't sent anything back. It was his first time leaving me on "read," and my brain swirled for a few minutes trying to figure out if he might actually be mad or upset that I hadn't told him earlier, but I convinced myself he was likely busy at work and headed down to the kitchen. Pesca was already there and quickly introduced me to the owners, who were busy setting up.

Fifteen minutes after that, my phone dinged again.

My stomach dropped, my face flushed, and my inner thighs tingled...*again.*

> Gennaro: Turn around

I finished pouring my glass of wine, spun around, and locked eyes with him from across the room.

He was busy at work alright, just not police work in Rome.

CHAPTER 12
Gennaro

I only had to study the picture she sent for a few seconds before confirming that the background was one of our apartment villas. Equal parts shocked and elated, I tried to form words to text as a response but they were failing me.

I had many questions, but one was at the forefront.

Why didn't she tell me she was staying?

"Everything ok?" I was still looking at her picture, but Mama must have noticed the expression on my face as she was running around getting set up for dinner.

I nodded quickly, still trying to process what my next move was going to be. I had pulled in a few hours ago and immediately started working with Giuseppe outside. Since it was a beautiful day, warm but not too hot with some cloud cover, we did more landscaping and outdoor mainte-nance than anything else.

We mowed the lawn, trimmed hedges and bushes—of which there were hundreds—weeded, cleaned the pool, and power washed the patios and walkways, including the courtyard where dinner was going to be hosted.

He asked why I hadn't come home last night like I

usually did on Fridays, and after telling him I went out with Marco after work I felt him give me a side eye.

"And?"

"And what?" I smiled.

"I don't think I've ever seen you go to a club or a bar without meeting someone," he reminded me.

Slightly offended by what felt like a man-whore implication, I asked, "What are you talking about? I don't even like people that much."

"Yea, but the ladies love you. I swear they're all attracted to your RBF."

"You're going to have to explain to me what RBF means," I shook my head, not quite following.

"Resting Bitch Face, but in your case, I'll change it to Resting Bastard Face," he smiled, beyond proud of himself.

Brothers.

"Ok, let me catch up. I'm generally unapproachable but women love that, and the more I don't want to talk to people, the more they talk to me. And *I'm* the problem here?"

"Who ever said it was a problem? I'm just jealous," he laughed and continued. "So, who did you *not* want to talk to last night?"

I didn't take the bait.

"No one actually." It wasn't a lie.

He rolled his eyes a bit, and then we started talking more about the villa, how things with Papa and Mama were, and how he felt about the villa work.

"To be honest, I thought I was going to hate it, but I kind of love how relaxing it is," he surprised me with his answer.

"Relaxing? I think you pronounced *stressful* wrong," I corrected him.

"Nah, me and Papa work well together. I do whatever

he tells me to do, and I get it done quickly," he said. "I like meeting all of the people who stay here, and every once in a while, there's a young, pretty one, so, *you know*."

I shook my head. It didn't matter how old he got, he was still, mentally, thirteen years old. And it didn't matter how old I got, I'd always butt heads with Papa. The fact was, I didn't do what *anyone* told me if I felt strongly enough against it. If he wanted me to power wash the patio but I thought the shutters needed painting instead, he'd shake his head in disgust. If I planned to string up patio lights and tiki torches for the family dinner, like I had today, he'd tell me it wasn't important and that I never listened to him.

That dynamic between us is what eventually made me hate working here. I loved the property itself, I loved our family's history, but I also like autonomy. I assume that same part of my personality transfers to meeting people. When someone tries telling me what to do, like a woman at a club trying to pull me onto a dance floor or asking me to buy her a drink, it's immediately a no. But if I notice her first, all bets are off. Like Mia, who was suddenly standing about fifteen feet away from me in the kitchen I grew up in.

"See, I told you. Every once in a while, a young, pretty one," Giuseppe said as he walked in behind me, nodding straight towards her. We had both showered, and while he'd been looking forward to dinner all day, I hadn't, because I generally hated sharing our house and home with strangers.

Until now.

I was watching her talk to Mama from across the room, trying to understand how I missed that she was staying in Tuscany.

"Quit being a stalker, you're staring at her. You're

gonna scare her away," Giuseppe knocked me out of my temporary coma.

He started to walk away, but I grabbed the tail end of his shirt and forcefully turned him around.

"The woman I *didn't* want to talk to last night, in the middle of a night club in Rome, is that one." His eyes widened and his mouth slowly curved into a "get the fuck out of here" smile. "I had absolutely no idea she was staying here. It never came up."

His thirteen-year-old tendencies erupted again. "This is amazing. What's her name?"

"Why?"

"Because if you know it, you actually like her. You have a tendency of forgetting to ask women their names when they're throwing themselves at you." His blunt response reminded me how much I loved him and sometimes despised him, simultaneously.

"It's Mia. Her name is Mia." I couldn't take my eyes off of her as I answered him.

"Ok, well I know I'm the younger brother, but if you want a shot, you may want to stop staring at her like a creep and go talk to her. Maybe she'll remember you."

If he only knew.

"She'll remember me," I confidently said. I took my phone out of my back pocket and pulled up her message. She looked gorgeous in the picture she sent, but even more so in person, standing across the room from me.

"Turn around," I typed and hit send.

She had started pouring a glass of wine when she heard the ding. After a few seconds staring at her phone, she slowly turned around, scanning the room quickly before spotting me. Eyes wide, her jaw dropped, and then she finally formed a huge smile.

In that same moment, though, Papa started clinking a wine glass, the signature start to the family dinner.

"*Attenzione per favore. Grazie a tutti per essere venuti. Speriamo che vi piacerebbe la cena, la compagnia e soprattutto i ricordi che farete,*" he said proudly.

When he remembered that most everyone there spoke only English, he repeated, "I'd like to have your attention please. A great big thank you to everyone for being here. We hope you enjoy the food, the company, and most of all, the memories you'll make."

He was a simple man, but there was no mistaking how much he loved this place and hosting others in it. Everyone clapped and smiled, including Mia, who looked over at me again, this time with a "What the hell is going on?" expression on her face.

At the same exact time I started walking towards her, Mama called out her name as well as the names of some of the other guests and invited them to gather around the island. The cooking class was about to begin. Normally at this time, I'd head to the outdoor patio with anyone who preferred eating the final product rather than helping cook it. It wasn't because I didn't enjoy cooking. I did. But I didn't usually enjoy it in a group setting.

Today was different.

"Gennaro, grab a bottle of red to bring out here," Papa called after me.

I took a bottle off the counter and handed it to him. "I'm actually going to stay in the kitchen today."

"Good, your mother will like that," he said.

"She's not the only one!" Giuseppe truly couldn't help himself, shouting as he walked outside.

Papa shot a look from me to Giuseppe and back again, but shook his head, not wanting to get involved.

"Gennaro! My boy, come over here," Mama's face lit up. "This is my oldest son. He's been in Rome the last couple of years as a police officer and comes home once in a while to help out." Then she began introducing me to everyone, starting with those closest to me. "Theo and Sophia came from Greece, Louis and Juliette from Paris, Alan and Diane and Mia from America, and of course you know Pesca."

My eyes scanned the crowd, smiling and saying hello, before landing on Mia for a few extra seconds. Then I walked over to Pesca to give her a big hug hello because I hadn't seen her in years. I was at a loss as to whether or not Mia and I should act like we knew each other, but Mama moved right into pasta making instructions, and I held off.

I stood to the right of Pesca, with Mia on her left side. She must have felt the absolutely scorching tension between us. I saw her look sideways at Mia and then towards me, with a quizzical, almost comical look on her face.

She leaned over and whispered something to Mia that caused her cheeks to flush and another beautiful smile to form. Then, she leaned over to me with an ever-so-casual, "Had a late-night last night, huh?"

Mama, still blissfully unaware that any of this was unfolding, began teaching everyone how to roll out the dough in order to make our family's favorite tagliatelle in a roasted eggplant and cherry tomato sauce.

Mia, clearly flustered, or incapable of rolling out dough (or perhaps both) asked for help. Pesca had stepped away to help the couple from Greece, and Mama motioned for me to slide over and help her. "Gennaro is the best cook of my three boys. He can help you."

She looked up at me and involuntarily licked her lips with a deep inhale. We still hadn't said a word to each other, but our body language and the chemistry bubbling between us said plenty.

"Looks like you need a little bit more flour so the pasta stops sticking to the counter," I said, reaching over to scoop some from the large bowl in the middle of the island. I sprinkled a bit over the dough and underneath it and then placed the palms of my hands over hers so she'd get a better feel of how to roll it out. Immediately, goosebumps formed along the length of her arms.

Her hair was slicked back, but I could still smell warm, sweet, musky perfume radiating from her. Her face looked sun kissed with the perfect amount of natural looking makeup, and her neck and shoulders were exposed with another off-the-shoulder top, this time paired with a long, flowing skirt.

She was even more gorgeous than I remembered her being this morning, which I wouldn't have thought possible. My head was spinning, still trying to understand how I missed that she was staying here, then wondering how long she planned to be here.

"I think I need a little bit more wine actually," she said, holding up her wine glass, looking directly at me. There was a slight smile on her face, which told me she wasn't mad, but I could feel an instant change in her demeanor, from confused and uncertain to frisky and confident.

Challenge accepted.

While everyone finished rolling their dough, Mama showed them how to run it through the pasta machine to form thin sheets. Then, she cut the tagliatelle by hand to a width in between a linguini and a fettuccine. When the eggplant had finished roasting, she scooped out the insides, creating a paste, and added it to the fresh cherry tomato sauce that was lightly bubbling on the stove top. After creating nests of tagliatelle and sprinkling them with a bit of semolina to prevent sticking, she had everyone begin on the appetizer.

It was a basic burrata caprese, but of course the burrata was freshly made alongside basil and tomatoes that were picked straight from the garden. Truthfully, everything tasted better in Tuscany. Quality and freshness were unmatched, and there was something to be said for cooking with *love*. That was Mama, she absolutely loved feeding people.

We had finally sat down on stools next to each other while everyone was busy plating their burrata, tomatoes, and basil when I asked, "Did we have a good time last night?"

She looked at me with slight confusion. "Is that a trick question?"

"Not at all. I had an incredible time, which is why I'm trying to figure out why you never told me you were staying. You said you were *leaving*, which I assumed meant back to the States."

"You know what they say about assuming, Gennaro, right?" she smiled, and I guessed this was some sort of an American thing.

"Uhm, no, I don't," my voice was laden with frustration, and she immediately noticed.

"I don't mean to be a smart-ass, I'm mostly kidding. I figured you were staying in Rome for work, and to be honest, I didn't want to feel like I was abandoning Pesca or changing my plans for the rest of my time here when I barely even knew you," she continued. "Speaking of which, how did Pesca not realize that you live where she picked me up?"

"She wouldn't have known. My parents barely know where I live. Only one of my brothers has even been down there to visit since I moved." I said, realizing how much that innately bothered me. "And besides that, I guess you never mentioned my name to her?"

"I guess not, but it wasn't on purpose." She was getting defensive, and I started to feel like all of this was getting misconstrued.

"Miscommunication, I guess," I said, realizing that I was mostly bothered because it seemed like she didn't actually want to see me again. My voice fell flat, and I put down my knife and separated myself by a few feet to wash some dishes. I wasn't often on this side of rejection. Maybe karma had it out for me this time around.

Everyone began to gather in the courtyard for dinner and wine. Mama had set the table already with name cards so we could all easily find our seats without any awkwardness—or so I thought, because we ended up sitting directly across from each other. Mama on my right, Giuseppe on my left, Papa to the left of him, then Pesca, and Mia across from me, with the rest of the guests filling the second half of the table.

It was Mama's turn to toast everyone while also detailing the menu. Thankfully we never did a go-around-the-table-and-introduce-yourself sort of thing. Instead, we began plating food to pass to each other, pouring wine, and making small talk. This always led to deeper conversations as the night progressed, thanks to lots of varying personalities, a good bit of cultural diversity, and a whole lot of wine.

Papa praised Giuseppe for stepping up around the villa, and Mama toasted me, like she always did, for attempting to keep the streets of Rome a little bit safer. Pesca joined in that salute, too, and introduced Mia as the daughter of some of her best friends from New York. Mia's face lit up when Pesca mentioned her parents, and then she effortlessly thanked her for being her *unofficial* tour guide, as well as Papa and Mama for being so welcoming to her. She raised her glass to cheers everyone and looked right at me as she lowered it back down without even so much as a smile.

Less than twenty-four hours prior, I felt like I had known her my entire life, and all of a sudden, she felt like a distant stranger again.

What the hell happened?

It was around nine-thirty in the evening when we finished and everyone began helping to clean up. Before I knew it, she was in the kitchen refusing to let Mama wash any dishes, and instead made her sit at the island with a glass of wine as a thank you for cooking. Pesca was there also, and because I felt like a bit of an outsider, I headed outside to the patio.

"Did she remember you?" Giuseppe wasted no time with his interrogation.

"She did, and I don't want to talk about it," I responded quickly.

What I did want to do was sit on the cushion-top bench underneath the string lights and across from the infinity pool to put my legs up, relax, and turn my mind off.

Within minutes, I heard a few of the dinner guests say goodnight to everyone, and then I heard Mama and Pesca talking, which could only mean Mia was right behind them. When I looked, though, I didn't see her.

Pesca moved closer to me and like the mind reader she was, said, "She said she was tired and went back to her villa." I shook my head. "What happened with you two?"

"From my recollection, we had one of the best nights of both of our lives," I stared ahead, sipping on the last of my third glass of wine, "but from how she's acting now, I have no idea, but whatever."

"Don't go doing that thing you always do," she said matter-of-factly.

"What's that?" I asked, genuinely having no idea what she was referring to.

"Tuning everyone and everything out when things don't exactly go your way."

Sometimes I feel like Pesca knows me better than my parents do.

"What should I do then? Because I feel like one big giant asshole."

"What everyone should do when things don't make sense, start a conversation about it." I decided she should have a self-help podcast at that exact moment.

I went to pick up my phone to send Mia a text and could instantly feel Pesca's eyes roll back into her skull.

"Do not make me throw that phone into the pool. You simply need to go talk to her in *person*." British accents have a way of making you want to listen, and this was no exception.

I finished my wine and walked through the kitchen to grab another bottle, along with two clean glasses. Thankfully, everyone who was still awake was outside, and I didn't have to field any questions.

I walked up a flight of stairs to the higher level of villa apartments, knowing exactly which one was hers, thanks to the picture she sent earlier. As I approached, I saw a few lights on and was instantly relieved *and* nervous.

What the hell was wrong with me?

She was still dressed in her outfit from earlier as I watched her pour a glass of water from a pitcher in the fridge. I knocked on the door lightly so I wouldn't scare her and could tell that, although I could see in, she couldn't see out. She squinted as she moved closer and her expression softened when she finally figured out it was me.

One small smile made me feel one thousand times better, and then, as though the last couple of hours hadn't happened, she opened the door, took my hand, and pulled me inside.

Mia stepped around me to draw the curtains, lowered the kitchen and living room lights, placed her water cup down, and motioned for me to do the same with the wine bottle and glasses I had brought over.

She came in close to my chest, neither of us having said a word to each other yet, and looked up at me. Her eyes burned with the same longing they had the previous night and this morning, and suddenly, I wasn't confused anymore. My hands gravitated towards both sides of her face, my fingers entwined in her hair, around the base of her neck, and I gently lifted her chin.

Instead of kissing her, I moved my mouth closer to her ear and whispered, "What do you want?"

She breathed me in and exhaled loudly with a very simple, yet direct answer.

"You."

"All of me?" I asked, and she nodded with zero hesitation.

"Every inch."

CHAPTER 13

Mia

I guess there was a small percentage of me hoping our third go-round would be less exciting, less thrilling, less *pleasurable*, but there I was, at one in the morning, with flushed cheeks, sweat streaming down the back of my neck, and legs shaking like a Jell-O mold.

The difference now, though, was that I was lying in the crook of his right shoulder with my arm slung over his stomach as he scratched up and down my back, and he was talking a whole lot more than he had the day prior.

"I'm *still* trying to understand why you didn't tell me you were staying," he said, his voice just above a whisper.

"I gave you the honest answer last night," I responded. "I didn't want to abandon Pesca to chase a temporary high. I knew we were leaving Rome that day, and I assumed you were working there throughout the weekend."

"Ah, so you can assume, but I can't?" he smiled as he responded, and I determined in that moment that, although his unapproachable side was kind of sexy, the soft, hidden one was my favorite. He was being vulnerable, clearly wanting to spend more time with me, but to what end I wasn't sure yet.

I nuzzled into him and hugged him a little tighter so he could feel how much I wanted to be there. "I tend to get shit on by men, if I'm being honest."

"The truth shall set you free. A man hater?" he asked with the slightest laugh.

"If by man hater you mean someone tired of dealing with men who are assholes, then sure." My response dripped matter-of-factness. "I'm always the doer. I came here mostly wanting to focus on *me*, which I am certainly not currently doing."

"I asked you last night if we had a good time, and you responded with a resounding yes, right?" He reminded me of last night's conversation, and I thought back to how incredible this entire thing had been. What were the chances we'd be here together again after a chance meeting in Rome the day before?

"There is no doubt I've enjoyed all of this," I responded after a few seconds of mentally strolling down memory lane.

"Well, if you're having a good time, and no one's forcing you to do anything you don't want to do, then you *are* focusing on yourself." It sounded so simple.

"There's so much to say, but I really don't want to over complicate everything, which is another thing I always do." I paused, waiting for him to say something, but he was still listening, so I continued. "We live in different countries and…"

I stopped. This was classic Mia. A few sex sessions in, and I was already trying to figure out what we "were" or what we were "going to be." Meanwhile, the delicious man in my Tuscan bed was likely concerned with how many different positions we'd be able to check off the list within the next two weeks.

"Don't do that; finish what you were going to say," he surprised me, likely the only man I've ever heard utter those words, and he meant them.

"We live in different countries, and I'm trying to understand if I really want to let myself enjoy this just to go home and have to live without it." I didn't realize exactly how I felt until I heard it come out of my mouth.

"See, I'm looking at it a little differently," he gently rolled me to my stomach, kneeled in between my legs, and started massaging long strokes up and down my hamstrings, the curves of my backside, all the way up to my shoulder blades.

"How so?" I moaned out of the corner of my mouth, if we could call it that. I love being touched and rubbed. It's my absolute favorite and a certified weakness.

"I'd rather experience all of the good and never have to wonder, 'What would have happened if?' You know, live in the moment and all of that," I felt a little bit of sarcastic snark, but knew he was right, that I wasn't listening to my own advice. He continued, "For instance, I'd rather know what it's like to make you finish for the fourth time in less than two days than have to worry about never getting the chance to do it again."

Gennaro slithered up my back, pressed his lips to my shoulder, and I moaned *again*. He took it as a signal for more, which it was. Strong hands attached to a body that smelled amazing was yet another weakness of mine, which reminded me of the cologne he was wearing. I thought about it for a millisecond before he rolled me back over, hooked his arms under my legs, and pulled me, *all of me*, towards his face.

I didn't say anything, just instinctively arched my back

and dug my heels into the bed to get as close to him as possible. Any self-conscious thoughts or worries I may have had were all but gone as my involuntary twitching got used to his tongue inside of me and I began masterfully riding the rhythm of his mouth. With my hands holding the back of his head and his fingers wrapped around my hips, I climbed to a pulsating finish within a couple of minutes, trying to muffle my screams in the process.

Devoid of energy, my muscles finally released and I rolled over to my side like the limp piece of flesh I felt like. My breathing became rhythmic as he pulled the blanket up and over my shoulder and curled up behind me. I quickly fell asleep and stayed asleep for the next eight hours.

When I woke up, the room was colder and felt emptier. I rolled over to discover I was alone in the bed. Having no idea what time it even was, I grabbed my phone off the end table.

10:08 am.

Jesus.

I immediately smiled when I saw a message from him on my lock screen.

> Gennaro: Questa è la seconda mattina consecutiva di fila che mi sveglio felice. Grazie.

I Google translated faster than a speeding bullet.

"This is the second morning in a row I have woken up happy. Thank you."

I was still topless with only a sheet covering me, so I snapped a quick picture and sent it to him.

> Mia: Anch'io

Pesca chimed in separately.

> Pesca: We are going to the market up the street if you want to take a walk?

> Mia: Absolutely, how should I dress?

I always need a solid plan.

> Pesca: Comfortably. You can hang by the pool when we get back, it's beautiful out. Meet you outside your apartment in 15 minutes

I threw myself in the shower for a quick but thorough body cleanse, flashing back to each of the times I had spent with him and found myself smiling.

Dammit.

I was falling for him.

I felt like half an idiot for it, but I was focused on enjoying life a little bit more and questioning it a little bit less.

I put on a black two-piece bathing suit with a pair of high-waisted cover-up pants and a duster cardigan, grabbed my purse, and walked out the door at the same time Pesca was walking up the hill.

"Ciao," she said, wearing her signature smile, woven hat, and sunglasses.

I smiled. She was my home away from home while I was here, and I was lucky to have her. I hesitated a bit before stammering, "I, uh, um, I'm not sure what I should share with you or not."

"Mia, you're a grown adult. So is he. As long as you're not being disrespectful of the property or of the other guests, all I want is for you to enjoy yourself. Truly."

We spent the ten-minute walk to the market talking about the previous night's dinner, and I learned a little bit more about Papa, Mama, Gennaro, and his brothers. Pesca also explained a bit more about Papa and Mama. They were innately different from each other with Papa being a hard head and Mama much softer and more go with the flow.

After thirty years, their relationship had developed into a relatively loving one, but it lacked much emotion, affection, or romance. They both took great pride in their family and their business as a whole, hosting international guests and maintaining such an impressive property, but it had taken a bit of a toll on their quality time together, as well as the brothers who witnessed it.

Gennaro definitely acted like the older brother he was, trying to keep it together for everyone, but he'd finally had enough. He ended up in Rome while Giovanni had "escaped" to Florence, which left Giuseppe trying to hold it down in their absence. The good part about that was that he seemed to be the easygoing one, letting most things roll off his back. Giuseppe didn't let Papa get under his skin, and he put the positives of working from home with his family at the forefront of his experience. He truly had no interest in working elsewhere.

If Pesca had a favorite of the Beletta sons, she didn't necessarily show it, but what I did notice was that she didn't have one bad word to say about any of them, including Gennaro. And, as my parents' close friend and an extended parent of my own who wanted me to "enjoy myself," I assumed she'd alert me to any red flags that might get in the way of some wholesome (and occasionally indecent) enjoyment.

The local market was tastefully decorated and had all of the essentials like wine, cheese, bread, and desserts. I walked around with Pesca, adding a variety of items to my basket. My only strategy for choosing the items was, "Does this item bring me joy?" If so, it was added.

Twenty minutes later, said basket was filled to the brim with freshly baked crusty (still warm!) loaves of bread; soft, creamy, mozzarella; crisp red onions; sweet red tomatoes; fragrant basil; a variety of hard cheeses; locally made prosciutto; olives; pesto; and some sweet pastries that could double as breakfast and dessert. I had put everything on the counter and turned around to the shelves behind me to pick out some wine when a beautiful woman floated down the aisle towards me after emerging from a door in the back. She wore a long flowing dress and dainty jewelry to complement red hair and an absolutely radiant smile that grew even bigger when she spotted Pesca.

They spoke for a few minutes, and Pesca explained to me that her family was very close to Papa and Mama. The woman helped me pick out the wine, added in a few extra cookies for me to enjoy with all of the other items I had gathered, and wished me well for the remainder of my vacation. I couldn't stop looking at her, and assumed it was because she was similar in age to me, but she seemed like an established woman, handling her business in one of the most beautiful places on earth.

What a concept. Doing something you absolutely loved, getting paid for it, and living in a place like this while you did it.

As we walked back to the villa, Pesca took a phone call while I took in the sight of everything around me. On one side was thick, dense tree-cover with dirt lined sidewalks. On the other were plush rolling hills and the vineyard that lined the front of Tenuta di Corsano where we were staying. I was so far away from my actual home, but this place was already imprinting itself on my heart. The closer we got to the front gate, the happier I felt myself becoming. I truly felt comfortable there.

On top of that, I could see Gennaro down the driveway, painting some door trim without a freaking shirt on.

"The exhibitionist." Pesca laughed to herself and rolled her eyes.

She may not have appreciated the view, but I absolutely did. As we walked up the gravel to where he was working, he spun his head around, met my gaze, smiled, and winked.

"When are you off duty?" Pesca asked him with just the right amount of sarcasm.

They got along well, and it made me happy. "I make my own hours around here, you know that," he smirked.

"I sure do, you've always been a rebel," she joked but without any misinformation attached. "I'm going to help Mama prep for dinner."

"What time is dinner?" I asked, consistently motivated by meal times.

"Whenever we show up," Gennaro answered, even though I was asking Pesca.

"When *we* show up? Is this when I'm officially introduced to the family as your forty-eight-hour girlfriend?" I laughed.

"Only if you want to be," his eyes might as well have burned a hole through me.

I smiled, tight lipped.

"In that case, can we swim a little bit first?" Pesca had already walked far enough down the hill to leave us to our sexually laced banter, so this question was directed towards him only.

"I was hoping you'd ask." He climbed down the ladder and grabbed his t-shirt off the chair it was draped over, but I walked right up to him and grabbed it back.

"You won't be needing this, sir." I stared at him with my mouth only a few inches away from his, trying not to smile.

He grabbed the back of my head firmly and pulled me in even closer than I already was.

"Let's go get wet," he said in a huffed whisper.

I took the bait this time.

"Already am—since this morning actually."

"Even better," he said without missing a beat.

My hormones subsided long enough to blurt out, "Let me go say hi to your parents in the kitchen first."

His eyebrows raised, and I instantly felt like a nerd. Maybe I'd care less if Pesca wasn't here, but I didn't want to be giving off the vibes we currently were within eyeshot of his family without spending a reasonable amount of time with them.

I guess that in my mind I was already pretending we were in a relationship, *which I always fricken' do*, but regardless of where any of this went, my relationship with Pesca and my parents reigned supreme. For now, at least.

"If you're not careful, you'll be in there the next four hours or so right up until dinner," he joked.

"Not if you come save me," I nudged him.

"I got you," he smiled. *That beautiful smile.*

"Stop doing that," I not so jokingly joked.

"I have no idea what you're talking about," he retorted. He smiled again with another small wink right after.

I walked down the hill and could hear pots and pans clanking in the kitchen. Pesca and Mama were already at work washing vegetables and rolling out pasta dough, but Papa was nowhere to be found.

"Ciao bella," Mama said to me with a big smile on her face. "How are your parents?"

This was exactly the reason I needed to come down here. "I think they're jealous that they're not with me."

We all laughed and spoke back and forth about what Pesca and I had planned for the rest of the two weeks I'd be there. And then, as though she knew me like the back of her hand, Pesca effortlessly and graciously told Mama that Gennaro and I had met, by chance, in Rome two nights prior. A sweet relief fell over me, because I wasn't sure how that was going to unfold in conversation.

Her eyes widened with the sweetest look of surprise on her face, and a smile remained for what seemed like minutes. She started rambling about how wonderful he was, how much she missed having him at the villa, and how proud she was of everything he had accomplished in such a short time. Mama also mentioned wanting to go visit him but never finding the time.

I took it as an opportunity to kindly let her know how much it would mean to him. "He actually mentioned to me how much he wants you all to visit for a weekend. There's a beautiful rooftop restaurant right down the street from him, too."

"He loves his scenery, that boy, but I'll never understand what's wrong with this view," she said motioning beyond the kitchen sink window to the patio, infinity pool, and vineyards behind it.

Again, Pesca chimed in, "Gigi, my dear friend, an incredible view in Rome doesn't take away from an exceptional one in Tuscany." They continued their prep but didn't say anything more. She certainly wasn't acting mad, but I could tell she didn't want to talk about it further.

"Can I help you both?" I broke the silence, wanting to be useful.

"Absolutely not," Mama said. "Please go use that pool since no one else does. And take this with you." She handed me a plate of cheeses and bread, a bottle of wine, and two glasses.

If this was Tuscan life, then I agreed with Mama. I understood parental disagreements and wanting to experience different things as you aged, but there seemed to be some information missing.

What really prevented him from enjoying this place?

I walked up the patio steps to the pool area, put the cheese, bread, and wine underneath the umbrella cover, and dipped my toe in the water.

Sweet serenity.

I located a basket of towels, took two, and spread them over a pair of chairs closer to the deep end. I slipped out of my loose knit pants and duster cardigan—which were now way too warm for the afternoon heat wave—and was thankful Pesca had suggested I wear my bathing suit earlier.

With eyes closed, lying comfortably on a lounge chair, I felt the sun radiating on my skin, willing it to give me the tan I desperately needed. About five minutes later I heard footsteps next to me, which sent chills (*the good kind*) up and down my body.

My eyes still closed, I smiled and asked, "What took you so long?"

A voice I didn't recognize responded, "I didn't know you were waiting for me."

My eyes quickly opened, temporarily blinded by the sun, before Giuseppe's face came into view.

CHAPTER 14
Gennaro

I walked into the kitchen expecting to see Mama, Pesca, and Mia talking, but no one was there. There was sauce simmering on the stove and everything was set for dinner later, but it was quiet as could be, which meant everyone was either outside or getting ready.

I peered out the kitchen sink window, looking up the patio stairs to the pool landing, and found Mia's long legs stretched across a lounge chair. I realized she was talking out loud, and when I looked at the chair next to her, I could see the back of Giuseppe's head. My eyes instinctively rolled--squeezing my temples with my thumb and middle finger—before walking outside.

"No fraternizing with the villa guests, little brother," I partially joked so it would come out sounding kinder than I meant it.

"You weren't ever particularly good at taking your own advice," he retorted instantly, with a whole lot less kindness than I had given him. "But I have to get in the shower anyway. We've got some special guests for dinner tonight."

I could feel him eyeing me, but I purposely ignored him. By the second day of us spending time together, we were usually wearing on each other's nerves. This weekend was no exception, clearly.

"Not sure how you put up with his moody ass, Mia, but bless you for trying to." He high-fived her like they'd known each other for years.

She high-fived him back with her trademark smile. "It's been exhausting," she responded with plenty of sarcasm, "but the rewards have been well worth the struggle." Her big, bright eyes looked me up and down like she was ready to devour me.

Giuseppe walked towards his villa, out of sight, leaving Mia and me alone on the veranda. Like every other time before it, the sexual tension immediately sprouted between us. It felt like we were two teenagers alone in a basement, not knowing what to do next but hoping to do *all* of it, immediately. Not wanting to in any way appear like an insatiable fifteen-year-old, I poured each of us a glass of wine.

"This will be my second one," she warned while taking the glass from my hand. "One more after that and I can't be held accountable for any poor decision making that occurs prior to another family dinner."

"Well, here's the good news," I pushed her legs with a gentle nudge upwards to her chest so I had enough room to sit on the chair, facing her. Then, after sitting, I grabbed the backs of her knees, loosened them, and stretched her legs out to rest over the tops of my thighs. "It's not a family dinner with villa guests where we're cooking. There will only be a few of us, which means it'll go faster, and then we can spend all the time we want together afterwards."

I didn't realize I wanted her to, but she pulled herself

off the back cushion of the chair, slid closer to me, and wrapped her legs around my waist. Just a few inches away from my mouth, she whispered, "As long as I get to stare at you for the next few hours and you're inside me sometime after that, I'm good."

And then she kissed me, hard.

If this was after one and a quarter glasses of wine, I wasn't sure my dick could handle her after three.

Who was I kidding?

I'd handle her perfectly. It was knowing what to do as her time at the villa ticked on that I wasn't sure how I'd handle. But I'd figure it out as it came.

"I want to go swimming," I told her, a faint smile at both corners of my mouth. I kissed her quickly, got up, dove in, and swam to the infinity edge which overlooked the vineyards.

The weather was simply perfect. A hot day was beginning to cool off, but it was still warm, in the low twenties with a mostly clear, blue sky. Some clouds floated high, but the blue sky over the deep green vineyard rows where the birds sang to each other was all one needed to set his senses on fire.

I heard a splash of water behind me and turned around in time for her soaking wet head of hair to rise out of the pool water. She smiled and effortlessly swam towards me. We were in the deep end, so I held on to the edge with one hand and grabbed her waist with the other, pulling her close. She wrapped her legs around my side, with one arm around my neck, looking out over the edge towards the vineyards. I could smell her perfume radiating off of her skin, and it made me want her even more, but I maintained composure long enough to situate her in between my body and the pool wall. Bracing both of our weightless bodies by holding onto the edge, her legs still wrapped around me, I looked into her eyes and told her quite honestly, "I've never appreciated this, all of it, until right now."

I closed my eyes and breathed deeply trying to remember the last time I had even been in the pool for any other reason than to quickly cool off after working all day. And, in that moment, I realized everything that had gone wrong with my view of this entire property.

I never was allotted the time to actually enjoy it.

I resented it for taking all of my adulthood and most of my childhood, without having one single say in any of it. I was born into it. It was a way of life. Protect the land, protect the family name, protect the future of it, always. But I was never given a choice. I hated anyone making decisions for me about anything, and because of that, I've grown to resent it all. I forgot how to truly appreciate it because I was too focused on the parts of it that bothered me.

To be fair, it was a bit easier to enjoy it with a beautiful woman next to me sharing in my appreciation for it. The last day and a half had become less of "What do I have to do next?" and more of "What do I *get* to do next?" and "When do I get to do it with *her* again?"

The beauty of it all shined brighter because of her.

Everything shined brighter when it reflected off of her.

"You ok?" she asked, sweetly. I slowly opened my eyes, not realizing I'd closed them while taking in the realization.

"I've never been better," I honestly responded. I floated in close to her, gently pinning her back to the wall of the pool and slowly tracing my lips over hers. I felt her inhale as I nibbled her bottom lip, and then I sucked the air back out of her with my tongue.

I could kiss her for hours.

My knees felt weak, but thankfully, floating in the pool helped to support me.

I hadn't drunk enough wine to be tipsy, but that's how I felt.

Weightless, light as air, and *free.*

Until his voice interrupted my real-life fantasy and brought me right back to reality.

"Ma che cazzo fai." Papa looked at me, shaking his head in utter disgust at whatever he had witnessed. If there were an equivalent of a cold shower for someone already in a cool pool, it was my father asking me what the fuck I was doing during one of my happiest moments of life to date.

I refused to answer, lowered my head, and closed my eyes, trying to release the immediate ball of tension his mere presence provoked. I felt Mia cower and sort of hide in my chest, definitely embarrassed and rightfully so. We were twenty-four and twenty-eight years old, feeling like we had to hide from my parents. I added this moment to the reasons why I had left this place.

Did I like Rome better than Tuscany? Absolutely not. But I loved the freedom it offered, the autonomy, and the solitude within a sea of people, whereas here, it was the complete opposite. We were in the middle of nowhere but with everyone involved in our business. Expansive, vast land felt crowded, and fresh air flowing atop rolling green hills lacked the crisp refreshment you'd expect or desire.

He had already walked back inside the house, his brief run-in providing all of the aggravation I'd come to expect after years of dealing with him. Oftentimes, I wondered how my mother put up with his negativity and innate need to control everything. He wasn't happy unless he was telling people what to do or watching people do what he told them to do. It went against every grain of my being. I didn't need to be in control of everything, but I absolutely didn't want anyone dictating what I did, when I did it, or how I did it.

We didn't see eye to eye, and I doubted we ever would. I self-soothed my aggravation by kissing her again. Harder this time. It felt like every ounce of rage for my father coming out as electricity burning through our lips.

"I need you now," I told her.

Her eyes widened and scanned the landscape around her.

"Not here. In your room. Now." It wasn't a question, it was a statement. And I needed her to agree to it.

She breathed deeply, and I could tell she was thinking about it but felt uncomfortable. Her fingers trailed my chest and shoulders until she reached my neck and looked right into my eyes.

"I want everything you're thinking about, but now isn't the right time," her words stung, even though I knew she was right. "Maybe you should go talk to him."

"There's no point," I said with an exasperated sigh. My dick must have assumed by this point that I was recently diagnosed with ADHD. One minute I was asking him to get up and go, and the next, "Down boy, false alarm."

All I felt in that moment was exhaustion from mental mind-fuckery. It was easier policing the streets of Rome on any given day of the week.

"I get it, I really do. Maybe I'd feel different if Pesca wasn't here as a backup parent, but we need to chill out. I don't want to be obnoxious about it all, especially if he's feeling the way he is." She had a way of calming me down when I needed it, and it made me want her even more.

"I'm going to go shower and get ready for dinner," she continued, "but I'm only going if you're going."

"Are you asking me to be your date, Mia?" I smiled.

"Yes, I am," she smiled right back at me coyly but with

tactful, passionate desire burning underneath the surface. It was without a doubt one of my favorite things about her.

"I'd love to," I played along, "under one condition."

"What's that?" she asked with a slight eyebrow raise.

"Wear something red," I requested, "please."

Her head cocked to the side as she thought about my request, and then she slyly smiled. "I can do that."

We got out, quickly dried off, and kissed each other goodbye with a small peck, as though we were still being watched. Part of me didn't care, while another part of me absolutely did, for a variety of reasons, but I tried to push past it to enjoy the rest of the night.

I watched her walk up the hill towards her villa as I headed towards the kitchen to drop off the quarter-full wine bottle and wine glasses.

Papa and Mama were huddled together speaking intently, and looked up at me like I'd interrupted them, which I had. Normally, I buried things. I didn't freely talk about things, especially right after they occurred. I was somewhat of a volcano, and I often let the volcano fill with lava until it exploded.

For whatever reason, this time I didn't want to bury anything. Maybe I wanted to prove my point that this was the exact reason I didn't want to stay here or, more accurately, couldn't stay here. Regardless of the why, my thoughts came flying out of my mouth.

"What's wrong with *me*?" I asked him, even though it wasn't a question. "What's wrong with this entire place?"

I didn't give either of them a chance to say anything before continuing.

"You make it absolutely impossible to enjoy anything here. When I lived here and worked here full time, it was never enough. That by itself made me want to get the hell out, and I did, but I still come back, weekend after weekend, to help. I do it because I love both of you, and I'm grateful for the life you've given me. But this place, and all of the unrealistic expectations you have because of it, have made it completely unenjoyable." I barely took a breath. "I've done what you've asked of me since I was old enough to walk. I gave up opportunities to learn or work anywhere else to help you out here. I even gave up my ability to have normal relationships because of your requests. No, your demands. And I'm done doing all of it. I'm leaving tomorrow, and I'll come back again for Christmas."

Papa was stone-faced and Mama just stood there, tears streaming down her face.

A few seconds passed before he finally asked, "Because of *her*?" He was referring to Mia, with a disgusted look on his face.

"You really don't ever listen to a goddamn word I say. Where did her name come up in anything I said?"

"It didn't have to. I know you better than you think I do, and I can just tell," he said, emotionless. In the same tone of voice, he continued, "I don't need you to come back. Giuseppe's been doing a good job. And don't come running back here after she goes home and you're bored in the middle of Rome. I don't need you here and after this conversation—I don't want you here."

Mama's tears turned to a full-blown cry, telling us to both stop, but once things got going with us like this, there was no stopping. Not until a few days or weeks or sometimes months went by. Even then, we wouldn't talk about it; we'd just bury it and act like it didn't happen.

"I'm going to take a shower," I announced.

"Are you coming for dinner?" Mama asked, her face long, drawn, and red from crying.

"Yes, because I told Mia I was going. Otherwise, I'd get

in my car and drive back tonight." It wasn't meant to sound like a dig, but it sure came out as one.

I walked to my room, blasted some music to distract my brain from everything running through it, and got in a scalding hot shower meant to do the same.

A solid fifteen minutes later, I willed myself to dry off and get dressed, with her as my only motivation. I pulled on dark jeans, a crimson red button-down that hugged my arms and chest tightly, the front of it tucked into my jeans and the rest hanging loose. I ran some hair wax through my hair so it would stay in place without hardening completely and sprayed four more sprays of cologne than I normally did. I knew she loved it, and I loved when I could feel, hear, and see her breathing me in.

It was about a half hour later when I returned to the kitchen, wanting to get a few glasses of wine in me before dinner started. I had to deal with Papa, Giuseppe and his ill-timed humor, *and* Giovanni was coming in from Florence, although he was the absolute least of my stressors these days.

I felt someone hovering behind me and turned to find Pesca standing there holding a wine glass out. "To the top, please," she said with *the* look. I've seen it plenty of times before, and it meant Papa, Mama, or both of them had gotten her ear after I left the kitchen earlier.

"I know how much you love when anyone tells you to relax, so I won't. Just pour yourself one to the top, too." I smiled. She was as effective as a squeezable anti-stress ball.

We sat next to each other at the island talking about Rome and police work as Papa and Mama prepared dinner together by the sink. I realized that, besides Mia, not one person in the house had asked me about any of it. I was telling her about my apartment, my partner, and some arrests I had made when I saw Mia walk down the stairs.

I expected her presence to—at some point—stop affecting me so profoundly, but it hadn't yet happened. She had on a two-piece outfit, skin-tight but tasteful, with a thick-strapped cropped tank, a high-waisted skirt, and the same ankle tie shoes she wore the night we met. Her long hair was freshly washed and wavy, with one side pinned up and the rest of it pushed to the opposite side. She completed it all with gold chandelier earrings, a chunky gold necklace, a bracelet to match, and a lot of gold rings. She really didn't do much of anything in an understated manner, and I couldn't get enough of it.

She smiled and quietly said "hello" as she walked past Papa, Mama, and Pesca, but her eyes were burning a hole right through me. She either had a glass of wine (or two) while she was getting ready, or she discovered some newfound desire. Hell, maybe both.

I caught a whiff of her sweet, sensual perfume as she walked towards me, and our mouths both curved into smiles. We walked together into the dining room, partially out of sight, and stood in front of each other. We weren't touching, but we were staring.

"Should I ask?"

"Ask what?" she blinked at me, and anyone who didn't know her better would think she was as sweet and innocent as she appeared.

"Didn't I ask you to wear red?" I reminded her, with my head cocked to the side.

"I am wearing red," she said, without taking her eyes off of me.

"How much wine have you drunk?" I laughed.

"Not enough," she answered, still staring.

"Well, I hate to break it to you, but you might be colorblind." I grabbed her hand and twirled her around, "This very beautiful outfit is black."

"You didn't specify which part of my outfit had to be red."

Blood immediately rushed to parts it shouldn't rush to ahead of a family dinner, and I found myself at a loss for words. She instinctively licked her bottom lip while looking at mine and grabbing the waistband of my jeans. At this point I was convinced she didn't do any of this on purpose —she was merely a sexual being with a very obvious love language—*physical touch*.

"*Fanculo*," I whispered slowly, shaking my head.

"Yes, that's the plan," she said before walking back into the kitchen.

Every inch of her was perfect, from her hair to her feet. She was every bit as sweet as she was sexy, but it permeated so much more than her physical traits. She always knew what to say, how to say it, and when to say it. She continued to calm me down when I needed it most. She knew how to get through to me to my core. She touched on every need, want, and desire I had, some of which I didn't even know were there until a couple of days ago.

My heart was beating fast and my mind went blank as I tried to shake it off. It couldn't be possible. *Absolutely not.*

There was no way I could fall in love with someone in two days.

There was no way I could fall in love with someone who lived in a different country, who I'd likely never see again.

There was no possible way—until I saw her with her arm around Mama.

Mama was laughing, Pesca was laughing, and even Papa had the slightest smile on his face.

I realized in that moment that knowing her for only

two days meant absolutely nothing when she brought such comfort to my life.

It was absolutely possible, because it had happened.

I had fallen for her.

The impossible part would be figuring out what to do about it.

CHAPTER 15
Mia

Somewhere between the bold earring choice and the ample sprays of perfume, both of which consistently made me feel like I could take on the world, I decided I was going to try to help fix the Beletta family tension.

Was it my place to get involved?

Not in the least.

Had that ever stopped me?

Absolutely not.

I was always guilty of overstepping, which usually stemmed from the close-knit relationships I had with everyone around me. As a sounding board for a majority of my friends and family, I often felt like the chosen vent receptacle. The skill I lacked, though, was listening, hearing, and understanding *without* letting the problems of others affect me—or, more accurately, without trying to help fix them.

Given all I had learned from Pesca about the family, paired with the warmth and love I felt radiating from them, I felt connected to it. All of it. Perhaps most of all, I fully understood the passion behind their family history.

They had a purpose, a goal, a vision, which was, quite simply, to allow people to slow down while embracing the importance of family time. Good food and drinks along with the visual beauty of the property, which was merely a bonus.

Sure, they made a living allowing others to enjoy their beautiful way of life, but they genuinely and authentically let us in to fully experience it. Of utmost importance through it all, though, was keeping their family bond strong, indestructible even, an undeniable Italian characteristic at its core.

It was clear that this last goal was slowly but surely slipping through Papa's and Mama's fingertips.

A tale as old as time: the tighter you try to hold on to something by force, the more likely it is to slip away. There was a lot of underlying resentment topped with strong personalities and a huge lack of communication. I had a front-seat view of it all, and to be fair, with the exception of the...*ahem*...quality time I had spent with Gennaro, I could see all of this in a relatively neutral light with a fresh set of eyes.

Two loving, supportive parents trying to keep a family together, but that family was made up of three men, a gender not historically known for thorough communication. The stone-faced nature of Papa alongside the easily agitated Gennaro, escape artist Giovanni, makes-a-joke-out-of-anything Giuseppe, and matriarch who didn't want to ruffle any feathers along the way didn't lend itself to effective or immediate conflict resolution.

Papa thought himself in charge but had proven himself to be an ineffective leader who demanded things from everyone without ever refilling anyone's cup. Gennaro hated being controlled, so he'd fight back, which created the wildly evident friction between them. Giovanni dealt with conflict by running away from it, and Giuseppe attempted to use his likable personality and humorous disposition to lighten the mood temporarily, rather than attempting an approach that might allow for long-lasting change. Mama, clearly exhausted by all of it, wore the weight of it on her shoulders, without the ability to get through to any of them.

From what I could tell, these dynamics had gone on for years and years, and from what I knew about successful, solid relationships, theirs was quite the opposite.

What I had witnessed with my own parents was two people consistently working together to get things done without expectations. My dad, previously the breadwinner, had lost his job at the height of his career and the top of his pay grade. When he was out of work he moved (quietly) into an alternate role where he took on some of mom's responsibilities around the house while she went to work and provided our house with income and benefits. Not once did I ever hear either of them pointing the finger about who *did* what, who *needed* to do what, or who *should* do what.

They just did it, quite like a tango. They worked together to create a seamless dance, or so it appeared from the outside, at least. They never let us see them sweat. It took years for them to get to that point, though, as well as a too-close-for-comfort dip in income that threatened our financial well-being as a family.

So, in this moment, as I watched the Beletta family approaching their too-close-for-comfort dip in family cohesion, I could feel that they needed their own "aha" moment.

"Mr. Beletta, I want to more fully introduce myself." I looked at him directly, confidently but kindly with a smile on my face. "You know my parents well. I'm Mia. I'm so happy to finally be here."

I studied him intently. His golden-brown olive skin was wrinkled, but a handsome face stared back at me with blazing blue eyes that I could tell had a lot of love in them.

He studied me back similarly, and the corners of his mouth raised slightly. He offered his hand for me to shake, but I went right in for a big hug and a kiss on the cheek, as I always did.

"You can call me Rocco," he said with a full smile and a playful curiosity in his eyes.

"Ok, Rocco. I'm sure this is a terrible thing to ask, but can I have some ice for my wine?"

He let out a belly laugh so loud that Mama and Pesca turned around to see what had caused it.

"Have you tried my wine yet?" he asked with a slightly offended but joking tone.

"I sure have, and it's delicious," I smiled back.

"But?" he asked, and I could instantly see where Gennaro got his charming yet occasionally smart-ass personality. It made me light up inside to chip away at the handsome boulder standing in front of me.

"But I like drinks that are cold," I shrugged, matter-of-factly. Truth was, this wine *was* delicious. I had enjoyed it for two days in a row without any need for ice. But my inner sleuth was using it as a way in, or more accurately, as a way to teach. Would he listen and understand what my needs were, even if they were different from his? Or would he insist on me doing what he deemed the proper way to do things?

As I continued to study his face, I could tell how much this small interaction had challenged him, which meant I had my work cut out for me.

"*Dio aiutami,*" he said, looking up at the ceiling and

pressing his hands together like he was praying. I accurately assumed he was asking for God to help him, and I chimed in with "Thou shall not judge, Rocco," a smile, and a shoulder shrug.

When I looked back across the room, Gennaro was still standing where I had left him, but he had a huge smile plastered across his face. I winked at him and tilted my head to the side, ushering him to come inside and join us. He started walking towards me, but Giuseppe had walked in behind him from the patio, calling his name.

With one finger in the air, he signaled for me to wait for him, and turned back around to talk to his brother. I couldn't make out what either of them was saying, but it was an intense conversation. Giuseppe's face went from shock and surprise to uncertainty and then to anger. Gennaro had his back to me the entire time, but I saw his hand ball up into a fist before leaning his head back the same way Papa had done a bit ago.

Something wasn't jiving, but this time, it wasn't Papa's fault. He was too busy arguing with me about putting ice in red wine. I didn't want to be nosy, so I turned back around to the kitchen island and pulled a stool up next to Pesca. She smiled and pushed my glass of wine, now complete with a few cubes of ice, towards me. "Well if that wasn't one of the funniest things I've seen in a while. Here's your chilled wine, Madame."

"All part of my plan," I smiled before taking a large sip.

She smiled and shook her head. "Which plan is that exactly?"

"There are way too many good people in this house for all of these negative vibes to be floating around. I want to try and help fix it." In that exact moment, I was confident of my ability to do so.

"I've been trying to do it for years," she said with a bit

of an exasperated, doubtful tone, "but you might have an advantage here."

I was still sipping, taking it all in, while Gennaro and Giuseppe were still intensely talking in the background, and Papa and Mama were whispering in the corner.

"Which advantage is that?" I asked, partially knowing the answer.

"You've got the two thickest ones to actually listen to you." She tilted her head to the side and raised her eyebrows. "And I haven't seen that happen in all of the years I've been an honorary member of this family."

"Is giving in to my wine ice cube request considered listening?" I joked, trying to play it off, since I knew it was the exact reason I participated in the entire interaction the way I did.

"For him, it absolutely is." She motioned towards Gennaro, who was walking towards us. "And, as for this one, he would have left to go back to Rome after the pool debacle this afternoon. He's only still here because you're here. It may be a small start, but it's a start. I can feel a bit of a shake up," she continued. "I just haven't quite figured out how the rest of the night is going to play out."

It sounded a little ominous, but I shrugged and sipped some more. I was over my three-glass limit, which meant I should slow down. I wasn't a *bad* drunk by any means. I merely got a bit louder and more carefree, and my mood could go either overtly emotional or overtly sexual. There was rarely an in-between. Since I was intent on healing years of family trauma in the next two weeks, I figured I should be at my most level-headed self.

Gennaro walked right up to the island, grabbed a rocks glass, and poured gin over ice this time rather than wine. He drank all of it in one gulp and all but slammed the glass back down when he finished. His fist was gripping the glass so tightly I was afraid it might shatter. When I looked at his face, his jaw was clenched, clearly aggravated about something. I placed my hand on his wrist, and he softened for a second, but then looked at me, inhaled deeply and then exhaled slowly. He licked his bottom lip, finally let go of the glass, and seemed to be in deep thought.

"I won't ask if you're ok, because you're obviously not, but is it something you want to talk about?" I tried to calm him down without the ever-so-agitating female ability to do the complete opposite.

He opened his mouth to start talking and then instantly shut it. His gaze was fixated on the staircase across the kitchen that led to the upstairs family room, upper row of villas, and main parking lot. As if she were in slow motion, I watched gorgeously toned legs saunter down the stairs. They were covered by a long, pastel-colored floral maxi skirt and two very high side slits. A white spaghetti strapped bodysuit was tucked into the skirt, and the entire outfit was topped off with dainty jewelry and flat sandals.

By the time she made it to the bottom of the staircase and her face was exposed, I immediately recognized her from the market Pesca and I had shopped at earlier in the day.

"Francesca! *Benvenuta, bevi un bicchiere di vino.*" Mama ushered her to the island next to Pesca and me.

When she noticed us sitting there, she smiled and greeted us. "*Ciao*, Pesca!" Francesca kindly declined the wine offer from Mama and settled on a glass of San Pellegrino instead. I looked back to Gennaro, who had not said a word and was now looking at the floor with his hands in his pockets.

I trailed my eyes over to Pesca, who darted her gaze back to me in a shared, "What the hell is going on?" moment of uncertainty between the both of us.

Something was off—and neither of us could put a finger on what it was.

Mama seemed unphased by all of it. She was either the greatest actress of all time or completely oblivious to the incredibly thick tension that surrounded all of us. When I glanced over at Papa, the smile I had evoked from him earlier had completely dissipated.

Then, as an added bonus round of strong personalities and generally uncomfortable scenarios, both of Gennaro's brothers walked through the patio door on the other side of the room.

Gang's all here.

I was still trying to figure out why Francesca was there, and was partially confused, with my Spidey sense all the way ticked.

Within ten to fifteen minutes of more small talk with Pesca, Mama, and Francesca, and prior to anyone introducing me to Giovanni, that last glass of wine started tasting a whole lot like "Let's figure out why he wanted me to wear something red" instead of "Let's stage a family intervention to help these people remember why they love each other."

When I looked back towards the dining room, I found Gennaro sitting on a couch past the dining room table with Giovanni and Giuseppe. It seemed like they were engaged in another deep conversation, but my last glass of wine convinced me to head over anyway.

"Be right back," I whispered to Pesca. I felt her side-eye me but she didn't try to stop me.

As I slowly approached the back of the couch he was sitting on, I slid my hands over his shoulders. At the same time that he looked up at me, I noticed Giovanni squinting his eyes, looking at Giuseppe. Giuseppe responded with a head shake and a shoulder shrug, and I instantly felt like an idiot.

"Sorry, didn't mean to interrupt. I…" Mama yelled in from the kitchen at the same time my voice trailed off, "Can someone get a small basket of ripe tomatoes from the garden?"

Gennaro squeezed my hand and immediately stood up. "Come with me." I smiled, wanting nothing more than a little bit of silence, some time alone with him, and to turn my brain off from whatever was buzzing inside the house. But before we went, I leaned over to his brother and extended my hand. "I assume you're Giovanni?" He nodded and shook it. "I'm Mia. It's nice to meet you." I wasn't sure why he was surprised by the action, but I added it to the list of things that had confused me over the past few hours.

Immediate relief washed over both of us as we opened the doors to a cool breeze that swept through the patio, paired with the warmth from the patio lights and the sound of the pool filter in the background. We walked the stone path alongside the pool that led to the garden, but rather than stop at the small gated entrance to it, Gennaro intertwined his fingers with mine and walked me a bit further down and around the side of the last villa. It was completely dark with the exception of light reflecting off the pool from the half moon.

The anxiety, stress, and aggravation that built up over the course of the previous couple of hours had reached their peak as he pushed me against the side of the stone building and pinned my arms above my head. He hadn't touched me this firmly in all the time we'd spent together, but I could feel immediately it wasn't directed *at* me, it was just being taken out *on* me.

As he inched his body closer to mine, I felt unmistakable movement in his jeans. He was rock hard, breathing heavily, salivating almost, and we hadn't even started to do anything yet.

"I need you, like I did before," he whispered. I went to respond, but he quickly shushed me by thrusting his tongue between my lips, sucking on my top one and finishing by biting the bottom one. Then he stood there, hovering an inch from my face, looking down at me, still holding my arms over my head. It was his version of asking for permission to keep going.

I didn't have any words. Instead, I growled softly in my throat, while my body softened and my head rolled back, exposing my neck. My eyes caught his right as he smiled, beyond pleased with the non-verbal permission I had given him. Then, he grabbed my wrists with one hand, freeing his other, trailing it down the side of my face, over my lips, down my neck, collarbone, over and then immediately under the thin material that covered my chest. His mouth met the delicate skin of my neck as he massaged me, tracing the edge of his thumb over my nipple.

He had an uncanny way of knowing how to touch me and how long to before moving to the next part of me. I felt like a rabid animal, foaming at the mouth, without any idea what the hell was happening around me.

And I didn't care.

I wanted him as much as he clearly wanted me, which was evident by the way my hips had magnetized to him. Wherever his body went, my hips followed. If time had slowed, I likely would have felt all of the sensations pulsating through my body at that moment. My breathing consisted of rhythmic panting, my chest now completely exposed with my top bunched over my sternum, and my inner thighs seized like they couldn't wait to wrap themselves around him. But all I felt was the combination of my heart pounding alongside incessant breathing.

He slid his right hand up over my thigh, under my skirt, cupping me and rubbing lightly to feel what kind of material he was working with. His eyes grew wide, and he breathed in erratically after realizing there was a lace-up tie preventing access. He released my arms from above my head and used his other free hand to hike my skirt up and over my hips before kneeling down in front of me.

Licking his bottom lip again, he looked up at me with devilish eyes and a grin. "*Rossa…*"

"Told you," I smiled back down at him with my fingers woven through his hair, and I could feel his entire body release like mine had a few minutes prior. When we were together, the entire world stopped spinning. I looked up at the sky and could make out thousands of stars. It was a perfectly clear night with a cool breeze, and as I went to deeply inhale the air, I felt his mouth on the inside of my thigh, his fingers untying the lace-up crotch of the bright red teddy I had thrown in my suitcase at the last possible moment.

Never in my wildest dreams, hopes, or expectations did I think it would have made its debut here, at this exact moment.

His tongue trailed a few inches along the length of my upper thigh towards the now unlaced opening of the red lingerie. I briefly thought of the tomatoes we were supposed to be fetching for Mama, but I truly couldn't have cared less about them.

I stopped worrying about what I should be doing, how I should be acting, the respect I was supposed to be showing, and generally what anyone would think of the decisions I was making.

His tongue was swirling inside of me, parts I rarely felt

comfortable letting anyone else explore, but he continued to demonstrate how he was so different from any man I had met before him. He effortlessly mixed unbridled passion and desire with deliberate movements that brought out my inner animal.

In that moment, I realized how much I trusted him, and I allowed myself to focus on every sensation he was forcing me to feel. His mouth had made its way to the top of me, where he sucked every millimeter of exposed flesh. Shortly after that, as he flicked his tongue back and forth without changing the speed or direction, my legs stretched and tensed up, which caused my ass to clench. I only briefly realized how hard I was pulling his hair in an effort to brace myself as he brought me over the edge.

I let out an exasperated cry before releasing the rest of whatever breath was left in me and falling down on my own knees in front of him. At the same time, I buried my face in his chest, grabbed his belt buckle, and unbuttoned and unzipped his pants in what felt like seconds. I had no energy left to *ride* anything, but he must have anticipated that, because he laid me back gently on the grass which was, thankfully, dry. My skirt still bunched over my hips, the rest of me, easily accessible thanks to the convenient opening of the lingerie, all but begged him to come inside.

I pushed down his jeans and underwear, and he sprung out the top of it. Pushing both of my legs open, he slid his body in between them and crawled up to meet my face with his. He slowed down for a few seconds, allowing our eyes to adjust to the darkness of the evening light. He smiled, kissed me sweetly, and slid up and in me in one swift, hard motion.

With my legs wrapped around his waist, my arms wrapped around his neck, and his face buried in mine, he rhythmically pounded me. With his hand over my mouth to muffle my cries, he eventually pulled out and finished to the side of me.

He released his weight on top of me, his skin glistening with a light layer of sweat. Slightly soldered to each other, our lips trailed whatever inch of the other we could make contact with, and my arms ended up wrapping around his neck, holding him tight.

The entire interaction took maybe fifteen minutes, but it had impacted me in ways I knew I would remember forever.

I was wildly infatuated with this man, and beyond that, I had a higher level of trust in him than anyone I had ever been with. I was desired, I was wanted, and above all, I was protected and respected.

As I mentally checked off all these boxes in my head, I realized this was the exact type of man I had always wanted.

Confident yet kind, strong but soft when necessary, intelligent but with the innate ability to communicate, with an attraction I'd never felt before.

"Gennaro! *Pomodori!*" Mama was yelling for him, which temporarily snapped me out of my thoughts.

I stood up, pulling both my shirt and my skirt down and attempting to fix my hair while he did the same for himself.

We grabbed some tomatoes on our way back down. Thankfully, everyone was still inside. But as we neared closer to the patio and then the back door, we heard commotion.

Francesca was standing in between Papa and Giuseppe, attempting to push them both back as they screamed at each other in Italian.

Gennaro ran in to separate them further while yelling, "What the hell is going on?"

Giovanni remained on the couch, clearly entertained by what he was watching, while Mama and Pesca were hiding in the kitchen, visibly appalled.

"She's pregnant!" Papa yelled in between breaths.

Gennaro scrunched his face like he misunderstood something. "Who is?" he asked.

From the couch, crossing one leg over the other, setting down his now-empty wine glass on the coffee table and looking directly back at Gennaro, Giovanni chimed in calmly.

"Your wife."

CHAPTER 16
Gennaro

My cheeks were still flushed from rolling around in the grass like I was in high school again, but if they weren't red from that, they would have turned their own shade of crimson given the frustration, anger, and mostly confusion I was feeling.

I realized I was still holding Mia's hand about the same time I noticed both Papa and Francesca staring at me intently, their eyes gazing at our interlocked fingers. While I was aggravated for having to hide whatever I was doing as a grown-ass adult, I did also feel the smallest amount of guilt for parading it around directly in front of Francesca, given our history.

But then, I snapped out of it.

She's pregnant?

Who was the father? And more importantly, why did I care? Or did I?

What a mind-fuck.

I released Mia's hand, gripped my temples with mine, took a deep breath, and then attempted to calm everyone down, like I always did. "You're pregnant?" I asked, looking directly at Francesca.

"Yes," she responded, calmly.

"And who is the father?" I'll admit, I was somewhat interested in her response.

She squirmed, uneasy, her eyes darting back and forth, which clearly meant she wasn't about to tell me the truth. "I'm not sure."

"Ok, and?" I asked, and, not wanting to be rude, followed up with "I don't mean that the way it came out, but I don't understand how that news ended up with the three of you yelling at each other."

"Because she's lying to you. She knows who the father is," Giuseppe chimed in and put his arm around her waist. "The baby is mine."

I turned to look at Papa since he was emitting a combination of grunts and Italian curse words. He had one knuckle in his mouth while the other hand was balled into a fist.

"*Vergognoso*." He shook his head in complete disbelief of what was unfolding right in front of him.

With similar disbelief, I waited for someone else to say something, but no one jumped in. I felt Mia's fingers release from my grip as she took a step back. I was so intent on trying to figure out what the hell was going on in front of me, I forgot that she had heard Giovanni utter the words, "Your wife."

When I looked at her face, it immediately ripped a hole through my heart. She squinted her eyes with uncertainty and then, in what seemed like slow motion, the realization of what was unfolding in front of her turned into pure, unadulterated anger.

"No, no, no, no, no," I started stammering. "Mia, it's not what you think."

She calmly put a hand up, looked directly into my eyes, shook her head, and told me, "Stop" before telling everyone else, "I'm sure you all want to talk about whatever is going on as a family, and none of this has anything to do with me. Thank you for the dinner invitation, but I'm going to head back to my apartment for now." she glanced at Pesca, who looked as confused as she did and confirmed her confusion by chiming in, "Same here. I'm going to take my wine to go, though."

A little humor for the road. Pesca for the win, as usual.

I was partially turned on and partially concerned by how calm Mia was, since the calmer a woman is in an emotionally charged situation, the worse it is for everyone involved at a later date. Luckily, I knew she wasn't heading back to the States for another two weeks, and since I knew where she was staying, I could head to her apartment later to try and have an honest conversation.

As for right now, I needed to wrap my head around Francesca's pregnancy, why she and Giuseppe were screwing around, and why, or even if, it bothered me. I didn't necessarily know where to start, but apparently Giovanni did.

Mia and Pesca had left, and as if he were the one inconvenienced with this news, he asked, "Can we eat first? I came here to eat a good meal. The daily drama is the reason I usually stay in Florence. So, since I'm not married nor did I get anyone pregnant, I really don't feel like sticking around for the rest of this nonsense."

He really was an asshole sometimes.

Papa stared at him blankly before squinting his eyes and shaking his head while Mama swooped in towards Francesca to ask how she was feeling and seat her at the table. That was Mama, always concerned and forever trying to protect people.

We all sat down and started to eat, with the exception of Papa, who looked like he'd rather be doing anything else.

Mama broke the silence, ensuring Francesca, "Whatever you need, we are here."

Almost immediately, Francesca began crying. Giovanni responded with an exaggerated eye roll. Giuseppe threatened to punch him in the face. And Papa, still staring straight ahead, said absolutely nothing.

"I guess this explains why you randomly had a change of heart and offered to stay here while I went to Rome?" I asked before sticking a forkful of salad in my mouth, complete with tomatoes from the garden I just had sex next to.

The timeline fit, but he didn't respond to the actual question.

"We already have names picked out—Rocco if it's a boy, after Papa, or Marianna, if it's a girl, after her mom," Giuseppe continued. I was looking at Francesca. Her hand was still intertwined with Mama's, resting on her lap, but she was looking far off into the distance, completely spaced out.

Papa finally chimed in. "*Questo è folle!*" he bellowed, and he was right, this was insane for sure.

Truth was, the thing that bothered Mia the most, me having a "wife," was the exact thing none of us were mentioning at the table. Our family secret was about to come to the surface, but not in the manner we always assumed it would.

When Francesca and I had both turned eighteen, our parents married us off to one another in an effort to preserve our shared acreage for years to come. Neither of us wanted to do it, but we had no say in the matter. Well, technically we did, but unless we wanted to be disowned from our respective families, we really didn't.

The Belettas owned the vineyards, villas, and rolling hills of farmland. The Taglias owned their own farmland, barns with animals, and the thriving market that Francesca was running. Our combined land was highly sought after by real estate developers, specifically those who wanted to build rental properties to increase their monthly revenues.

Papa, as old school as he was, wanted nothing to do with any of that. He wanted to preserve the history, the culture, and the authenticity behind our family legacies, the properties, and the livelihood they contributed to. By marrying us, with a signed written agreement that neither party would ever sell their portion of the land to a non-family member, we'd be able to preserve the combined hundreds of acres for years to come, regardless of how many times real estate developers would try to sway us otherwise.

As an eighteen-year-old boy, I had no interest or desire in ever getting married for love, so the marriage portion wasn't a huge deal to me. Feeling *forced* to stay here for the rest of my adult life was what suffocated me.

Francesca was mostly concerned about getting the fairy tale wedding and reception that usually came with a marriage but it was something I vehemently refused. You could force me to get married via paperwork, you could force me to stay here for the indefinite future, but you couldn't force me to make a mockery of myself and someone else and pretend the entire marriage was anything but a political familial advance.

So, we had a short civil ceremony to marry ourselves on paper, essentially. And ever since that day, Papa and I hadn't seen eye to eye. I immediately shut down when forced to do *anything*, and forcing me to do something with this level of importance and long-term ramifications made it even worse.

Francesca, though, having grown up with an even more traditional family than we did, was essentially heart-broken that I wasn't elated to be "married" to her. We didn't live together, we didn't act married, we didn't spend time together. I stayed in my own villa, alone, the way I liked it. She remained on her own property, the way her father liked it.

So, my occasional run-ins with her when I would visit the market for last-minute items always ended with moody exchanges, bad vibes, and a whole lot of resentment on both parts. She hated me for not treating her like my "wife," and I couldn't stand that she was ok with someone else telling each of us who we should be marrying.

I had buried all of this over the course of the last decade, so much so that I didn't even think of it much anymore. I knew why she'd give me an attitude when she'd see me, which I would brush off since it certainly wasn't my idea and I didn't feel like dealing with the slack.

I was absolutely falling for Mia, but she lived in a different country. Because of that, I hadn't once thought about any of this marriage-on-paper stuff in the last few days. Being with her long-term seemed like a pipe dream, and I was intent on enjoying what I could with no regrets, regardless of how deeply my feelings seemed to be growing with each passing day. Francesca was the farthest thing from my thoughts, as she usually was.

Which wasn't the case for Giuseppe, it would appear.

I looked over at him across the table and suddenly it felt like I had time traveled back fifteen or so years. His face was long, drawn, and worried, like he had gotten in trouble for doing something stupid, which was usually the case when we were growing up. But, as I kept staring at him, I noticed the most prominent emotion coming to the surface—sadness.

"G, why the face?" I asked. With Papa turning into a solid brick of silence, as per usual, I had to take the reins to get anything accomplished.

"This is not how I wanted this all to happen," he said, lowered his head like he was ashamed of himself.

As if he could smell blood in the water, Giovanni took the opportunity to pummel him when he was down. "You didn't *want* to sleep with your brother's wife?"

Francesca winced, Giuseppe started breathing heavily, Mama whimpered, and Papa slammed his fists on the table. This was why nothing was ever accomplished in this family and all we did was harbor resentment for each other.

"Ok, we can stop pretending like we have a normal marriage or that either of us have any interest in each other romantically," I said, not mincing words, "and I mean that wholeheartedly, without any disrespect." Francesca could not have appeared any more uncomfortable, but I wasn't sure why.

Now that I was thinking about it, she usually acted weird around me, but I assumed it was because we both always hated being forced into this entire "agreement." I had practiced what I learned from family observation through the years, and because of that, I never really bothered to talk about it with her. I simply stayed away.

Mama chimed in telling me not to be rude, and while she and I usually saw eye to eye—with this, we didn't.

"I didn't say anything rude," I continued. "I'm just being honest. You can't force two people to get 'married' and then expect everything to magically work out. I refuse to pretend like it's anything more than it is."

"You can actually," Mama began, but Papa cut her off.

"*Lascia perdere*," he said with a short yet domineering head shake. And forget it, she did.

I rolled my eyes and felt the aggravation beginning to boil over. The two of them getting pregnant had now affected my entire night, and all I could think about was getting to Mia's apartment to talk to her.

"Ok, so what are we doing here? They're pregnant, it's not mine, and everyone's looking at me like I should be doing something about it," I started fuming, "which is standard practice around here, but I'm not taking the bait. This isn't my problem."

My eyes blinked to Giuseppe. "Little brother, what's the move?"

He looked back at me with worry in his eyes, like he was still a teenager, and quietly stammered, "I...I'm excited about it. I want to be with her, I just don't know how that happens with, you know."

"No, I don't know," I wasn't about to let everyone else off the hook. "You don't know how it happens with what?"

"With you two being married," he trailed.

Giovanni, with his consistently epic timing, said, "That's usually something you'd think about before bedding someone. A, is this person married? and B, but more importantly, is this person married to my fucking brother?"

Giuseppe's head fell back, and I could see the anxiety written all over his flushed cheeks and bloodshot eyes along with incessant foot tapping under the table. He brought his palms to his cheeks and then crossed his fingers over his mouth before speaking again. "Why can't we be the ones who are married instead?"

Papa burst into laughter and Francesca squirmed in her chair, still saying nothing.

I was concerned about whatever was going through her

head but found myself paying more attention to the aggra-vation Papa was causing everyone, especially me.

"What could you possibly be laughing at?" I asked him, narrowing my eyes as I looked in his direction. As much as I tried not to get involved, I always was. You could add this to the many reasons he and I never got along.

"*Stai zitto*," he said slowly. It felt like he was challenging me to say something more, even though he had told me to "shut up."

"Yea, I know you'd love for me to." I continued, "So you could spend the rest of your life telling everyone what to do with theirs. It'd be easier that way, wouldn't it? Your entire family would be miserable, but it would be easier for you."

My blood continued to boil and my anxiety levels kept rising, but I continued. "Let me do all of you a favor. I don't want to be in this bullshit marriage, I never have. We all know that. So, whatever you've got to do to get rid of it is fine by me. I wish you both the best, and there are abso-lutely no hard feelings, because I simply don't care. I want you to have a healthy pregnancy," I said, looking directly at Francesca. Then, to Giuseppe, "And I want you to figure out how to properly take care of a family with a whole lot more conviction than you currently have. You grew up these last few months while I've been in Rome, but now it's time to level up again."

Giovanni sat there nodding his head, with one leg crossed over the other like he was agreeing to terms being rattled off in a business meeting. "And you, try to be a little less of a judgmental asshole."

"What the hell did I do?" he asked, pretending to be shocked but with the smallest smirk on his face.

"You didn't *do* anything. You just are," I said matter-of-factly. It was true. He was a sarcastic jackass. It came naturally to him.

Papa sat there shaking his head, and Mama had finally loosened her grip on Francesca's hand. Nothing else was going to get solved tonight. Tensions were too high and we'd all activated our fight modes. I was used to this after the last twenty plus years of going through it.

"I'm leaving tonight to head back to Rome because I've got work in the morning," I told them. "I'll be back next weekend so we can figure the rest of this out." I was partially lying. I was coming back next weekend because Mia was still going to be here, but they didn't need to know that part.

I stood up, pushed my chair back in, finished the half glass of red wine that was still on the table in front of me, and then walked into the kitchen to clean it. As I was rinsing it out I looked through the window towards the pool where I had been with Mia a few hours earlier and felt so defeated. What a shit show this day had turned into.

"Gennaro?" I whipped around to see Francesca standing by the kitchen island, out of sight from the dining room table where everyone still remained. She was whispering, clearly not wanting to be heard. "Can you talk with me upstairs?"

"Yeah sure, I'm heading out there now anyway." We climbed the back-kitchen steps and walked into the family room when she grabbed my hand to turn me around to face her.

I froze in place briefly, because in all the years we've known each other, "Hello, how are you?" hugs and kisses were the only type of touching we had ever really done, like we were brother and sister or something.

She began to interlock her fingers with mine while looking up at me, and I instantly felt my stomach tighten.

I knew exactly where this was going.

"I don't know how to say this," she began, "mostly because you've made it really clear how you feel about everything." Struggling to find more words and looking like she was about to burst into tears, she continued. "I've always wanted to be a mother, so I'm excited to be pregnant…" Her voice trailed off.

I tried to soften my response because I knew she was having a difficult time, but I didn't want to be dealing with any of this. "Ok, well that's a good thing at least."

She shook her head and confirmed my thoughts. "I just always envisioned it being your baby, not Giuseppe's."

I exhaled deeply, loudly, and remained there for about ten seconds, just staring at the wall, not sure how to make it out of this conversation without hurting the already heightened emotions of a pregnant woman. But if one thing was certain on my end, it was that I was done solving everyone else's problems.

I let go of her hand and stepped back a bit to look at her from afar.

"The situation we're in, you and I, and our 'marriage,' is neither of our faults, but *this* situation," I pointed towards her stomach, "is the direct result of you and Giuseppe doing whatever you did." It sounded harsh, but it was the truth. "You and he need to figure it out."

I began turning the door knob to head outside towards Mia's apartment when she blurted out, "But I love *you*."

My thoughts from earlier were confirmed, so I was prepared with my response, even though it would initially project as a hurtful one. But deep down, I knew she didn't love me. She barely even knew me. What she was in love with was the idea of being with me, given our family history, everyone knowing each other, and the ease and convenience it all provided.

In fact, hearing her utter the words "I love you" when she barely knew anything about me only turned me off more. It was a phrase of desperation, lacking authenticity or any actual heartfelt feelings.

I had learned more of Mia, and she of me, in the last few days than I had ever cared to know or attempted to know about Francesca, and vice versa.

I wasn't about to mince my words in my response. Giuseppe had to man up, and she needed to grow up.

"You don't love me," I began. "You love the idea of me. I don't love you or the idea of us ever being together. I never will."

Tears streamed down her face.

"Go focus on your family," I said. "Giuseppe deserves that much."

And he did. He hadn't backed away from his part in it, and he hadn't denied it. If anything, he was afraid of my response to it. Truthfully, I didn't blame him for falling for Francesca. I hadn't been kind to her, but that's because the thought of her had been shoved down my throat since I turned eighteen. She was beautiful, kind, smart, and business savvy, which were all incredible qualities. I even felt a flicker of hope that she'd be able to help refine and mature Giuseppe even more in the coming years.

Now, it was her turn to visualize the same.

I turned back towards the door, opened it, and closed it quietly behind me. Before I walked away, I watched her slowly lower herself onto the couch, her head in her hands, tears having turned into a full sob.

Then, I walked up the path towards Mia's apartment, prepared to use all of the feelings, emotions, and kindness I was unable to muster in the last hour or so in an effort to explain to her exactly what had happened.

As I neared her door, the lack of interior lighting

became wildly apparent. She was already sleeping? Couldn't be.

"She left." I whirled around to find Pesca standing behind me, her hands in jacket pockets. She often walked at night after dinner, and I could tell she had just gotten back from another.

"She what?" I asked, stunned.

"We were supposed to go to Florence tomorrow, but she wanted to leave tonight. Her neighbors happened to be leaving when we came up from dinner, and they offered to give her a ride."

I walked to the nearest patio table situated in the gravel across from the top row of villas and collapsed into one of its wrought iron chairs. I put my head in my hands, exhaled, and felt a twinge of the kind of heart pain that I'd always heard about but never experienced. It was probably karma repaying me for the brutal mishandling of Francesca's heart from earlier, but I didn't necessarily think that to be a fair exchange.

I felt ridiculous saying it out loud, but I could tell Pesca was concerned. When she sat in the chair next to me, I took it as my go-ahead to make the admission, even though it left me vulnerable to her judgment.

"I think I've fallen in love with her," I said, like a little boy afraid of the consequences of his confession.

She smiled, warmly, then raised her eyebrows with the perfect touch of sarcasm. "Oh, you think?"

I immediately felt better.

"I haven't seen two people fall for each other like this since…" her voice trailed off.

"Since what?"

"Since Michael and I fell in love the night we first met," she blinked slowly, looking at the stars, and smiled again.

I couldn't imagine finally finding your "person," loving someone as deeply as they each loved each other, only to lose them a short time later.

"So, you don't think this is ridiculous then?" I asked as someone who rarely searched for validation or approval from others, but desperately needed hers at this exact moment.

"The only ridiculous thing you could do right now," she said calmly, "is to let her go without telling her how you feel."

"She thinks I'm actually married though," I retorted. "She's not going to trust anything I tell her."

"Listen, I didn't know anything about you being 'married' to Francesca until tonight, but I know how these things work and why your parents probably wanted it," she continued with her level-headed explanation. "But anyone paying attention would see that not one part of your heart was reserved for either Francesca or the forced marriage between the two of you. In fact, your distaste for this place is a lot more understandable, now that I know all of this."

I nodded in agreement but not convinced that Mia would understand the same.

"What do I do now, then?" I asked her.

"For someone who always has the answers to everything, you are certainly struggling right now, aren't you?" She was enjoying this a little bit too much.

I stared back at her with a minimal smile, my brain exhausted and my heart hurting.

"Go pretend you're Pesca Garmo, and spend the next few days in Florence with her, my treat," she said without an ounce of uncertainty. She texted me the name and address of the hotel and handed me her credit card.

"I'm not taking that," I said.

"Yes, you are," she was petite but mighty, and I didn't

bother arguing with her further. "All I want to know is that both of you get there safely. Then, don't think about anything else until it's time to come back home."

"I'm supposed to be working this week," I rattled.

"Looks like you've got to call out the next few days, family emergency and all that," she said with a shrug.

"Ok, ok. I'm going," I got up to say goodbye and squeezed her tight. "Thank you for everything."

"You don't have to thank me for anything," she said, and then after a few seconds of thought added, "but if you want to do something, promise me not to make your life more complicated than it has to be. Michael and I found our love was deepest when we focused on the simplest of things. Go there, be with her, talk to her, and just enjoy things together. The rest will work itself out."

"I can absolutely do that," I responded.

And I did.

I packed a small backpack of clothes, got in my car, and drove. I didn't think about Papa or Francesca or Giuseppe or my bullshit "marriage." I simply thought about spending time with her.

And, like magic, those heart twinges began to subside.

CHAPTER 17
Mia

I was grateful Alan and Diane offered to let me tag along, especially after only speaking to them briefly at the first villa dinner. Since I was heading to Florence a night earlier than Pesca and I originally planned, she would meet me there in the morning. It was late and dark out, so I closed my eyes, pretending to be sleeping in order to avoid conversations I didn't have the energy to participate in.

"Your wife."

It echoed in my brain, and my heart felt like it was seizing. I caught my breath, quickly realizing I had drifted off to sleep during the last twenty minutes of driving. My eyes blinked, bringing a landscape of beautiful rows of historic buildings and thousands of city lights into clear vision as we pulled into the Plaza Hotel Lucchesi.

Italy has an uncanny way of making you focus on the simple beauty of things. It doesn't necessarily minimize your problems or make you forget about them, but it helps to retrain your brain to focus on the things that bring you joy instead.

I was thousands of miles away from my actual home,

and while I'd normally check in with them daily, I hadn't spoken to my parents or my friends in a couple of days. I was reeling from the after effects of lusting after a beautiful man I randomly met. That's all it was, after all, right? Lust? It couldn't be anything more when I hadn't even had enough conversation with him to know he was married.

Married. "Your wife."

My stomach gurgled. I needed to check in with my "people" and regroup.

"Your room is actually available early," Alan smiled at me, interrupting my nauseating trip down memory lane. I think we were both thankful to be able to head right to our respective rooms without the need to force conversation. A lovely couple just trying to enjoy their vacation, I was positive they didn't need to be bothered by the ridiculous lust-affair triangle I had accidentally found myself in.

I thanked Alan for the drive and rode the elevator up to my room. I opened a large white door to be greeted with simple, modern decor that instantly calmed me. A brownish-gray wood floor led me past a dark-gray-tiled bathroom on the left with a soaking tub, large shower, and oversized white and gray marble countertop, complete with gold fixtures.

On the opposite side of the bathroom wall was a small side table with a gorgeous, freshly picked arrangement of gardenias and hydrangeas, a bottle of red wine, two wine glasses, a wine opener, and a soft, inviting armchair perched in the corner. A king-size bed cozied up to the sitting area, adorned with an elegant ivory comforter and about six pillows more than necessary, which was exactly how I liked it.

The wall opposite the bed boasted an enormous gold floor-length mirror, and in between both hung a crystal chandelier. Long tan curtains with a gold shimmer flanked both sides of the large sliding glass door leading to an outdoor patio and balcony overlooking the famous Arno River.

It was small, but modern, clean, comfortable, and elegant with incredible views.

I couldn't have asked for more.

But that short moment of contentment opened the floodgates to *wanting* more. I flashed back to the two of us in the pool earlier that day, the lines of his muscles trailing from his traps to his shoulders, back, and arms. His dark brown hair, soaking wet from swimming, and his light brown eyes that seemed to glow like warm embers, especially when he looked at me. His smile, which melted parts of me I didn't know existed, replayed in slow motion in my mind, over and over and over again.

I dropped my suitcase next to the bed, took my phone out of my back pocket, opened the slider, and stepped outside to breathe in fresh air while getting my thoughts under control. Another short-lived burst of clarity was followed with memories of us on *his* apartment balcony in Rome. It at once felt like no time had passed and an entire adventure that happened a lifetime ago.

I quickly shook my head from side to side, stopping myself from free falling down the rabbit hole that was attempting to welcome me.

> Mia: Gonna need you to remind me that becoming a lesbian won't solve my relationship issues

While I waited for Allie to respond, I texted my mom and dad in a group chat:

> Mia: Just made it to Florence

> Mia: (A day early)

> Mom: What happened?

Why did they always know?

> Mia: Nothing, I wanted to come tonight so I could get more time exploring tomorrow morning

> Mom: You're lying but ok. Just be careful, tell Pesca I said hi. Send pics tomorrow. Get a good night's sleep.

> Dad: I hope you've overdosed on pizza by now

I smiled. The man had a pizza obsession, which was where I got mine.

> Mia: I will overdose tomorrow in your honor

> Dad: That's my girl

And then, the G.O.A.T. chimed in:

> Allie: I'm going to need some more context and detail before I support your latest She-Woman-Man-Haters-Club initiation attempt

> Mia: He's married

> Allie: Hot cop from Rome?!

> Mia: Yes, hot cop from Rome. Married. Has a wife...

> Allie: Wow - the dudes in Italy are as shitty as the ones here

> Allie: Kinda makes me feel better about my choices earlier in life

Allie: We were doomed from the start, glad I got my ho phase out early

Allie: Sorry, haven't taken my meds today, can you tell?

Allie: Anyway, where are you now?

Mia: In Florence a day early, I excused myself from their family dinner before it started and after we ::eggplant emoji::

Allie: You ::eggplant emoji::'ed?

Mia: Yea, next to the pomodoros

Allie: You had sex next to tomatoes?

Mia: Kind of, we were outside on the side of one of the villa apartments, next to the garden. We were supposed to be grabbing tomatoes for dinner.

Allie: And your vagina just fell onto his eggplant instead??

Mia: Not quite.

Allie: How many times have you eggplant-ed?

Mia: I've lost count

Allie: Is it the best eggplant you've ever had?

Mia: By far

Allie: Ok, well...how married is he really?

Mia: ALLIE

> Allie: What???? I'm a benefit-of-the-doubt kind of girl. Maybe it's not quite as cut and dry as we think it should be.

> Allie: Doesn't Pesca know him and the family?

> Allie: I feel like she'd have warned you if he was a super dick, no?

It was a good point, and I had asked Pesca about it briefly when we walked back up to our apartments. She didn't have any clue about the "marriage," and in fact, she didn't seem quite as concerned as I was, which was out of character for her. We were all follow-the-rules kind of people, but something about her response to it seemed lax, like she wasn't all that worried about it.

Maybe there was an explanation? But I couldn't fathom what it could be. How many times would you have sex with someone, *while they were staying in your family's home,* without giving them so much as a heads up? It didn't make sense.

> Mia: I guess that's the thing, she didn't seem that concerned about it when we found out

> Allie: Ok, so you're saying there's a chance

> Mia: I have no idea what the hell I'm saying actually

I sent her a picture of the balcony view overlooking the river.

> Mia: All I know is that I have a river view, a balcony, a soaking tub, and a complimentary bottle of wine

> Mia; I'm gonna go play some music, take a bath, and turn my brain off

> Allie: You promised yourself you were going to enjoy everything

> Allie: All of it

> Allie: Keep that at the front of your mind

> Allie: I'm not telling you to bang a married man, but keep that brain off until you come home

> Mia: Yes, boss

I didn't really have any more clarity than I did a few minutes prior, but I felt better. I also reminded myself that I didn't *knowingly* have sex with a married man, so technically, I was not at fault. He was.

Another message came in with a ding, as I turned on my Bluetooth speaker and pressed "shuffle" on my most recent playlist.

> Pesca: Did you get there safely?

> Mia: Oh shit, yes, sorry

> Mia: Hotel is beautiful! Room is beautiful. Thank you!

> Pesca: Great, see you tomorrow

A short pause…

> Pesca: Room service should be delivering a bottle of wine shortly

I smiled, about to tell her the wine was already here when I heard a knock at the door.

Well, I could certainly make do with two complimentary bottles of wine.

I opened the door without looking through the peephole, and before I knew it, was surrounded by notes of Acqua dell'Elba Classico. The about-to-get-tipsy-on-wine smile I was sporting five seconds prior immediately changed to deer-in-headlights-what-is-he-doing-here eyes. My cheeks turned hot, I caught my own breath in my throat, my stomach turned—too soon to tell if it was a good or bad turn—and my knees actually felt weak.

Gennaro lifted his head from the ground and met my gaze in what felt like slow motion. Two caramel brown eyes stared back at me, saying so much without saying anything at all. He wore a white, long-sleeved thermal shirt, dark jeans, and tan boots, his gold chain necklace peeking out of the crew neckline.

I suddenly felt like a glass of ice water was more important than the bottle of wine I was holding.

"What are you doing here?" I managed to string some words together.

"I obviously have some explaining to do," he didn't break eye contact. "Can I come in?"

I didn't *want* him to go, but I knew he probably *should.*

My phone dinged in the hand that wasn't holding the wine. I peeked quickly at it and saw Pesca's name on my lock screen, so I opened it.

> Pesca: He smells better than wine, and he won't give you a hangover.

> Pesca: Vivi il momento, right?

If my voice of reason wasn't being reasonable, I could blame the next thirty-six hours of potentially bad decision making on her.

Perfect.

I smiled at my phone again and turned the screen off. Then, I looked up at him and moved to one side, motioning for him to come in. Locking the door behind us, I turned back around to see him standing next to the foot of the bed. I had yet to see him in any lighting that didn't suit him, but his tanned olive skin in a white shirt next to an ivory bed underneath an ornate crystal chandelier had me needing a fresh pair of underwear.

I swallowed with much difficulty since my throat was bone dry, but then, thankfully, I had a slight moment of clarity.

"If you're waiting for me to say something, you're gonna be waiting a while," I shrugged my shoulders and shook my head. This was not my issue to begin to address, and I wasn't about to go down the dark hole of apologizing for anyone else's actions. I turned around to the table against the wall and began opening the bottle of wine I was holding, waiting for him to say something…*anything*. The cork came out easily, and I poured two glasses. It smelled incredible, begging to be sipped, but Pesca was right. He smelled better.

Gennaro was standing behind me now, and there was no mistaking the scent surrounding me. His rugged hands, marred with calluses from manual labor, traced over my shoulders and down my arms before he intertwined his fingers with my own. Then, he stepped away and grabbed the wine glasses.

"Turn around, Mia," he said in a soft growl. My heart was already beating out of my chest.

I turned around as I was told, but only because he said it kindly and was holding the wine.

He handed me a glass and took a sip of his own, so I did the same.

Looking into my eyes, which I felt deep in my soul, he asked, "Do you trust me?"

I kept my gaze on his while my brain processed the question. It wasn't what I expected him to say to break the ice, but he was asking in a way that made it clear he truly cared about the answer.

I revisited our last few days together in my mind, reliving every which way he touched me, looked at me, devoured me, held me, and smiled at me. Mostly, the way he spoke to me. I *had* trusted him. I remembered holding on to his thick hand as we walked from the night club in Rome towards the rooftop terrace, weaving in and out of strangers on the street, having just met but with full confidence in his ability to keep me safe.

Now, as I stood in front of him, working through what happened a few hours prior, unsure of what the hell was going on with Francesca, I did what Allie told me.

I turned my brain off, because I absolutely felt safe in his presence.

I felt that same confident feeling I felt on the streets of Rome. I looked up at him, his body towering over mine like a fortress, which essentially answered the question for me. He was a protector by nature and I felt safe, cared for, highly regarded, and respected. He hadn't given me a reason not to feel that way since the moment I met him, so I decided he deserved a chance to explain himself.

"Yes, I trust you," I said, still staring straight back at him, my heart beating even stronger and faster than before.

He took my wine glass, placed it next to his on the end table next to the bed, turned back to face me, lifted his arm up and over his head, grabbed the neck of his shirt, and pulled it over his head before throwing it on the floor. He stood there, giving me the space I needed to process what I wanted to do next, but all I could manage was moving closer to him, closing my eyes, breathing him in deeply, and resting my head on his chest.

I felt his hands travel up my neck, holding my head gently before tilting it towards his. He looked at my lips for a couple of seconds and then sucked me in completely. His gentle hold became firm, like he had no intention of letting my mouth escape his. In that moment, I felt the rest of my body release into him. I didn't know what was coming next, and I didn't care.

I was living for right now. I was living for the sweet taste of a man who wanted me, who drove to me, who was ready to explain things to me, unlike anyone who had come before him.

There was not a single other place on planet Earth where I wanted to be.

Was it lust? Was it love? Did I even care?

I didn't.

I let him take charge in order to start explaining things the best way he knew how to.

And did he ever.

CHAPTER 18

Gennaro

Nerves aren't something I deal with often, but as soon as I pulled out of the villa parking lot and began the drive to Florence, a wave of anxiety rushed over me unlike anything I had ever felt. The stomach twangs I felt earlier had now paired with pressure in my chest topped with a dollop of what-the-fuck-am-I-doing? There was a generally easy-to-understand explanation for most of what was going on, but I didn't know what kind of mood Mia would be in when I arrived or if she'd even want to see me. For someone who was usually in control of all situations, this all felt entirely out of my comfort zone.

I had called the hotel as soon as I left the villa to confirm there was a last-minute room available, which was a solid backup plan I was hoping I wouldn't need. My body was craving a couple glasses of wine to relax and turn my brain off a bit, but on the other hand, I didn't want to stop thinking about her. Her face, her red lingerie, the tomato garden and surrounding areas, all of it. My memory bank offered a photo slideshow of the last few days, but I forced a control+alt+delete reboot, not allowing myself to get worked up when I had no idea what the rest of the night would look like.

I was thankful for Pesca though, as always, for helping me feel a little less alone.

Arranged marriage hidden from mostly everyone? *Check.*

Falling in love with someone who lived in a different country in three days? *Also check.*

I truly couldn't believe I had gotten involved with a villa "guest," but I obviously didn't know she was one when I met her in the middle of a night club in Rome. The fact that she knew Pesca made it different, too. I hadn't fallen for a complete stranger, which gave me a bit more confidence in my feelings, since Pesca spoke so highly of her. But regardless, I was now calling out of work, driving to Florence, about to knock on the hotel room door of a woman who may want to punch me in the face, with a bottle of wine in one hand and hope and a prayer in the other.

The Gennaro of years past wouldn't even recognize the Gennaro of today. But isn't that what life's about? Growing, evolving, taking risks, and living in the goddamn moment? It's exhausting, if I'm being honest with myself. I flashed back to how easy life would be living on property, doing the same work day in and day out, marrying Francesca as I was told, and growing old together.

Yeah, easy. And ridiculously boring.

While I still wasn't sure if anything could work between us, I was damn sure going to try. She'd know exactly how I felt, in every possible way, before she left to go home.

I wasn't used to sounding like a self-help book, which was also out of my comfort zone, but after an hour of trying to talk myself off a few ledges, I arrived at the hotel. Check-in at that time of evening was thankfully quick, so I went up to my room first, dropped off my backpack, show-ered quickly, grabbed the bottle of wine, and left for Mia's room.

Pesca had texted me a few minutes earlier confirming Mia had arrived and which room she was in. It was not lost on me how creepy this all would be without her as my wing-woman.

Pesca: Room 1119. I told her she's getting a wine delivery.

Gennaro: I feel like a stalker but I'm on my way

Pesca: Everyone likes wine. Stop overthinking.

Gennaro: It's not the wine that I'm worried about

Pesca: It's not the wine she'll be excited to see

My nerves intensified as I walked down the hallway to her room, but when I heard that she was listening to an Italian Pop playlist from the other side of her door, it calmed me down. Her footsteps quieted as soon as I knocked on the door, and her big smile faded into wide eyes and raised eyebrows when she opened it and saw my face staring back at her.

I doubted myself and this entire idea in the seconds that followed, until she asked me what I was doing there. I answered that I owed her an explanation if she'd allow me to give her one, and she moved to the side to let me in after receiving a couple of texts from Pesca.

Before long, after a few more short exchanges laced with sexual tension, I was standing shirtless alongside the bed, her head in my hands, her eyes locked on mine, with lips begging to be kissed. Tilting her head back, my hands wrapped behind her neck, my thumbs tracing her jawline, I leaned in slowly, my lips lightly skimming hers in between deep, pounding breaths. The touch of our tongues had set our hearts on fire, and after ensuring she was comfortable with me being there, trusting me fully, it felt like they were beating in tandem.

I had a lot of explaining to do, but letting our bodies explore each other first seemed a better plan. She had changed out of the outfit she wore to the villa dinner into a loose-fitting sweater and drawstring pants to match. Her bra was thrown across the bed, and her nipples were peeking through the thin material of her shirt accordingly. An inner animal growled underneath the surface, but I kept him caged for the time being. The purpose was to show her what she meant to me, how much I cared for her, how much I respected her, and how much I wanted her.

As I grabbed the bottom of her shirt and lifted it over her head, one of my favorite songs streamed through the Bluetooth speaker. It was romantic and sexy, starting slow and picking up halfway in. Her skin shivered as she stood there shirtless, so I drew her in closer, whispering some of the lyrics in her ear.

She instinctively wrapped her arms around my waist, and I lightly scratched her back with long, slow strokes until goosebumps formed. My hands slipped beneath the back waistband of her pants, traveling the length of her curves, cupping the base of her ass. I squeezed, digging my fingers into both cheeks, pulling her closer to me. Then, I lifted her just enough for her mouth to reach mine before setting her back down on the edge of the bed and pulling off her pants entirely.

She was completely naked, her long hair draped over

one shoulder, and her hands resting over her lap. I kneeled in front of her and tilted her head up so that her gaze met mine.

"I want you to watch me devour you," I said without losing eye contact. "As long as you want it." Her eyes glazed over, so I asked the actual question: "Do you want me to?"

"Yes," she answered quietly.

"Yes to what, Mia?" I was finding my rhythm now, having left all of my uncertainties in the hotel's hallway.

"I want you to take all of me," she sounded more confident this time, but I wanted to make sure.

"Do you trust me completely?" I asked one last time.

"Oh my god, yes, do it now." Her breath grew heavier as I watched the rise and fall of her chest and her still hard nipples. My hands met her skin at the smallest part of her waist before I slid them down and around her hips, over her thighs, and to her knees where I spread her legs wide. I hooked my arms underneath her hamstrings and pulled her forcefully towards my face. Her back now laid flat on the bed, with a good portion of her bottom hanging off the edge of it, her legs wrapped around my neck, clinging to me for support.

I kissed the sensitive skin of her inner thighs slowly, heading straight towards her bikini line. She clenched ever so slightly after feeling the light scratch of my beard hovering over her skin, grabbed the back of my head, weaved her fingers through my hair, and simultaneously let both of her legs fall to the side. Her body felt like it had collapsed into me, ready and willing for me to help her release.

So, that's exactly what I did.

My tongue trailed the length of her, slow to start until I heard her breath reach a distinct rhythm. When I stopped for just a second, she stopped breathing, which, in my experience, was code for *"If you don't keep doing what you were doing, I'm going to murder you."* I continued licking the length of her over and over at a medium pace, always ending a tongue stroke right on her spot. When her rhythmic breathing pattern returned, I slipped my middle finger inside of her, stroking upwards to the soft, spongey g-spot that was begging to be touched.

My unrelenting tongue and consistent finger stroke combined to turn her panting into a full-out moan. Her hands were cupping her own tits, her legs tightening further around my neck, so I didn't dare stop. Minutes later, her quiet scream turned into a whimper before her entire body seized up, twitched a few times, and then released. When I looked up, her eyes had changed color yet again—a deeper shade of green this time—and were staring back at me looking anything but finished, even though her body certainly was. She reached down, grasped both sides of my neck, and pulled me towards her.

She kissed me deeply, pulled my ear to her mouth and whispered, "Do *you* trust *me?*"

I moved my head back in position over hers, looking directly at her with a side smile, and responded with "Absolutely."

She smiled and then rolled me onto my back. Straddling me and teasing me with her nipples skimming over my lips, I thought back to the morning after in Rome, but this time, she turned around to face the mirror across from the bed. I propped my arm underneath my head with a front-row view of her slowly lowering herself onto me before peering into the mirror to watch her ride me in reverse.

With her hands propped on the bed in front of her, long strands of hair falling in front of her face, now beginning to stick to her neck, she rocked her hips forward and backward gliding effortlessly up and down the length of me. She was still soaking wet, her skin glistening to follow suit.

The mirror's reflection displayed her sensual beauty perfectly. Mia pulled her hair over one shoulder, running that same hand down the length of her neck, over her chest, and across her stomach before using her middle and ring fingers to rub herself while still riding me.

Our eyes met each other's through the mirror, and I could tell she was looking to see how close I was to finishing. "I'm right there," I reassured her. She picked up a little speed and found her rhythm with one hand on the bed still supporting her weight, the other rubbing herself more quickly. It was like a ballroom dance, feeling the rise and fall of each other's movements before bursting at the seems and climaxing at the same exact time.

I squeezed the sides of her hips before tugging on her waist to pull her closer to me. Our skin was sticking and our faces flushed as our breathing attempted to return to a normal pattern.

I lay on my back as she lay on her side facing me, her arm draped over my bicep and the heel of her hand propping up her head. Nibbling on her bottom lip, looking down at me, she appeared content, and looked effortlessly beautiful. Had I not been exhausted myself, my dick probably would have reacted to her again.

"I need you to know," I began, before she put her finger to my lips and shook her head.

"Not now," she said quietly. "Respectfully, not now. I just want to look at you."

My eyebrows raised, somewhat shocked by her response. I felt most women would be yelling or carrying on, demanding the truth by now, but she had surprised me since I met her a couple of days ago. Why would this be any different?

So, we stayed right where we were, listening to music, sipping on wine, kissing each other deeply, and oddly enough, just staring at each other.

I had never done anything like this before, always having someplace I needed to be or, more accurately, finding anywhere else I *could* be to quickly leave an "after" situation.

But not with Mia.

She was different.

She was excitement and comfort.

She was a challenge and a cure.

She was confident and compassionate.

She was strength, and she was absolute beauty.

She was the best of everything, nothing at all I had ever experienced, and everything I was terrified of losing.

CHAPTER 19

Mia

Opening the door and seeing his face had brought me comfort, sure, but mostly confidence. Confidence in what we were feeling for each other and where this could potentially go, so long as there was an actual explanation for him having a "wife." Sure, Pesca supporting it all helped me feel a whole lot more secure than I would have had I met a complete stranger, but honestly, I was still keen on trusting my gut.

His face staring back at me as I opened the door brought pure shock, not because I wasn't completely longing for it but because I wasn't expecting it. Historically, I'd been the chaser, always trying to prove my worth to men who didn't deserve me. Always trying to give them the benefit of the doubt when they didn't do something they said they would. Always the one putting in the hard work, allowing them to skate by with minimal effort.

Here I was, lying in bed with an exceptional man who I knew, deep in my soul, was a good human. I felt at peace when I was with him. He listened to me. He understood me. When we spoke to each other, he paid attention. When

I looked at him, he looked back at me with a profound longing. When I let him inside me, he filled me completely —physically and emotionally.

It was the stuff I had read about in books but never experienced in real life. I felt complete the last few days because of him, and truthfully, hearing the phrase "your wife" ripped me apart, because I knew how badly I wanted him for myself.

The morning after we'd fallen asleep wrapped up in each other in between sateen sheets, my eyes blinked open, slowly remembering where I was and who I was with. There was no "morning after" regret, but I knew I was ready for his explanation.

He was still sound asleep, though, so I quietly got out of bed, quickly freshened up in the bathroom, threw on a loose, long t-shirt, and opened the doors to the balcony. The air was warm, but the breeze coming off the river had a morning chill to it. The sound of the water echoed down the river, and the buildings that lined it were visible, thanks to the bright morning sun.

I dozed off for about twenty minutes after collapsing into a cushioned patio chair, watching the current while replaying everything in my mind—including how we met, how such few words had turned into such strong feelings, and then, conversely, had caused such uncertainty.

The sun began to radiate warmth, turning my skin the lightest shade of red-kissed bronze, when the sound of the patio door opening woke me up. He was wearing black, loose-fitting drawstring pants and a white v-neck t-shirt, which at this point was now my favorite clothing item he owned. The most attractive part of him at that exact moment though? He was holding two cups of coffee—a double espresso for him and an Americano for me.

"An Americano for the Americana?" I smiled.

"Just wanted you to have more to sip on so you could relax longer," he said before turning around and peering over the balcony, taking in the calm beauty that was the Arno River.

I fell asleep staring at him last night, and it was clear I still hadn't had enough. I devoured the sight of him from behind, his "*Impavido*" tattoo peeking through the thin, white material of his shirt. The outline of his muscular frame led straight down to what could only be described as a *perfect* ass. I was never one to notice an ass on a man, but I swiftly understood that to be because I had never seen one like this before.

His handsome face connected to muscles in the most perfect way with solid thighs, toned calves, strong hands, and a flat but not quite defined midsection—like he knew how to enjoy food whenever he felt like it but also worked out on occasion. He had the best of everything, as far as I was concerned. Thick in all of the right places, always smelling incredible, and when we were not physically touching, I wanted to be.

I was addicted.

But uncertainty won in that moment, and I temporarily snapped out of it.

"I'm ready to know now."

He slowly turned around, nodded, set his cup down on the table, and sat across from me. I wasn't sure what I was prepared to hear, but I felt my guard go all the way up. And, as he was beginning to do consistently, he anticipated it.

Leaning forward with his elbows resting on his knees, he looked directly in my eyes and said—without even an ounce of hesitation—"My parents arranged the marriage between Francesca and me when we turned eighteen in order to preserve land ownership for another generation, at least." He stopped to observe my reaction, but besides my eyes blinking while staring at him and trying to comprehend what was he saying, I didn't have one.

"Her family owns hundreds of acres next to ours, and we see real estate developers constantly trying to buy it up. I think you know enough about Papa to know none of that interests him, so since I'm the oldest and the first one to turn eighteen, he basically *told* me that's what was expected of me, without ever giving me an option to decline it." His head fell as he buried his face in his hands.

I winced. It sounded like a tale from the eighteen-hundreds, although that was probably my ignorance towards world history talking. In any case, it still seemed ancient and he could tell my brain cells were burning while I processed it.

"Francesca wanted every part of this, and I wanted none of it. Since the moment we turned eighteen, she's tried to make it a thing even though I made it very clear that we were married on paper but weren't going to act like it in real life. Which obviously is incredibly hard to do. The more I pulled away, the more she threw herself at me, my family, and the entire situation. It's a large part of why I ended up in Rome. I've never even had a girlfriend because I didn't want to bring her back home and have to deal with it. And now…" he trailed off.

"And now?" I tried helping him out.

"You're here," he sounded defeated and comforted at the same time.

"I'm hardly a girlfriend though." We had known each other for just a few days, and in less than two weeks I would be heading back to the States. Where was this going? His reaction to what I said seemed to sting though, and in turn, it hurt my heart.

"I'm not saying you're a girlfriend, I just…" he trailed

off, standing up, looking out over the balcony again. I stood up to be closer to him. His voice sounded pained, and he was getting frustrated, agitated even.

I knew enough about him and the time we'd spent together to know I cared about him deeply. If I was being honest with myself, I more than cared about him. But I felt myself holding back emotions, because I was either still petrified of getting hurt or falling into old patterns where I'd end up being the one who did too much. Actually, it was probably both.

I *was* living in the moment, because I had let him into my hotel room, I had let him have his way with my body, and I had let him begin to explain the entire situation, which I swore I wasn't going to do anymore.

No more second chances, right?

I was all over the place. I felt like I was doing to him what had always been done to me. Pulling someone in just enough and then wildly disappointing them with less than heartfelt responses.

I exhaled loudly, my eyes darting upwards towards the sky.

What would Allie say?

I couldn't text her in the middle of him baring his soul and family secrets, but I imagined it would go a little something like this:

> Mia: Mayday, mayday. His wife is actually from an arranged marriage his parents forced on him when he turned 18

> Allie: I wasn't aware Jerry Springer aired in Italia

> Mia: Seriously, what do I do?

Allie: I'm missing some information here, how do you know this?

Mia: ::photo of him leaning over balcony::

Allie: What in the hot-ass Italian man world is he doing there?

Mia: Surprised me last night

Allie: And now he's telling you he's unhappily and arranged-ly married?

Mia: How do you know it's unhappily?

Allie: Because he's standing on your balcony dipshit

Mia: Oh right

Allie: Keep up

Allie: You know the people who wish for opportunities to present themselves so they can escape the shit hands they were dealt in life?

Mia: Yea...

Allie: You're it for him

Mia: So I'm just an opportunity then...

Allie: You're doing it again

Mia: What?

Allie: Over-fucking-thinking

Mia: I hate you

Allie: Hate you too

Allie: Keep listening to your gut, but I swear you already know what you want to happen. You're just fighting it to protect your heart.

Mia: You say that like it's a bad thing

Allie: The only bad thing that can come out of this is regretting something you didn't do by the time you get home

Allie: If it all turns out to be shit, you quite literally never have to see him again

I put my mental text exchange on hold and slipped my arms around him from behind, resting the side of my head on his shoulder. We both looked out towards the river, our breathing synching effortlessly. I felt the rise and fall of his chest and listened to his heartbeat. He grabbed my hands, intertwined his fingers with mine, brought them to his lips, and kissed them gently.

One thing was for sure, if he was truly like any of the men I had dealt with in the past, he'd have bowed out by now. He'd have gotten laid a few times, had somewhere to be in the morning, and wouldn't have driven here to explain anything. He'd have already moved on to something easier or more convenient.

I felt *that* in my gut, for sure.

He turned around, pulling me towards him, his face hovering in front of mine, scoping out the scene for a go-ahead sign. When my eyes closed, my chin tilted upwards, and my lips parted, his hands traveled from my waist to my neck to firmly hold me in place. His lips caressed mine softly at first and with purpose in the moments following. I could sense from the way he kissed me that he was as confused as I was. Wanting each other, but respecting each other, wondering what the hell we were doing, and where it was going from here.

But one thing remained—I still trusted him. And, it made me comfortable enough to ask the question I was about to ask.

"I feel like we've got a hell of a lot to learn about each other, but do you actually think there's a way for us to be together?" I shook my head like I already knew the answer and wanted him to make me feel better about it. "Take the married portion out of it; you live here and I live there. That's hard enough by itself."

"All I know right now is that I want to try." He didn't take his eyes off of me as he continued. "Three days with you has made me want things I never thought I would."

"Like what?" I was never satisfied with a short answer. I wanted all of the details, *all of the time*.

"A real relationship, for one," he started.

I opened my mouth to interject with a "but" so I could kindly remind him that people who live five thousand miles apart can't have a real relationship, but he put his finger to my mouth and shut me *all the way up*.

"But nothing," he shook his head. "You asked me a question, let me answer it."

Hot damn.

"You're everything I want. The way you talk, your confidence, your humor, your love of family, your intelligence. I can take you around any family member or friend and it's effortless. That's what I've always wanted. And the way I'm attracted to you is an epic bonus. It's only been three days, but I know when I know."

"You know what?" I was half dying for him to confirm what I was thinking and also partially scared shitless of the admission. We couldn't be falling in love in three days. Absolutely not. This was some serial killer shit.

There I went again.
Inner Critic was ripping me a new one.

> *Mia: Shut the hell up; I'm trying not to get us killed
> or broken-hearted*
> *Inner Critic: Would you make up your fucking mind
> already?*

"I know when I know, and you'll know when I want you to." He kissed me again, and while it felt like a kiss to shut me up and stop asking questions, I was more than ok with it.

My phone dinged from the table behind us. I didn't want to break free from his arms, his lips, or the thoughts that were circling around in my head. This beautiful man was saying all of the right things and making me feel all of the right ways, and I didn't want to forget any part of it but, I wanted to make sure Pesca didn't need me since she was supposed to be arriving today. He kissed the top of my head and then excused himself to the bathroom while I checked the message.

Pesca: Everything ok over there?

Mia: Define "ok"

Pesca: If it helps, I had no idea they were "married"

Pesca: If it also helps, I know he doesn't want it

Pesca: And if it helps further, I know the only place he wants to be right now is there with you

Pesca: Which brings me to my next point, I'm going to stay here

> Mia: You don't have to do that

> Pesca: I usually don't insert my nose where it doesn't belong, but there's something there between you two. And I feel like you need to see what it is, without any distractions.

> Mia: I feel the same

> Pesca: Let me know what time to pick you up from the bus station tomorrow

> Mia: <3 will let you know!

"Everything ok?" he walked back onto the terrace as I put my phone down. I smiled as I looked back at him.

"Pesca is going to stay there." Now *I* was inspecting *his* face for a go-ahead. He returned a smile and raised me a slow head nod. "What are you thinking?" I asked.

It's every man's favorite question, isn't it?

"I love Pesca, but I love the idea of us spending time together, alone, a little bit more." He pushed a piece of hair away from my face and kissed me again. "I'm going to ask Giovanni for a few recommendations on where to eat and what to see."

I was a little taken aback. "You want him to know you're here with me?"

"I don't care who knows," he said without a flinch, "the same way they didn't care that I was the one forced to marry someone I didn't want to marry." He shrugged, kissed me again, and ushered me inside. "Go get dressed."

"Demanding, aren't we?" I joked.

"Only when I want something bad enough," he replied with another one of his perfect eyebrow raises.

I loved this game we played together, the battle of the wits. "So, you want me dressed this time?"

"The sooner we go out and get *cultured*, the sooner we can get back here so I can undress you again," he said matter-of-factly. "Now go get dressed, Mia Luciano."

CHAPTER 20
Gennaro

The most endearing parts of Italy were without a doubt the architecture, the scenery, the entertainment, and of course, the food. No matter which city you visited, you'd be able to appreciate the exquisite building design, intricate wooden trim and moldings, magnificent stained-glass windows, and textured walkways, all of which radiated historical beauty.

Add to that the music emanating from random street performers, the divine smells permeating the bakeries and restaurants, the pops of color shining brightly from a gelato or landscape display, and the couples walking arm in arm, falling in love with their surroundings and each other.

Now I got to enjoy it with an incredible woman walking next to me. I slipped my fingers between hers, grabbing full hold of her hand as I felt *myself* falling deeper. But into what, exactly? I refused to admit it out loud, to myself, to her, to anyone besides Pesca, apparently.

"Are you hungry?" I distracted myself with thoughts of food, which was the Italian way, after all.

"I know we're still learning about each other, but," she

smiled without even the smallest shred of shame, "I'm always hungry."

"I do love that about you." I shot her a small wink, because there were few things that made me happier than a woman who could eat. "I got a text from Giovanni because his law office isn't too far from here. He mentioned a spot to meet him for lunch if you want to do that?" I surveyed her face and body for a physical reaction, but she confidently responded, "Families usually love me, and of all the Belettas, Giovanni worries me the least." She shrugged with a smile.

I wrapped my arm around her neck and pulled her in for a kiss before exhaling loudly. We walked a few more Florence blocks towards the San Lorenzo Market. It was a large, two-story building that oozed with culture and buzzed with people, locals and tourists alike. Set up like a flea market, the bottom floor consisted mostly of shops and stores alongside live performers. Upstairs boasted a modern Italian food court.

"*Ciao*, Gennaro!" He slapped my ass after quietly sneaking up on us. Mia laughed and I glared, which was standard practice between us. "Mia, welcome to Firenze!" He kissed her once on each cheek and threw his arm around her shoulders.

"Let's hit the Chianti wine booth first and then grab a seat for lunch." For being the quiet one, he really seemed to come alive as a tour guide.

I reminded him kindly, "You realize it's the middle of your workday right?"

"Absolutely do. It's merely another benefit of *not* working for our father. I can do whatever the hell I want here, and I do it well." He certainly did.

Since Giovanni worked nearby, he came to the market relatively often, evident in the way that he waved to shop owners on our way up and the seats he effortlessly snatched as another couple was leaving. Pulling one extra seat over, he ushered for Mia and me to sit down and ordered directly from the owner. He effortlessly impressed us both by returning with three flights of Chianti to sample. "Hope you like red wine, Mia."

"I've gotten into it more since I've been here, and I really like Papa's," she said, referring to the villa dinner, "even though he strongly disapproved when I asked for ice."

"Yea, well, he strongly disapproves of mostly everything." His nonchalant honesty is refreshing. You always know what he's thinking and don't have to guess or sugarcoat anything. He appreciates conversations where others do the same, which is why I knew he and Mia would get along just fine. "So, what do you do for work back at home?"

"Well I *was* an event planner," she said as she started on her Chianti flight, "but I was partially let go and partially decided to leave before I came here."

"What do you *want* to be doing, then?" he asked like a somewhat concerned parent.

"Honestly, I have no idea. I haven't thought about it since I got here." She shrugged, confident with her response.

A few minutes of small talk later, and me doing more listening than talking, he put us both on the spot. "So, can I ask, if you're technically married to Francesca," he looked at me and then to Mia, "and you live in the States, what's your plan here? Or do you even have one?"

I wasn't feeling confident that I was prepared for this conversation.

"We've known each other for three days," I began, but he interrupted.

"And? I have never in the history of ever seen you like this with a woman." He motioned from me to Mia and back again with his palm in the air, shaking his head side to side. My appreciation of his nonchalant honesty was beginning to fade, even though he was right.

A server came over, and we all ordered pasta dishes with a prosciutto and buffalo mozzarella appetizer. It was a nice distraction, and while I was about to chime in and finish that part of the conversation, Mia did it for me.

"I came here without any intention of meeting anyone. I went to a nightclub by myself in Rome, wanting to see the sights, and I met him by complete accident." When she had something to say or a point to prove, she knew exactly how to do it. "The villa is the most beautiful thing I've ever seen, and everyone has been nice, all things considered." She turned towards me. "I've never felt like *this* about anyone, either."

It was more than I thought she'd say, but the Chianti probably gave her a little added liquid courage. Giovanni was smirking with a slightly raised eyebrow. "I'd usually have something negative to say right now," he said, looking directly at me. "Gennaro can confirm that," turning back to her, "but I actually believe every word coming out of your mouth."

"I can die a happy woman," she rolled her eyes with a smile and some sarcasm, which was the best way to deal with Giovanni. He loved it, and the longer they spoke back and forth, the more apparent it was that he really liked her. She kept asking questions to learn more about him and, in turn, me.

"Are you dating anyone here?"

"Dating is a strong word, Mia," he shrugged unapologetically, "and I learned that from my big brother. Unless it's with the right person, it's not worth the time and energy. I'm more of a hang-out guy. When the right one comes along, I'll know." She nodded in understanding, then asked a few more questions about the type of law he practiced, how long he had been there, and so on. It was easy, simple conversation, which was a positive change for once.

When our appetizer came, Mia divided up equal portions and handed us each a plate before making her own. We all agreed which glass of the wine flight was our favorite and bought a couple bottles to bring back home or, in our case, to the hotel.

My phone dinged, and seeing Marco's name reminded me I would have normally been at work at this time. I opened the message to see a single photo of my closed locker at work with some question marks. I slyly snapped a photo of Mia as she sipped on more wine and sent it back to him.

Marco: Ma che cazzo! (Get the fuck out of here!)

Gennaro: She's staying at my parents'. I found her in the kitchen there on Saturday.

Marco: And now you're where?

Gennaro: Florence

Marco: When the hell are you coming back to work?

Gennaro: Never

Gennaro: Kidding, be there Wednesday

Marco: I'm not used to you meeting women or spending time anywhere but the villa

> Gennaro: I'm not use to meeting women like this one

> Marco: Oh, shit

> Gennaro: What?

> Marco: Sei finito

> Marco: See you Wednesday

That was the second time I had been told that I was "finished," but in fact, I was just getting started.

About a half hour later, I was fixated on Mia and Giovanni's conversation. Listening to them playfully interviewing each other taught me that Mia's family consisted of her parents, an older brother and sister, and herself. They hailed from New York and also lived in New Jersey, which she said made them "hybrid" Italian-Americans. Sometimes Italian-Americans got a bad rap from the "real" Italians, but I always thought that to be bullshit. They knew how to celebrate their history, as much as they knew about it, and they added their own flare to it. I loved it, actually.

The way she talked about them was enviable. Pure love, adoration, with only a handful of eye rolls as she explained some of their personality conflicts, which every family had.

Clearly.

Remembering that her parents were great friends with Pesca was another positive, since level-headed, fun people usually traveled in packs. I didn't necessarily realize I was doing it as I did it, but I was envisioning where different parts of her life could fit in with mine.

"I've got to get back to work." We had finished our last bites of pasta and were feeling a little buzzed from the

Chianti sampler. It appeared to be a regular Monday for Giovanni though, because he was filled with energy, kissing us both goodbye, and whispering something into Mia's ear that made her smile.

"See you at home this weekend?" I was surprised he asked since he didn't usually go home on back-to-back weekends.

I nodded my head yes while looking in Mia's direction and asked, "You don't usually do two in a row. What's the occasion?"

"What's the occasion? One brother is married to someone he doesn't want to be married to who's impregnated by another brother, while the first brother is clearly in love with someone new," he smiled. "I don't blame you for that one bit, but this shit is great! Like a movie. I have to see how it ends." He winked at both of us and left faster than my mouth could string together an insult in reply.

When I turned back towards Mia, she was smiling with wide eyes before burying her head in her hands. Clearly embarrassed, I pulled her towards my chest, kissed the top of her head, and suggested we keep walking. She looked up at me, smiled sweetly, and nodded. I took it as a go-ahead to ignore Giovanni's commentary about being in love. If and when I decided to talk to her about that, it would not be in the middle of a marketplace restaurant with my brother around, of that I was absolutely certain.

We walked hand in hand through the side streets of Florence after visiting the duomo and stopping in to a few small shops along the way. I found myself with my arm wrapped around her, my hand resting on the small of her back, or my lips on hers multiple times throughout our walk. I could feel tension growing in my thighs when she kissed me back, alongside the smell of her hair and perfumed skin, and felt happier than ever.

Complete even.

Up until this moment, my life had consisted mostly of family tasks, school, family tasks, work, family tasks, and occasional reunions with my friends. It was the same cycle over and over again, rarely including things I actually considered fun or fulfilling. I was edging closer to thirty years old and simply going through the motions.

Maybe part of it was because I hadn't met anyone who inspired me to want more, until now.

We were looking through one of the shops when Mia wandered off ahead of me trying to find some souvenirs for her family. I was looking through a rack of random jewelry when one piece in particular caught my attention. I didn't hesitate to secretly buy it when she was buried head-first into a display of silk scarfs. I slipped it into my pocket without her seeing, not sure when exactly I'd give it to her. I'd do it when the time felt right. Then it hit me. I had never in my life bought anyone jewelry. I shook my head, fully confident in my pick and still surprised by how the last few days had taken direct aim at my heart.

It was mid-afternoon, and we decided to stop for a coffee after she paid for the scarves she had picked out. Most of our Chianti buzz had worn off, and we were both in need of a midday pick-me-up. My brain was in a fog, albeit a happy one. Feelings of "new love" were creeping up on me, and I couldn't get enough of her. I knew I had to go back to work and wouldn't see her again for a few days, so I decided to soothe the uncertainty with some fresh pastries and an espresso.

"Do they run Ubers back to Tuscany from here?" she asked me, somewhat nervously.

"I'll drive you myself." As though I'd actually let her get in an Uber alone.

"You're not driving back there and then heading to

Rome for work afterwards, absolutely not," she said, shaking her head defiantly.

"Why not?" I loved when she got passionate or aggravated about something. The way she strung words together to prove a point was unmatched by anyone I had ever met.

"Because it's unnecessary, and if I hadn't met you, I would have to be figuring this stuff out on my own," she continued. "Part of this trip *was* meant for me to hone my independence, you know."

The corners of my mouth turned into a full-blown smile, but I shook my head and looked away. She was sassy, sexy, and stoic all at the same time. She didn't like admitting defeat and had a whole lot of pride, but somehow, she managed all of that with the perfect amount of softness. I loved the combination of it all.

"How about we compromise and I drive you to Siena. Pesca can pick you up there?" I tried meeting her in the middle.

"Do I have a choice?" she asked playfully.

"For this? No. I'm not letting you travel alone if you don't have to." The gentlemanly protector in me was on full blast.

She stared at me for a few seconds before conceding.

"Let me pay for dinner tonight then," she suggested.

I wasn't budging on that either. "Absolutely not."

"The coffee then," she tried.

"Nope."

"Now you're being ridiculous." I guess she had a few more feminist qualities than I had realized, but this was how I grew up. It wasn't that women *couldn't* pay for themselves, it was just a sign of adoration when we didn't *let* them.

"I don't know who you're used to back at home, but you're not home right now. You're not paying for anything, you're not taking an Uber, and if you roll your eyes again, I'm taking you back to the hotel and keeping you there all night long." I smiled and tilted my head while keeping my eyes on her so she knew I was messing around.

When she played right back, it was all the more evidence I needed to confirm she was the perfect match for me. "That's supposed to be a punishment?"

"Depends how you look at it," I teased.

"Well, since you're demanding shit left and right here, take me back to the hotel, have me as an appetizer, take me to a nice dinner, and then have me for dessert, too."

"Thought you'd never ask." I grabbed her hand, our bottles of wine, and stood up to head back towards the hotel, but not before asking her, "You didn't bring that red lingerie with you, did you?"

"I didn't," she said as she positioned her body right in front of mine, then leaned into my ear and whispered, "but I've got something better."

CHAPTER 21

Mia

He was effortlessly sexy, leaning over the railing, shirtless, with his tattoo and muscle definition on full, delicious display. After returning to our hotel room and pouring some wine, he stepped onto the balcony and I excused myself to the bathroom. I opened the gift shop bag where, buried underneath the scarves I had bought was a small, *very small*, lace teddy. As Gennaro had been looking through the front of the store, I noticed a rack of intricate lace underwear, bras, and a few pieces of lingerie. One of them had an "L/G" size label on it, and I hoped my *grande* boobs would fit inside it.

"Fit" was a strong word in this particular instance, but I was able to shove them in there. The small pieces of lace, paired with satin strings, connected to form sexy cut-outs that barely covered my nipples and lady parts. Strings from the top of the nipple triangles tied around my neck to form a halter and behind my back to keep the girls in place, as much as possible. A two-inch-wide piece of lace connected the bra top to the panty portion (could a triangular piece of fabric be considered a panty?) and strings tied on either side of my hips, like a string-bikini bottom.

I slapped my cheeks a few times, brushed my teeth, and let my hair fall from the clip that had secured it for most of the day. A quick washcloth cleanse, a thin layer of lip gloss, and a few sprays of perfume had me feeling like a new woman. I quickly thought back to the few times in my life that I had gotten to this point with someone. Every single one of those times had ended in tears, disappointment, and regret.

As I stared at my reflection, I felt different. A more mature version of myself was staring back, confident even. I wasn't dressing up to receive validation from anyone. I wasn't dressing up to convince him to be with me. I was dressing up because he had already made me feel like half a goddess, and I wanted to return the favor.

I opened the door of the bathroom and peeked outside. He was sitting in one of the patio chairs with a glass of wine in his right hand, his left arm reaching behind his head, scratching it lightly. His legs were outstretched, resting on the patio table. On my way out, I slipped on a pair of black strappy heels that were packed in my suitcase, took a large sip of wine, let out a deep exhale, and opened the balcony door.

"You know, I was…" his voice trailed off as soon as he saw me. His big brown eyes slowly surveyed every inch of me, and his jaw instinctively dropped. He took his chin in his hand, tracing his own lip with his thumb while he calculated what his first move would be. If the first few seconds made me feel unsure of myself in any way, the following few hours were about to make up for it.

He stood up and held his hand out to mine. When I grabbed it, he slowly spun me around. Even with my back to him, I could feel his soulful eyes burning holes through me. He pulled me in close, with his hand on the small of my back, and then pushed me gently towards the wall of the balcony behind me. With both of his hands resting on the wall on either side of my head, his mouth hovered over mine before he whispered, "I want you, Mia."

I moved my mouth closer to his, sucked his bottom lip, and whispered back, "*Ti voglio anch'io.*" I wanted him, too, and thankfully Google translate had taught me a few key phrases while I was slipping myself into patches of lace and satin strings. My ability to speak three Italian words apparently had a direct correlation to his dick, which was now rock hard and pressing against my inner thigh.

I'd enroll in an Italian course as soon as I got home.

In what seemed like an instant, he had transformed from his usually low-key, even-keeled temperament to what felt like an untamed animal. His breath was heavy, and I could feel his heart beating rapidly against mine as he pulled me in closer. With both arms wrapped around me and his tongue trailing the length of my neck, goosebumps formed on my skin. I lightly moaned, which was all he needed to hear to keep going, even harder.

He used his knee to part my thighs, guiding me to a wide-leg stance. At the same time, his fingers trailed from the tops of my thighs to the sides of my hips before he grabbed the sides of my waist to pull me in even closer to him. I had never been kissed like this before. It was passion, it was desire, it was hunger and, the feeling was mutual. I salivated at the thought of him, wondering what was coming next.

Ever the mind reader, he kissed me while gently gripping the base of my neck to lift my lips towards his, and then he dropped to his knees. Still dressed in dark jeans and a black belt with no shirt on, I looked down, my hair dangling in front of my face, as I watched him kiss me through the small lace patchwork. With his hands on my hips, his kisses turned into long licks after pushing the lace to one side, and my light moan turned into a loud one. Anyone enjoying the evening on their own balcony would have heard us, clear as day, thanks to the sound-waves the river carried down its canal.

I didn't care one bit, especially since they had about twenty more minutes of listening to do.

When we finished, lying together on the lounge chair completely naked with bruised knees and sticky skin, he broke the silence. "Where the hell did you get that outfit?"

"You liked that, huh?" I was still reeling, feeling both flirty and tired.

"Liked it? I *like* pastries. That? That was perfection. I *loved* it," he continued. "And I..." His voice trailed off as his head shook from side to side and looked towards the sky. It seemed like he wanted to say something else, but I was happy just to see how content he looked in the moment.

"Let's go inside. This cement patio beat the shit out of my legs and knees," I joked.

"I'll fix that," he stood up, holding his hand out towards mine. "Let's take a hot bath."

An hour later, I was still soaking in the bathtub. The hot water had turned lukewarm, but the bathroom itself was still filled with steam. We spent about a half hour together, washing each other, kissing, and talking before my stomach started growling. "What are you in the mood to eat?"

One of my favorite questions.

He ordered food from the restaurant downstairs and went down to grab it. I picked up my phone to be met with a slew of new messages.

Mom and dad checking on me.

Brother and sister making sure I was still alive.

Allie being Allie.

> Allie: Did you guys elope yet?

> Mia: If by elope you mean double orgasms on a hotel balcony, then yes

> Allie: Hot damn

And Pesca checking on my well-being *and* tomorrow's pick-up.

> Pesca: I am assuming no news is good news?

> Mia: You are correct Madame. ::heart face emoji::

> Pesca: Good. What time am I picking you up tomorrow?

> Mia: 11 ok? He said in Siena

> Pesca: Yep, he knows where we usually park, see you there

I pulled myself out of the soaking tub with the little bit of energy I had left. I wrapped a towel around my head and walked out of the bathroom naked at the same time he put the key in the door. With a bag of food and a smile on his face, he looked at my ass like it was a freshly baked focaccia that needed devouring.

"I am calorically deficient," I said, smiling at him with a finger in the air. Every moment I wasn't having sex with him, I wanted to be. But as every woman knows, once you achieve the after-sex clean feeling from a bath or shower, you don't want to dirty yourself up again for at least a couple of hours.

I quickly lotioned and dressed myself as he set the food up outside on the balcony. I watched him pour two glasses of wine, and it wasn't lost on me that during every relationship or more accurately—*situationship*—I'd been in prior to this one, I was always the one doing the work. Being wined and dined wasn't half bad, and it continually tugged at my heart strings. He was the perfect mixture of respectful gentleman, care-taker, and protector, and Jesus Christ did he know how to make my body crave him.

I hadn't ever successfully finished during sex before he came along, and now all I could think about was never getting to experience him again after my trip was over. I found exactly what I had been looking for my whole adult life, and he lived five thousand miles away.

He smiled sweetly at me as I walked onto the balcony. "It's not black lace lingerie, but I love it just the same," he said, motioning towards the t-shirt I was wearing, which was his, and smelled exactly like him.

I looked at the table, which was filled with two pasta dishes, a small pizza, salad, dessert, and more wine. We clinked our glasses together with a "*Salute,*" kissed each other, and ate every last morsel of food.

The rest of the night we moved back and forth from the balcony to the bed, lying with each other and talking endlessly.

I learned more about his younger years. He seemed like a heartthrob who was very selective in who he gave his attention to, if anyone. The arranged marriage with Francesca really took its toll on him, and from that point forward, he hadn't envisioned himself in a normal relationship. The more she pressed, the less he envisioned the possibility of them being together. He hated pressure of any kind, similar to my not wanting anyone to tell me what to do, unless I happened to ask them.

We had so much in common. Our turn-ons, our turn-offs, and most importantly, what we wanted out of life.

We were two level-headed people who tried to do the right thing but never wanted anyone to take advantage of them.

We were two people who had a hard time trusting others fully.

Our chemistry was intense and undeniable though, and the comfort I felt being wrapped in his arms was something I had never experienced with anyone else. I felt cared for, protected, wanted, desired, and respected.

Being around him brought out the best in me.

I felt confident.

I felt understood.

Quite simply, I felt *valued*.

My heart felt a pang of pressure, and I caught my breath in my throat. I knew what was happening, but I couldn't admit it to myself.

I kissed him goodnight, backed into him, and clung to his arm that was draped over the side of me. With his chin nuzzled in between my neck and shoulder, his breathing became rhythmic within minutes. I matched the rise and fall of his chest and didn't open my eyes again until the morning sunlight beamed through the curtains.

I was lying on my side facing him with an arm draped over his chest when his phone began ringing. He slowly woke from the very deep sleep he was still in, patting the end table next to him. Once his hand found his phone, he grabbed it and brought it within a few inches of his face. Our eyes focused at the same time to see her name displayed on the screen.

It was Francesca.

CHAPTER 22
Gennaro

The good news was that the day could only go up from here since the mere sight of her name incited rage deep within me.

If I didn't answer, though, it would look like I was hiding something, which I wasn't. "*Pronto?*" I answered abruptly with absolutely no kindness attached to it.

She went off. Stringing together more words than I had ever heard her speak before, Francesca lit into me. I was thankful that all of it was in Italian, and besides widening her eyes, Mia didn't have much of a reaction. I maintained much of my composure, listening to her vent about Giuseppe being, well, Giuseppe.

From what I could tell, he had been drinking a lot, which I couldn't necessarily blame him for. He often felt like he lived in my and Giovanni's shadows, and now, after helping for half a year with a majority of the property, he was still being viewed as an outcast.

Granted, bedding your brother's "wife" and impregnating her was frowned upon in most parts of the world, but an honest assessment of our familial situation would confirm that worse things could have happened. The two families who wanted to guarantee land ownership were now going to have offspring together. The wrong name being listed on the marriage certificate was a mere inconvenience, and at worst, a reason for everyone to talk more shit about us than they usually did.

When her voice began tapering off, I told her I'd be there this weekend and we'd figure out a solution. I already knew that solution was to initiate an annulment of the marriage, and for her and Giuseppe to wed for real, but I also knew it wasn't what she wanted to hear.

I hung up the phone and rolled over to Mia. "*Mi dispiace.*" I quickly remembered I wasn't speaking to Francesca anymore and repeated myself in English: "I'm sorry."

"What was that all about?" She followed it up with a kiss, and it felt good to know she trusted me.

"Where to begin? My wife on paper who's pregnant by my brother doesn't know how to handle his drinking, needs to start getting things ready for the baby, and somehow that has become a responsibility of mine." I thought to myself briefly and finished, "I think that's about it."

"Maybe you should kidnap me and we can go missing," she smiled and rolled over top of me, pressing her lips to mine again.

I pretended to growl at her and lightly bit the bottom of her lip. "Didn't we already determine I can't kidnap the willing?"

"Fine, I'll put up a little bit of a fight," she winked.

If only that were a viable option.

"The last thing I want to do is leave this room, but we better get on the road if we want to meet Pesca by eleven."

"Yes, boss," she responded. "*Andiamo.*"

Pesca was beginning to feel like a favorite aunt ready to defend us when our own parents couldn't possibly understand the choices we were making. So, she was a happy face to behold when we saw her at our drop-off point.

"Did you love it?" She hugged Mia tightly and gave me a small wink and a nod over her shoulder.

"The hotel was incredible! So was the marketplace, and the shops." She continued looking back at me and smiling. "And the company. All of it was amazing."

"I am delighted," she said with that calming British accent of hers. "We'll have a nice few relaxing days, and then there's another villa dinner this weekend for new guests." Looking over at me, she asked "Are you coming back this weekend or staying for work?"

"I'll have to see," I responded. "I'm working through Friday for sure and have to see what's waiting for me when I get there today."

"Ok, I brought you some eggs, cheese, and vegetables so hopefully you don't have to go shopping," she said, handing me a basket before hugging me goodbye. "Drive safely."

Pesca waited in the car, telling us not to rush, but I could tell by the look on Mia's face she still felt a little uncomfortable. "She's been great, but I still sort of feel like I'm doing something I'm not supposed to around her." It was a weird feeling to go from balcony sex to timid high schoolers unsure of what to do next, so I tried to help us both out. I grabbed her hand, turned her around, and spun my back to Pesca's car.

I knew Pesca well enough that she wasn't peeking at us in her rearview mirror like a creep, but I pulled Mia in close to me, tilting her mouth towards mine. "I've lived here my whole life and never spent time in Florence like that," I said quite honestly, "thank you for that, and for everything else." Her cheeks flushed red and she shook her head, so I kissed her. Then, I breathed her in deeply, knowing how long the next few days were about to feel.

———

My phone had been dinging the entire ride back to Rome, but I was enjoying driving with the windows open and music playing. I parked my car with an hour to spare before I had to report for my shift, grabbed my backpack from the trunk, the food Pesca had brought, and walked from the large parking structure into my apartment building. Once on the elevator, I checked to see who had messaged.

Her name made my stomach flip, which is not something I remembered ever feeling before.

> Mia: Mi manchi già

I smiled.

> Gennaro: I miss you already…too

> Mia: Google translate strikes again

> Gennaro: I appreciate the dedication

> Gennaro: Almost as much as I appreciate black lace

> Mia: If you had to pick between the red or the black which one are you going with?

> Gennaro: If you had to pick between pasta and pizza which one are *you* going with?

Mia: I see what you did there

Gennaro: ::wink emoji::

I could talk to her all day long, but I opened up Marco's message next:

Marco: Do I get my partner back today?

Gennaro: Yes, be there in a half hour

Marco: I'll need a debriefing

Gennaro: On...?

Marco: Just tell me if we're doing a bachelor's party or not?

Gennaro: ::stop sign emoji::

And finally, the group text with Vincenzo and Salvatore, reminding me how long it had been since I'd seen or talked to them.

Vincenzo: What's everyone doing this weekend?

Gennaro: I'll be up there at some point

Salvatore: I need at least 14 beers, let's have an Osteria night

Gennaro: That was a very specific number

Salvatore: I've had a rough few weeks

Vincenzo: You've had a rough life

Salvatore: Thank you for noticing

Gennaro: Let's do Saturday

Gennaro: We've got a villa dinner that night, and then we'll meet you afterwards

Vincenzo: Who's "we"?

Oh, shit.

Gennaro: You'll see

Salvatore: Does she have a sister or a friend?

Vincenzo: How do you know it's a she?

Salvatore: Is this your way of telling me he's gay?

Vincenzo: Jesus Christ, I mean how do you know he's not bringing one of his brothers?

Salvatore: Are you G?

Gennaro: Gay? No

Gennaro: ::shrugs emoji::

Salvatore: See you assholes Saturday

Vincenzo: ::beer emoji::

It took me less than a second after opening the door of my apartment to remember that the last time I was here, was with her. The bed was a mess, pillows were thrown on the floor, and dirty towels were hanging from hooks. I took a quick shower, vacuumed the floors that were covered in a fair amount of her long dark hair, and put in a load of wash that included the sheets we had rolled around in. Thinking about it, I was truly amazed by how fast and slow it had gone.

I felt like I'd known her my entire life, yet I hadn't even known her for a full week.

I shook my head, looking back to make sure everything was in order, and, as quickly as I had walked in, I walked right back out to head to work. The elevator doors were closing when I heard, "*Tenga la porta!*" I held it open as requested and looked up to see Giustino's grumpy face, which grew into a wide smile after realizing it was me.

"Gennaro!" He hugged me harder than I ever remember my father doing. "I haven't seen you in a while. It's the new girl, isn't it?" I let out a loud laugh.

"Well, I went back to the villa this past weekend, but yes, the last two days were with her."

"American?" He inquired with a raised eyebrow. I wasn't quite sure where he was going with it, but I played along.

"God Bless America, right?" I responded.

A series of odd sounds, hand slaps, and shoulder nudges later, I understood fully that Giustino was a ladies' man back in his prime. How much *respect* he had for women was questionable, but he certainly loved spending time with them. After skirting around most of the specifics, I gave him a few details to satisfy his inner perv and made my way to the precinct for my next interrogation.

It was around two in the afternoon, and I was already exhausted with an eight hour shift ahead of me. "*Bentornato!*" Marco's voice echoed throughout the locker room. When I turned around to greet him, he immediately began his assault. "Just tell me how many times."

I punched him in the shoulder. "What are you, fifteen?"

"We have gone out together so many times and I've never *ever* seen you with anyone, which means we only ever talk about me and my horrible taste in women," he continued, matter-of-factly. "Thankfully, it's your turn now. Let me hear it."

I battled with myself for a few seconds about how much I wanted to admit to him. On one hand, guys don't usually talk about this stuff in detail, but on the other, I wanted an unbiased opinion on what the hell I was getting myself into.

I inhaled and held my breath for a few seconds while he examined me, not sure what I was going to tell him.

"I think I fell in love with an American." I grimaced, waiting for his reaction. I didn't necessarily need him to understand me, but I wasn't in the mood for any relentless ball breaking.

He looked me up and down, and I could tell was choosing his next words carefully.

"Are you waiting for me to tell you that you're a dumb-ass?" he asked, his facial expression still inquisitive.

"I have no idea what the hell I'm waiting for you to tell me. Just don't bust my balls. I'm tired." I wasn't usually dramatic, but the last five days had finally caught up to me.

"G, you have to be one of the most level-headed, patient, confident guys I know," he replied, his expression softened from overly curious to empathetic, "and the look on your face right now is…"

"What?" I asked, interrupting him.

I need some of Sal's fourteen beers.

"You're acting like you got her pregnant or something," he said. "If you fell for her, what's wrong with that?"

I was a little surprised by the direction the conversation had taken. "She's only here for another week and then she leaves. What is the point of falling for someone who doesn't live here?" I was tired and suddenly aggravated.

He sat on the bench across from me. "Ok, first you need like twelve hours of sleep, a pizza, or both," he said, surveying my face. "I know you well enough to know you turn into a dickhead whenever you're hungry or tired. And second, have you ever heard of long-distance relationships or, dare I say, moving to be close to one another?"

My head rolled backwards, looking up at the ceiling, ingesting all of what he was saying. I knew what I was feeling was love, but I also honestly knew I wasn't in the leave-Italy-and-move-to-the-States stage of my life. If it were a few years ago, I might have considered it, but now, having graduated from the academy with an entirely new career, it wasn't something I'd be willing to do.

How would that be fair to her?

"I could never move there, and after learning more about her and how close she is with her family, I doubt she'd move here," I spewed.

"Focus on each single day. If you waste time worrying about it now, you're going to regret not enjoying the rest of the time she has left," he shrugged—and he was right.

I was getting ahead of myself, which I normally didn't do, but his simple questions had my brain reeling. I also had never had quite this deep of a conversation with him before. Our time together was usually spent venting about work and family while I watched him soak up the daily attention from being a police officer.

"I think it's cool you finally found someone you enjoy being around that much," he added. "Now I feel a little less like a man-whore."

"To be clear, I'm not trying to bed her just to bed her." He looked back at me and shrugged his shoulders.

"No idea what you're talking about man." He clapped his hands and pointed towards the door with his thumb for us to get moving towards roll call. "Stop overthinking and enjoy what you can. Oh, and let's go get a pizza."

A few hours into our shift and one shared pizza later, I took my phone out to send a quick message to her.

Gennaro: What's happening at the villa today?

Mia: ::picture of her lounging by the pool::

I bit my knuckle.

Gennaro: Mi stai ammazzando...

Mia: Hold on lemme Google translate that

Mia: I'm killing YOU?

Mia: My body hurts in places I didn't know existed

I smiled from ear to ear.

Gennaro: I'd apologize but I'm not sorry

Mia: ::picture of her sipping on some wine::

Gennaro: ::picture at work with Marco::

Mia: Men in uniform...

Mia: You look like you smell delicious

Gennaro: A little old lady did just tell me I smelled good when we got a pizza

Mia: She's got good taste

Mia: Be careful

Mia: Call me when you're done if you can

Gennaro: It'll be late

Mia: I'm a big girl

Mia: I'll leave my ringer on

Thinking about that phone call got me through the next six hours effortlessly. I clocked out, headed back home, and was thankful for the groceries Pesca had given me. I made a quick potato and egg omelet, showered, pulled the sheets from the dryer, and made the bed. Music was playing in the background. I poured myself a gin and seltzer, grabbed my phone, sat on the balcony, and Face-Timed her.

I didn't text before to see if she was ready, as was standard practice, but I was glad I hadn't.

When she answered, she was in bed, with no makeup on, under the covers. With her hand over her face, she said, "I assumed this would be a phone call."

"You assumed wrong, Mia Luciano," I growled.

"If you could stop saying my full name like that, I'd appreciate it," she responded in her classic sarcastic tone.

"Does it bother you?"

"It bothers my insides a little," she smiled.

"How *are* your insides?"

"Probably rearranged, but I'll worry about that when I get home."

Her words hit me right in the gut. "Don't mention going home, please."

"Ok, let's focus on when I'm going to see you again," she suggested.

"I have to work late on Friday, so I'll probably come Saturday morning." And then I remembered to ask, "Do you want to meet some of my friends Saturday night?"

Her smile grew. "I would love to, Gennaro Beletta."

"How come you can say my name and I can't say yours?" If anyone were watching my facial expressions as I flirted back and forth with her, they'd be mortified for me, I was sure of it.

"I make the rules here, sir."

"Since when?" I asked with an incredulous look on my face.

"Since I rocked your world with black lace and satin ties."

We talked for an hour before we started dozing off. Our "goodbye" was the kind that took ten minutes longer than necessary, where neither party wanted to be the one to hang up the phone. I shook my head, my smile reflecting back at me in the mirror as I brushed my teeth. The stress from the day had completely dissipated after looking at her face for an hour. And then, as I crawled into bed, I realized I still had two more days of work before I'd be able to see her again.

I mentioned I'd be getting there Saturday morning, but decided I'd surprise her Friday night instead.

And surprise her I did.

CHAPTER 23

Mia

The beauty that emanated from the villa and the peace it brought me was unmatched by any other place I had traveled to in my life. I had spent the last few days with Pesca and Mama, trying to help out in the kitchen more than they would let me, so I ended up poolside and sunbathing for a fair number of hours as a result. It was my favorite spot on the whole property thanks to the calm ripples in the pool water, the bird's chirping in the not so far away distance, and the picturesque rolling hill vineyards that surrounded it. Add to that a couple glasses of wine, perfect weather, and amazing food, and I was all but vacationing in an HGTV special.

I had gotten myself into a nice little routine, having breakfast in my own villa and then catching up on life or doing something productive to help Mama out. Yesterday, Pesca and I drove around to explore the smaller towns close by, then ate dinner at the Osteria down the street. She knew the owner and introduced me as a friend of the Beletta family. He was a kind, funny, and respectfully flirty older man, talking to me about living in the States and asking how I liked it in Tuscany. When I couldn't stop listing all of the things I loved, he shot Pesca a quick glance, joking how it's never the ones who grow up here who love it. It seemed like he was referring to the Belettas, but I convinced myself I was reaching.

I spent a majority of Friday poolside, which I absolutely needed. Traveling and a lack of sleep had caught up to me a second time after finally adjusting to the time difference. Spending the last week or so having the most sex in my entire adult life was a win in *many* columns, but not the restful one.

Ever since I had left Gennaro earlier in the week, we texted back and forth throughout the day and Facetimed at night when he was back home in his apartment. While the tension was always palpable, I loved that it stayed flirty without him attempting to get me naked on the phone. In fact, it seemed we had some of our best conversations during those evening Facetimes, when we couldn't be distracted by wanting each other physically.

Truthfully, it made me trust him even more. I didn't know many men who genuinely wanted to talk on a phone for hours on end, especially when it wasn't going to result in a *release* of any kind. He didn't seem to *only* want sex, and because he didn't, it made me want it with him even more.

I turned the shower water off and wrapped myself in a towel, pleased with the reflection staring back at me in the bathroom mirror. I was sun-kissed but not burnt and had a natural looking glow about me. A not-so-quick skincare regimen later, my face looked like a glazed donut. Some lip balm, body butter, and body spray sealed the deal, and I couldn't wait to get into bed. A day of sun and a big dinner with Papa, Mama, and Pesca was enough to exhaust a girl. I had a book lined up to read while I waited for Gennaro to Facetime when he got home from work.

But he didn't.

Years of "dating" trauma had prepared me for this moment, since it undoubtedly always came. Conversations that started out exciting reached a predictable pattern, then ended with someone bailing. But where I used to overanalyze and turn into a half-mental case, I leaned into my new mantra instead.

He was probably still working, he'd be here in the morning, and I had a comfortable bed and a good book waiting for me. I slipped into loose, black satin shorts with a matching tank top, and layered a cozy duster cardigan over top of it. In no time at all, I had become proficient in managing warm Italian days that turned into cool Italian nights.

With the ceiling fan on low, I propped up some pillows, climbed into bed, and resisted the urge to get under the covers. It was just shy of ten o'clock, and while I was tired, I wasn't quite ready to go to sleep—or so I thought.

My brain started computing the light knocking at the door before I was able to generate any physical movement. For a brief moment, I forgot where I was until my eyes blinked open, the fan still circulating, the end table light on, and my book lying next to me like a rejected outcast without so much as a crease in its spine. Next to it was my phone, the screen of which was lit up. I grabbed it, saw his name, smiled, and then realized it was quarter past eleven. I had fallen asleep for a little over an hour after reading a maximum of three sentences.

His messages spanned a half hour, from quarter to eleven to this exact moment. There were also two missed calls and three dots were currently bubbling as he continued typing.

> Gennaro: Special delivery

5 minutes later

> Gennaro: This will require you to open the door

10 minutes later

> Gennaro: Mia Luciano

> Gennaro: I will break down the door if you don't wake up

5 minutes later

> Gennaro: I decided not to break down the door since I'd be the one to fix it anyway

> Gennaro: But it'd be cool if you'd let me in

And the latest…

> Gennaro: This is the first and last time I ever surprise your sleepy ass

I climbed out of bed without any idea of what I looked like, hoping there were some remnants of toothpaste, lip balm, and body spray lingering. As I opened my bedroom door, his ridiculously gorgeous face was staring back at me through the glass window of the villa door. Wearing dark gray sweatpants, a matching hooded sweatshirt, and black sneakers, his hair looked perfect, which I knew to mean he was freshly showered and smelled delicious. My heart skipped several beats, and I felt undeniable pressure in my thighs.

I opened the door with a shy, sweet smile as he pretended to be mad that I left him waiting outside my door for a half hour. "I could have texted before I left," he shrugged, "but I figured that would ruin the surprise." He dragged his hand up and down, indicating himself like Vanna White, and continued, "It's me. I'm the surprise."

I thoroughly enjoyed this side of his personality, his humor on full display. Words failed me as I smiled back at him, pressing my lips together and holding in a full burst of laughter as my cheeks burned in the process. "Ok, I'll try again tomorrow." He pretended to walk away, and as I reached out to turn him back around, he snatched my hand like a jiu-jitsu instructor, pulling me into a headlock and kissing me like the three days since we had seen each other had actually been three months.

"I'd pretend to threaten you if you ever left me out here looking like an asshole again," he kissed again, "but I know how much you love being told what to do."

"You think you know me pretty well for one week, don't you?" I grazed my lips over his neck, slipped both arms around his lower back, and hovered close to his mouth waiting for him to kiss me again.

"Invite me in so I can show you how well I know you." His bold eyes turned a sweet, sinister shade of caramel brown, and I could hear him growl ever so slightly.

"But you're going to mess up my hair." I kept up the charade, because it simply came naturally to us.

He played along effortlessly, "I'm gonna do a lot more than that."

I woke up early, thanks to the loud flock of birds yammering right outside the villa door. The sun was taunting me, its blinding rays peering through the curtains. Still, there was nowhere else in the world I wanted to be, regardless of the time. I rolled from my left side to my right, away from the window, now facing the back of him. I scooted closer, acting as the big spoon, with my arm draped over the small of his waist, trailing kisses across his tattooed back muscles. He stirred, grabbed my hand, kissed the side of my thumb, and then rested our intertwined fingers alongside his chest.

Within minutes, I had fallen back asleep.

When my eyes opened again, the sun was shining as brightly as it was earlier, and while the birds had finally given it a rest, they had been replaced by the sound of a mower. I nudged him awake, partially because I wanted to look at him but also because I wasn't sure if he was supposed to be out there helping. Papa had spoken to me briefly the day before, and since it felt like the possible start of a breakthrough, I selfishly didn't want our progress to be ruined if Gennaro didn't show up on time.

"Are you supposed to be helping them outside?" I whispered, trying not to wake him up while simultaneously waking him up.

"Not until eight," he grunted.

Oh dear.

"It's nine, baby."

There it was. A "baby." I pulled the covers off of us and stood up on sore legs. I immediately remembered why my entire body hurt and why "baby" flew off of my tongue so effortlessly. How could I forget, really? This man had finished me twice in two hours.

After making him a quick plate of food as a late dinner, he decided to indulge further with me for dessert. With one leg hanging off the kitchen table and another propped up on the chair in front of it, I held on to his head for support as he kneeled down in front of me, licking and sucking, until I completely came undone.

Quickly after that, he ushered me into the bedroom where what started in the actual bed ended up with me bent over an armchair and out of breath, after finishing for a second time on the floor. My knees were bruised, my thighs trembled, and my jaw was a little tight, too.

I hadn't had a sip of wine either, which meant one thing.

I was really, really comfortable with him.

"Did you say nine?" he finally clocked in.

"I sure did," I said, turning the shower water on.

"*Fuck me.*" He shot out of bed and threw his clothes on.

"Did that already," I smiled, proud of my early morning wit.

He smiled back and headed towards the bathroom. "Will you get grossed out if I use your toothbrush? I don't feel like walking to my room to get mine."

"Our mouths were in worse places last night. Go ahead," I answered.

"Worse is a strong word." He splashed water on his face, drank what was left of the glass of water on the nightstand on his way out, and teased, "and I'm planning to put my mouth in all of those places again later."

"Oh yea? What time?" I asked, mostly jokingly, but also curious as to what we'd do together later on.

"Actually, I wanted to bring you to meet my two best friends tonight at the Osteria up the road."

I smiled and confidently responded, "Can't wait."

"I gotta get out there, but I'll be around all day. Come distract me as you see fit." He kissed the top of my head, lightly patted my ass, and walked out in a hurry, leaving his backpack and phone in my room.

I showered, made myself a quick breakfast of almond cookies, fruit, and yogurt, brewed an espresso, and texted Pesca to see what she was up to.

> Mia: Mom? It's your adopted daughter
>
> Mia: What are you doing?
>
> Pesca: Getting eggs fresh out of a chicken's arse
>
> Pesca: Heading to the kitchen next
>
> Mia: Meet you there

I walked the short distance from my villa along the gravel pathway to the main house, then down the steps to the kitchen. Pesca was helping Mama out, as she usually was, prepping food for the evening's villa dinner. Papa was in the living room rifling through a notebook, taking notes, and shouting at someone on the phone. When he was finished, he hung up in a huff, came in, shouted it all right back to Mama, and walked back out. She stood there looking stunned, and since I couldn't speak or understand a lick of Italian without Google Translate nearby, I was at a loss for what to say, if anything.

Pesca chimed in, speaking nearly fluent Italian, and as I studied both of their expressions, I was unsuccessful at decoding the issue. Mama looked sad and frustrated and Papa was angry, although from all I knew of him, that was the norm. After excusing herself out the back door, Pesca and I remained in the kitchen. I looked towards her with inquisitive eyes, and she motioned for me to hold on. After peering out the kitchen sink window to get eyes on both of them, she turned around and quietly told me, "They're still arguing over Gennaro, Francesca, and Giuseppe."

My heart sank and my face flushed, but while my first instinct was to blame myself, I knew all too well Gennaro wouldn't stay married to her if she was pregnant with Giuseppe's baby, even *without* me in the picture. While I was perhaps the current scapegoat, this entire scenario would likely be happening even if I'd never showed up here. In fact, Gennaro would probably have been in Rome for most of it and wouldn't even know yet.

"What's there to argue about?" I asked without hesitation. "And by that, I mean, who exactly are they mad at?"

"I think they're mad in general. With Papa, he's lost control of the situation. For him, it was essentially a business transaction." Her face looked about as sad as my heart felt.

I grimaced at the thought. *How did he have the right?*

"And for Mama, she's just always in the middle of it all. She'd love for Francesca and Giuseppe to be happily together but…" Her voice trailed off.

"But?" I asked with a tilted head and accusatory eyes.

"Francesca can't kick her Gennaro habit, apparently." She looked at me for my reaction, but what could I say? "No, he's mine"? I was a passionate gal, but I wasn't psychotic. I had feelings for him, a lot of them, but I knew my time here was limited, and neither one of us had promised the other dual citizenship.

"I can't blame her," I matter-of-factly said. The slow shrug of my shoulders and Pesca's raised eyebrows in response showed me she agreed. As we finished cleaning up, the back door slammed, and in walked Mama, followed by Papa.

They continued their passionate Italian shouting match before realizing we were both still in the kitchen. By the looks of it, Pesca had understood every word they had spoken. Their eyes darting back and forth slowly with their mouths ajar told me it was something she hadn't previously known. Afterwards, though, their tones softened, and they began speaking quietly before Mama broke into a soft whimper.

My heart was breaking, and I had no idea why.

I told them all I'd leave out of respect for their privacy, but Mama said no and patted the seat next to her. Pesca took a seat on the other side of me. My anxiety levels were rising, but for what? It felt like I was about to be dragged into some family drama, more than I already had been. What felt like an hour was actually just a few seconds as I waited for her to begin speaking.

"Mia, you are a true joy. Pesca loves you and speaks so highly of you, and I love you the same now that I've met you, especially knowing your parents like I do," she said slowly with her hand on top of mine. "I can see a difference, a good one, in Gennaro when he's around you." Her voice trailed off and she looked around the room trying to find her words.

"I want nothing more than for my boys to be happy. I'm not proud of the marriage we set up between him and Francesca, but the reason we did it all those years ago and the reason it didn't seem so odd to me—was because Papa and I had one, too."

My eyebrows raised slightly. I wasn't expecting to hear it, but the more I thought about it, the less surprising it was. I had never seen them particularly affectionate towards each other, even though they certainly worked well together. The more I reviewed their interactions in my mind, it did, in fact, seem like their relationship was more business than personal.

She continued, "Our parents forced it all those years ago, and because it's what we knew, we did the same to Gennaro, but," she briefly hesitated, "none of the boys know this."

"How come?" I asked.

"We never wanted them to doubt our love or the bond of our family, I guess," she responded.

I didn't want to speak out of turn or be too honest for my own good, which was often the case, but I wasn't entirely sure how they thought the boys viewing their existing marriage and the way they operated would be any better. Knowing their marriage was arranged made things a whole lot clearer to me now, and if I was Gennaro, I *might* be able to better understand why I was assigned a wife at the age of eighteen.

Pesca chimed in, "Mama, the boys aren't boys anymore. They're grown men." She paused for a second to collect herself. "May I speak honestly?"

"Always," Mama assured her.

"The more you try to control things," she said, looking briefly at Papa, "the more they're going to resist. You haven't given them the opportunity to understand why things are the way they are, and now it seems to all be unraveling." I exhaled deeply. She said everything I was thinking but didn't feel comfortable saying as a week-old honorary family member.

She continued, "You two have grown to love each other, right? You have this big beautiful property that you're very proud of and three boys that have grown into wonderful men in their own ways. That's an accomplishment, too. Any hesitation or embarrassment you feel when you think of telling them," she finished, "Are your own fears getting in the way. I know these guys well. They'll be nothing but supportive. And, in fact, I think the truth will help tremendously."

Mama was still whimpering but nodding her head, and when I looked at Papa, who had a very solemn expression on his face, he lifted his head and looked right back at me. He rattled off some Italian to Pesca and Mama while pointing at me. They both shook their heads and put their hands up as if to say, "Stop."

I asked Pesca what he said.

She thought about whether or not she wanted to repeat it, but Papa nodded his head in my direction, so she did. "He wants to know if you're in love with Gennaro." I knew her well enough to know that she wasn't upset by the question itself, only slightly embarrassed he had brought it up.

To be fair, I had the same thought myself. Gennaro and I had felt intense feelings in an incredibly short amount of time, but crazier things had happened in life. Everyone always spews, "When you're not looking, that's when you'll find what you've been looking for," and it had proven to be true.

I sat there thinking of leaving this place, and short of my family being five thousand miles away, it broke my heart. Shit, I hadn't seen him for barely two hours, and I already missed him. I hadn't been in love—real love—ever before, and now I understood why.

It felt crazy, and while I had been put on the spot, I knew wholeheartedly the answer to Papa's question. There was nothing about Gennaro that I didn't like. He understood me. He listened to me. He respected me. He hadn't given me any reason to think that anything he told me had been a lie. I had uncovered his inner mushy side but knew without a doubt he'd protect me fiercely whenever necessary. It was everything I always dreamed love to be.

Was it too soon?

Who was to decide that?

More importantly, why did I feel I had to bare my soul in the middle of a kitchen without the person we were talking about being present?

I spoke my truth, and I did so confidently, without giving in to old, outdated family traditions.

"I love many things about your son, Papa," I paused to

catch my breath, "But I want him to be the first person to know *exactly* how I feel, when *I'm* ready to say it."

I wasn't sure if he was satisfied by the response or taken aback by the slight defiance I showed in not answering his question directly. Either way, it felt good to stay true to myself.

I thanked them for their honesty and excused myself to my villa. I didn't even know what time it was, but I already needed a glass of wine.

With my emotions all over the place, I decided to skip the wine and organize my bedroom instead. I shook out the blankets, made the bed, fluffed the pillows, organized my suitcase, and smiled when I saw Gennaro's backpack still sitting on the armchair across the room.

His phone had gone off a few times in a row while I was cleaning, and while I didn't want to intrude, I realized he may not have noticed he left it in here. I pushed my suitcase into the corner, clothes folded neatly, content with my quick clean-up, and walked over to grab it and bring it to him.

My smile faded when I saw who had been texting him.

Six-plus messages from Francesca, and they were still rolling in.

My stomach turned, feeling unsettled. It aggravated me, but was I being irrational?

Was there something he hadn't told me? Or was she on a never-ending mission fueled by increased pregnancy hormones?

I put his phone back down and decided against bringing it to him. With her name on the lock screen, I'd look like I was being nosy. Instead, I walked into the kitchen, cut up some bread with fresh mozzarella and tomatoes, and poured that glass of wine after all.

Emotional eating and drinking is *my* therapy.

Who gave a shit that I had eaten breakfast just over an hour ago? Not me, clearly.

The real question was, which part of the morning had stressed me the most?

Learning about Papa and Mama's arranged marriage and having to keep it from Gennaro?

Papa putting me on the spot asking if I was in love with Gennaro?

Francesca and her never-ending communication attempts?

Or the fact that I *was* in love with him and couldn't shake the feeling that something was still *off* with Francesca, even though I believed everything he had told me?

CHAPTER 24

Gennaro

I was knee deep in tall grass, weed whacking alongside the entrance to our property, when I heard a car horn in the distance. If I had any doubts about who it was, those doubts floated away as he pressed on said horn, screaming "Gennarooooo!" with his middle finger in the air. I gave Salvatore a middle finger right back as he slowed down and put the car in park.

One big bear hug later, he exclaimed, "Man, I'm excited to get together tonight. Are we eating dinner at the Osteria?" I hugged him back and smiled. "I actually have a dinner date already, and I was planning to meet you guys at the bar for drinks afterwards, if that's cool."

"Yea, of course," he nodded his head and then shrugged. "Can't promise I won't show up early to bust your balls, though."

"I'm not surprised," I responded, then asked, "What's Vin been up to?"

"You're both too busy policing the streets of Italy, but he's been having some issues at home," he shrugged with genuine concern. "I'm sure he'll tell you later. Oh, also, does your girl have any friends or sisters? Ask her to bring one or two." He was relentless.

Fully ready for the blowback, I responded, "Might take a while for them to arrive. They'd be coming from the States."

His mouth hung open and then formed into a smile. "If someone had *paid* me to predict which one of us would hook up with an American first, my money would not be on you." He pretended he was kidding, but then, with complete honesty, said, "You're not even that *nice.*"

"I think she'd beg to differ," I said, giving him another middle finger for good luck.

He got back in his car and drove off. I didn't love coming back to Tuscany as much as I had to, but Sal definitely made it more bearable. His easy-going nature made things enjoyable. He wasn't necessarily the guy you wanted around if you had actual issues that needed solving, but if a light-hearted, good time was what you were looking for, Sal was your guy.

The sun had finally come out from behind the clouds, and I wondered if Mia was down by the pool. I felt around in my back pocket for my phone to see if she had texted or called me and quickly realized I'd left it in her room. It was as good a reason as any to finish this section of the land-scaping and then head back down.

A half hour later, I had sweat pouring down the sides of my face and my back, even after having taken my sweat-shirt off. The white t-shirt that remained was soaked, and I was certain I smelled like a giant pile of dirt and grass clip-pings. I pulled the t-shirt up and over my head, rinsed it off with a hose, and once it was saturated with cold water, draped it back over my neck. It cooled me off instantly, but I definitely needed a hot shower.

As I walked towards her villa, I found her sitting at a

small patio table in the gravel, her feet propped up on a chair, her back to me, reading a book. "Psssst," I whispered as I closed in on her. She tilted her head back and looked up at me. Instinctively, I grabbed the side of her face gently and kissed her upside down.

"I can't smell good," I smiled at her and she smiled back, but I still apologized. "Sorry about that."

I took a seat across from her so I could ogle at her effortlessly beautiful face. She had no makeup on, her hair was messy, and she was wearing a pair of tan linen pants with the same white spaghetti strap bodysuit she wore on the streets of Rome when I first laid eyes on her. Oversized sunglasses made it a little difficult to see the expression on her face, but a small smile remained. Her body language, though, was off.

"You ok?" I asked. She quickly responded with a "yes," asking how the day had been so far and what time she should be ready for dinner. I was happy she seemed eager to go, but I could absolutely tell that she was upset about something. I told her we'd head over for dinner a little after seven and then meet up with Salvatore and Vincenzo for drinks after.

"You left your backpack and phone in my room in case you were looking for either of them," she said matter-of-factly, still looking at her book and barely at me.

"Mind if I shower in there?" I asked her, searching her facial expressions for a hint as to what she was feeling or why.

"Not at all, go ahead," she added. "I'm going to finish this chapter and I'll be right in."

I left my dirty shoes and sweatshirt outside, took my pants off right inside her door so as not to alarm any other guests who were around, and then added them to the pile outside. It was nice not to have to sneak around, but somehow, I still felt like I was doing something forbidden.

Maybe that's why I enjoyed it so much.

What I did *not* enjoy, though, was seeing Francesca's name on my phone with no fewer than nine missed text messages and two missed calls.

Immediately, I knew this was the reason for Mia's mood swing. I opened my phone to see what her newest issue was, only to be met with the same old shit.

> Francesca: When are you coming back this weekend?

> Francesca: Hello?

> Francesca: Your brother is still drinking too much

> Francesca: You need to talk to him

> Francesca: I don't want to tell Papa & Mama

> Francesca: It'll upset them

> Francesca: OMG why are you not answering me??

> Francesca: And also, I'm fine and the baby is fine, thanks for asking

> Francesca: Whatever

By the time I finished reading them, Mia had walked inside. She must have seen me shaking my head in disgust because she asked me what was wrong. Without mincing words and because I hated for stupid shit to linger more than it had to, I said, "If you saw her name on my phone, please don't be bothered by it." I handed it to her to read. "Here. Look. It's the same shit over and over again."

"I don't need to read through your messages," she said in a somewhat monotone voice. "I trust what you've told me; I just don't trust her."

"I'd prefer to not even waste time on this to be honest, and while I'm usually not a have-sex-to-avoid-my-problems kind of guy," I hesitated slightly, "I'd really like you in the shower with me right now."

Her eyes widened, her jaw dropped, and after about five seconds of deliberation, she untied the top of her pants and let them drop to the floor.

The two of us simply understood one another.

My hands found every curve of her beautiful body with ease. My mouth knew what her skin tasted like, right down to the temperature of her lips as they kissed me back. My fingers knew the pressure and speed she preferred, from a thumb to one to multiple. My dick knew which position made her legs go weak and which position left her twitching. My ears knew what her breath sounded like when she was excited, when she was about to finish, and after she had finished.

Afterwards, with her bent over the built-in shower bench and one of my legs propped up beside her, I pulled out, fully committing myself to learning everything else I could about her.

Our shower session was a quick one, and served a bit more as a necessary release of stress for me as Francesca continued to aggravate me from afar. Always the gentleman, I didn't want to leave Mia hanging, but she kindly reminded me she had finished twice the night before, or technically, early this morning.

"Let me give you a massage then," I suggested. Her eyes rolled back into her head at the thought, so we laid down on the bed, her completely naked and me with a towel wrapped around my waist. I poured some lotion in my hands and began rubbing her back in long strokes.

"I have some questions for you," I said, breaking the repetitive sounds of her light moans every time I got to her shoulder blades.

"Go ahead, masseur," she joked.

"Ok, I'm gonna start easy. What's your favorite color?"

"I don't have one."

"Beach or pool?"

"Beach for the sounds, pool for the no-sand-in-your-ass refreshment factor."

"Pizza or pasta?"

"Both."

"Red or white wine?"

"Papa got me on red."

"Favorite music?"

"Depends on the mood."

"Give or receive?"

"Give, except for this moment right now."

"Go out or stay in?"

"Both."

"What's your favorite thing about me?"

"That I don't think you're full of shit."

I smiled.

"What's your second favorite thing about me?"

"Is this a dick reference?"

"Not unless it's your second favorite thing about me."

"I love how you make me feel. That's generic, I know, but it's made up of a lot of small things."

"Like what?"

"You pay attention when I talk. You make me feel like I'm the only person in the room when we're together. You do what you say you're going to do. You have a big heart. You smell great. You have great lips. And…"

"And?"

"Fine. You've got a perfectly sized dick and you use it better than anyone ever has. You happy?"

"Only if you mean it."

She rolled over and kissed me deeply.

My mouth curved into a smile as it usually did when I was around her.

"One more question, if I may?" I was on a roll.

She smiled back and nodded her head for me to continue. "Have you thought about what we're going to do when you leave?" My gut wrenched, unsure of what her response might be.

Her eyes swept the corners of the room before she finally answered, "To be honest, I haven't. It's sort of been my mantra while I'm here to only worry about the day at hand, which is wildly out of my comfort zone," she paused. "But that doesn't mean I haven't thought about what *you* want to happen."

It was a safe, smart response to gauge my interest, and I appreciated her strategy.

"Well we've still got a solid week together. Let's focus on that." She squinted at me like she was unsatisfied with my response. "I'd be lying if I said I hadn't given thought to coming to visit you, though."

She moved in closer, wrapped her arms around me, and kissed me deeply.

I hadn't felt happiness or contentment like this as an adult ever before.

———

The adoration I felt for her continued, staring into her eyes over a small table with a dimly lit candle at the Osteria that illuminated her face perfectly. Watching her eat had become one of my favorite activities. Surrounded by a pizza *and* a pasta dish to share alongside a few empty glasses of red wine, we had been non-stop talking since we sat down.

My commitment to learning more about her continued as she told me about her best friend Allie, described her apartment to me, and what she liked (and didn't like) about growing up in and living in New Jersey and New York. Thankfully, we had been granted two full hours of quiet time *before* I heard the two assholes come barreling through the restaurant.

"*Ciaoooo* Gennaro!" It appeared that Sal had already dabbled in some homemade wine while he took a shower and got ready like the old days. And if I was a betting man, I'd say Vin was mostly sober, the stone-faced designated driver.

As they rounded the corner and found our table, Sal practically lunged for Mia, yanking her out of her seat for a big hug. Vin sat down, looking back and forth from them to me, and eventually extended his arm to shake her hand. It wasn't necessarily out of the ordinary since he was the least sociable out of all of us, but he seemed a little more pissed off than usual.

I looked at Mia, who had a big smile on her face and explained, "You met my brothers by blood, but these are the ones who know everything about me. They're a lot less dramatic than the other ones, too."

Vin chimed in. "I don't know *everything*," he said, nodding towards Mia. "Do I?"

"Well that's why you're here, right?" I wasn't about to take his or anyone's shit tonight. "She's been here for a week. How much sooner did you want a progress report?"

He didn't answer out loud, but his facial expression

said plenty. I pushed some wine in his direction. "Try some, it'll take the edge off," I suggested firmly.

He downed the whole thing in about three seconds and stretched his arm out for more. I poured it but knew without a doubt something else was wrong, and was thankful that Sal had Mia's attention instead.

We moved from the table to the bar area, the same one you'd always find us at back in the old days. "*Ciaooo*," we yelled to the owner, Carmine, but his eyes weren't focused on us. His mouth curved into a big smile, as he looked past Vincenzo and myself.

I followed his gaze and saw Mia smiling right back at him. "Carmine!" She shouted reaching across the bar top, grabbing his face in both hands, planting a big kiss on his cheek. He turned about three shades of red, and the smile on his face remained.

I was waving cash in front of him and finally yelled, "*Ayeee*, can't we get any good service around here? And, how do you two know each other anyway?"

Mia explained Pesca had introduced her to him earlier in the week, and he retorted, "*Lasciami in pace*, I'm busy!" He winked at me, soaking up every ounce of a young, beautiful woman's attention. I couldn't blame him, especially coming from her.

"Leave you alone? Get us our drinks, old man!" I joked as he grabbed Sal, Vin, and me our usual Peronis and Mia a Pirlo, which I recognized to be the same drink she had at the club in Rome.

I watched them interact as she asked about his kids, how today's lunch and dinner had gone, and what he decided to do about the issues he was having on the farm. It was clear they'd made an impact on one another. She looked directly at him when she spoke to him, like I wasn't even in the room. I loved that about her. She focused on what was right in front of her. She made true connections with people. She was a genuine soul.

I smiled and surveyed them a bit longer before I asked, "Hey, I don't mean to interrupt, but can I get my date back?" Carmine's eyes grew three times in size and his mouth opened into an even bigger smile than he had before.

"How the hell did you land this one?" he asked with his hand underneath her chin.

"I'm still trying to figure that out, actually," I said, my eyes panning back to Mia.

She grinned and rolled her eyes in a playful manner before replying, "I'm a sucker for good hearted Italian men I guess." Somehow, she made *both* of us blush this time.

He was an old buck but a good man who worked hard and sacrificed a lot for his family. He was one of the most eligible Tuscan bachelors back in the day, but the passing of his wife a few years back had taken a toll on him, and his seventy-four years of age were showing. She was extra kind to him, and it made me fall even harder for her. I was incredibly content sharing the joy of Mia with Carmine.

"So, what's going on with this?" Vin snapped me out of it, pointing towards her again. I was used to his mood swings, but I really wasn't feeling like dealing with them tonight.

"What is your issue? I met her in Rome, and didn't realize she was staying here until I came back the next day. We've been hanging out ever since. That's it." I had an attitude in my voice because the tone he was using was aggravating the hell out of me.

"That's it? You've literally never brought a chick around here ever, and on top of that, your *wife* owns a store next door." Like I needed the reminder.

"You can't stand Francesca, and now all of a sudden

she's my *wife?* Cut the shit. What's the actual problem?" I stared at him, grateful yet again that Mia's attention was on someone else instead of his grumpy ass. And, for maybe the first time ever, I was beyond thankful for Sal's big mouth and lack of a filter.

"Has he told you about *his* wife yet?" Vin had gotten married to a girl we went to school with almost two years ago. They hadn't dated for very long, and I always thought they weren't the right match, but she was pretty and he fell for her strictly based on physical appearance.

As I could have predicted, arm candy turned out to be a selfish, shitty excuse for a spouse. She'd spend all day doing quite literally nothing while he worked, and he'd come home, still having to cook and clean for himself. They didn't have kids, thankfully, but he hadn't been happy in a long time.

Vin stared into the mirror behind the bar, and I looked from Sal back to him. "What about your wife?"

He hesitated a few seconds before responding, "She's been messing around with one of the guys we grew up with."

"Jesus, man, how'd you find that out?" I asked. I felt for him, because he was a good guy who loved hard but had a history of loving the wrong type of woman.

"She's been in her own world more than she normally is. We haven't had sex in months. She's always sleeping by the time I get home and gone by the time I wake up. I felt like she was avoiding me, and then one day I noticed her phone going off constantly when I was running about a half hour late for work," he continued. "When I grabbed it to give it to her, I saw his name on it. I opened it and saw way too much shit that I'd have preferred not to."

"Let's go fuck him up!" Sal interjected, which was comical because Sal hadn't fought someone in his entire life. Peronis had a way of making you a hard ass when you really weren't one, but at least his heart was in the right place.

"Vin, do you really love her?" I asked directly.

He answered quickly, "That's a loaded question. Of course, I do."

"There's nothing loaded about it. Are you sad to be losing her, or are you uncomfortable thinking about starting again?" He paused to think while I continued, "What do you truly love about her? What can you not live without? If you don't have a good response for that, it's not *her* you're in love with. You were just comfortable having her there."

"Jesus Christ, when did you become a therapist?" He was laughing but also poking at me. At the same time, I felt Mia slide her arm up over my shoulder and around my neck before turning my chin to meet her face and planting a kiss directly on my lips. Vin's eyes grew wide, and he threw his head back with his lips pressed together and hands up as if to say, "Ok, didn't realize it was that serious."

"I don't mean to sound like I know everything, because I don't. I always swore I'd never fall in love and never get married, for *real*, but that's because I was convinced it would end up as one huge steaming pile of shit." We had never talked about relationships this deeply before, so while it was a bit weird, he seemed to still be listening and I continued. "It only ends up a steaming pile of shit if you pick the wrong person and you don't understand one another."

Mia chimed in, "Vincenzo, how's it feel to be the big brother he never had?" She smiled and added, "I've never heard a guy speak so highly of a friend as Gennaro has of you." And then, she hopped off her bar stool. It was a rhetorical question, and while I wasn't sure if she heard anything we had talked about, I was absolutely certain her heart was in the right place when she brought it up. As I looked back at Vin, I could tell he had finally softened a bit.

"I'm really happy for you, G," he smiled. "I can tell why you've kept her to yourself for a week."

It was about an hour after he had angrily walked into the restaurant at this point, but he'd already started working through his issues. We spoke a bit more about Mia, and I brought him up to speed with the Francesca and Giuseppe situation, which made him feel a little better about his own. I was convinced Mia had some superpowers, allowing people to fall in love with her in the shortest timeframe possible. She and Sal were now dancing to Italian love songs playing from the speakers overhead while Vin and Carmine watched with goofy smiles on their faces.

It's what I never envisioned for myself. The person I *wanted* to be with fitting in perfectly with my own crew, but that's exactly what she did. Genuinely, effortlessly, and easily, she had weaved her way into my life, my heart, and with any luck, my future.

CHAPTER 25
Mia

I was beginning to lose count of how many times we'd woken up next to each other, but the more we did, the more comfortable it felt. Meeting his best friends seemed to push it, whatever "it" was, to the next level. Sure, he could have introduced me knowing I live far enough away that, once I left, no one would ever have to bring me up in conversation or accidentally run into me again. Truthfully, though, his friends didn't give off those types of vibes any more than he did, which was to say, not at all.

They seemed genuine and kind, maybe a little crazy, but the good kind. And mostly, I could tell they all viciously protected one another. It very much reminded me of my relationship with Allie, and was another plus in the positive column.

As I was lying there recounting the events of the day before, I remembered how frustrated I was by Francesca's texts and how easily he diffused my anxiety about them. Did I trust what he was saying? Yes. I had been involved with people in my life plenty of times who didn't know how or when to quit, which wasn't a reflection of me. I also knew he'd likely not even engage with her if she wasn't so close to the inner workings of their family—and *married* to him.

It sounded weird even in my brain, and then I started second-guessing everything all over again. Was I being a completely lovestruck idiot? It was time to check in with the boss.

> Mia: You're probably sleeping but...

Allie: ::sends picture of her daughter lying across her horizontally in bed::

Allie: I haven't slept in about two years

Allie: What's up?

> Mia: I'm just doing what I usually do

Allie: Stop it

> Mia: Kind of hard not to overthink

> Mia: The "wife" keeps texting and calling him

Allie: ::eye roll emoji::

Allie: I don't mean to talk shit about someone I don't know but maybe next time try to not bang your husband's brother and get pregnant and then maybe you wouldn't be having these issues

Allie: What has he been saying to her?

> Mia: Nothing of importance

> Mia: Basically says it's not his problem and that she and his brother need to figure it out

Allie: Team...

Allie: Wait, what the hell is his name?

Mia: Gennaro

Allie: Team G fo sho

Allie: Has he been hiding his phone or something?

Mia: No, he actually left it in my room all day yesterday

Mia: I saw her texts on his lock screen throughout the morning

Allie: Ok, and what did he do when he read them?

Mia: Just shook his head, said it's the same shit over and over, and offered for me to read them

Allie: Did you?

Mia: No, I'm not turning into a chick who reads messages

Mia: I either trust you or I don't

Allie: Ok killer, so do you trust him or do you not?

Mia: I see what you did there

Mia: I do

Allie: So what doesn't feel right?

Allie: STOP

Allie: OVER

Allie: THINKING

Allie: You've got less than a week left

Allie: Do all of the things

Allie: Have ALL of the sex

Allie: Let him love on you, hard

Allie: Let him bang you…harder ::cry laugh emoji::

Allie: If you come back home and never hear from again, so be it

Allie: I highly doubt that'll happen though

Allie: Like, in my gut, I don't think that's gonna happen

Allie: It seems like too much work for someone as hot as he is, when he could go hand pick someone from the streets of Rome and screw them if that's all he wanted

"Come here," he rolled over and put his arm around my waist.

Mia: Couldn't love you more

Mia: Gotta go - he just woke up

Allie: ::eggplant emoji::

"Yes?" I playfully asked as I rolled over on top of him with my hand over my mouth.

He put his over his own. "You're right, let's go fix that."

I gave him a quick, closed-mouth morning-breath-is-disgusting kiss and went into the bathroom to start the shower. As I was brushing my teeth he walked in behind me, completely naked, and from the feel of it, completely hard.

His hands slid up and over the back of my satin sleep shorts before wrapping around the front of me. Teasing me for a bit with some long strokes of his thumb, he looked directly at me in the mirror reflection. As soon as my breathing changed and our eyes met, he smiled, stopped abruptly, and brushed his teeth instead. When he was done, he teased some more. "I'm so sorry, were we in the middle of something?"

"Don't do that." I said with conviction and a smile.

He spun me around, pinning one of my hands behind my back and using his other to gently hold the base of my neck, lifting my mouth towards his. "I don't ever start something that I don't plan to finish." His lips were millimeters from mine, and I refused to give in. I stared into his eyes, deeply, and let him finish talking instead. "Don't ever forget that."

He kissed me in a way that relayed every intention he had with me that morning, and he was right. He did *not* start anything without finishing it. Twenty minutes later, I was naked on the bed, my cheeks flushed, my hair matted to my neck, my legs in a figure-four position, and my backside exposed to the cool air. He had showered a *second* time to freshen up after the complete undoing of our first rinse. As he walked out of the bathroom, he climbed up behind me and whispered in my ear, "Better get dressed if you plan on doing anything outside of this room today."

I exhaled, "I do like this room…a lot."

"I want to take you to one of my favorite towns. Go get dressed." I liked when he took charge, and I did as I was instructed. Twenty minutes later we walked out at the same exact time Papa, Mama, and Pesca were heading to their car. Awkwardness ensued for a few seconds before Pesca broke the silence. "We're heading to Siena if you want to come."

"I'm going to take Mia to Bagno Vignoni and then I'm leaving to head back tonight." Just like that, I was reminded today was Sunday and he had work tomorrow. "Do you need anything else done, Papa?"

"No, *grazie*." He seemed like he was trying to be pleasant, and I couldn't help but wonder whether our kitchen conversation from yesterday had helped in some way. Mama chimed in, "There's food for you to take back with you on the counter in the kitchen," and then Pesca reminded me that we were leaving early the next morning.

After we said goodbye to everyone, he took my hand in his, started walking towards the car, and asked where Pesca and I were heading. "Venice. I had 'gondola ride' on my list of to-dos for this trip."

He let out a small laugh. "What else is on that list?"

"Experience villa life in Tuscany. I can check that off. Unlimited pizza, pasta, wine, and gelato, which is another victory. A gondola ride is the only thing left," I said, quite proudly.

"That's the only thing left?" He stopped walking and pulled me in close to his chest. I looked up at him, intently studying the look in his eyes.

"Well, technically, I had one other thing, but I accomplished that the second night I was here," I remembered.

"And what was that?" He was genuinely curious about my list, which I found to be pretty adorable.

"Can't tell you," I smiled.

"Come on," he pleaded.

I thought about it briefly and responded, "I had a bonus section for having sex with a hot Italian." My cheeks turned a light shade of pink as I looked towards him for a reaction.

"So, all I am is a good roll in the hay, huh?" He looked at me wide-eyed and playfully.

"You're just a little bit more than that." I took a step closer to him. As he had done earlier in the bathroom, I answered his question with only my lips and my tongue. Pulling his face in towards mine, I trailed the length of his neck to his jawline to his mouth. What began quickly and firmly turned into slow, soft, sensual motions that I hoped relayed how *much* more he actually was to me. When my eyes opened, his were still closed, an obvious longing in his still-parted lips.

My message had landed.

There was no turning back now. We were in this together. He had my heart; I had his. And while we hadn't spoken the words, we certainly felt them.

———

Floating along the canals of Venice on a gondola as I listened to an older gentleman singing "O Sole Mio" in the distance was a surreal moment for me. I had dreamt of it since I was old enough to appreciate the art of travel and history in general, and I was finally here. Pesca and I had left around eight in the morning to get on a train from Florence to Venice and checked in to our hotel room early. After dropping off our bags, we turned right back around to go explore some.

Gennaro had wined and dined me the day before as he showed me around Bagno Vignoni, with a late lunch, early dinner, and multiple glasses of wine at a cliffside restaurant overlooking the hills of Tuscany. It felt like I had unbuckled my "don't get your heart broken" seatbelt as we traveled at excessive speeds on a narrow highway. It was fun, exhilarating, and something I would always look back on fondly, so long as one wrong move didn't end up in some sort of disaster, but I had promised him I wasn't going to think that way. I pushed those thoughts to the back of wherever those thoughts should go.

It took us about an hour to say goodbye to each other as he geared up to head back to Rome. He offered to stay until the morning and said that he didn't mind leaving early to get to work on time, but I still had to pack and check in with my family, and I was severely tired. Part of me thought a little time apart would be good to pump the brakes a few times.

I immediately regretted that decision when it was time to fall asleep. I missed his strong arm draped over the small of my waist and his light breath on my shoulder. In any case, I slept soundly, which gave me all the energy I needed to take the two-hour train ride to Venice and immediately hop on a gondola.

I let him know we had gotten there safely.

Mia: ::picture with gondolas in the background::

Mia: Here I am about to knock things off my Italian bucket list

Mia: Just missing you

Gennaro: I promise you that I'll take you back there and we'll ride one together

Mia: Is that your way of making sure I visit you again?

Gennaro: ::shrugs emoji::

Gennaro: (Did it work?)

Mia: Too soon to tell

Gennaro: Fair enough

Pesca and I began peacefully floating, thanks to our *gondolier*, and almost instantly my whole body felt at peace. The weather was incredibly beautiful, not too warm and not too cold, with the perfect amount of sun peeking through the clouds. Since it was a Monday, there weren't too many people around, either. I took a few short video clips of the ride and then put my phone away to enjoy the moment I was in.

"What's on that mind of yours?" Pesca asked, and for the first time in a while, I could honestly answer, "Nothing at all. I'm just really freaking happy."

She smiled, and we settled in for the rest of the ride, which lasted about a half hour. Afterwards, we enjoyed lunch and window shopped along some smaller side streets before heading to the Piazza San Marco where random street performers were playing music, juggling, or handing out roses, taking pictures with them, and then attempting to charge money afterwards.

The following day, we took a short boat ride over to Murano for a glass blowing demonstration. It was amazing to watch how something so delicate was forged from fine grains of sand. What was even more amazing was the cost of it.

I walked through the gallery after the demonstration, taking note of pieces ranging in price from hundreds to thousands of dollars and smiled to myself. A shop assistant asked if I needed help, and I resisted the urge to tell him I'd need a personal loan to afford any of it. "Which way to the gift shop?" Surely, I'd be able to find a small piece of glass there for less than a mortgage payment. I settled on a small keychain and was checking out when Gennaro texted.

Gennaro: How's that bucket list doing?

Mia: I'm happy I'm here but...

Mia: It's not my favorite place

Gennaro: I hear that a lot about Venice

Gennaro: It's for very specific interests

Gennaro: Did you love the gondola ride?

Mia: It was my favorite part and worth the trip by itself

Gennaro: When are you leaving?

Mia: We're staying over one more night and then heading back tomorrow.

Three bubbles popped up, and then stopped, and then popped up again, and then stopped. I paid for my keychain and still didn't have a message when we got back on the boat. I put my phone away. Pesca and I decided to have an early dinner. We listened to some live music in the piazza and dabbled in some more wine, and then we headed back to the hotel to get a whole lot of necessary rest.

I took a quick shower to wash the touristy day away, brushed my teeth, and crawled into bed. Pesca was nose first in a book, so I caught up on my phone, which I hadn't looked at in about three hours.

Allie was checking in to see if I had any updates, Mom and Dad were ensuring I was still alive of course, and I had three missed messages from Gennaro.

Gennaro: Sorry got distracted with a call at work

> Gennaro: I know it's a longer train ride for you but would you want to ride down to Rome and stay with me for a few days?

Two hours passed before he followed it up.

> Gennaro: You fell in love with your gondolier didn't you...

I laughed out loud and accidentally startled Pesca.

"Let me guess," she smirked, her eyes cutting holes through me.

I put both hands up like I was completely innocent and asked, "How long is the train ride from here to Rome?"

"About four hours," she answered quickly with zero judgment. "Planning an extended tour of the Colosseum?"

"I don't think it's the Colosseum I'm interested in," I replied.

"I'm sure it's not, darling." She shut her light off, rolled over, and went to sleep.

> Mia: The gondolier wasn't quite as charming as you are

> Gennaro: What a shame

> Mia: I also wouldn't sit on a train for four hours just to see him, so you're in luck there, too

> Gennaro: Does that mean you're coming?

> Mia: It absolutely does

I spent the nearly four-hour train ride with earbuds in, listening to music and snoozing on and off. Pesca had done the same for the first half before she got off in Florence, so I didn't feel guilty about it. She hugged me goodbye and told me just to have fun. "We don't have any other formal trips planned. Stay there as long as you want, and don't worry about me. You're not *abandoning* me."

"How'd you know I was thinking that?" I smiled.

"I know most things," she winked, and I didn't doubt for a second that she did.

I sent Gennaro a message letting him know I'd be there sometime around two in the afternoon. He told me where to go from the train station and who to ask for when I got to his building since he was at work until eight. It was exciting and nerve wracking all at once and I subconsciously hoped the hotel staff wouldn't assume me to be a prostitute.

Getting off the train in Rome wasn't as overwhelming as I thought it would be, but I was certain that him patrolling the streets not too far away helped. I had a little bit of a safety net with him there, and I felt more confident because of it. A fifteen-minute walk from the train station brought me back to the street I had first seen him on nearly two weeks prior. I smiled wide and tried to simultaneously bury the hollow feeling in my heart, knowing that my time here was running out.

As I approached the front door of the building, I was thankful that, for the first time in my life, I had packed lightly, with only a small shoulder bag, a couple of outfits (all of which were dirty at this point), and one extra pair of shoes besides the sneakers I was wearing. Gennaro must have called and given them my basic description because I was treated like half a celebrity as soon as I walked in.

"Mia?" A sweet, older lady called from behind a desk.

I immediately smiled. "Yes, hi!"

"Welcome! Mr. Beletta asked me to let you into his apartment. Come with me." I guess being a cop has its perks.

We exchanged general pleasantries on the elevator ride up, and I was happy that I didn't feel an ounce of judgment. In fact, she mentioned how quiet and courteous Gennaro always was, which gave off a bit of an "I've never done this for him before" vibe. It was another plus in the positive column, which was growing longer by the day.

She opened his door with a spare key and motioned for me to enter. After asking if I needed anything, she let me know her name was Gina and gave me the number to the front desk if I changed my mind.

When I closed the door behind me and turned around, his immaculate apartment impressed me for a second time. Spotless yet comfortably inviting, it smelled almost as good as he did.

Never in my life had I met a man with his shit together more than Gennaro Beletta.

CHAPTER 26
Gennaro

A woman I had met by pure chance on a side street in Rome had me daydreaming, looking at my phone more often, and randomly smiling to myself by the mere thought of her. I felt like a little kid, hoping my work shift would end quickly, the same way I used to wait for Christmas morning to arrive. I was anxious, excited, and couldn't wait to turn the key to my apartment door and see her there, wondering what tonight would bring, since it seemed every moment I spent with her kept getting better and better.

My phone dinged, temporarily knocking me out of my stupor.

Mia: ::picture from living room couch::

Gennaro: Gonna be the longest six hours of my life

Mia: You and me both

Gennaro: Make yourself at home

> Gennaro: Fridge is full, wine bottles under the island, glasses to the right of the fridge, remote for music or TV is next to the candle on the coffee table

> Mia: Stop, you're turning me on already

> Gennaro: That was easy

> Mia: Wasn't it?

> Mia: ::video sent::

> Mia: :: video sent::

She was killing me softly.

I clicked on the first video, immediately greeted by her beautiful smile, with the phone propped up on the kitchen island counter as she opened a bottle of red, poured herself a glass, and clinked the camera lens with a pretend "*Salute.*" The second video showed her holding a bowl of Mama's pasta leftovers as she walked towards the balcony, past perfectly folded stacks of clean clothes on the living room table.

I wasn't much of a gender role guy, but there was a nice feeling knowing there was a "woman's touch" in my place. She had made herself right at home, like I wanted her to. Another smile creeped up on me, and then more messages came through.

> Mia: I don't want to keep bothering you while you're working but

> Mia: ...a girl could get used to this place

> Gennaro: Bother me??

> Gennaro: Stop it

> Gennaro: I love that apartment

> Gennaro: And I love it just a little bit more with you in it

Mia: Just a little?

> Gennaro: Ok, a lot more

> Gennaro: ::picture in cop car with Marco behind him::

Mia: Those eyes...

Mia: They're my favorite thing to look at

Marco kept asking what I was smiling about, but I shook my head in a vow of silence. "She has a full hold on you, G. I love to see it."

Truth was, so did I.

We got a call at that exact moment, which I was somewhat grateful for. It took a couple of hours to break up some fights with a few arrests, and it felt good to do police work when the next day, I'd be right back to manual labor at the villa.

We stopped for some pizza afterwards, and when I didn't have any new messages from her I assumed she had fallen asleep. My thoughts were confirmed when I sent a text and received a photo response curled up on the couch underneath a blanket with sleepy eyes.

> Gennaro: Guess who's getting out a little early?

Mia: ::picture smiling, laying down on the couch::

> Gennaro: Looks like you're well rested

Mia: I'm ready for you

Gennaro: We'll see about that

Gennaro: See you soon

She had a way with words *and* visuals, *and with my body*, apparently.

I put my key in the door about forty-five minutes later and opened it to see something I had never once even imagined but was somehow everything I had always wanted. Music was playing, a candle was burning, and on the island was a small plate of bread slices, nuts, cheese, roasted peppers, olives, and two glasses filled with red wine. The ingredients for what looked like spaghetti aglio e olio were on the counter, and she was dancing to music that was now loudly playing from the living room speakers.

I stood there for the few seconds it took her to realize I was watching her. Her long, wavy hair that I now knew the exact scent of draped down her back, and she was dressed in one of my t-shirts, barefoot and making dinner.

It was heaven on earth.

I cleared my throat, trying not to startle her, as she whipped around with a big wide-eyed grin. "I didn't even hear you come in! My father would *not* be thrilled at my lack of security precautions," she joked.

"Well, I kind of live here." Holding up my key chain, I smiled. "Have a key and everything, see?"

I dropped my bag, scooped her close to me holding the small of her back in one hand and an ass cheek in the other, and put my mouth on hers. A few seconds later, she responded with a smirk, "You've got to be the only man who works ten hours policing the streets of a major city and still manages to look and smell like this." Her eyes damn near rolled into the back of her head.

"I cheated and showered at the precinct. I've got a locker full of stuff for the few times Marco and I have gone out straight from work." I smiled as she looked me up and down. "I also didn't want to waste any time when I got back here."

"Oh yea? What did you plan to spend your time on?" She grabbed my waistband and pulled me in closer for another kiss.

"Well, I had no idea my new roommate would be making dinner, so I didn't account for all of this." I pointed towards the island with the tray of antipasto and the wine. "I think I'll enjoy some wine first, antipasto second, dinner third, and dessert after that."

"I forgot to make dessert actually," she said as she turned back towards the stove to put the spaghetti in the water.

I sipped some of the wine she had poured for me before closing in on her, the heat of our bodies burning nearly as hot as the boiling pot of water in front of us. I bent down slightly, trailing the palm of my hand from the back of her knees up the back of her legs to the bottom of her ass. I inhaled sharply when I realized she wasn't wearing any underwear, but contained myself as we were hovering around bubbling water.

Sitting across from each other at the corner of the island, we talked, laughed, and ate her expertly prepared dinner that was so good it had me reaching for a second helping within minutes.

I was used to my mother's delicious food, but the good cooking of a woman who I had fallen for hit just a little bit differently.

After the sun had fully set behind the city buildings she curled up next to me on the couch in between my legs with her head resting on my chest. With the overhead lights dimmed and a few candles burning on the coffee table, we talked back and forth about life. She asked me if I really saw myself staying in Rome long term, and I thoughtfully responded by saying, "I don't have a reason not to."

I was subtly referencing her being back in the States, but I wasn't quite sure that she picked that part up. We spoke about me visiting her there and meeting her family. We discussed marriage, not necessarily to each other but in generalities, since I never pictured it for myself besides the on-paper sham with Francesca.

She persistently asked about my dating past, and I finally admitted that women were oftentimes more interested in me than I was in them, which was kind of difficult to say without sounding like a giant arrogant asshole. It was the truth, though. I just didn't care to waste my time on all of it.

"I messed around in school a bunch when I was younger, and all my friends rag on me for it, but I've never been much for wanting to deal with people's emotions and feelings after a hookup. Once I came down here, I felt myself mature a lot more, and unless it felt like something worth my while, I didn't bother wasting my time. I became more of a wingman for Marco than anything else."

Everything I had told her when we first met, or that she had learned about me from my family and friends, was still holding true because she seemed satisfied with our conversation. Francesca was a roadblock for sure, but not an insurmountable one. We had finally hit our stride. There were no doubts, there were no uncertainties, and we kept leaning into each other.

It was around eleven when we went out to the balcony

for a bit of fresh evening air and to take in the city lights. The wind was blowing through her hair, and she had a blanket wrapped around her since the temperature had chilled a bit. Music was still playing from the speakers inside, and after having excused myself to the "bathroom" I came back outside with a small bag. I was the tiniest bit nervous, which seemed to make *her* the tiniest bit nervous in return.

When I started talking, though, she knew exactly *why* I was.

"Mia, I don't know how to say this, and I'm not entirely sure whether or not you want to hear it." I looked to her for permission to keep going, and when she nodded her head towards me, I continued. "I fell in love with the sight of you two weeks ago, right down that street over there." We both looked down, and it was indeed, exactly where her Uber had dropped her off. She smiled and I kept going. "The more I've tried to convince myself of every reason I *shouldn't* fall for you, the more I do."

She blinked slowly and looked like she might be holding back tears, but when I saw her smile again, I handed her the bag. "Here, just open it." She took it from me, recognizing that the name stamped on the bag was the same store where she bought the black lace teddy from in Florence.

"When did you get this?" she asked, in full amazement that she had missed the entire transaction at the store.

"Uhm, you were headfirst in the scarves display or picking out black lingerie. I'm not too sure, but I kind of love that we were both surprising each other and didn't realize it," I responded.

Her cheeks flushed, and for some reason, my heart was beating incessantly. She removed the single piece of tissue paper and found the small black box at the bottom of the bag.

After opening it, her eyes immediately welled with tears.

It felt like a whirlwind, this entire thing. Two weeks had already changed the course of our lives, but whatever uncertainty we had felt throughout them had completely vanished. I knew there was not a single place on Earth where we were meant to be other than where we were.

I felt it deeply.

Her smile grew wide as a few tears escaped her eyes and trickled down her cheeks, and when she looked up at me, I instinctively and quickly wiped them away with my thumbs. "I don't even think you need Google translate for that one," I joked.

It was a gold chain that read "*Ti Amo*" in a delicate script.

She laughed, shook her head no, and asked me to put it on her. I clasped the gold chain at the base of her neck and spun her around. The look on her face was all I needed to see. She took a few deep breaths and was about to speak, but I put up my hand to stop her.

"I don't want you to say anything. Not right now at least." I wiped the last tear that escaped and kissed her gently. "I want to thank you for reminding me to *enjoy* life. I've had more fun the last couple of weeks than I remember having in the last ten years."

I stopped, licked my lips, looked up at the sky, and continued, "I've never felt this way about anyone because I never thought it was possible, but I realize now that it wasn't possible because I never envisioned it with someone like you. Jesus, I didn't even know someone like you actually existed."

I trailed off again, mostly shocked that I was speaking

as vulnerably and emotionally as I was. Men get a bad rap for communicating as little as possible, sure, but she effortlessly brought it out of me. I rested my hands at the base of her neck, my fingers woven through her hair, and tilted her face up towards me.

"I have no idea where this is going. I just need you to know that I love you," I said, looking into her eyes and speaking directly into her heart, *"Ti amo."*

She hugged me tightly with her head on my chest before looking back up at me again. With my hands on either side of her face, I kissed her the best way I knew how to and the same way I did everything else in life, *passionately.*

"This is everything I've always wanted, and nothing I ever thought was possible," she whispered. "And for once, I'm not afraid of any of it."

We were living for the now, doing our best not to care what anyone thought or would think about our whirlwind romance. We weren't wasting time worrying about "what ifs" or what would happen when she went back home.

I leaned into her, and she leaned into me. Trusting each other was the key to the bond we now shared that felt unbreakable. I was a grown adult, but I felt like my life had *finally* started, with a woman I could absolutely see forever with.

And now, I wanted to start forever as soon as possible.

CHAPTER 27
Mia

Something changes when you fall in love. Well, technically, a lot of things change, but something deep within your soul simply feels different. *You feel whole.*

I woke up the next morning and could immediately feel that he wasn't in the bed next to me. The sun was shining through the windows the same way it had the first morning I woke up there a couple of weeks ago. This time though, I heard music playing from the living room, I smelled breakfast cooking, and rather than a feeling of uncertainty, I felt deep contentment.

The bed was empty beside me, but my heart was full. For the first time in my life, as it related to a man, I *knew* I was exactly where I was meant to be.

And it had appeared when I promised myself I wouldn't be focused on it.

"When you stop looking, you're going to find exactly what it is you've been searching for."

I flashed back to the exact moment in my parents' kitchen half a year ago when my mom rattled that phrase off to me after yet another heartbreak. To be fair, I had heard it or read it often throughout my adult life, and despite all evidence to the contrary, I believed it to be true.

When you lose something at home, you find it when you least expect it. When you get lost driving, you find something else along the journey that you didn't even know you were looking for. It's a common theme that's hard to remember until it rings true for you, depending on what you *are* looking for.

Walking into the kitchen towards a shirtless, tattooed, sun-kissed man who had poured me coffee and cooked me breakfast with place settings that included a fresh bouquet of flowers in a small crystal vase was everything I didn't know I wanted. Mostly, though, just as he said the night before, I didn't know he *existed*. My expectations of men were so low based on what had come before him that by not *trying* to find someone and not *forcing* myself to feel something for someone, I had allowed my heart to open wide enough to naturally let the person who was meant for it inside.

I wrapped my arms around the front of him as he was cooking eggs, the side of my head resting on his back. It was one of my favorite positions—the strength of his back brought me physical comfort while the echo of his beating heart brought me emotional relief. He put his free hand over one of my arms and squeezed me. I was so tuned in to him, his body, and his mind, and I knew at that moment that I absolutely loved him, too.

I promised myself to wait to tell him, though, and decided that later in the day or tomorrow I'd write how I felt instead. I had a tendency of writing more clearly than I spoke, and I didn't want to misconstrue or forget anything.

We spent the morning together, indulging in his skill-fully prepared breakfast, sipping on coffee, and flipping through photo albums on our phones. We waded through pictures of our family and friends, my apartment, some old coworkers, and food pictures (of which I had many) for at least an hour. It was our way of introducing each other to our regular lives, since relatively soon we'd be five thousand miles away from each other and had no definitive future visit planned.

As he got ready for work, he told me he wanted to take me out for dinner. "Be ready by eight, and make sure you're hungry."

"Hungry for what, exactly?" I playfully asked.

He stepped in closer to me, his mouth hovering directly over mine as he looked into my eyes. "Anything you feel like eating." He kissed me with a hand at the back of my neck, and I felt myself melt into him. "Don't get into too much trouble while I'm gone."

"Can I do anything for you while you're at work? I can clean or" he abruptly cut me off with a finger to my mouth.

"You're on vacation. There's a pool on the rooftop, there's a gym up there, too. There are a bunch of cafes down the road if you want to get out for lunch. Do whatever makes you happy." I inhaled, exhaled deeply, and kissed him again. Before he walked out, he said, "If there's a knock at the door later and you're here, it'll be Gina from downstairs. Answer it, if you don't mind. Otherwise, she'll leave it right outside the door for when you get back."

"Leave what?" I asked.

"You'll see." He winked, kissed me one more time, grabbed his bag, and walked out.

A few hours later, I had cleaned up breakfast and coffee cups, made the bed, organized my suitcase, and put my hand on my new necklace no fewer than five times to make sure it was still there. Which reminded me, this was a big development that I needed to share with Allie.

> Mia: ::picture of necklace::

Allie: Ooooh, that's beautiful

Two minute delay.

Allie: Wait a second, that means "I love you" not "love"

> Mia: Correct

Allie: ...did you buy it for yourself as a form of self-care?

> Mia: I did not

Allie: ...did the hot Italian man you're trying not to be in love with give it to you?

> Mia: Maybe

Allie: What color is my bridesmaid dress gonna be?

Allie: And can you make sure my partner in the wedding knows how to have fun, please?

Allie: I need a solid night of partying and I'm not putting up with anyone who's a pain in the ass

> Mia: Getting a little ahead of ourselves, no?

Allie: You tell me

Allie: I've never gotten an "I love you" necklace in my life...so...

I was smiling at my phone and shaking my head when I heard a knock at the door. Gina was on the other side when I opened it, holding a perfectly wrapped white gift box with a black satin bow. My eyes grew wide and my mouth fell open. I felt like I was living my very own "Pretty Woman" moment, minus the whole hooker thing.

"You are one lucky woman," she sweetly smiled. "He asked me to help, but he had very specific ideas in mind. I hope they're the right size! If you need anything changed, come down and let me know."

I nodded my head, but not many discernible words came out. I took the box into the bedroom and stared at it for a few seconds. I'm not a superficial gal at all, and to be honest, I usually enjoy giving gifts more than receiving them, but the thought behind this got to me.

Somehow, I had met my thoughtful match.

Somehow, the girl who was *always* the planner had someone a few steps ahead of her.

It was a little uncomfortable but mostly fulfilling, in the best way possible. I untied the ribbon and lifted the top of the box. Underneath tissue paper and a sticker that read "Pinko Boutique" were two dresses. One was a deep purple satin drape neck with ruched sides, spaghetti straps, and an asymmetrical bottom. The other, a black high-neck halter that tied around the neck with a loose body skimming fit that fell perfectly over my hips and bottom.

A text came in as I was trying them both on.

> Gennaro: Special delivery

I sat on the edge of the bed with my phone in my hand, smiling at it.

> Mia: You managed two secret gifts in less than 24 hours

> Mia: And I'm a pretty hard person to surprise

Gennaro: ::shrugs emoji::

Gennaro: As long as you like them

> Mia: I love them...but which one should I wear tonight?

Gennaro: Whichever one you like best

Gennaro: Wanted you to have some options

> Mia: You sure you're not gay?

Gennaro: Positive baby

Gennaro: Although you're the third person to ask me that

Gennaro: Meet me downstairs later at 8, ok?

> Mia: You got it

Both dress options required a little bit of a sweat session to at least trick myself into forgetting how much pizza and pasta I had eaten in two weeks. Before I went to the gym though, I went downstairs to thank Gina and ask her opinion.

"Did you open it?" She exclaimed as soon as I rounded the corner. I absolutely loved her energy.

Smiling back at her, I responded, "I did. Thank you so much for helping. I love them both, but woman to woman, any insight as to *which one* I should wear tonight?" I asked.

I searched her face for clues that she might know what

we were doing or where we were going, but her eyes squinted slightly, focusing only on the question at hand. She was in her late fifties, subtly gorgeous still, which meant she was a knock-out back in her prime, and I was prepared to take her suggestion quite seriously.

"Well, in my experience, *women* prefer wearing colors that everyone will obviously notice. *Men,* though, prefer spicy colors *underneath* that only *they* know about." She looked up at me with one eyebrow raised. "Know what I mean?"

Did I ever.

"Any lingerie stores close by?" I smiled and asked her without hesitation.

She winked and sent me on my way.

Maybe Gina would have to be invited to the wedding, too.

It had never taken me longer to get ready in my entire life, but when I was finished, there was not a doubt in my mind that he'd enjoy looking at me as much as I currently did. My legs were slightly sore from the gym and looked more toned than I remembered them being prior to my workout, which I snuck in after visiting the lingerie store Gina recommended.

It was five minutes to eight, two hours after I had hopped into the shower, and I was more than satisfied with the reflection staring back at me.

Gennaro: I'm downstairs

Gennaro: Don't rush

Gennaro: Reservation is 8:15

Mia: On my way

When the elevator door opened, he turned around in what felt like slow motion. I stepped off confidently and walked towards him, dressed in the black halter dress; black ankle tie shoes (the same ones I wore the night we met); a messy updo with long pieces hanging down the front of my face; smoky eye makeup; a glossy, dark nude lip; long dangling earrings; and a few stacked bracelets.

Someone else walked past me, straining his neck as he did, but my eyes were fixated on Gennaro and his on mine before running them up and down the length of me.

He pulled me in close without hesitation, his mouth on my collarbone, and inhaled me. "*Buona scelta*," he whispered into my ear and then pulled back to translate, "Nice choice."

"Gina helped," I smiled and nodded towards her. She was behind the desk, quietly clapping, with a big grin on her face. Gennaro thanked her, grabbed my hand, and we walked out the door.

"Where are we headed?" I asked without a care in the world as to where he was taking me, so long as we were together.

"I want to redo the rooftop down the street from the night we met," he said, adding, "but do it correctly this time."

I hadn't found any fault in our original time there, but if he was keen on improving it, so be it. Following his lead, we walked a few blocks down the street, rode the same elevator, and sat at what appeared to be the best available in the entire place. A guitar player and singer were nestled in a corner not too far away, singing Italian love songs.

"I wanted to sit down and enjoy a meal this time." He looked over the railing and pointed towards the cityscape of lights before turning back towards me. "And I wanted to enjoy it while I get to look at you." His eyes felt like they were burning a hole right through me, and my cheeks flushed bright red.

He was right. This rooftop *did* deserve a redo. It was as exhilarating as it was the first night we met, with the added comfort that came from knowing him better and trusting him fully. Being on an actual *date* made it even better. We ate, we drank, and we talked for two hours straight.

"So, you're going to come visit me in New Jersey?" I smiled at him as I sipped the last of my third glass of wine. My cheeks were still red, but not from shyness this time. I was equal parts enamored with and turned on by the thought of him showing up at the Newark International Airport and then magically ending up in my bed. There was no time better to ask than on a rooftop in Rome when crushed, fermented grapes were helping me feel no pain.

"Let's figure out a good time to do it. I'll put in for vacation and book my flight," he responded without hesitation. My heart fluttered, which, up until this point of adulthood, I didn't think actually happened in real life. Then, he stood up and held out his hand.

"We're leaving?" I asked.

"No, we're dancing." He took my hand in his and pulled me in close to him. The lyrics to Ed Sheeran's "Perfect" began pouring out of the singer's mouth at the same time. Her voice, paired with the strings of the guitar, delivered the simplistic beauty that only an Italian acoustic version could. We slowly danced next to our table, alongside the balcony railing, with city lights reflecting in our eyes as if no one else on the rooftop existed.

Then, he tilted my chin towards him and kissed me, his fingers wrapped behind my neck and his thumb alongside my cheek. When he pulled away, my eyes parted slowly, and he surveyed the look on my face. "I wasn't sure that night could get any better, but I wanted to try," he said, his lips meeting mine again. He continued, "Glad I did."

It was surreal.

Meeting him, staying at his family's villa, spending more time with him, the effort, the special gifts, the surprises, all of it had made me fall deeply in love with him.

I couldn't believe it had happened, how it had happened, and what it meant for our future. But I'd write down my feelings the best I knew how in the morning after he went to work, and I'd give him the letter when the time was right.

As for this moment, I was planning how and when to show him the deep purple colored lingerie hidden underneath the dress he gave me.

"I'm glad you did, too." I kissed his neck and looked up at him. "The dresses were a perfect touch. I had trouble picking between them, but decided the purple color was meant for *underneath* the black dress."

His eyes widened and he cocked his head to the side, "Oh?"

I shrugged with a sly smile.

He signaled for the check, paid quickly, left a larger-than-necessary tip, and led me back through the restaurant towards the elevators. As we approached, a few couples got off and walked past us into the restaurant. If any of them had committed a murder that night, I wouldn't have been able to speak to what they looked like because my eyes were glued to him.

He kissed me again as we walked into the now-empty elevator and pressed the "close door" button before anyone could join us. As the doors shut, I pushed him towards the back wall, took his hand, and slid it up and under my dress. My thighs pulsed as his fingers trailed the length of me.

I watched him intently as he realized the lacy material was being held together by just a few snaps. His eyes grew wide, and he instinctively sucked his bottom lip, but the doors opened before he could do anything about it. His breathing turned frantic, and the long, fast strides he took walking home told me everything I needed to know about his plans for the rest of the night.

The following few hours were a blur thanks to an animalistic side of him I hadn't fully seen before. He wanted me badly, and I let him have every part of me. If there was a type of intimacy meant for two people who dreaded the thought of not seeing one another for a while, this was it.

My body, my mind, my heart, my soul, all of it had been snatched up by Gennaro Beletta. He loved me, protected me, and cared for me. And if there were any possibility of his words not relaying those truths, his body made up for it.

I had finally found every single thing I ever wanted in a man, and I was terrified by the thought of not having him.

That was the risk of love after all, giving yourself to another person and hoping to never find out what it would feel like to be without them.

It was too late to turn back now.

I was his.

He was mine.

Learning to live in the moment while *planning* a little less and *doing* a little more had brought me straight to him.

The rest?

Well, the rest would have to sort itself out.

CHAPTER 28
Gennaro

I woke up with what felt like an elephant on my chest, and it took me a short while to figure out why. One of the best nights I'd ever had was almost *too* good. It was Friday, I still had a shift to work before we could drive back to Tuscany together, and her flight home was Sunday. That meant we had only two nights and one full day left to spend with each other.

I had no questions or hesitations about my feelings for her, and I had been honest with her about them. She was still wearing the necklace I had given her, which I took to be a good sign that she felt the same. I *had* told her not to respond after telling her how I felt, but I'd be lying if I said I wasn't wondering why she still hadn't said anything.

It was uncomfortable because I was usually the one not reciprocating feelings towards someone else. I didn't doubt that she felt something, but I couldn't tell if things were changing a bit as we edged closer to her leaving. We had both said it a few times during our time together: "What are we doing?" and "How is this going to work?" We never quite came up with a viable solution and instead kept leaning towards the "We'll figure it out" option.

"What are you thinking about?" She had opened her eyes, still lying on her side facing me, and had a smile on her gorgeous, sleepy face. Her long hair was piled on top of her head, and while she had taken her makeup off before we fell asleep, she forgot to remove her earrings, which now draped over her neck. She was an absolute vision.

"A few things, actually," I said, quite honestly. "Two weeks together seems like it went by way too fast, I have no interest in going to work today, and I can't get enough of you." I pulled her on top of me, feeling the heat from her inner thighs on either side of my hips as she straddled me and the slow, accidental trace of her nipples along my chest as she leaned over to put her mouth on my neck.

A not-so-short while later, we were breathless on my bed.

Now, I had to face an eight-hour shift before seeing her again.

Mia: Do you have a secret stash of paper or a notebook somewhere in this immaculate apartment?

Gennaro: Top drawer of the small table by the front door

Gennaro: Are you writing me a love letter?

Mia: Maybe

Mia: ::Shrugs emoji::

"Telltale sign you've got it bad: when you smile at your phone like an idiot," Marco interrupted.

I didn't even disagree with him.

"She's leaving Sunday, man." I looked out the window while he drove us around the outskirts of Rome, as we usually did right before lunch.

"Well, you're planning to see each other again, right?" He asked like it was no big deal that she'd be five thousand miles away in less than three days.

"Yea, but…" I trailed off. I didn't want to sound like a soft ass, but it's exactly how I felt. I couldn't wait to get back home to her and dreaded thinking of her leaving.

Another text message came through.

> Mia: ::picture holding wine and the notebook she found, on the balcony deck::

> Gennaro: I wish I had a camera out there so I could watch you like a creep

> Mia: ::another picture, this time with a little more cleavage::

At least I knew our text conversations would be exciting, even if we weren't going to be together physically.

"Umm, hello?" I forgot I was in the middle of responding to Marco.

"Sorry, I… damn. I don't know. It was easier not getting involved with people," I joked, trying to make light of the situation.

He knew me too well after two years to accept that as a reality. "She's obviously not just 'people' to you, which is the issue," he continued. "I think it's awesome. You fell hard. And I don't blame you."

"Don't blame me?" I knew what he meant, but didn't quite know what he was referring to.

"She's got all the things. She's beautiful. She doesn't text you 487 times per day. And, didn't she do the laundry the other day while you were working?"

"Of all the things I've told you the last few days, her doing laundry was at the top of your list?" I shook my head. I knew he was kidding, but only partially.

"I listed beautiful and not over-texting first!" We laughed and continued on with our shift that felt like it was six days long, not six hours.

Back at my apartment, I heard music playing and her talking on the phone as I put the key in the door to open it. She whirled around with a big smile on her face, wearing cream-colored sweatpants and a coral tank top, her hair down, no makeup, barefoot.

It smelled like she had been cooking, but the door to the balcony was open and a candle was burning. She was clearly fumigating the place. I peeked at the plate on the counter, and my stomach growled as soon as I saw there were freshly made chicken cutlets on it.

She made chicken cutlets *and* aired out the place after she was done.

If she didn't have a scroll's worth of other good qualities, I'd probably have fallen in love with her based on those two things alone.

She hung up the phone as I turned around with a bite of chicken cutlet in my mouth.

"Like them?" she asked with a big smile on her face, then came close to give me a kiss. "Ohhh, you did *not* shower at the precinct today, did you?" she joked with a little bit of judgment and a wrinkled nose.

"Was in a rush to get home." I pulled her back in by her waistband and kissed her neck. "I'll go shower now, though. Want to eat and then head up there?"

"Wherever you're going, I'm coming," she said and kissed me again.

We pulled into the villa driveway around ten. My happiness to be back with her turned to absolute dread the minute I opened the car door. Loud yells streamed through the courtyard, which meant they were originating from the kitchen. I contemplated bypassing whatever was going on, but Giuseppe slammed the kitchen door and marched towards the gravel lot where we had parked, stringing together every Italian curse word ever created.

His face was beet red with tears streaming down it, his hands balled into fists. Mia was wide-eyed with concern, and to be honest, so was I, since he was usually the calm, relaxed one. "Whoa, whoa, what happened?" I placed my bag on the hood of my car, walked closer to him, and put both hands on his shoulders. It seemed to work to temporarily calm him down, because he began breathing more evenly and finally cooled off enough to get some adult sentences out of his mouth.

"Nothing I do is good enough for her," he said, pointing back towards the house. "She's insane!" And suddenly I knew it was him and Francesca yelling back and forth at each other, which I wasn't surprised by. She lived according to her bright red hair color and was either sweet as pie or a raging, five-alarm fire that couldn't be contained. The door swung open from the kitchen, and she came running at us.

Five-alarm fire it was.

"Don't you walk away from me, Giuseppe!" She still wasn't showing, but I wasn't well versed in pregnancy and therefore had no idea if she *should* be showing this early, so I didn't think much more about it. "Get back here!"

"Or what?" He shouted back at her. "You barely talk to me; you don't let me touch you. You're just *bitchy* all of the time. Is it because of pregnancy hormones or something? Or are you just insane? Tell me now and put me out of my misery."

I laughed under my breath. Giuseppe was pretty good when he got going, but mostly, I was happy to not have to deal with all of this bullshit myself. The worst thing for Mia and I would be figuring out how to navigate all the miles between us.

Francesca? She was a different animal. She was a hot head, and she was *always* right. Her parents raised her to believe she could do no wrong, and it showed in her demeanor, her actions, and the way she spoke, regardless of how much older she got. It was the most unattractive thing about her, and conversely, the thing I loved *most* about Mia. She didn't appear to have an immature, selfish bone in her body.

"How dare you talk to me like that!" She yelled back at him with her fist in the air.

He threw his hands up, shook his head, and said out loud, "Insane then. You're completely insane. I'd have a more productive conversation with these rocks than I ever could with you." He kicked some gravel, and she started crying loudly, which was another thing I couldn't stand about her.

Mia, still having said nothing and standing still, trying not to interfere, finally blurted out, "Can we grab a bottle of wine from the kitchen?" I smiled, grabbed my bag in one hand, her hand in the other, and walked toward the kitchen, leaving Francesca fake crying in the courtyard. I wasn't interested in playing her games, and I wasn't about to waste the short amount of time I had left with Mia on any of it.

When we walked into the kitchen, Papa, Mama, and Pesca were seated around the island, as they usually were. The ladies smiled big when they saw us. "What the hell happened with those two?" I asked after we hugged and kissed everyone hello.

Mama chimed in with a quick response. "They're not seeing eye to eye, I guess." I looked to Pesca for the *real* answer, and her raised eyebrows and half eye roll let me know she'd fill us in with what actually happened some other time. Then, she looked towards Mama and Papa, motioning her head towards Mia and me, as if to say, "Go ahead, tell them."

"Everything ok?" I asked inquisitively, trying to break the ice of whatever was brewing. Papa exhaled loudly and then motioned his hand towards Mama, giving her the go ahead. "Well," she let out a deep sigh, "I didn't think we'd ever tell you this, but it seems like it might be the right time."

My head swirled trying to figure out what it is they could possibly be sharing with us. Maybe Francesca and I were never actually married? Maybe they convinced Mia's parents to move here, and we'd solve that whole five-thou-sand-mile problem? Maybe Papa finally got a new weed whacker so that I could trim the walkways and driveway in less than four hours next time I had to do it?

No such luck on any of the above.

"Papa and I..." She trailed off before clearing her throat and blurting out, "Our marriage was an arranged one." Her eyes moved back and forth from me to Mia, waiting for a reaction, but neither of us had one.

I was both surprised and not.

The surprise factor came from them keeping it from us

all this time and then admitting it as quickly as she did, but I wasn't immune to the fact that they didn't have the most affectionate or romantic of marriages. Ever since I was young, I noticed that they weren't particularly touchy feely with each other, and to be honest, I wasn't sure I had ever seen them in a loving embrace that lasted more than a couple of seconds.

Their relationship had always centered around the villa, the business, and supporting the three of us. They were a "get-shit-done" sort of couple, not a "you're-my-best-friend-and-love-of-my-life" couple, which, now that I knew this information, made a whole lot of sense.

"Is there a reason you're telling us now? Rather than years ago?" I continued, to soften the statement a bit. "And I only mean that curiously, not as an accusation."

"I didn't want you to think we didn't *actually* love one another." She thought about it a little more before continuing. "Our marriage didn't start out the best, but we *made* the best out of it."

"So, do you?" I asked.

"Do we what?" she responded.

"Truly love one another?" I was confused. Was their *entire* relationship a sham? I could understand certain couples not being super affectionate, but I never doubted that Papa and Mama *loved* one another.

"I love your mother more than anything in the world," the usually quiet Papa chimed in to confirm his own feelings. When Mama started whimpering in response, I knew she felt the same.

"If I may," Pesca interjected before looking at them for permission to continue, "I think that was why they assumed you'd be fine with the arranged marriage with Francesca. They *were* able to find love for one another and wanted you to be able to as well."

I understood the thought process behind it, but life had clearly taken me in a different direction. Even if Mia had not shown up and completely changed my life's course, I still wouldn't have ever actually married Francesca for *real*. And, after seeing her latest display with Giuseppe, I didn't blame myself.

I had zero patience for dealing with "crazy." The world was crazy enough. What I longed for was unwavering support and comfort from an even-keeled woman who also happened to know every which way to turn me on.

"What does all of this mean exactly?" I snapped out of my own brief mental vacation.

Papa responded matter-of-factly, which surprised me since his go-to maneuver was to remain silent in a corner. "We just thought it would be important for you to know. We tried telling Giuseppe before, but the two of them started arguing before we could. We figure we'll tell Giovanni whenever he's back."

I was trying to understand if Papa was urging me to try to make it work with Francesca, as Mia was standing right next to me, but I pushed the thought towards the back of my mind. "To be honest, I don't really think it's a big deal. I'm glad you told me, but it probably would have been helpful to know years ago." I continued, "As far the two of them," I motioned towards the courtyard, "what do you plan on doing with that because they're out of control." The more emphasis I put on *them*, the more I hoped Papa would stop assuming I was going to magically fall in love with Francesca or try to make anything work.

Papa shrugged, clearly exhausted. Mama just looked sad, which was normal as of late, and Pesca said nothing, which I didn't blame her for because she was an innocent bystander to the recent shit show that was our family. Rather than sit there and aggravate myself thinking about it all, I thanked them for the honesty, albeit years later than it should have been delivered, grabbed a bottle of wine like Mia suggested, and said goodnight.

I led her up the kitchen stairs, through the living room, and out the front door towards the villa, successfully avoiding Giuseppe and Francesca, who were still arguing with each other in the courtyard. We walked into her villa, which now smelled exactly like the perfume she wore, and dropped our bags in the bedroom.

Before heading into the kitchen to open our well-deserved bottle of wine, I pulled her close, firmly grabbed her face with my fingers weaved into her hair, and spoke as honestly and passionately as I could so the meaning behind my message would relay. "*Tu sei la calma nella mia vita. Sono così contento di averti trovato. Cosa farei senza di te.*"

I breathed her in and then exhaled slowly, still holding the sides of her face, looking at her intently, wanting her to feel me and my words deep within her soul.

Her eyes, which had closed as I was speaking, slowly opened again. "You know I'm going to need a little translation for that, right?" She smiled sweetly as she moved my hand over to her mouth and kissed my thumb.

I repeated it in English. "You are the calm in my life," I said slowly and continued, "I'm so thankful that I found you, and I don't know what I'd do without you."

My face was buried in her hair, and my heart was beating incessantly. I breathed in and out slowly trying to regulate it. As I pulled away to look at her, I saw one tear escape the side of her eye and fall down her cheek. Brushing it away, I assured her, "I did *not* want you to cry tonight."

She inhaled, blinked, and studied my face. Then, after a few seconds of what felt like an internal deliberation, she asked me, "Did you *want* me to fall in love with you?"

I matched her coy smile. "I wanted you to feel comfortable enough to see if you *could* fall in love with me." I paused a bit before confirming the answer I already knew. "Did it work?"

She blinked away another tear and allowed herself to follow it up with an ear-to-ear, closed-mouth smile. Then, she nodded.

I reiterated what she already knew. "I love *you*, Mia."

She wrapped her arms around my waist, moved in as close as our bodies would allow, and reminded me why I had never let anyone else in.

"*Anch'io ti amo*," she said.

I exhaled slowly, closed my eyes, and vowed to never forget what this exact moment felt like.

She loved me, too.

And, for the first time in my life, I had everything I never dreamed of.

My life had been changed, significantly, in a very short amount of time, all for the better. One brief moment on the streets of Rome and a second-chance follow-up. I lived in the moment, and it led me to love.

It led me to her.

CHAPTER 29
Mia

After two weeks, the bird conversations that occurred daily outside my window as early as five in the morning, had become a familiar source of comfort. It was my last full day, and while I looked back at my time in Italy with such gratitude, I felt an immense sense of dread thinking of leaving him. I tiptoed to the window to take a peek at the weather. It was mostly cloudy, but they were moving quickly, the sun trying to peek through as they passed. The weather app on my phone predicted a high of eighty-two degrees and a mostly sunny day ahead of us.

I made myself a hot Americano, wrapped myself in my duster cardigan for some extra warmth, and walked outside in my slippers. Sitting at the small patio table, I stretched my legs onto the chair in front of me and leaned backwards, my face begging the sun to kiss its skin. As I sipped my coffee, I heard footsteps in the gravel. I opened my eyes and immediately noticed red hair in the not-so-far distance.

"*Ciao, Mia,*" Francesca said cheerlessly. "*Come stai questa mattina?*" When I didn't answer right away, she followed it up with "Oh, sorry, you only speak English. I forgot."

Shots fired.

I closed-mouth smiled while envisioning punching her in the face but didn't give in to the thought, refusing to give her, or anyone, the satisfaction of getting under my skin.

"Sipping coffee on this beautiful property," I said. "I can't be bad."

"You're leaving soon anyway, right?"

She had zero couth.

I smiled again. "Tomorrow, actually."

"What are you doing today? You should come by the market," she suggested.

I'd rather clean up cow shit.

"I have a full day planned. I'll be busy." I kept giving her breadcrumbs, and she kept persisting.

She shrugged a bit and then asked, "Busy doing what?" And then, by the power of the hot Italian Gods, the sun broke through the clouds and Gennaro walked out of my apartment, shirtless, wearing only pajama pants.

"Busy doing that," I motioned towards him and smirked. Him winking back at me only enhanced the complete gratification I felt in the moment.

She threw her hands up in the air and huffed and puffed all the way back down the hill after shouting, "*Che porco!*"

"Did she just call you a pig?" I asked him, unable to hide my smile.

He smiled back. "She absolutely did."

Gennaro had promised Papa he'd help around the property for a few hours and said he'd meet me by the pool sometime around lunch. Pesca and Mama had offered to take me into town to do some shopping, but after last night's drama and this morning's run-in with Francesca, I was all "people-d" out.

I had been to Rome, Florence, Bagno Vignoni, Venice, and back to Rome again. I had seen plenty, I had done plenty, and I had *felt* plenty. It was time to relax and turn my brain off so that I could enjoy the beauty of everything around me for one last day.

Somewhere around my third chair flip from my front to back, I was getting sufficiently bronzed under the Tuscan sun, and my stomach began rumbling accordingly. My phone had dinged a few minutes before, so I grabbed it to check.

> Gennaro: You hungry?

If this is what true love is like, sign me up again and again.

> Mia: Always

> Gennaro: Want anything in particular?

> Mia: You

> Mia: Wine

> Mia: Pasta

> Mia: In that order please

> Gennaro: Coming right up

About fifteen minutes later, I heard footsteps. I turned my head to the right, having been face down in the lounge chair, and watched him walk towards the pool landing with a bottle of wine and two glasses in one hand and a large bowl in the other. He was *still* shirtless, but this time with a bathing suit on in place of his pajama pants.

He placed the huge bowl of pasta down on the small table between us, and poured two glasses of wine. He took a few sips of his, kneeled down to kiss my forehead, and rubbed up and down my butt cheeks and the backs of my thighs with long, strong strokes as he kissed my lips.

"You're going to want to stop doing that unless you want to watch me sleep," I said, the side of my face squished into the towel I was resting my head on, my eyes mostly closed shut.

"I love watching you sleep, but yes, I would prefer to spend our last day doing other activities, definitely." He smirked and kissed me again. We sat next to each other for the next half hour, sipping on wine and sharing the bowl of pasta; room-temperature, hand-rolled cavatelli in a simple tomato sauce with chopped basil; and a dollop of freshly made ricotta.

The only thing more swoon-worthy than the dish itself was the beautiful man who delivered it to me.

"I'm sitting here trying to figure out how best to spend today," he began. "But the more I think about it, I don't really care what we're doing as long as we're doing it together."

"As long as Francesca doesn't keep trying to very blatantly get you in her bed, I don't care what we do, either," I joked.

"She's out of control lately," he said. "Maybe it's the pregnancy hormones or something, but I've never seen her like this."

I offered my own insight. "I'd bet that's because she's never had to see you with someone else before."

He nodded his head and realized I was right.

Escaping to Rome was out of sight and out of mind for her, but being back home a few weekends in a row where she had to watch us together had proven to be an entirely different animal. I guess I felt a little bad about it, but on the other hand, I didn't. If they had a normal marriage, and had I known he was "married" from the beginning, none of this would have even happened. I wasn't into breaking up happy homes, but the universe had presented this slightly messy situation to us for a reason.

I was sure of it, and I still wanted to see what that reason was.

The next few hours were pure bliss. We sipped on some more wine, we swam, we sat next to each other holding hands one minute and I climbed in between his legs with his arms around me the next. We talked a lot, even deciding on the best time for him to visit over the summer.

I suggested the Fourth of July since it was a fun American holiday, a good combination of family time and friend time, and included fireworks which were one of my absolute favorite things in the world. It was also only a month away, which seemed doable as far as a waiting period and sufficient time for him to put in a vacation request at work.

When we grew tired of the sun, we decided to head in. I took in the now-empty pasta bowl, glasses, and empty wine bottle, and he grabbed my bag and our towels after lining the chairs back up along the stone wall. For someone who was frequently aggravated by his father's rigid rules, he still abided by mostly all of them.

He stood next to me with a towel, waiting to dry the pasta bowl and wine glasses as I finished washing them. When they were finished, he moved close to me, pushed a few strands of hair that had escaped from my messy up-do to the side of my face, and put his lips on mine slowly, taking his time to lightly nibble before connecting his tongue with mine.

Of all the sensual, sexy things he did, the way he kissed me was by far my favorite. There was intent behind it, and he let his desires take over as they led his hands, fingers, lips, and tongue to where they longed to be. It was exploration, it was adoration, and it was when I felt most loved by him.

We were in somewhat of a trance when we heard a hard tapping on the island behind us. Our heads quickly turned to see who it was. Papa was glowering at us both.

"*Che vergogna. Voi due siete ridicoli.*" He said it slowly but with purpose and a complete look of judgmental disgust on his face. If there were any previous feelings I had of hope or promise that Papa would come around, this moment had diminished them. When he walked out, still mumbling and cursing to himself, I looked to Gennaro for a translation. He had closed his eyes and shook his head slowly. "It's not even worth repeating."

"Just give me the short version," I shrugged.

"I'm a disgrace, and the two of us together are ridiculous." He ran his fingers through his hair and rubbed his jaw, visibly aggravated.

I returned the head shake, completely perplexed that a parent would try so hard to dictate their kid's life. I couldn't relate to it in the least. My parents and I may not have always agreed on things, and sure, we'd have our generally playful, sporadically attitude-filled interactions, but we always ended up with a general understanding and acceptance of the others' intentions or decisions.

When I looked towards the ground, trying to find something productive to say in return, he pulled me closer and urged me, "Don't bother. I've been trying to make sense of him my entire life, and it's a waste of time." Then he suggested we head back to the room to shower. I knew he was putting a temporary Band-aid on a larger problem by losing ourselves in each other, but given the time I had left here, I was ok with it.

We quietly walked into my villa and locked the door behind us. Almost immediately, he grabbed one of my wrists and spun me around, pinning my back to one of the bedroom walls, his palm resting on the wall above my head. I curled one hand around his wrist and used my other to push him even closer to me by the small of his back. I wanted to feel how hard he was, which was easy to do given the thin material of the bathing suits we were still wearing.

As he kissed me with a slowly moving but perfectly pressured tongue, he pulled on one of the strings of my halter top. It mostly untied, loosening both cups of my top. He pulled on the opposite string to fully undo the knot and slid both pieces of triangular fabric lower, grazing my nipples with his thumbs as he did. He moved on to untie both sides of my bottom, the knots of which easily came undone, and as he bent down in front of me, I felt the cool breeze from his breath a few inches away from me.

My muscles tightened as I envisioned his mouth on me and in me. Within three seconds, I had clearly willed *that* vision to life as he grabbed my hips, held me in place while kneeling in front of me, and traced his tongue up and down the length of me. He licked and sucked, expertly, as he always did. My hands, now resting on his at the dip of my waist, gripped them firmly the closer I came to finishing.

He knew exactly what I was steering him towards.

When I screamed out and exhaled all of the breath I was holding in, one of my hands was squeezing his hair, and the other, his shoulder. He kissed my inner thighs before propping himself up, sitting on his knees, and looking up at me to survey my facial expression.

I hadn't ever done drugs in my life, but I assumed that I looked high as a kite. My eyes had rolled into the back of my head, my face was flushed, and I tried regulating my breathing as I lowered myself towards him.

He smelled of me, of sex, of pure desire, and I was ready to go for another round. So was he. As he spread his knees apart, still sitting on his feet, he sprung free, begging to be sat on. Helping to guide me on top of him, with both of us still seated on the floor, I placed my knees on either side of him. He supported his weight by leaning back on his hands, and I supported mine by leaning forward, holding onto the foot of the bed. I glided up and down him slowly but methodically to a rhythm I now knew to be his favorite.

When his face fell into my neck and his breathing became incessant, I could tell he was close. I felt him kiss along my collarbone as we both moaned deeply, and I desperately tried to ensure my thighs didn't give out before he finished. With sweat dripping down my neck and cleavage, I felt his body clench as he wrapped his arms around me. He exhaled loudly and held me close as I fell into him, rolling to our sides atop the rug that laid underneath the bed frame.

It may not have been the most comfortable position I had ever been in, but it was the most fulfilling finish for sure. I felt him still pulsating inside of me, my legs weak, still dripping sweat, as we tried to calm our breathing. When he slid out of me, I clenched my ass cheeks tightly, stretched out my legs, and saw stars. Somewhere during the last two weeks I discovered how to orgasm through my g-spot, the likes of which no other man in my life ever had the ability to guide me towards.

He was an Italian unicorn in many ways. The way he communicated, his chivalrous nature, how he protected me, his romantic and thoughtful ways, and *holy hell*, how he finished me. I'd have to upgrade my vast collection of vibrators when I got home, because for the first time in my life, the real thing was better.

After lying with each other for a few more minutes, we showered, got dressed, and had a few minutes to kill before dinner. I decided to pack up the majority of my stuff so that I didn't have to rush early in the morning. I could feel his demeanor change as I started, but unfortunately, leaving my family and career in the dust and never returning wasn't an option. When mostly everything was packed except a pair of pajamas and tomorrow's outfit, we left to head to the villa for dinner.

Papa, Mama, Pesca, Giovanni, and Giuseppe were all there. Francesca was not, which made me happier than I realized it would. I still didn't trust her, but mostly, I didn't want to be distracted by her dramatics. Giuseppe was a lot lighter and funnier without her around, too. I felt for him. He had a great personality, but he didn't seem quite ready to be a dad.

If I had to guess, he'd have preferred to find a nice girl and do some exploring with her the same way Gennaro and I had. Giovanni had been the first to leave home, and he was probably the most content out of all of them. Gennaro followed suit, and I was happy to help him do so. I knew that by watching his brothers, Giuseppe would eventually figure out his own happiness, too.

Everyone enjoyed each other's company. They toasted me and wished me a good trip home, urging me to return soon. Well, everyone except Papa. He sat there, stone-faced as ever, eating his food and grunting more things in Italian.

I tried to give him the benefit of the doubt, but at this

point he clearly didn't deserve it. Neither did Mama, if I was being honest. She was a typical mother, wanting her family to enjoy each other and get along. While he tried keeping everyone in a controlled choke hold, anyone paying attention could see her happiness was slowly withering away.

Gennaro and I helped clean the dishes and then decided to take a quick walk alone before dessert. Somewhere along the path, he stopped walking, held me tight, and looked up towards the sky. When I looked at his face, illuminated ever so slightly by the moonlight, I noticed a single tear pooled in the corners of his eyes.

I didn't say anything. I just held him tighter, moved in closer, and put the side of my head to his chest. His heartbeat quickened a little and it echoed deeply within me.

His heart was forever intertwined with mine.

In a very short amount of time, we became one. Not on paper, not per a marriage certificate, not according to anything other than what we felt for one another. He was undoubtedly my person, and I was his. I felt like I was a part of him, I knew how badly I wanted to be with him, and I kept pushing any other doubts away.

Distance wouldn't keep us apart.

Fear wouldn't keep us apart.

Francesca wouldn't keep us apart.

When we returned back to the house and walked into the kitchen hand in hand, Papa wouldn't take his eyes off of us. He was visibly agitated, pacing the floor of the dining room, breathing heavily and still mumbling. I looked towards Giovanni and Giuseppe for a hint as to what had happened, but they both shrugged. Mama was yet again whimpering in the corner, and Pesca was missing.

"What's going on?" Gennaro asked in a strong, confident tone that innately translated to *"I'm not wasting my time on bullshit, so what the hell is going on here?"*

Papa immediately started shouting in Italian, none of which I could translate even the slightest bit, but from the looks of everyone's wide-eyed expressions, it wasn't anything complimentary. He kept pointing at me, screaming so loudly that spit was spewing from the sides of his mouth. Gennaro put his arm out, pushing me behind him as though he were protecting me, but Papa kept coming closer.

"Che cazzo ti prende?!" he yelled at Papa, which I understood to be some form of "What the fuck?" Finally, Papa put me out of my misery by commenting on my lack of Italian speaking skills and then translating his horrid thoughts in English.

"I'll speak English for the American whore then. You don't belong here. And you'll never be accepted into this family by me." He continued, venom still spewing from his lips, "Your parents would be ashamed of how you've acted! Jumping in bed with my son, spreading your legs to a married man. You're a disgrace and you disgust me."

And then, to really send me on my way, "Get the fuck out of here!"

The words wouldn't stop ringing in my ears, and everything else that happened afterwards felt like a blur. Gennaro lunged towards Papa, with Giovanni and Giuseppe trying to hold him back. Tears streamed down my face, and my heart felt a burst of immense pressure before it shattered within the walls of my chest.

My face was hot with embarrassment, and my legs had gone weak for a second time. I was completely stunned, which didn't happen often, but I knew that frozen feeling would turn into some form of hysterics within the next few minutes. I willed my wobbling legs to help me up the back-kitchen steps, out of sight from all of them, before I started crying hysterically or otherwise lost my shit entirely.

As I reached the front door and grabbed the knob to open it, Pesca was turning it from the other side to come in. Her eyes nearly flew out of her skull when she saw the expression on my face turn into a full-fledged sob. She caught me as I fell into her arms, and after decoding my words through hysteria-infused tears, helped me back to my apartment.

"I want to go home," I said.

Before I could even recount what had happened, I was headed towards the airport.

CHAPTER 30
Gennaro

Love has a way of making you do crazy things, like falling for someone in two weeks who lives five thousand miles away, then coming to blows with your own father because of it. The words he strung together to completely demolish her character were some of the worst I had ever heard from him, and the rage I felt because of it was unmatched.

Arranging a *marriage* between myself and the neighbor's daughter actually bothered me less than hearing him lay into her. Thankfully, neither of us landed any fists with Giovanni and Giuseppe there to separate us, but I was still fuming, and my heart was still pounding, sweat dripping off my temples from pure adrenaline.

Giuseppe had taken him outside while Giovanni stood in front of me for the last fifteen minutes, likely making sure I didn't run after him. He knew me well. I was pretty even keeled until I wasn't, and right now, I was unhinged.

So unhinged, actually, that I hadn't even realized Mia wasn't in the room anymore. "Where did she go?" I asked Giovanni, as though he had seen anything while he was peeling me off of Papa and trying not to get hit in the face himself. "Go to her apartment and talk to her," he suggested. I nodded and started walking, but Mama stopped me.

She had bloodshot eyes and wet cheeks from tears that had been streaming down them, and she was still sniffling from crying. For the first time ever, her age struck me. My parents were getting older, and the discord between all of us was aging her even more. Still, I didn't know what to say to her. She was as responsible for arranging my marriage as Papa was, and she had yet to stand up to him on my behalf. Even saying that, I somehow felt *guilty* for it.

I knew she had a huge heart and meant well, but she didn't stand up for what she believed in, and at this point in my life, I wanted to be surrounded by people who understood me and supported me. I didn't always want to be fighting fights, against Papa, against Francesca, against anyone.

"I'm sorry" was all she could muster, but I wasn't even sure what she was sorry for.

"Mama, I love you. I always will, and I know it's not easy being in the middle." I could tell she was about to cry again, but I kept on. "But I don't want to be involved with any of this, if *that* is how he really feels. Life has changed, the world has changed, and he's still living in the early nineteen-hundreds. It's insane, really." I stepped back to observe her face, which was still blatantly sad.

I felt myself running out of patience because I was trying to talk sense into someone who hadn't done much to ever change her own situation. I knew that sounded judgmental of me, since she likely didn't have much of a choice back then, but it was never too late to stand up for what you believed in, and I didn't want her to live the rest of her life doing everything he dictated.

"Are you happy with your life?" I asked, truly wanting

her most honest response. She looked forward, clasping her hands together while holding a tissue, and then rested them on her chest. "Are you *happy?*" I asked her again.

She took a deep breath and finally responded, "I do what I have to for you, for your brothers, for Papa, for this place. That's all I ever really think about."

"You didn't answer the question," I pressed on.

"I'm happiest when you boys are happy," she sighed, and I felt more rage being added to the pile.

"Are *you* happy? That is the question," I continued. "Not us, not Papa, just you. When your life nears its end, are you going to look back and feel happy knowing you had what *you* needed to feel fulfilled? Have you ever traveled outside of here? Do you ever go to dinner with friends? Have you ever seen your old family members? *Yours.* Not Papas, just yours?"

I studied her face again and couldn't take it anymore. "I'll help you out. *No,* you're not happy. Since you were born you've been told by everyone else around you what you can and cannot do. Your marriage was arranged, and you live every day here according to what *he* says is important and not once, not once, in my nearly thirty years, have I *ever* seen him do anything for *you,* outside of taking care of this place."

"It's just the way it is" was all she could manage to say. "It's just the way it is."

I knew the old school way was set in traditions, most of which were outdated, and I knew Mama doing things outside of them would be considered taboo. I felt for her, I truly did, but I wasn't about to live the rest of my life in the same manner. Papa hated the way I lived my life because I did the very thing he never had the courage to do.

I did what I wanted to do, and that didn't mean I did it selfishly or without regard for family and friends and responsibilities. It meant that I took the best part of our traditions, learned from them, grew with them, and left the outdated ones behind me. It was the most beautiful part of living, after all—learning. Learning what you wanted, learning what you didn't want, and learning how to share your life with someone who felt similarly to you.

It was exactly what I had found with Mia in two short weeks, and it was precisely what I refused to let walk out on me because my father didn't agree with it.

"I don't want to leave you here, but I need to go find Mia." I hugged Mama tightly. "I think you'd agree that regardless of how he feels about the situation, the things he said were completely out of line." She nodded her head in agreement.

"*Ti voglio bene, Gennaro*," she said, patting the side of my face with her hand.

"*Anch'io, Mama*." I ran up the back steps as fast as my legs could carry me. At this point, it was a half hour since Papa had lost his ever-loving mind, and I truly had no idea what I was about to walk into.

I passed the parking lot and noticed Pesca's car was missing, but she hadn't been there since Mia and I had returned from our walk. My stomach twisted as I neared closer to her apartment door and realized every single light was off. I peered through the windows, thinking maybe she had fallen asleep on her bed, but it was perfectly made.

I checked my phone to see if she had called or messaged, but there was nothing. I called her instead.

Six rings felt like six years, and the sound of her voice on her voicemail message ripped through me like a hot knife. I called Pesca next, and when she answered I could tell she was driving. Her voice was quiet.

"Are you with her?" I asked, in desperate need of an answer.

"Yes," she all but whispered, "but we're headed to the airport." I found my stomach in my throat, which made it difficult to swallow.

"Her flight isn't until tomorrow! You have to turn around." I was partially yelling and partially fighting back tears.

"She wanted to come early." I heard her exhale and was certain it was because she was now accidentally caught in the middle. While I knew she was on *both* of our sides as far as being together was concerned, I wasn't sure what Mia had told her about Papa.

"Did she tell you what he said?" I asked her and without even letting her answer, continued with "He's lost his goddamn mind!"

"She gave me the brief version, but seeing what she looked like, I imagined it was a lot worse than she even was able to relay." I noticed someone walking up the gravel path and immediately tensed at the thought of it being Papa, but a few strides later, I could tell it was Giuseppe.

"I can't have her leave like this," I said. "There's no way she can leave like this," I was rambling, trying to figure out what to do. If this were a movie scene, I'd be getting into my own car and driving 150 kph to intercept her at the airport, but in my heart, it didn't seem like the right thing to do. "Let me talk to her please."

Pesca avoided putting her on the phone. "I don't think she wants to get in the middle of the family any more than she feels like she has. She has lots of feelings for you, G. The distance is one thing, Papa is another." She paused and then continued, "I left right after dinner because he started going on and on about the two of you when you were out for a walk. My blood was boiling. I couldn't take it anymore."

"So, what the hell should I do here? I can't just *let her*

go." My heart felt ribbons of sharp pain the likes of which I'd never experienced.

"She was leaving tomorrow anyway," Pesca reminded me. "Keep in touch with her to let her know where you stand, but…" she hesitated and then continued, "she's going to need some time. Maybe you do, too. Your family is going through it right now, and the problems aren't going to go away the next time you run back to Rome. They're here to stay unless you all figure out a solution."

"Please ask her to check her messages." I felt deflated, the wind completely knocked out of my sails. "And thank you, for everything. Sorry you're in the middle of it."

"Nothing to apologize for. You're like family. I know how deeply you care for her."

"And?" I pushed her to finish.

"I know how deeply she cares for you. To me, that's what is most important. You want Papa's and Mama's blessing. I would, too, but not to the detriment of your own happiness."

"I hear you. *Grazie*, Pesca." She managed to calm me down a bit, but when I looked up, Giuseppe's facial expression riled me up all over again.

"Papa wants to see you," he said a decibel or two over a whisper.

I put both hands to my face, trying to rub the angst away, to no avail. "I don't give a *shit* what he wants right now, and you can go tell him that," I said confidently with absolutely zero remorse. Then, I walked into her apartment. He started to follow me, but I turned around with a straight arm to his chest. "Don't. I don't want to be near anyone right now."

He shrugged, turned around, and walked back towards the main house. I knew if he actually relayed that message to Papa, I'd hear him shouting from all the way up here. I didn't care about that either.

Right now, I wanted to soak up whatever was left of her. Remnants of her perfume taunted me as soon as I opened the door. I battled back and forth between immense depression and an absolute longing. Longing for her, for the time we had spent together a mere hour earlier and how quickly it all changed.

In truth, saying goodbye to her in any fashion, whether it was tomorrow or tonight would have ripped me from limb to limb. I was prepared for that but I was not prepared for it to happen in the manner it did, with words spoken the way Papa had delivered them.

I moved towards her made bed, grabbing a pillow and inhaling the scent that remained on it. Some strands of her hair were still stuck to it, too, which wounded me in ways I didn't think were possible. In her bathroom, I found near empty bottles of shampoo, conditioner, and body wash, all of which I smelled, further tormenting myself.

Used towels were hanging from the shower door, and as I turned back around to walk out, I saw her long cardigan sweater hanging off a hook from the back of the bathroom door. The fabric was worn and not recently washed, and I knew it would smell exactly like her. When I pulled it to my face and closed my eyes, it felt like she was still here.

I took the sweater with me and walked into the living room where I found a small white envelope on the coffee table. When I got closer to it, I could make out a small "G" in the corner. My heart in my throat, I sat down on the couch and held it in my hands for a few minutes before opening it. I wasn't sure if she wrote it before or after the debacle with Papa, but then I remembered her asking for paper in my apartment and knew it was from yesterday.

I took a picture of the envelope and sent it to her, assuming she would either be sleeping or too upset to want to speak to me. When I saw my phone's screen light up a few seconds later, I almost choked on air.

> Mia: I am really sorry I left without saying goodbye to you but I just needed to get out of there

> Mia: I hope you understand

> Gennaro: I do but I need to see you again

I waited close to ten minutes, but she didn't respond. So, I turned to the letter she had left instead.

Absolutely nothing could have prepared me for what she had written.

G.

I'm having trouble figuring out where I want to begin, but I guess that's because there is so much to say.

First, though, thank you.

I sort of gave up on the fairy tale of finding my "person" a long time ago.

I assumed I'd never find someone who could meet what I consider very basic needs for a solid relationship.

But, you've blown them all away...every last one of them.

You are kind, chivalrous, respectful, and an absolute gentleman.

You are thoughtful, romantic, affectionate, and the most passionate man I have ever known.

You are handsome. So goddamn handsome, and I'm smiling as I write this because in two weeks you've become my favorite thing to look at.

You're a family man, and you've given so much, to so many, for so long.

You stand for what you believe in and you do so without apology.

You follow through with everything you say you're going to do and you do so effortlessly.

When I think of you, I see a future that I never quite envisioned for myself, because I never thought it was possible.

Thanks to you, though, I've been living for the moments. For the now.

These moments led me directly to you and have been the two happiest weeks of my entire life.

You've taught me how to think a little bit less and enjoy a little bit more.

I've watched you confidently support your family, without sacrificing your own identity. Your love of this place is so evident, when you're given the opportunity to actually enjoy it. I am so proud of you for living true to yourself and your needs, while finding a balance between the two.

On top of all of this, you've given me confidence in return.

Confidence to be myself.

Confidence to be comfortable not knowing the outcomes of things.

Confidence to live one day at a time.

Vivi il momento...

Of all the moments of my life, you have become my favorite one.

From the moment my eyes met yours on a random street, to dancing in a night club, to kissing on a rooftop in Rome, to reconnecting in an unassuming kitchen in Tuscany, my life has forever changed.

My "moments" highlight reel has been forever altered, because moments like these will always be hard to top.

My hope, though, is that we never stop trying.

We continue to fall in love over and over again.

We continue to make new memories.

We continue to live in the moment, with each other, until our moments are done.

I love you.

I've known it from the moment I looked into your eyes and somehow immediately trusted you, even when I tried to convince myself I couldn't or shouldn't.

I never believed "love at first sight" to be real, but you've proven it to be true. Through your actions, through your words, and through your touch...

I love every last thing about you.
I love who I am when I'm with you.
And I love thinking of my life with you in it.
I don't know when I'll actually give this to you, but whenever you finally read it, please trust and believe that I mean every word.
My heart is yours.
Forever.
Mia

The world had stopped, if only for a few minutes. I texted her again to let her know I had read it.

> Gennaro: My heart is yours
>
> Gennaro: Forever

And then, I went to find Papa.

He had dictated my life for as long as he possibly could. Until now.

I was going to annul the marriage between Francesca and me. I was staying in Rome full-time and was done attempting to help out around the property.

Was it extreme?

Maybe, but I wasn't going to let someone else tell me how to live my life anymore.

I had accidentally found the person who had been the missing piece to genuine happiness.

I had preached to Mia to live in the moment and live for the *now*.

What was happening *now*, for me, would dictate the rest of my life, and what I knew, above anything else, was that the rest of my life was going to include her. It *needed* to include her, whether Papa, or anyone else, liked it or not.

I walked towards the kitchen with the letter in my hand, knowing fully what I planned to tell him.

I never got the chance to, though.

While I was busy planning my next moves, life was busy laughing at me.

With sirens in the distance and loud screams coming from the terrace, my heart shattered for a second time that night, in a way I never expected it to, and in a way I would not soon recover from.

Epilogue

MIA

"I really need to dust that fan."

I couldn't remember the last time I had moved off of the couch on this particular day. My stomach grumbled from a lack of nutrition, and my phone continued to alert me to more text messages that had gone unanswered as I watched the blades of the ceiling fan circle in what felt like slow motion. My thoughts had turned relatively basic, boring, and somewhat depressing in the two weeks that followed my arrival back home. The apartment I was previously excited to call my own now paled in comparison to the beauty and comfort I felt back in both Tuscany and Rome.

If there were such a thing as a vacation hangover, I had been experiencing it ever since wheels touched back down at Newark International Airport. Withdrawal symptoms had reached their peak, causing food to taste bland, sunshine to seem dull, and my heart to consistently feel like an anvil was crushing it.

I looked over to the vividly colored wall art that had

previously brought me joy and shook my head. Then, she returned.

> *Inner Critic: If you thought a $49 piece of Home*
> *Goods wall art was going to make you smile*
> *after that disaster, you are sorely mistaken*
> *Mia: I thought I left your negative ass in Italy*
> *Inner Critic: You thought wrong*
> *Inner Critic: Although I did like you a lot better over*
> *there*
> *Inner Critic: By the way, when's the last time you*
> *showered? You smell terrible*

She was right, after all. I *did* smell terrible.

I needed a shower.

I needed to respond to my messages.

I needed to figure out my next move, because two weeks of feeling sorry for myself had been enough.

What was I feeling sorry *for* anyway?

I stood up, walked to the bathroom, and let the hot beads of water soften the tension that had a vice grip on my neck and shoulders. I briefly flashed back to *his* bathroom and *his* shower as I stood there breathing in steam, but stopped myself. Voluntarily torturing myself with memories wasn't going to help move me forward.

But what would?

Allie.

I turned the water off, grabbed a bath towel that needed a few wash cycles itself, and realized the first step in climbing out of the depressing hole I was buried in was to start cleaning.

Cleaning?

Yes. This whole place needed some uplifting refreshment, and so did I.

I started my first load of laundry, did a quick round of dusting as well as a vacuum run, opened the curtains and blinds in both my bedroom and living room, and turned on my Bluetooth speaker.

I let out a few choice words when the first song my phone decided to play was an Italian one, and quickly changed it to early 2000s Pop instead.

The crooning sounds of Justin Timberlake and J.C. Chasez calmed me enough to finally pick up my phone.

> Mia: Want to meet for lunch tomorrow?

> Allie: You bet your ass I do

> Allie: On one condition

> Mia: What's that?

> Allie: You don't show up like a sad sack of potatoes

> Mia: I love potatoes

> Allie: So do I

> Allie: But I prefer to eat them

> Mia: Fries before guys

> Allie: ::forehead slap emoji::

Mom and Dad had checked in as had my brother, sister, and Pesca. I knew she was concerned for me, so I lied and told her I felt better now that I was home. She didn't believe me, of course, and I wasn't remotely surprised by it.

> Pesca: Don't go convincing yourself that what you felt isn't real

> Mia: Oh, it was real alright

> Mia: Because it hurts like a mother f'er

> Pesca: Then, don't go convincing yourself that the story has to end here

> Mia: You need to start writing either romance or self-help books

> Pesca: Too much work

> Pesca: It would interfere with my wine consumption

> Pesca: ::photo of the courtyard and her holding a glass of wine::

> Mia: Why are you torturing me?

> Pesca: Zoom in, back right

Gennaro was a small blip on the picture, shirtless and cleaning gutters.

I suddenly had the urge to become a wet pile of Italian leaves.

My heart felt the anvil pressure again, which I realized was, in fact, an unadulterated longing to be with him, to be there, to relive it all again.

I missed all of it, and in my heart, I didn't question what we felt for each other. I knew it was real. I just didn't see how any of it could actually work.

My original hurdle was the ability to have a vacation *fling* and not overanalyze it or attempt for it to become anything more. When I lived presently, though, with less expectations and less worry, was when a relationship naturally developed. I allowed him to see the real *me*, and he had fallen in love with every part.

When I opened his message, the anvil pressed on.

Gennaro: This isn't the end for us

Gennaro: It's just the beginning

Gennaro: Ti amo, Mia

How on earth he was so certain of that, I had no idea. My head fell backwards as I looked towards the now-dusted ceiling fan and then heard a rustling at my door followed by a quick knock.

Had I not just seen him in a photo cleaning gutters five thousand miles away I'd have assumed I was about to star in the closing scene of a late '90s Rom-Com.

When I opened the door, a large drawstring bag was perched along the doorframe. I had *totally* forgotten that I asked my landlord to hold my mail for the two weeks I was gone. I set it on my coffee table and separated bills from junk from personal pieces. At the bottom was one small box covered in varying stamps and postage stickers. The address label was handwritten, and one of the stamps read: *Italia.*

My stomach bubbled.

I pushed myself back towards the softest part of my couch and stared at it briefly before opening it. As I flipped over the flaps of the box, turquoise tissue paper peeked out at me. Lying on top of the tissue paper was a postcard. The front of it boasted a beautiful photo of an evening sky lit up by fireworks and the bottom right corner read "Arno River, Firenze." When I flipped it over, my eyes welled up.

Mia,
If you look up the definition of "fireworks"
you'll find a variety of descriptive words like spec–

tacular, explosive, a burst of energy, and a brilliant display.

You have lit up my entire world in the same way. Figuring out what happens next may not be easy, but the best things in life usually aren't. All I know, is that our story doesn't end here.

Ci rivedremo presto. Ti amo,

Gennaro

I Google Translated at lightning speed.

"I will see you again soon."

I peeled off the rest of the turquoise tissue paper to reveal a box of Acqua dell'Elba Classico. After ripping it open like a five-year-old on Christmas morning, I sprayed the air, and deeply inhaled.

It instantly transported me, and I felt immediate comfort.

He was right, and so was Pesca.

This wasn't the end of our story.

It was just the beginning.

Ciao!

Let's stay connected.

Scan the code below with your smartphone camera to visit my website and register for launch updates. You'll be the first to know when the **second book(!)** of this series is available for pre-order.

And, follow me on Instagram, Facebook, and TikTok for some behind the scenes snippets, recipes, teasers, and more.

@mary.belle.books

About the Author

Mary Belle writes relatable love stories with equal parts spice and humor. She is a wife and mother who spent most of her life idolizing love while getting her heart consistently crushed. Having found her ideal life partner, she (and he!) quickly realized that marriage is a whole lot harder than anyone ever lets on.

So, she's sharing her love of love, and all of the lessons learned along the way; that while it's anything but easy, it should always feel like it's worth the hardships.

And, even more than that, the hardships should always lend themselves to growth.

That's life.

Forever learning and forever growing—that's where true happiness is found.

Mary lives with her husband and daughter in New York, where she celebrates all of life's moments (quite literally all of them) with a good meal. This is her first novel.

instagram.com/mary.belle.books

tiktok.com/@mary.belle.books

facebook.com/mary.belle.books

Acknowledgments

Realizing a dream is a feat in itself at times. As we grow, many of our dreams grow with us.

Others do not…

When I was little, I used to dream of going to Harvard to be a hairstylist and "make-over-ist."

From then until now, my life, dreams, wishes, and expectations have taken many twists and turns, but what has remained constant is the support of unforgettable people, throughout all stages, who have helped me get here.

Allow me to start from the beginning (please get cozy).

To my parents, who have an uncanny way of being supportive without ever being overbearing. You listen, you lend a suggestion here and there (even if you don't think it'll be taken), and you continue to do so, without fail, with every year that I grow older.

Having saved nearly every single poem, story, or piece of artwork I created from pre-K through college, you have shown interest in my interests, without ever throwing away the hope (literally and figuratively) that those interests would blossom into my true calling. And, at times when I've struggled through certain jobs or relationships or personal battles, you've reminded me of the importance of focusing on the good parts, forgetting the bad parts, and never letting anything "dull my shine."

It is my true hope that this book reminds you that things can only shine bright in nurturing environments. I would not change a single blessed aspect of my childhood, as all of those roads led me here. "Thank you" will never be enough, but I hope to remind you of my never-ending gratitude until the end of time. Perhaps, if I sell enough books, we'll never have to mention that pesky Post-it ever again.

To my brother and sister, who—despite the winding roads of life that could potentially lead us further and further away from our original home base—have done quite the opposite. We are all very different and very similar at the same time. I'm still not quite sure how we manage that, but I do take solace in the fact that we'll protect each other to the end. Thank you for loving me, even when we've slightly hated each other (in temporary spurts, you know).

Honorable mention to my brother in law—for your endless technology assistance, fabulous dance moves, and Gennaro-level cologne application.

Mostly though, thanks to all of you for giving me a tribe of mini best friends; Lex, Carm, Chicky, and Lily Lus. I hope that one day I'm half as famous as they think I am.

To my entire extended family, from grandparents, all of whom are now in Heaven, to my aunts, uncles, cousins, and beyond. In varying ways, you have all helped me realize my true potential. From kind comments to introducing me to your in-laws or friends, many of whom always exclaimed, "I've heard so much about you!" you've always made me feel *special*.

To my closest friends, of which there are many and can't possibly be listed in typed form without adding an extra three thousand words:

Leesh— my oldest and dearest since 1989, half of the inspo behind *Allie*, and the epitome of "You don't have to talk all of the time, but when you do, you pick up right where you left off." You skipped front row *NSync tickets to come to my Sweet Sixteen and I will never forget it. With the kindest soul and the biggest heart, you're raising incredible girls, which speaks to how special you are at your core.

Rams—we buried a bumblebee together sometime in the seventh grade and haven't looked back since. Along the road of our friendship, we've gone long stretches with distance between us, branching out on our own, even while attending the same college, but always find our way back to each other. I'll forever be grateful for your honesty, your grit, and your focus, which have always inspired me.

Horn—it would take another novel to explain our relationship, or to thank you for it, but being the other half of *Allie* inspo should say plenty. You have been my constant since 2002 when we bonded over the New York Yankees and North Jersey accents in our dorm's common area. We've waded through friend, family, and relationship drama while celebrating each other's achievements along the way. When we have moments of self-doubt, we remind each other to "woman the f up" and get it done. Our entire friendship can be summed up by our maiden jet ski voyage—knowing what we're each capable of and pushing each other to showcase our true potential, even when we doubt ourselves. My life would truly not be the same without you in it.

Burkie—your crazy ass has always inspired me to loosen up, just a little (unless it comes to drawing on car windows). Your ability to continually push through the daily stressors of life while still finding shit to smile about is what I draw from on particularly bad days, and it is what helps me to just keep pushing through. I am in awe of all you accomplish, and I can promise that no matter how successful an attorney you continue to become, I will always refer to you as Gillian Anderson who humped my leg on a dance floor and made us astronaut meat sauce dinner.

Jane—you are my "I hated you before I loved you" friend but would you look at us now! The Irish potato to my Italian cannoli, I am forever thankful for our rowdy college days that have morphed into judgment-free parenting advice sessions. If I were to ever pick a real life couple to write a romance novel about, it would, without a doubt, be based on you and Jake.

Dawna & Elvira—the two of you have always been my biggest cheerleaders and are the true definition of "women supporting women." You fill my heart with more joy, pride, and #bossbabe-ness than you'll ever know.

Co-workers and friends I've met through my vast career of random occupations (LOL)—what a ride. I've taken something I've learned from each and every stage to help get me here. Thank you for the memories, the emotional overeating and indulging, and the constant reminders that "whatever you choose to do, you'll be great at," as I left one for the next.

To every boy who has broken my heart in one way or the other; in my fictional dreams or in real life, thank you.

You led me straight to…

My husband—I've been in love with you ever since your football picture hung on our refrigerator back in the nineties. We fell hard and quickly for each other when our paths crossed again later in life (thanks, Gram). Having fallen off track for a few years in between, we still came out the other side. I'll spend the rest of my life paying as much attention and care to your heart, your needs, and your happiness as I do creating the fictional characters of my romance novels.

For any of you wondering if there are any "real" men who actually communicate as much as *Gennaro* does, the answer is yes. I married one of them. And, thanks to a lot of hard work on both of our parts, I get to be married to him for the rest of my days. Forever is not long enough, but I'll take whatever I can get, so long as it includes the nook, coolie rubs, homemade dinners, and motorcycle rides. I'd choose *you* over and over again. *Ti amerò per sempre.*

To my "in-laws," who are very much a bonus "real" family, and my incredibly smart, kind, and kick-ass (literally) niece, Lina—I would not have been able to write this book without your support in keeping *Marinasaurusmaximus* a happy little girl during her many extended visits.

To Rosie especially—I'll never stop thanking you for giving birth to and raising the greatest man I've ever known and for not giving up, on either of us, when we both needed you the most.

To author Jennifer Probst—your books, *Write Naked, Write True,* and *What I Wish I'd Known* were the first I read as I embarked on my journey of *Pretending I Know How the Hell to Become an Author, First Edition.* Your responses to a few of my DMs sparked a light inside of me that I had found my "people," and I will never forget that simple act of kindness.

To my editor, writing coach, author cheerleader, and virtual friend Elizabeth Lyons—I'd quite simply be lost without you. I have adored you since your very first Instagram audio message and have trusted you ever since. You are an incredible teacher and mentor, and I feel so, so lucky to have had you by my side as my dream has come to life. I hope we share a coffee (decaf for you) and a muffin (gluten-free for you) together soon. And, if anyone reading this has always wanted to write a book, go ahead and purchase *Write the Damn Book Already* and enroll in every course, workshop, and training Liz offers. Thank me later.

To my beta readers, Stephanie and Nicole—your enthusiasm, suggestions, and excitement as I pushed through to finish this have been all the motivation I needed in the final stages of writing the story.

To Peach—for your knowledge of Italy, sharing it with us, and generally just being one of the most intelligent, independent, and reliable women I know. I hope *Pesca* made you proud.

To Italy (yes, I'm talking to the entire country) and especially Tenuta di Corsano (Liliana, Francesca, and Nanni, may he rest in eternal peace)—you are the inspiration behind this entire novel, and have left a permanent imprint on my heart and soul. I hope to visit you again soon.

To my Instagram family—you are strangers who have become friends. On days I felt like quitting, your kind words of encouragement kept pushing me through. Never underestimate the power a "like," "comment," or DM can have for a small business owner or entrepreneur as they struggle through their journey of self-discovery.

To everyone who bought this book—thank you doesn't quite cut it. I enjoy writing, and I can tell a good story, but I wasn't quite sure how that would translate into romance novel form. I hope following Mia and Gennaro's journey allows you to escape this crazy world, if only for a little bit, while making you fall in love with one of my favorite places.

And finally, to my daughter, Marina Rose—you have changed me for the better. From the day I became pregnant with you to the day you entered the world officially to present day as you sit next to me while I'm typing, muttering to yourself, "Mom…dis is boring," you challenge me to be a touch more patient and a little less rigid and structured.

I always thought "Vivi il Momento" became a *thing* for me when I was searching for a tattoo design, but as I write this, I realize it started the day you were born. You forced me to be just a little more comfortable with not having all of the answers all of the time. You forced me to realize that no matter how much we plan, life keeps throwing us curve balls. And in doing so, you've taught me that the sum of all life's little moments is what makes life itself grand.

You, my girl, are a bright light that will continue to shine long after my days are done. My hope, at the very least, is that this book will always remind you to follow your heart, chase your dreams, cast away the doubts, and believe in yourself. When you believe in yourself, you truly love yourself. And loving *yourself* is the first step to finding a partner who will love you in a way that puts any romance novel—even one I write—to shame.

Grazie mille a tutti.

Thank you all so much.